PENGUIN BOOKS

Alex Grecian is the author of the long-running and critically acclaimed comic book series *Proof*. He lives in the American Midwest with his wife and son. *The Harvest Man* is his fourth novel, following on from *The Devil's Workshop*, *The Black Country* and *The Yard*.

The Harvest Man

ALEX GRECIAN

PENGUIN BOOKS

PENGUIN BOOKS

UK | USA | Canada | Ireland | Australia
India | New Zealand | South Africa

Penguin Books is part of the Penguin Random House group of companies
whose addresses can be found at global.penguinrandomhouse.com.

First published in the United States of America by G. P. Putnam's Sons 2015
First published in Great Britain by Penguin Books 2015

001

Copyright © Alex Grecian 2015

The moral right of the author has been asserted

Set in 12.5/14.75 pt Garamond MT Std
Typeset by Jouve (UK), Milton Keynes
Printed in Great Britain by Clays Ltd, St Ives plc

A CIP catalogue record for this book is available from the British Library

B FORMAT PBK ISBN: 978–1–405–91508–3
A FORMAT PBK ISBN: 978–1–405–92046–9
ROYAL PBK FORMAT ISBN: 978–1–405–91509–0

www.greenpenguin.co.uk

For Roxane, who always has my back.

When children are playing alone on the green,
In comes the playmate that never was seen.
When children are happy and lonely and good,
The Friend of the Children comes out of the wood.

Nobody heard him, and nobody saw,
His is a picture you never could draw,
But he's sure to be present, abroad or at home,
When children are happy and playing alone.

He lies in the laurels, he runs on the grass,
He sings when you tinkle the musical glass;
Whene'er you are happy and cannot tell why,
The Friend of the Children is sure to be by!

He loves to be little, he hates to be big,
'Tis he that inhabits the caves that you dig;
'Tis he when you play with your soldiers of tin
That sides with the Frenchmen and never can win.

'Tis he, when at night you go off to your bed,
Bids you go to sleep and not trouble your head;
For wherever they're lying, in cupboard or shelf,
'Tis he will take care of your playthings himself!

– Robert Louis Stevenson, 'The Unseen Playmate',
A Child's Garden of Verses (1885)

Night

Mother and Father were sharing a bed. The Harvest Man hesitated in the open bedroom door, staring down at his bare feet, his face flushing scarlet beneath the plague mask. Mother and Father had always slept in separate rooms. He was certain of it. But perhaps their habits had changed over time. That made perfect sense. If they had remained the same, he felt sure he would have found them long ago.

Mother stirred in her sleep and the Harvest Man finally moved. He wasn't ready for her to wake up. He uncorked a bottle of ether and placed a folded facecloth over the rim, tipped the bottle up and held it until cold liquid soaked through to his fingers. He set the open bottle on the floor next to the doorjamb, where he knew the liquid would silently turn to gas.

Everything always changing, things disappearing without a trace.

He moved forward in slow motion, keeping his head and shoulders straight up and down, only bending at the knees. He made no sound. Mother stirred again, rolled on to her back, and the Harvest Man moved around the foot of the bed to her side. He preferred to deal with Father first. Father was bigger and stronger and, if he woke early, he always caused trouble. But Father was snoring and

Mother was moving, on the verge of waking. Better to tend to her.

He knelt by the bed and gazed at Mother's sleeping face. The room was dark, but the window was open and the moon shone bright. He could see well enough even through his thick lenses. Mother was pretty. He thought she had always been pretty, but she didn't look like he remembered. It took him a moment to categorize the differences. Fortunately, he had a very good memory for faces. Mother's nose was slightly larger now, and was turned up at the tip. Her eyes were spaced closer together and her lips were thinner. She had lost a little weight, and her forehead was wider, her hair a different colour, her neck longer, her cheekbones more prominent. He shook his head and the heavy beak at the front of his mask moved back and forth. Why did they always make so much work for him? They shouldn't change so very much. It always made him cross.

Mother opened her eyes and they were not the same colour as he remembered. He hesitated, confused, but when she opened her mouth he clapped the ether-soaked cloth over it, held it tight to her face. She struggled for a moment, then relaxed, and her arm fell limp over the side of the bed. He picked up her hand and placed it on her chest.

Around on the other side of the bed, Father shifted his position, and so the Harvest Man leaned far across Mother's limp body, stretched out his arm, the moist cloth pinched between the ends of his two longest fingers, and shared the ether fumes with Father. When both parents were insensible, he left that room and explored the house.

He had been in a hurry earlier and had bolted for the attic without taking his customary tour.

There were two children, both boys, sleeping in a small bed tucked under the staircase. He pushed the plague mask up to the top of his head so he could see them better, enjoying the feel of fresh air on his cheeks and chin. He rubbed his ear. Sometimes it still itched where the top of it had been pulled away. The mask's goggles rested against the back of his head and the long pointed beak stood straight up like the face of a baby bird straining for food. The Harvest Man stood and watched the children's chests move gently up and down. He gazed without affection at the nearest boy's chapped lips, which were parted, the upper lip deeply grooved and dark pink. The boy's eyelids fluttered. The Harvest Man placed his drying face-cloth between the children, trusting that the remaining essence of ether would keep them from waking.

He climbed up the stairs above the sleeping boys and retrieved his boots and knife and a coiled length of stout rope from the attic. He sat on the top step and pulled the boots on. He tugged the plague mask back down into place and adjusted it so that it wouldn't slip from his face while he worked.

He decided to ignore the boys. He didn't know them. They might be his brothers, but he couldn't remember their faces and so it would do no good to remove their masks. He would ask Mother and Father about the other children when they woke later. Then they could determine together what was to be done. As a family.

But first things first. Before they could be a family again, he would have to remove Mother's and Father's

3

masks to reveal their true features. He smiled, excited, and stood, picked up the curved knife and the rope and trotted down the stairs, no longer concerned about making noise. He couldn't wait to see his parents' faces again.

How happy they would be that he had finally found them.

Day One

From breakfast on through all the day
At home among my friends I stay,
But every night I go abroad
Afar into the land of Nod.

All by myself I have to go,
With none to tell me what to do –
All alone beside the streams
And up the mountain-sides of dreams.

The strangest things are there for me,
Both things to eat and things to see,
And many frightening sights abroad
Till morning in the land of Nod.

Try as I like to find the way,
I never can get back by day,
Nor can remember plain and clear
The curious music that I hear.

– Robert Louis Stevenson, 'The Land of Nod',
A Child's Garden of Verses (1885)

I

In the late spring of 1890, number 184 Regent's Park Road was a flurry of activity. Upon receiving news of the arrival of twin grandchildren, Mr and Mrs Leland Carlyle ordered their luggage to be packed for an immediate holiday in London and took up residence across the park from their daughter's home in Primrose Hill. Mrs Carlyle visited Claire Day early each morning and stayed on past tea most evenings. She found the household in a state of disarray (or, as she put it to her son-in-law, a state of near vacancy) and determined that her first order of business was to hire a staff. Fiona Kingsley, the young lady who had stayed at number 184 to look after Claire during the pregnancy, was sent back to her father's home. Within three days, a new governess had been acquired, along with a cook, a scullery maid and a head of housekeeping by the name of Miss Harris. Mrs Carlyle also arranged for three boys from the local reformatory to help clean the house once a week between seven thirty and nine in the morning.

Overnight the household became too large to be sustained on the salary of a policeman, and Detective Inspector Walter Day began to feel vaguely anxious. The two babies woke at odd hours, and Day, who was a light sleeper, rose with them and tried to stay out of the way as the governess tended to them. He did not remember the governess's name, nor did he know the names of the cook and scullery maid. Nobody had bothered to introduce him to Claire's staff and he felt certain he was going to have to let them all go once his in-laws departed. He made no effort to get to know them.

Violence had recently been visited upon the Day home in the form of a double murder, and reasonable precautions had been taken against future ugliness of the sort. A retired inspector by the name of McKraken had volunteered to stand guard on the house. He kept to himself, but his presence added to the general quality of congestion at number 184.

Some sensation had returned to Day's right leg and he got around with a degree of confidence using a cane. The commissioner of police, Sir Edward Bradford, had assigned Day a number of tasks designed to supplement the efforts of the rest of the Murder Squad and, clearly, to keep him sitting at a desk for the bulk of his shifts. Day had petitioned Sir Edward for a meeting on several occasions, hoping to convince the commissioner to give him more challenging work, but he had been ignored. Everyone at the Yard was bustling about, working to catch a murderer known only as the Harvest Man, and boxing up all non-essential items for transport to the new headquarters that was being built for them – was, in fact, nearly finished – on the Victoria Embankment. Nobody was sitting still except for Day; change was everywhere. The flow of life, he felt, had plucked him off his feet and deposited him on some deserted beach.

Feeling useless both at home and at the Yard, Day began to spend much of his time at the Chalk Farm Tavern above the canal. That is where Nevil Hammersmith found him at teatime on the first Tuesday of May. Day was at a table in the back, talking with a trio of young solicitors. He had lost track of the amount of ale they'd had and he doubted the other men would make it back to their office in Camden Town. When he saw Hammersmith at the tavern door, he stood and moved stiffly around the table. Hammersmith saw him and made his way across the room, through a maze of mismatched tables and chairs. They greeted each other warmly and Day introduced him to Haun, Moore and Peck, the solicitors. After shaking hands all round, those three men politely gathered their glasses and retired to the counter near the front of the pub, surrendering the table to the inspector and his friend.

'I'm headed to Bridewell right now,' Hammersmith said. 'I assume you've heard the news?'

'I'm sure I haven't. Nobody tells me anything any more.'

Hammersmith blinked and pulled out a chair. 'You look rough,' he said.

'Do I? And how have you been, Nevil? Breathing well enough?'

'I've been careful,' Hammersmith said. He had been promoted from constable to sergeant after helping Day catch a child murderer, but then almost immediately dismissed from the Yard. In the brief course of his duties he had been poisoned on two occasions, bludgeoned, nearly frozen to death and stabbed in the chest with a pair of scissors. It had all been too much for the commissioner of police to bear. 'I don't move as quickly as I once did.'

'Nor do I,' Day said.

'How's the leg?'

'Better than it was. Will you have a pint?'

'Tea for me.'

'Good. And then you must tell me your news.'

Day called over the proprietor and ordered a pot of Imperial and brown bread. The man nodded and hurried away. Hammersmith watched him go, then leaned forward across the table. 'Never mind the news. That can wait. I want to know, are you with me?'

'With you?'

'Now I'm sufficiently mobile,' Hammersmith said, 'I'm going to find him.'

He didn't have to explain. Day knew who he was talking about and he unconsciously rubbed his leg. The scars there were ugly and they ached, and he had been told he would never walk properly again. The most dangerous man in London had held Day captive in a devil's workshop deep beneath the city, had tortured and taunted him. Day had barely escaped with his life.

Hammersmith had come even closer to an early death. His chest was a battleground of dried black stitchwork. Both men knew that Jack the Ripper was still at large, still roamed the streets, and had not finished his deadly work.

'Come with me now,' Hammersmith said. 'Together we can catch him.'

He leaned back as the tavern's proprietor reappeared with a wooden tray. The jittery little man set a teapot in the centre of the table and ringed it with two cups and saucers, a plate of brown and white bread, lemons, a jug of milk, and tiny pots filled with sugar, jam, and thick white butter.

'Thank you,' Day said. 'And a shot of whisky?'

The man nodded and took the now empty tray back to his counter, out of earshot. Day and Hammersmith busied themselves with the tea for a moment. Day poured in a spot of milk and swirled the dark tea in after it. He spooned in sugar and stirred slowly back and forth, watching the murky liquid fold over on itself, ripple outward, and lap gently against the side of the cup. He set the spoon down and sipped, his eyes averted from Hammersmith's face. When he lowered the cup at last, he wiped his lips and sighed.

'It's my leg,' Day said. 'I'd be useless to you.'

'Hardly useless. You're the brains of our little outfit, you know. We can catch him, you and I. You figure his game and I'll ferret him out.'

'Sir Edward's been giving me busywork.'

'Yet here you are.'

'I can't help you.'

'You know I'll do it without you. But I'd rather have you with me.'

'I have two babies, Nevil.'

Hammersmith said nothing.

'And if I do go with you? If he catches me again . . .' Day shivered, remembering long hours underground, a scalpel, a laughing madman. 'If he kills me this time, Claire and the babies will have nothing. They'll be put out in the street.'

'Do you really believe that?'

Day filled his cup again and sipped. Claire's parents would jump at the chance to have her back home with them. Her father no doubt already had a proper match in mind for her. She'd be remarried within a year and the twins would be raised by some other man. They would take that stranger's name and call him Father. Day set his cup down and opened his mouth to respond, but there were no words. The pub's proprietor arrived just in time with the whisky. Day took the shot, swallowed it and handed back the empty glass.

'Another, would you?'

'Right away.' The proprietor walked back across the room, wiping the glass with a dirty cloth.

Day looked again at Hammersmith, who held up a hand and nodded. 'I apologize,' Hammersmith said. 'You have a family. Of course you have a family. And so many other considerations I do not. My God, the Ripper even knows where you live. You must be constantly on edge. It's only . . . I'm frustrated.'

'I know you are. I am, too.'

'Yes, you're the only one who knows my frustration. That's why –'

'It's not just fear, Nevil.'

'I know.'

'It's really not. They're hunting this other monster now.'

'The Harvest Man.'

'Yes. He killed another family last week. The things he did . . .'

'You'll catch him.'

'And I want to help you. But our fellow Jack, he's all but disappeared.'

'Doesn't that frighten you? What's he up to, do you think?'

'He's killing them. Somehow. He must be. Or planning to, at any rate.'

Jack the Ripper was embroiled in a personal war with a

secret society of vigilantes who called themselves Karst-phanomen. The notion that the Karstphanomen might have won, that Jack might be dead or captured, did not cross Day's or Hammersmith's mind. Jack was far too dangerous to go quietly.

'He hates them,' Day said. 'And I honestly can't muster much sympathy for them. It's the Karstphanomen's fault he's at large right now. Their own damn fault he's killing them off.'

'He'll make a mistake and I'll be on him before he can hide again.'

'I know you will. At least, you'll catch him if he really does make a mistake, but I don't share your faith that he will.'

Hammersmith opened his mouth to respond, but Day held a hand up, quieting him, as the proprietor appeared once again with a shot glass on his tray. Day took the drink and closed his eyes, held the whisky in his mouth as it warmed, then finally swallowed it. He opened his eyes again and took a deep breath.

'I must do my job. And only my job. Sir Edward won't acknowledge that Jack's even still alive. I can't make him see the truth and I can't risk my job.'

'Then I'm on my own.'

'Get one of the others. Constable Bentley might help.'

'I'm not a policeman any more, remember? Nobody's going to help me. Not officially.'

'Then give it up. For your own sake. It's too much for you. He'll leave you alone if you let him be, but if you don't, he'll get to you before you can find him. I know him. He's almost . . .'

'What?'

'Never mind.'

'No, what were you going to say?'

'I don't think he is a man. I think he's something else.'

'A woman? He's not a woman. I heard his voice.'

'No.' Day sighed. 'That's not what I meant. Forget I said anything. Just let it be. For God's sake, Nevil, you had your chest split open. You're lucky to be alive. Heal yourself and, when you're better, petition Sir Edward for your old job back. He's fond of you. He'll consider it. I'll put in a word for you, you know I will. So will some of the others. Kett, Blacker, maybe even Tiffany.'

'What you said. I'm lucky to be alive. There's a reason I am. I think it's to catch that monster. Someone has to. He can't be left to roam. If I'm alive, then I must make myself matter.'

Hammersmith pushed his chair back and stood, fished sixpence from his pocket and tossed it on the table. 'For the tea,' he said. He walked away without another word, out of the door and into the sudden blinding sunlight. Disappointment shimmered like heat from his shoulders. The door closed behind him and the tavern was once more plunged into brown silence.

Day motioned for another shot of whisky, stared glumly at Hammersmith's untouched cup of tea and waited for the man to bring his drink. It occurred to him, too late, that Hammersmith had come to deliver news. He wondered what it might have been.

2

Dr Kingsley stood in the doorway with his eyes closed, sniffing the air. He had got a glimpse when he first stepped into the house and he knew that ahead of him lay the parlour, big and empty, a rectangular rug covering the floor, and a fireplace directly ahead of him, its chimneypiece caved in, obstructing the hearth. To his right was another door and he had no way of knowing what was on the other side of it. To his left was a short hall that widened out into a dining room, where the family would have had their meals. Also to his left, between the parlour and the dining room, was a staircase. Policemen moved up and down the stairs in a constant stream. Kingsley smelled old food, an animal of some sort, and rot. There was a faint chemical scent in the air and something else, something sweet and dark, lurked just beneath the rest of it. There were bodies decaying somewhere in the house. But of course there were. If not, the policemen would be somewhere else, swarming about some other place, some other bodies.

All bodies ended.

'Do you feel all right, Doctor?'

Kingsley hung his head and opened his eyes. He looked up at his giant companion. 'I'm fine, Henry, thank you. I was concentrating. You must let me think without interrupting.'

'What were you thinking about?'

'I was thinking about . . . Well, I admit my mind was wandering a bit. But I was smelling the air in this house.'

'It smells terrible,' Henry said. 'It's full of terrible things and you should try not to breathe it or those things will get inside your body.' As if in agreement, the magpie on Henry's shoulder squawked.

'Actually, you're not wrong,' Kingsley said. 'The air carries particles of decay, along with little bits of everything else that's been stirred up by people walking through the area. By sniffing those particles, I'm sometimes able to tell how long a body's been dead before I see it.'

'Why do you need to do that? You can just go up the stairs and look at it instead of smelling it so much.'

'I'm honing my skills, Henry. I'm sharpening my instruments.'

'Oh.'

Kingsley saw the big man struggling to understand. He waited for Henry to ask him what kind of instruments he played, but Henry smiled at him and nodded. He was learning. Kingsley smiled back and walked forward, looked at the useless fireplace, moved to his left, and passed two policemen who said something to him that he didn't hear. He went up the steps with Henry behind him. Kingsley's black leather bag swung in his hand, pulling him forward and up. At the top of the stairs, he looked right and left and he turned to the left, towards the stench of rotten meat, and marched past the blue-uniformed bodies that were upright and healthy and moving about, onward to a room at the end of the hall.

Inside, an enormous bed filled his frame of view. At

least, it looked enormous to him. It was butted up against the wall all the way at the back, under a picture window that looked out on the semidetached house beside it, so close he thought he could reach out and touch it through the glass. On the bed under the window, two people, a man and a woman, lay curled in each other's arms. Their lower extremities were properly covered with a heavy woollen blanket, yellow and brown, a floral pattern embroidered about the edges. Their shoulders rested on the windowsill behind them and their heads leaned in to touch, a tender gesture of love or comfort. But thick rope was coiled about them, snaking under the bed and back up, holding the bodies in place. Where their foreheads met, the skin had been peeled back so that the exposed muscle of one head joined the muscle of the other. The couple melted together in a parody of love, their torsos angled in towards the centre of the bed, their arms draped over each other's abdomens.

Henry gasped and Kingsley turned around. The simple giant was using one hand to cover his bird's eyes, and the magpie was flapping its wings in irritation. A tear escaped Henry's eye and rolled down his cheek. Kingsley sighed.

'Henry, would you like to wait downstairs for me?'

'I can't, Doctor. I'm supposed to help you.'

Kingsley glanced back at the bodies and frowned. 'This is more than you signed on for. I can handle things here.'

'It's my job, sir.' Tears were spilling down Henry's face now, but he was doing his best to put on a brave smile. It looked more like a grimace of fear and sorrow.

Kingsley tried a different tack. 'Oliver's still young.'

Henry looked at the bird and nodded. 'He's little.'

'You're responsible for him. He shouldn't be around a thing like this.'

'It's bad for him to see it.'

'Very bad. Perhaps you should take Oliver downstairs and make sure he's all right. We wouldn't want him to have nightmares.'

'No, sir, we wouldn't. Are you sure you'll be . . .'

'I'll be fine.'

Henry nodded and scooped the magpie from his shoulder. He cradled the bird in his arms and went to the stairs and down. Kingsley shook his head at Henry's back. The giant had been living on the street, but had helped catch a murderer, and Walter Day had taken pity on him, found a small strange home for him to live in and asked Kingsley to find work for him. As an assistant, Henry was nearly useless, but he helped to remind Kingsley of the human aspect of what he did.

Kingsley took a step towards the bed. The woman lying there had long dark hair, wild and tangled and brushed back from her vulnerable brow. The man's hair was receding, sandy brown, shaggy over his ears. Their eyelids had been cut away and their naked eyes, as if surprised by the frowning doctor in front of them, popped. Kingsley noted with regret that the woman's eyes were startling green, sun-dappled seas that must once have sparkled with life. Even as he watched, the colour appeared to drain from them.

He looked down at the floor. Bits of gore, grey and purple and pink and glassy yellow, were strewn haphazardly over the two-foot space between the bed and the wall. A streamer of something red clung to the skirting board. There was the end of a nose, what seemed to be an upper lip, a dimple cut whole from a man's cheek, still rough with stubble.

Kingsley took another look at the faceless couple in their bed and turned his back on them. He crouched and ran his fingers over the floor, placed his palms flat and bent so that his cheek nearly touched the boards. He watched the slowly moving pattern of light from the window. He stood up again and turned to a constable who was standing just outside the bedroom door.

'Where's Inspector Day?'

The policeman jumped and smiled at him nervously. He did not look at the corpses behind Kingsley. 'It's Inspector Tiffany on duty, sir. Want me to fetch him?'

'Not particularly.'

'Um, then what?'

Kingsley sighed and waved his hand at nothing in particular. 'Yes, very well. Please fetch Inspector Tiffany for me.'

'Right away, sir.'

The constable hurried away. Kingsley fished a handkerchief from his pocket and held it over his nose and mouth while he took a deep breath. He heard footsteps on the stairs and he counted slowly in his head, listened as two men came towards him along the landing. Tiffany entered the room, glanced once at the bodies and approached Kingsley, stepping carefully around a chunk of human gristle.

'You asked for me?'

'Yes,' Kingsley said. 'I mean no offence, Inspector, but would you mind telling me, where is Walter Day?'

'He's not been working lately,' Tiffany said. He was a

hard-edged man, gone grey all along his hairline, an inoffensive moustache kept carefully in line above his lip. 'I mean to say, he's working, but at his desk. Until he's ready, you know.'

'Ready for what?'

'Well, you know. You know what happened.'

'Yes. But what's he preparing for?'

'For work, I suppose. For this.' Tiffany held his arms out, taking in the bloody smears on the wall above the bed. 'He had a rough time of it. He's settling his mind, I suppose.'

'I'd like an opportunity to settle my own mind, come to think of it. This is a bit much, isn't it?'

'This one's ugly,' Tiffany said.

'Ugly doesn't begin to touch on what's happened here.'

'Is it him, you think?'

'The Harvest Man?'

'Yeah,' Tiffany said. 'Him.'

'Indeed.'

'It does look like the others.'

'Just like them . . .' Kingsley's voice trailed away at the end of the sentence and he turned around to look at the door, at the narrow wedge of landing he could see outside the room. 'The bodies are set in the same sort of tableau.'

'That's it, then, do you think? He's making tableaux?'

'That's what I thought. At least, initially. But I can find no trace of photographic equipment having been used. No indication that a camera was set up. It would have to have been placed right around here on the floor and its legs would have made marks.'

'Could still be a tableau vivant,' Tiffany said. 'We don't

have to assume he was taking photographs. Could've been for an audience of one: hisself.'

'It's possible,' Kingsley said. 'Let's not rule it out.' He glanced down. 'Were there children in the house?'

Tiffany nodded.

'Oh,' Kingsley said. He was unable to think of any other words to sum up his sudden fear. He could think of nothing worse than a murdered child.

'But it's different this time,' Tiffany said. 'It's why I wasn't sure. Not absolutely. Follow me.'

He led the way out of the room and across the landing to a staircase. Tucked under it was a narrow bed, pushed up against the wall, its blankets rumpled and wadded. A miniature cupboard was situated near the bed at the base of the steps, one door hanging open, clothing pouring out on to the floor, the top of it stacked with children's things: a toy ark, tiny wooden animals spilling out of it; a larger wooden horse, from a different set, one leg broken off; a pink teacup with a chip on the handle; a stuffed dog with button eyes, its head resting in the lap of an ancient baby doll that had no eyes at all; a single shoe, smudged with mud, its buckle scratched and dull.

To Kingsley's great relief there were no small bodies in sight.

'I think there were two of them,' Tiffany said. 'Two pillows, two sets of the same puzzles in there with the toys. And no signs of anyone else in the house.'

'But where are they now?'

'That's just it. Can't find 'em anywhere.'

Kingsley looked up at the ceiling. 'These stairs lead to an attic?'

'Yeah. First thing we looked for, knowing how this bloke likes to do his deeds.'

'They're not up there, then? The children?'

'No.'

'Did he . . .' Kingsley paused to take a deep breath. 'He didn't take them with him, do you think?'

'We've checked the ground outside. There was a little rain last night, but no footprints out there, nothing disturbed. He's vanished same as he always does, but so have these kids.'

'Maybe they weren't in the house when it happened.'

'Come here.'

Tiffany turned again and led the way back to the landing. Just outside the bedroom that housed the two mutilated bodies, he pointed down. Kingsley dropped to one knee and squinted at the dark corner where the doorjamb met the floor.

'It's a partial footprint,' he said.

'That's what it looks like to me.'

The long outside edge of a tiny foot, ridged with whorls and topped with the impression of two perfect little toes, was inked in blood. Kingsley set down his bag and fished out his lens, he hunched low over the print and stuck out his tongue, licked his lower lip while he peered through the curved glass.

'Most definitely the foot of a child.'

'Any way of telling whether it's a boy or a girl?'

'No,' Kingsley said. 'He or she was perhaps seven years old. No younger than five, I'd say, and no older than eight or nine if it was a boy. If it was a girl, depending on nutrition and medical history, she might be as old as twelve.'

'And barefoot.'

'Yes. Of course, barefoot.'

'Possibly injured, too.'

'If it's the child's blood. Considering the scene here, there's no reason to assume anything yet.'

'Good thing it's warm out.'

'If there are two of them, at least they're together.'

'Might be,' Tiffany said. 'Might not be.'

Kingsley stood and looked past the bed, past the embracing corpses, out through the window behind them at the bright blue sky. 'If he's got them . . .'

'He's never taken anyone before.'

'Even so . . .'

'I've got every constable on alert. We're going from door to door. We'll find a neighbour who knows them, knows their names. Might even find the children themselves if someone took 'em in last night.'

'We can't simply wait.'

'Not much else we can do right now.'

'There is one thing.'

'What's that?'

'Find Inspector Day and bring him here.'

'I told you –'

'Inspector Tiffany,' Kingsley said. 'Get Day here as soon as you possibly can. I insist on it.'

Tiffany opened his mouth, then closed it and nodded. He walked back across the landing and down the stairs. Kingsley entered the bloody room again. He took a tape measure from his bag and got to work.

3

Fiona Kingsley stepped through the front doors of the Marylebone bazaar. She brushed her hair behind her ear and waited for her eyes to adjust to the electric lights, listened to the babble and the bustle of hundreds of people all packed into the passages between stalls. She smiled at a man with a waxed moustache that curled out past his ears, his eyebrows shaped so that they vaulted across his forehead in a single expanse of black fur. He smiled back, but his gaze quickly moved on when it became apparent that she wasn't there to buy one of the tins of hair care products arranged on the counter in front of him. She pushed past his stall and between two stout old ladies who were marvelling at a gramophone on display at the next stall over. A salesman was winding the big handle, and Fiona stopped for a moment to watch as the turning cylinder produced tinkling music out of thin air. The effect was unsettling, and Fiona wondered who bought such things. She felt certain the sound of it would grow tiresome very quickly once the novelty of the thing wore off. She moved on again, pausing here and there to admire the carved handles of Indian parasols or to stroke a length of soft Chinese silk with her knuckles. She finally found what she had come for, on the second floor of the bazaar near a window at the back. A beam of sunshine pointed the way to a small kiosk with a sign that declared it to be Goodpenny's Finest

Stationery, its counter organized like a single place setting. In the centre was a letter of introduction from Lord Walpole, engraved on fine letterhead and precisely aligned two inches from the edge of the counter's polished surface. Next to the paper was a silver letter opener, Her Majesty's likeness etched on its handle, and above it was a creamy white envelope that rested alongside a tin of sealing wax and a stamp. All of this was artfully suggested to fit within a leather wallet that was open to show off its many compartments and enclosures. Below, a glassed-in cabinet enclosed a range of pocket watches, tiepins, cufflinks and assorted other fine accessories. A small round man with a soupçon of a moustache inscribed across the expanse of his upper lip sat on a stool behind the counter regarding Fiona without any indication that he cared whether she was there to purchase his wares or merely to window-shop. She liked that about him and took it as a sign that he was confident in the quality of his products.

'I would like to purchase a small wallet, please.'

'There's no need to shout,' the man said. But his voice was low and gentle and he smiled at her.

'I'm sorry,' Fiona said. 'I hadn't realized I was shouting.'

'You weren't. I was simply advising you that there's no need. The rumours of my hearing problem are quite erroneous. My ears work just as well as yours do, I'm sure.' He hopped off his stool and stepped towards her, his back straight and his little round tummy curving out ahead of him. 'What sort of locket would you like? I have three here, one with a lovely cameo of Her Majesty in silhouette. Please keep in mind I can engrave it for you, but you'll have to leave it for delivery.'

Fiona put her hand to her mouth to hide a grin. She bit her lip and pointed to a small black card case near the back of the cabinet. 'I'm afraid I've changed my mind,' she said. 'Could I possibly look at a wallet instead?'

'Ah, yes. The ability to change one's mind is the hallmark of a nimble intellect.' He bent and she saw his hands through the glass as he fumbled blindly about, feeling for the wallet, his line of sight blocked by the frame of the cabinet. At last he drew out the wallet and set it on the counter between them, moving the letter of introduction carefully out of the way.

'Is it the proper size to carry calling cards?'

'No, no, my dear. This is meant to carry calling cards. Just the right size for twenty of them to fit without causing an unsightly bulge in a gentleman's pocket. It comes with a full complement of plain cards, so you may customize them with your own information as you wish or simply replace these with something you've had properly printed.' He opened it to show her a little stack of ivory-coloured cards, a small filigree design in one corner, but otherwise blank.

'How much is it?'

The man leaned back and found his stool without taking his eyes off her face. He sat and frowned at her for a moment and then smiled again. 'You tell me. What would you pay for such a thing?'

'I have three crowns and tuppence. Is that enough?'

He sniffed. 'Did your mistress send you here today?'

Fiona looked down at her dress and boots. Her forehead creased as she looked up and around at the other women on the landing. Even the poorest ladies wore their finest frocks and polished their shoes for a day of shopping at the bazaar, but Fiona had paid no attention at all to her wardrobe before leaving the house. She felt a twinge of sadness. Her father did his best with her, but he had not been able to teach her proper dress and behaviour for a lady. She had learned all she could from Claire Day, but of course it wasn't Claire's duty to act as her mother.

'No, sir,' she said. She looked down at the counter, suddenly ashamed. 'It's for me.'

'For you? A man's card case?'

'For a friend of mine, I mean.'

'Well, if he's mean, you shouldn't buy him things with your own money.'

She looked up, alarmed. 'Oh, no, he's not mean at all.'

'Then you shouldn't have said he was. That's quite misleading and you might injure his reputation.'

'I'm very sorry.'

'That's better.' He pursed his lips and pushed them in and out, staring at a corner of the ceiling behind her for a long moment. She held her breath, not sure what to say to him or what he might *believe* she'd said if she did say anything. At last his gaze returned to her face and he smiled. 'One crown ought to be enough,' he said.

'Oh, are you sure? It looks so much more dear than that.'

'Thank you, young lady. I made it myself. And I've decided I want you to have it and I want you to keep some of your money, too. I would feel bad about myself if I took it all from you. You may need to purchase something else for this mean young man you seem so fond of.'

Fiona laughed. 'Thank you, sir.'

'He's a lucky boy.'

Fiona blushed and looked down at the counter again. She busied herself with her change purse and handed over a crown. Goodpenny took it and slipped it into his waistcoat pocket without looking at it. 'I'll wrap this for you,' he said.

'Oh. Would you mind . . . I mean, would it be possible to keep the cards out?'

'If you don't want the cards, if you've got printed cards to use in their place, I can keep them myself and put them to some use.'

'But I do want them. I won't waste them, I promise.'

'Very well, then. Give me a moment.'

He took the case and walked with it to the back of the stall where there was a giant roll of butcher paper bolted to the wall at eye level. He laid the case against the roll as if measuring how much he'd need to wrap it, then yanked and tore off a length of paper, which he brought back to the counter. He laid the paper down and creased it at the edge of the wood and tore it into two neat pieces, one smaller than the other. His fingers moved quickly and confidently, and in a moment the card case was wrapped twice over in the larger piece of paper. He bent and came up with a spool of bright green ribbon from behind the counter, which he wound around the little bundle, then he scraped the ribbon with his thumbnail until it curled around itself. He tapped the stack of blank cards together and wrapped them all up in the smaller piece of paper, and handed both packages over to Fiona with a flourish.

'May I ask your name?'

'Kingsley. I'm Fiona Kingsley.'

'I am pleased to make your acquaintance, Miss Tinsley.

I am Alastair Goodpenny.' He pointed to the sign above that carried his name. 'I hope you'll call on me again if you've a need for stationery or fine jewellery. Ask for me if I'm not at my post here.'

'I will.'

'And please bring your young man around sometime so that I may inform him of his very good fortune in having earned your admiration.'

'I'm sure I'd be the lucky one, if he only knew that I existed, Mr Goodpenny.'

'Ah,' he said. 'Well, it is better to have good fortune and not realize it than to have no fortune at all.'

Fiona nodded. But it occurred to her that the young man they were discussing had perhaps the worst fortune of anyone she had ever met.

She looked at the little parcels in her hands. 'Perhaps this will serve as a charm for him.'

'It most assuredly will,' Mr Goodpenny said. 'All of the items I sell are good luck for someone.'

Fiona waved goodbye to him and made her winding way back to the stairs and down, and out by the front doors of the bazaar. She took a deep breath when the sunlight hit her face and she closed her eyes and wished that Mr Goodpenny might be right and that Nevil Hammersmith would be safe from harm. For once in his unlucky life.

4

The warder hurried to open the gate, and Nevil Hammersmith stepped into the courtyard of HM Prison Bridewell. He stood and waited as the gate was closed behind him and then shook hands with the warder.

'Morning, Bill,' he said. 'I appreciate this.'

'Of course,' Bill said. 'I still owe you. Just keep it quiet. Don't want to lose my position.'

He jerked his head at the high stone walls behind them and led the way up the winding path and through a thick iron door. It, too, closed behind Hammersmith, who breathed in the cool dry air and stuck his hands in his pockets. He was wearing a thin black overcoat with an unfashionably large collar and cotton trousers that were a bit too short. His shoes were scratched and worn, buffed to a blue sheen around the heels, but dirty grey at the toes. His mop of uncombed hair fell into his eyes, but he hardly seemed to notice.

The warder glanced up at him and motioned for Hammersmith to turn and follow a wide hall around the corner. The walls were thick and soundproofed to increase the prisoners' sense of isolation, to impress upon the men a need for contemplation and regard. One wing of the prison had been destroyed by a runaway locomotive and was being rebuilt. Hammersmith could hear the men working, their voices echoing faintly down the halls. They walked silently through a large room filled with battered wooden tables and chairs, through several more doors and finally stopped outside a cell at the end of a long corridor.

'He's in there. On the floor at the back.'

Hammersmith looked up and down the empty hall and stepped inside the cell. He waited for his eyes to adjust to the dim light from a high window, barely four inches across and five feet off the ground, through which a pale shaft of light shone. Against the wall to Hammersmith's left hand was a narrow cot, metal slats with a hard straw mat and a blanket. The only other furnishing was a wooden bucket on the floor in the far corner. Hammersmith didn't need to be told what the bucket was for. A man's naked body lay across the cot, his knees on the floor and his arms stretched out so that his knuckles touched the wall behind the slats. His face was buried in the grey blanket. Three of his toes had been broken and were splayed out at different angles. Something glinted in the dim light and Hammersmith narrowed his eyes, saw a pair of spectacles in the dark at the intersection of the wall and the floor beneath the cot.

'You're sure it's him?'

'It's him,' Bill said. 'It's Adrian March, all right.'

March had been Walter Day's mentor, had introduced him to the Yard and got him his position as an inspector. But Adrian March had also belonged to a secret society of torturers and murderers. Day had been forced to arrest his mentor, his old friend. Hammersmith suspected that Day was still punishing himself for what he had been forced to do.

'Did he fall?'

'Roll him over, you'll see.'

'What will I see?'

'His tongue.'

'Nothing else? Only his tongue?'

'It were enough. He choked on it.'

'Self-inflicted?'

'Not judging by the expression on his face, it weren't. He saw something bad, something that frightened him. My guess? Whoever or whatever that was . . . that's what kilt him.'

Hammersmith winced and looked away from the body. Across from the cot on the opposite wall was an odd configuration of blue lines on the stone. Hammersmith stared at the lines until they made sense to him, formed a symbol he'd seen before: a faint chalk outline in the shape of a circle. Under the circle was a crude arrow that pointed down. A giant number zero pointing roughly in the direction of Adrian March's body. Hammersmith drew in a quick involuntary breath and turned to the warder.

'He wasn't cut?'

'Not a bit,' Bill said. 'Someone came in here while I was at my meal and shoved his tongue down his throat. Didn't touch one other hair on his head and left again before I returned. Like a ghost.'

'Very much like a ghost.'

'You think it was one? An actual ghost?'

'I think it was someone most people think is dead and gone. Better he should have stayed that way.'

'Whoever it was, it looks to me like Inspector March put up a fight. You can see he thrashed around some, maybe while he was choking, maybe before that. Broke his toes and one of his fingers. You can't see the finger from here. It's around the other side of him, but it's broke.'

'What about his eyes?'

'They're bulging straight out of his head like they might pop, but they're still in there. Like I said, roll him over.'

'No. I've seen what I came to see.'

Hammersmith turned and pushed past the warder and down the hall. He called back over his shoulder. 'Do I need you to let me back out with that key?'

'Can't get out of a prison without a key, Nevil.'

'Then hurry up. Let me out.'

Bill hustled and passed him and got to the iron door first. He inserted his key, turned it and swung the door open, gesturing for Hammersmith to walk ahead.

'Once I'm away,' Hammersmith said, 'raise the alarm.'

'They'll only call you right back here to investigate the bloody thing.'

They went through the front door and down the path to the gate. Bill lingered there and Hammersmith looked away from him, through the opening in the fence.

'They won't call me out this time,' he said. 'Not any more. I've been sacked.'

'Sacked? You didn't tell me you got the empty. What're you doing here if you ain't a policeman no more?'

'Not a thing, Bill. I was never here.' Hammersmith raised a finger to his lips.

'Damnedest thing,' Bill said. 'You're the last one I'd expect would get the sack.'

Hammersmith patted the warder on his shoulder and crammed his hands back in his pockets and walked away from the prison. He listened for the echo of the metal gates as they closed behind him.

5

Bill Pycroft closed the outer doors behind Hammersmith and they locked automatically. He took his time walking back to Adrian March's cell. Once there, he turned March over and laid him on his cot. He arranged the former inspector on his back and pulled a blanket up over his chest.

He left the cell and went to a small cupboard at the end of the passage, where he picked up a bucket of soapy water and a brush. Back in the cell, he scrubbed the blue chalk marks off the wall. He stood on the end of the cot and dumped the dirty water from the bucket out the narrow window. He put it back where it belonged, along with the brush, and locked the cupboard. He surveyed his work carefully and nodded to himself. He'd more than earned the twenty quid he'd been paid for this. He pulled the cell door shut and went to sound the alarm:

'Inspector March has killed himself in his cell!'

As he ran along the outer corridor, he pulled a chunk of blue chalk from his pocket and dropped it in a rubbish bin.

6

By the time Day reached the crime scene, he was desperate for a glass of water. His tongue was dry and his head was pounding and his fingers were trembling. There was a hollowed-out sensation in his chest. He didn't hear what the runner said to him, but he gave the boy a ha'penny and stepped inside the house. Henry Mayhew was there, leaning against the doorjamb. The big man grinned and scooped Day up for a bear hug. As his toes left the floor a wave of dizziness and nausea washed over Day. He patted Henry on the back and swallowed hard. Henry let him down and they exchanged greetings. Day took a moment to regain his balance and smiled at the black-and-white bird that was Henry's constant companion. From across the room, a constable recognized him and motioned for Day to follow him up the stairs and across the landing to a room where Dr Kingsley stood silhouetted against a big picture window, leaning over two figures on a bed.

The smell was overpowering: coppery blood and emptied bowels and an acrid chemical trace beneath it like a distant memory. Day felt the sudden rush of vomit and tried to turn away. He dropped his cane and put his hands over his mouth, but too late. He spewed through his fingers, down his right sleeve, and on to the floor. He spat and wiped his mouth with his left sleeve.

Kingsley straightened up and surveyed the new mess,

but didn't approach the inspector. 'Someone probably should have warned you,' he said. 'It's not a pretty sight.'

Footsteps sounded on the landing and Day turned to see Inspector Tiffany approaching. Tiffany held a finger up under his nostrils and touched Day's elbow to steady himself while he looked past him into the room. He reeled back and gave Day a black look. 'What've you done to my scene?'

'Sorry,' Day said. 'Don't know what happened.'

Tiffany sniffed. 'By the smell of you, what happened is no great mystery. Why don't you get down to the kitchen and clean yourself up? Have your jacket brushed out.'

Day nodded. He stooped to pick up his cane and limped past Tiffany to the stairs. He stopped halfway down, his hand on the wall. He took a deep breath and held it in his lungs. His throat hurt and he felt sloppy, panicky, like he was underwater. He let the air out and passed a hand over his mouth and leaned heavily on the banister the rest of the way down the stairs. In the kitchen, a girl jumped up from the long low table and took his jacket from him without a word. She folded it over her arm and bustled out of the room. Day went to the pitcher on the sideboard and dipped a cloth into it. He unfastened his cuffs and wiped his sleeve until it was drenched, then pushed it up past his elbow and rinsed his hands and arms in the basin. He splashed water on his face and tipped the pitcher up, drinking until it was empty, letting the water run off his chin and down the front of his shirt. He heard someone in the hallway approaching the kitchen.

'I don't know if I've seen anything worse than this.' Kingsley's voice was grim.

Day turned and grimaced at the doctor. 'It's bad up there.'

'I meant you,' Kingsley said. 'I've disinterred better-looking corpses.'

'Sorry.'

'Desk work clearly doesn't suit you.'

'I've not much choice in the matter.'

'Well, I'd appreciate your opinion on this one. If Inspector Tiffany's agreeable, that is. A day or two away from the desk. Maybe more, if we don't catch this mad-man before he kills another family.'

'Jimmy Tiffany's a good man. You don't need me.'

'I think I do.' Kingsley pulled out a chair and sat.

Day set the pitcher down and pulled his wet sleeve back into place, fastened the cuff. He leaned his cane against the table and sat opposite Kingsley. 'What makes you think I can do you any good?'

'It's not just the bodies,' Kingsley said.

'Did he do something different this time? Wait. I'm getting ahead of myself. Am I wrong in assuming this is the work of the Harvest Man?'

'You are not wrong. This is unquestionably his work. There's a broken window at the back of the house and scuff marks in the dust up in the attic where he waited for the family to come home and go to sleep. We may take it for granted that he acted much as he did in the other three houses . . .'

Kingsley continued to talk and Day sat silent, drying, absorbing what information he could, trying to remember the basic facts he already knew. A killer had escaped from prison with three other men and had used the ensuing confusion to evade police. He was still at large. He had no known name, and his records had been lost, but he had been called the Harvest Man by other inmates. The Harvest Man broke into people's homes while they were out during the day and hid in their attics, waiting until the household was asleep before emerging. He somehow made them groggy and unable to react while he methodically cut away their faces, a piece at a time.

'How do you think he keeps them still before he ties them down?'

'This one is fresher than the others. There's still a lingering odour of ether. He's sedating these people.'

'So they go to sleep and then he keeps them asleep.'

'Which gives him all the time in the world with them.'

'To harvest them.'

'I don't think that's where he got his name.'

'Why do they call him the Harvest Man, then?'

'It's a spider,' Kingsley said. 'Opiliones. A breed of arachnid-like creatures that live in people's attics, out of the way, unseen, prey on common household pests, I think.'

'Of course,' Day said. 'Every one of the victims has had an attic.'

'That fact is not lost on me,' Kingsley said.

'Nor on me.' Tiffany entered the kitchen and picked up the water pitcher, saw it was empty and shot a damning look in Day's direction. 'And there are signs he spent time in this attic. Broken cobwebs, scuffs in the dust, like that. But there are hundreds of attics in London. Thousands of them. An attic is a natural place to hide, if there's one near to hand.'

'So, what, you think he's just been lucky all his victims had attics? You believe in coincidence?'

'Don't you, Dr Kingsley? I've certainly seen enough of them.'

'I reserve judgement,' Kingsley said. 'What do you think, Inspector Day?'

'I don't think it's coincidence. He specifically chooses houses with attics,' Day said. He could feel himself engaging with the puzzle, his nausea ebbing as he tried to imagine himself in the killer's shoes. 'That must be his first priority. Or, at least, an early priority as he goes about looking for victims.'

'So he's always interested in the houses?' Tiffany pulled out a chair next to Kingsley and sat, staring at Day all the while. Day put his hands in his lap, hiding his sopping right sleeve from view.

'More than that, don't you think?'

'I'd like to know what you think,' Tiffany said.

'I don't know why the attic's so important to him, but I do think the houses play a part in whatever his reasoning is.'

'Sure,' Tiffany said. 'He seems like a reasonable bloke.'

'He chooses the house and he chooses the family. The two go hand in hand for him. He needs both circumstances to be right before he acts. And I imagine there are details about the members of each family that have to fit his criteria.'

'That's a lot of things for a murderer to concern himself with,' Tiffany said. 'I mean, most of them I've met barely have a single thing that sets them off. All you have to do to be killed is jingle a pocket full of coins.'

'Yes,' Day said. 'That's what sets this man apart from other killers, makes him that much harder to catch and more dangerous. But it's also why we haven't seen even more murders like this one since he escaped prison. The conditions have to be just so for him. It must take time for him to deliberate and then make his move.'

'Supposing you're right,' Tiffany said. 'Why? Why these particular conditions? What is it about the house and the family? I heard what the doctor said about spiders feeding on common pests. Does he think he's a spider? Does he think those people upstairs, that man and woman he chopped to little bits, does he think they're pests? Insects? What?'

'No, I wouldn't guess he's delusional in quite that way. I don't know whether he starts with the house or the family inside it. I don't know what it is about the house. Aside from the obvious fact that he wants it to have an attic.'

'But beyond that? You make it sound more complicated.'

'It is,' Day said. 'He's searching for something.'

'How would you know that? What's he looking for?'

'Right now he may be looking for those children,' Kingsley said. 'That should be our priority.'

'What children?'

'I'm sorry, Inspector Day,' Kingsley said. 'There are two missing children. I should say, we think there are two. We don't know much of anything yet, but Tiffany's men are making enquiries. It's a large part of why we asked for you.'

'To be clear, two children have gone missing from this house?'

'Yes. We think so.'

Day leaned forward. 'What do you know about them?'

Tiffany broke in, swiping his hand through the air. 'I have constables looking.'

'Nobody's implying that you and your men aren't doing the job,' Kingsley said. 'But does it hurt to have another pair of eyes?'

Tiffany sat back and frowned, not objecting, but not agreeing.

Day looked at each of the men in turn. 'You said the children were a part of why you asked me here. What's the whole reason?'

Kingsley stared at Day without speaking.

Day nodded. There were politics involved here, and though Kingsley was the bluntest of men, it wouldn't do to antagonize Inspector Tiffany too much. 'I apologize,' Day said. 'Long day. Long month, actually. It doesn't matter. Tell me about the children. You're right, that's most important.'

'As I say, we know nothing about the children,' Kingsley said. 'Not really.'

'There are two beds upstairs,' Tiffany said. 'And there are two bodies, but they're both adults and both in the same bed. The other bed's smaller, child-sized.'

'You've looked . . .'

'We've searched the entire house, knocked on every door up and down this street and the next.'

'Speaking of those two bodies upstairs,' Kingsley said, 'I must get back to them. And I probably ought to send poor Henry home. He's not of much use to me here. Please excuse me, gentlemen. Godspeed.'

41

The two inspectors watched Kingsley rise and leave the room, listened for his tread on the stairs. Tiffany leaned forward and put his elbows on the table, tented his fingers under his chin. 'What's happened to you, man?'

'What do you mean?'

'Look at you,' Tiffany said. 'You're a disgrace.'

'The bodies caught me off guard, is all. The smell of it.'

'You've seen bodies before. We all have, and worse than this.'

'Never worse than this,' Day said.

'All right. Perhaps not worse than this, but certainly not much better.'

'It's not a thing I really care to become used to.'

'You'll never get off the desk with that attitude.'

'Maybe I don't want to leave desk duty.'

'Please,' Tiffany said. He laid his hands palm down on the table. 'We both know you've been hobbled.'

Day sniffed and changed the subject. 'Do you think he took them? The Harvest Man, I mean. Do you think he has the children with him?'

'He's never taken anyone out of a house before.'

'Not that we'd know if he did.'

'True,' Tiffany said. 'We don't know much. There was a bloody footprint, a small one, child-sized, near the bedroom door.'

'An injured child?'

'Or it just stepped in its parents' blood.'

'Please don't call the child *it*.'

'I don't know whether they're boys or girls. What should I call them?'

'Let's just find them.'

42

'I have two constables looking for more footprints outside. Unless the killer carried them out, the children may have left signs, but so far no luck.'

'They ran away. They saw what was happening, saw it was too late to act on their parents' behalf, and they got themselves out of the house.'

'I hope so,' Tiffany said.

'They're hiding somewhere nearby.'

'Why nearby?'

'So they can watch and come home when the Harvest Man leaves. I'd bet anything on it.'

'But he's left already and they haven't come back.'

'Because we're here now.'

'They're scared of us?'

'Of course they are.'

'My constables are at your disposal. The two in the garden are. Take them and find those children. I've got to get back to the investigation.'

They both rose as the girl came wordlessly back into the kitchen, holding Day's jacket up to the light from the window. It looked passably clean. She helped him on with it and he thanked her. Tiffany nodded at him and turned to leave.

'You know,' Day said, 'those children . . .'

Tiffany didn't turn back to look at Day, but he stopped at the kitchen door. 'What?'

'They saw him. They must have seen him. We could finally get a description of this madman.'

Tiffany passed through the door and into the hall beyond. His voice wafted back through the air. 'That fact is not lost on me, Mr Day. Please find those children as quickly as you can.'

7

Why did he do it that way, do you think?'

Dr Kingsley straightened his back and swivelled his head a few degrees in the direction of the bedroom door. 'Who did what?'

'The murderer. He did it messy.'

Kingsley sighed and turned his head the rest of the way so he could see the doorway. Constable Bentley leaned there against the jamb, his hands in his pockets.

'He did indeed do messy work here,' Kingsley said.

'Is there clues about who he is, him what done it?'

'Look right there.' Kingsley pointed to a long smudge of gore near the corner of the bed. 'Do you see these ridges in the blood?'

'It's a boot print, is what that is, Doctor.'

'Yes. A boot print.'

'And you can tell from that print whose boots they is?'

'I can indeed. You'll note the distinctive pattern here of wear along the outer edge. This narrows down the suspects to one pair of boots among a thousand.'

'You're some kinda genius, you are. To be able to see all that. So who done it, then?'

'You, Constable. This is a print from your own boot. You've walked through the blood over there, you see?' He pointed. 'Then you picked up a bit of the man's face on the tip of your right boot and deposited it over here, which caused you to slip just a bit and smear through this small pool of blood right here.'

Bentley backed away, his palms up. 'No, sir. Wasn't me did all this. No, sir!'

'Of course not. I'm not implying that you killed these people, you fool. But you might just as well have been the murderer's accomplice, since any evidence I might have found here you've completely obliterated by tramping through the room like a bloody elephant.'

'Weren't only me in here.'

'No. The lot of you have ruined this crime scene. As you've ruined half the crime scenes I've been to.'

'You got your work to do and we got ours.'

'Yes, but could you possibly see fit to stop obstructing my work as you carry out your own?'

'You mean, there's no clues left here at all?'

'Oh, I don't know, Constable. Please go away and let me concentrate. I might still find a clue intact.'

'I can tell you right off the murderer's a madman. Full of hate.'

'We can't know that.'

'Sure we can. It looks to me like he cut bits off 'em and then laid the bits on the floor and kept on cuttin' and cuttin' the bits, even though they was off already. Just choppin' and choppin'. He musta hated these people to go on killin' 'em even after they was dead.'

'You're substituting assumptions for facts and then treating them as history. That won't do.'

'How so? If I was Inspector Day, you'd be hangin' on me words.'

'You're not Inspector Day.'

'Looka all these pieces of people underfoot. There's a nose. But over there's another bit of nose, might be the same damn nose.'

'It is the same nose,' Kingsley said.

'That's hate,' Bentley said. 'You're a doctor. So I respect that. You see sickness. You see it in the body and you must see it in the mind. People come to you, think they got somethin' wrong in their bodies, but it's in their minds. But me, I'm police. And I see hate. I see it every day. Hardly nobody I see but they're fulla hate, and I see what they do to their neighbour with that hate. They use it like a weapon, see? That's what this is. A bit of that man's nose here and a bit of that same nose there. Hate.'

'This is, in fact, the woman's nose that you're pointing to now. Or parts of it.' Kingsley rocked back on his heels and contemplated his bloody fingertips. 'And I don't know that it is hatred on display here.'

'What else could it be?'

'It could be that the doctor's busy and you're in his way.' Inspector Tiffany crossed the landing and tapped Bentley on the shoulder. 'Get back to work, you. You're wasting Dr Kingsley's time and your own.'

'Wasn't trying to waste time. Trying to understand why we're here, is all.' But Bentley tipped his hat to Kingsley and elbowed his way past Tiffany and down the stairs.

'Sorry,' Tiffany said. 'He doesn't know any better.'

'Actually, I suppose I can appreciate his point of view. I tend to come to a thing like this with the idea that I'm looking at a manifestation of some brain injury or an imbalance of spirits. It's easy to forget that people

46

are capable of the worst acts when they think they're justified.'

'You think young Bentley's right, then?'

'No. Not this time. This is a seriously deranged individual. Your man's hypothesis leaves off the most telling point, which is that whoever did this did it while the people were alive and he did it in stages.'

'Stages? You mean like he was putting on a show?'

'No, I mean he did it bit by bit. He cut off this part of the woman's nose' – Kingsley turned his lens and used the handle to point at a piece of flesh on the floor near the corner of the bed – 'then went back and cut off this part.' He pointed at another chunk of meat. 'Then this and this and this.'

'You're saying . . .'

'I'm saying he took these poor people apart a little at a time, while they lay there helplessly and they may have even watched him do it. I only hope the ether kept them asleep the entire time.'

'But I thought –'

'You thought what Bentley thought. That he cut them and then cut the pieces of them. But no, he cut them and then cut them deeper and deeper until there was nothing left to cut.'

'He's mad.'

'He is assuredly mad. And when he ran out of things to cut, he became angry. That's when he killed them.'

'Good Lord.'

'By that point, death must have been a mercy.'

'You can tell all that?'

'I can. Their blood continued to flow as the night wore on. It must have taken hours.'

'And you're saying there was no hate involved in a thing like that?'

'I don't think so. I think he was moulding them. Or trying to.'

'Moulding them as what?'

'Perhaps he's an artist.'

'I'm not interested in art,' Tiffany said. 'I'm interested in catching this bastard.'

'Ah,' Kingsley said. 'Then I'll get back to it.'

8

Fiona Kingsley climbed the steps at 184 Regent's Park Road and stood, hesitating, before the blue door. An older man stood at attention there. He glanced at her and nodded a greeting. She nodded back, then turned and looked down the street towards the park, but it was out of sight around the bend. She sat down on the top step and opened her bag, took out a large sketch pad and, after another minute of rummaging, found a thick pencil. She looked up again at the guard on the door, but he wasn't paying attention to her. Fiona took a deep breath and closed her eyes, and when she opened them again she focused on a tree across the road. She found a blank page in her pad and held her pencil loosely, barely touched it to the paper as she set down guidelines for her drawing. She didn't hear the door open behind her.

'I didn't hear you knock.'

Fiona jumped and dropped her pencil. She turned and goggled at Claire, who stood just inside the open doorway.

'I startled you,' Claire said. 'I'm so sorry. I didn't mean to.'

'It's not your fault,' Fiona said. 'I was lost in thought.'

'That tree must be very interesting.'

'I like trees. I tend to trust them more than I do people.'

'Oh.'

'Well, except for you,' Fiona said. 'And a few others.'

The guard raised his eyebrows. 'A sensible attitude to take, young lady.'

Claire smiled. 'Thank you, Inspector. Fiona, are you going to come inside?'

Fiona nodded and picked up her pencil, tucked the sketch pad under her arm and stood. She hoisted her bag, ducked her head as she passed the guard and followed Claire into the front room. Claire gestured towards a day-bed that was angled in the far corner of the room beneath a small, framed portrait of the twin babies, and Fiona perched on the edge of the bed. She set her bag next to her and folded her hands atop the sketch pad on her lap. Claire sat opposite her in a comfortable chair before the fireplace and arranged her skirts so that they wouldn't bunch under her.

'I hope I didn't leave you out there for a very long time,' Claire said.

'Oh, not at all,' Fiona said. 'I never even knocked.'

'Then I couldn't possibly have known you were there.'

'Of course not. I wanted to see the children, but then I realized I had no idea what your new nanny's name is and I got confused and sat down and decided to draw a tree rather than bother anyone.'

'But you're never a bother,' Claire said. 'I do miss having you here. All these strangers about . . . I much prefer my friend's company.'

'Me, too.' Fiona grinned and looked away at the floor. Her gaze travelled around the room, along the skirting boards. 'It seems . . . It looks very clean in here. I mean, after . . .'

'I so rarely come in here any more. I thought I might brave it today, with you here to keep me company.'

'Did you ever actually see . . .'

'The body? No, thank goodness.'

Fiona had briefly seen both the corpses that had been left in the Days' home and she had not been able to forget them. One of the victims had been opened up and displayed like a trophy in the front room. The other, young Constable Rupert Winthrop, who had been assigned to protect Claire, had been left in a pool of blood on the kitchen floor. Commissioner of Police Sir Edward Bradford had personally overseen the removal of both bodies and had paid to have the rooms cleaned and redecorated, but their invisible influence remained.

'And what of Constable Winthrop?' Fiona kept her eyes down, examining the tops of the new patent leather shoes she had changed into. 'Did you see him? His body?'

'I never did. But knowing he died in that room . . . Well, I don't enter the kitchen any more, either.'

'That's two rooms you don't use.' Fiona tried a timid smile. 'You should find a tenant and get some use out of them.'

Claire smiled back at her. 'I suppose there will come a day when I won't let past events bother me so much, but quite honestly I'd simply rather move away.'

'I can't blame you one bit. Are you able?'

'My parents insist on it, but you know Walter can't afford a place big enough and he wouldn't care to impose on my father again. For now, we have a guard on the door, that nice Inspector McKraken, and a houseful of new people, all of which makes me feel the slightest bit more secure until we decide what we can do.'

Claire sighed, then sat up straighter and clapped her hands together as if the noise would dispel the ghosts they both felt there. 'On a happier note, the babies are doing splendidly.'

Fiona perked up. 'I'd love to see them.'

'They're sleeping.' Claire put a finger to her lips. 'Nanny will be cross if we wake them just now.'

'Oh.'

'But do stay until they wake. Keep me company.'

'Of course. I'd be glad to. Father's out examining a crime scene. The Harvest Man has killed again, only Father won't allow me to sketch anything. He's changed his mind about my being there and seeing the bodies. Thinks it's somehow improper.' In fact, Fiona still woke every night screaming, the image of Constable Winthrop's body vivid in her mind. Dr Kingsley had told her he feared for her sanity and could no longer allow her to be exposed to the consequences of evil deeds.

'I can't say that I disagree with him. It all sounds perfectly horrible,' Claire said.

'It is, but when I sketch the bodies for him it feels important to me. It takes on a different aspect. A body becomes a part of a task, rather than a dead person, if that makes any sense at all.'

Claire started to nod, but grimaced and raised her eyebrows. 'No, I'm afraid it doesn't. I thought it might, but it doesn't.'

'Well, at any rate, I'm out of a job and I'm not needed

here with you any longer and I find myself completely irrelevant in every way.'

'I'm in a similar predicament. All I do is make up awful rhymes to read to the babies. They seem to like it, but Walter barely listens when I read to him.'

'I'm sure he . . . Oh, wait, I almost forgot!' She bent and opened the top of her bag and pulled out a small bound volume, which she handed over to Claire. 'I brought this for you. Well, for you and the babies.'

'You shouldn't have.'

'It's Robert Louis Stevenson. He often writes about the strangest things, but these are lovely.'

'*A Child's Garden of Verses*,' Claire said, reading from the spine of the book.

'Very much like the things you write.'

'Not at all like my humble rhymes, I'm sure.'

'I thought they might inspire you.'

'Oh, thank you so much. You're too kind, really.'

'There's one I particularly like about shadows.'

'I wrote one about shadows, too,' Claire said.

'Did you? I want to read one of yours.'

'I couldn't let you.'

'You most certainly could.'

'Well, if you insist.'

Claire jumped up and scurried from the room. Fiona waited a moment, tapped her finger against the cover of her pad and opened it to the page where she had drawn the faint beginnings of a tree. She pressed her pencil hard against the paper and drew the outline of the tree, then moved her hand up and down, drawing long irregular lines from top to bottom. Later, she would scribble short horizontal lines between the verticals to indicate bark. She liked to give a thing as much texture as she could, liked to imagine she might actually be able to reach out and touch the image, as if it were real. She stuck the tip of her tongue out against her upper teeth and frowned. What shape to make the leaves?

'Here's one I just finished this morning.'

Fiona looked up as Claire entered the room carrying a piece of paper with a jagged edge, as if she'd recently torn it out of a book or diary. She handed it over to Fiona, but turned and left the room the moment she let go of the paper. Fiona read out loud.

> She has a little curl in the middle of her head,
> And she has a string of pearls in a darling shade of red.
> The smallest silken stockings to adorn her little feet,
> But her eyes: so wide and merry for a creature so petite!
> Tiny hat and tiny dress and tiny woollen bib.
> How like a little girl she seems within her little crib!

'It's a doll,' Fiona said. 'It's a child's doll.'

Claire stuck her head back into the room, grinned and nodded; she had been waiting just around the corner in the hallway. 'It's exactly the doll that my mother gave the girls. But I can't give it to them yet, because I worry they might choke on the pearls.'

'Does it really have a pearl necklace? It sounds terribly expensive.'

'Oh, it must have been. Entirely inappropriate, really. Here, I'll show you.' Claire bustled out of the room. Fiona opened her tablet again and turned to a new page. She pursed her lips and loosely sketched an image from her head, got the basic shapes down on the page and built them up into the form of a baby doll, added features and hair and outlined the sketch so that it was fully formed. It was the work of perhaps five minutes, and she stopped when she heard footsteps approaching.

Claire entered the room, carrying a miniature bassinet with a lace ruffle around it, and set it down at Fiona's side. Fiona peered into the top and saw a wee baby girl made of wood with a horsehair wig, and painted eyes and lips, and a tiny wardrobe that was better than anything she had ever owned for herself.

'It's beautiful,' she said.

'It's too much,' Claire said.

'Well, maybe that, too. But it inspired your poem.'

'For what that's worth, I suppose. Only doggerel, after all.'

'Oh, but I like it. And I think girls like to read about this sort of thing. It's smaller than they are, you know. Children like things that are smaller than they are.'

'Well, then, you're right. This poem is a very small thing indeed.'

'That's not what I meant at all. But your inspiration became my inspiration.'

'What do you have there?'

'It's nothing. I just wanted to draw what you described. And I do think it's close, don't you?'

Claire took the sketch pad and looked at the new drawing on the topmost page. 'Why, that's it exactly.'

'The face is not the same. But you didn't describe the

face. And, of course, it needs more details. I just barely started drawing it.'

'I like it.'

'A thought has occurred to me,' Fiona said. 'You should publish your nursery rhymes so other children can see them.'

Claire paused, then laughed, a single sharp bark that shattered the stillness.

'But I'm serious,' Fiona said. 'You really should consider publishing these, Claire.'

'They're just for the girls. Only they don't understand them, of course.'

'You'll think about it, though? I think it's a marvellous idea. And then I'd be able to point to a book of your rhymes and say, "I knew her before she was a beloved children's author."'

Claire laughed. 'Oh, I've missed having you here, Fiona. You will stay for dinner, won't you?'

'If you'll have me. I don't know what else to do with myself today.'

'Wonderful. Let me tell Cook. Oh, come with me. I should introduce you to the nanny so you'll remember her name and not sit on our porch the next time you visit.'

9

Bishop's Road was busy. Vendors packed the pavement with carts and boys ran up and down crying their wares. Carriages threaded the narrow avenue between pedestrians, who strolled about, window-shopping and haggling with the vendors. The Harvest Man stayed close to the buildings on the south side of the road and kept his eyes fixed on the family across the street. The sun on his face was warm and the air stirred with life and movement. He felt nervous. He stepped from shadow to shadow and dodged the shoppers crowding the path.

The family was in no hurry. They ambled along, making it difficult for the Harvest Man to watch them without seeming conspicuous. The woman carried a big wicker basket over one arm, her other hand in the crook of her husband's elbow. The children, one boy and one girl, were obedient. They stayed near their parents, only occasionally darting off to look at some vendor's display of penny toys or fresh fruit. The Harvest Man took no notice of them. He stared intently at the mother and father, tried to gauge the shapes of their skulls beneath the masks they wore. It was hard to see clearly at such a distance, but the masks didn't fool him. He could distinguish the woman's lovely cheekbones even from yards away, and the man's wide forehead, his strong jaw. Those were features they couldn't hope to hide from him. He had chosen the right people this time, his own parents, spotted amongst the teeming masses. He was nearly sure of it.

The mother moved away from her husband, walking carefully in the street in her pattens, the children close behind her, while the man stopped to relight his pipe. He stretched and glanced up and down the thoroughfare and looked directly at the Harvest Man, but then away again, apparently without noticing the strange spindly creature in the shadows. He ambled along after his family and nodded politely whenever his wife held up some new item for his appraisal, but he didn't seem interested in shopping.

At four o'clock, the mother and two children left the father and entered a tea shop. The father took out his watch and checked the time, then tucked it back in his waistcoat and hurried away. The Harvest Man had to choose quickly. He decided the mother would be some time in the tea shop. She would have to get the children settled and find something for them to eat before she could enjoy her tea. So he followed the father, kept well back and skittered along in the man's wake until they reached a pub. The father went inside and the Harvest Man followed him only as far as the main entrance. He glanced in at the door and turned and trotted back the way he had come. The pub was no place for a child to be.

Back at the tea shop, he took up a post behind a vendor selling ladies' dresses, simple handmade cotton things in several sizes, all hanging loose from a makeshift awning. The Harvest Man's stomach rumbled, but he ignored it. He hardly ever paid attention to things like hunger or weariness. He knew that he would eventually find his way into an attic where there would be all manner of things to catch and eat, and a cosy corner in which to doze while he waited for the night.

The foot traffic had begun to thin by the time the woman and her children emerged from the tea shop. She led them along the street, picking up a spool of thread from this stall and a tin of beef from that. She went inside Arthur Burgess and Sons, taking the children with her, and didn't emerge for more than half an hour. She wasn't carrying anything new and the Harvest Man assumed she had ordered grocery items to be delivered to the home the next morning. He made a mental note to be sure to finish his work long before the delivery boy arrived.

After that, the day's shopping was done. Father reappeared, walking along in their direction, and after many glad greetings and kisses all round, the little family made their way to the end of the street and turned the corner. The Harvest Man shadowed them, easier to do now that the sun had begun to set. He was eager to finally see their house, hoped he might remember once living there with them. No house had triggered a memory yet, but he knew it would eventually happen, he would one day see the home he had spent so many happy childhood years in, and on that day his long ordeal would be over. He would strip the masks from his parents' faces and their drawn-out game of hide-and-seek would be ended at last. There would be shrieks of joy and he would be welcomed back into his family's embrace. He would never let them leave him again. This game was not so much fun any more.

The family, and their bizarre tagalong, walked for a quarter of a mile in a southerly direction. The little girl skipped ahead and the boy amused himself by picking up a stick from the ground and dragging it along the path behind him, making a clattering sound against the stones. The Harvest Man longed to snatch it away from him and strike him with it, teach him that silence should be a virtue among children (only look at his own example), but he didn't. He remained far behind them and carefully out of sight.

They turned another corner, and another, and walked on until the Harvest Man felt quite lost. Finally they stopped in front of a tidy blue cottage with white trim and a little fence. An ideal home, exactly proportioned for a family of four. The father unlatched the gate and the mother swung her basket as she stepped through and up the steps to the white door. She opened it and ushered the children inside. The father came after her and held the door for her and hesitated on the threshold, peering about him into the descending gloom as if he sensed the trespasser in his neighbourhood. The Harvest Man was nearly invisible behind shrubbery and the father's glance swept right past him. The man lit his pipe again and took a deep breath and picked tobacco from his upper lip. Then he turned and went inside the house and closed the door behind him.

The Harvest Man put his hand on the shrubbery and pushed at it as he emerged. He stood in the street for a long moment, staring up at the house. He then turned and walked away without a backward glance. This was not his home. And this was not his family. He knew because the house had no attic.

He would have to find a safe place to sleep and then he would begin his search anew the next day. He had lost so much time in prison, his nerves jangled with a sense of urgency. He was looking so hard, moving faster than he ever had before, examining so many possibilities that he felt exhausted to his core.

A single tear rolled down his cheek and he wiped it away with his sleeve. He set his shoulders and picked up his pace. He would stay strong for his parents. He would be a brave boy and faithful, too, and he would find them. They were waiting for him somewhere.

10

Day stood at the edge of a wide and sprawling wood and peered into the green, hoping to see some sign of the missing children. The sun was going down. Treetops swayed in the breeze and small creatures skittered here and there in the underbrush, but he saw nothing unusual, nothing that didn't belong. He looked down at his boots. Mud squelched up around the soles, and the tip of his cane had sunk an inch into the ground. His brain felt like it had swollen, pushing against the inside of his skull. He wondered what would happen if he never moved again. Perhaps the mud would suck him down under and he would slowly be lost to sight.

He reached for his flask.

'Walter!'

Day turned his head and saw Nevil Hammersmith approaching from the road. 'Nevil. But I just saw you.' Day drew his hand back from his waistcoat, leaving the flask in his pocket.

'I went by the murder scene. Bentley told me you were out here somewhere.'

'There were children. Two of them. Little boys, roughly eight and ten years old. I talked to the neighbours. They say the boys like to play in the wood out here, but I can't see any trace of them.'

'There's a lot of mud.'

'Yes. But no footprints.'

Hammersmith looked behind them at the rows of homes lining the street. 'Is it possible they weren't heavy enough to leave tracks?'

'I suppose so.'

'They could be anywhere.'

'No, I don't think so. The wood is dark and safe. They know the terrain. The city at night would be strange and frightening. I think they're in there.' Day pointed at the trees.

'Isn't it possible that he took them?'

'There's no evidence of the Harvest Man ever mutilating anyone outside their homes. He hides, ties up his victims, then leaves them. It's always a man and a woman. Together. If there are children in the house, they're also found dead, but not otherwise mistreated. I don't think he cares about them after he's done whatever it is he comes to do. It's all as highly ritualized as it is random.'

'So the children escaped his notice.'

'Otherwise they'd be dead.'

'But the Harvest Man is still at large and they may have seen him, may be witnesses,' Hammersmith said. 'Which puts them in serious danger. If there haven't been witnesses before, it's a different situation now and you can't know . . .'

'True.'

'I'll help you look for them.'

'Inspector Tiffany wouldn't care for that. You're not police any more.'

'Have I ever worried about Tiffany's feelings?' He paused. 'Have you?'

'You make a good point. And, frankly, I'd welcome the help. But you were looking for me for a reason.'

'I came to tell you that Inspector March is dead. Murdered in his cell. I meant to tell you before, but this doesn't seem like a good time, either.'

Day drew in a sharp breath. He bit his lower lip and sniffed. 'How was it done? I mean . . .'

'I think it was Jack, but it doesn't quite make sense. You may have some insight. I admit I'm at a loss.'

'You'll have to tell me everything.'

'I will.'

'Good. It can wait. But . . .'

'Yes, when we've found the children.'

Day nodded and walked away, moving south along the tree line. Hammersmith headed north. Day looked behind him and saw Hammersmith plunge into the wood and disappear.

Adrian March was dead. The news sank like a stone to his gut and sat there. He rolled his head from side to side, trying to ease the tension he felt. He wanted to grieve for his mentor, but still felt angry at March. He reached out and poked at the underbrush with his cane. The brambles were impassable. He kept walking, peering at the ground for clues, trying to concentrate on the job at hand. Eventually he came to a series of low flat rocks, arranged in a haphazard queue across the mud. Soil was smeared across the tops of the stones, a heavier deposit at the forward edge of each rock. Day stopped and stared at the wood. There was a gap between the trees, two feet across, the brambles trampled down, bent and broken.

He took out his flask, uncorked it. A stiff shot of brandy

worked its way down his throat, exploded heat across his abdomen and expanded out through his limbs, warm, then icy cold. He closed his eyes and cleared his mind, concentrated on two missing children who needed his help. He would sort his feelings about March later, when the time was right. Properly fortified and focused, he opened his eyes and limped across the stones, into the forest.

He used his cane to push the flattened brambles ahead of him, stepping carefully, watching for signs of recent passage. The canopy above him gradually cut off the diffuse sunlight, but just at the threshold of utter darkness Day saw a single familiar footprint, small and shallow. The side of a bare foot pressed into the mud, the impressions of three tiny round toes, deeper at one side, then tapering off so that the last toe was only half represented. A child running or skipping, not lingering long enough for his entire foot to rest in the mud. Day cleared the underbrush away from the print and bent down as low as he could, moving slowly around the print in concentric circles, looking for more signs of the children. There was nothing. Nor did he find any evidence that an adult had passed this way. Someone heavier would almost certainly have left deeper footprints. Day's own prints were clearly visible behind him, wherever he had stepped off the brambles. He grinned and let out a breath he didn't know he'd been holding. The children had escaped. The Harvest Man had not followed them into the wood.

He straightened up and hung his cane over a nearby branch. He raised his hands and cupped them around his mouth. 'Children!'

A brace of pheasants flew up out of the bushes directly ahead of him, a maelstrom of fluttering wings, and he reeled backwards, catching himself against the trunk of a tree. He waited for silence to descend again, listened, but he could hear no human sound.

'Simon!' He listened and called again. 'Robert! You're safe now! I'm a policeman, come to take you home!'

He listened again, shaking off the realization that he would not, in fact, be able to take them home. They would never go home again. Either a relative would be found for them or the boys were bound for the orphanage.

'Walter!' It was Hammersmith's faint voice, somewhere far away to the north.

'Nevil, they're here somewhere! They're alive and running! There's no sign of the . . .' He broke off. No need to frighten the children by mentioning their parents' killer.

'I'll come to you!' There was the distant sound of thrashing bush and branch. Day strained to hear the surrounding wood, hoping the children would cry out, give some indication of where they were hiding. There was nothing.

He backtracked to the footprint and found his cane. He held it out in front of him, aimed in the direction the little toes in the mud had pointed for him. Eventually Nevil emerged from the brambles and stood at his side, panting. The former sergeant's clothes had been torn. His hair stood straight up on end, his trousers were soaked with mud and there was a deep scratch along one cheek. Day smiled. Something about the sight of Hammersmith's habitual disarray comforted him. He held up a hand and pointed down at the mud. Hammersmith knelt, his knees squelching in the mire, and smoothed the air above the footprint as if he could make it more visible. He looked up and they smiled at each other.

'A good sign,' Hammersmith said.

Day nodded and held out his hand, helped Hammersmith back to his feet. Mud tumbled from Hammersmith's shins in a miniature avalanche that covered the tops of his boots.

'They were headed in this direction.' Day used his cane to point. 'But it's too dark in there to see anything.'

'What do we need to see? We'll go on that way and hope the children show themselves when we reach them.'

'Of course.'

'Lead the way.'

'I'll follow. You move faster than I can.'

'Not as fast as I used to.' Hammersmith held his hand against his chest.

'Still faster than me.'

Hammersmith nodded and bounded ahead, moving fast through the vegetation. Day didn't try to keep up. He hobbled along, listening to the darkness on either side of the path Hammersmith was making. The younger man was no doubt obliterating any sign of the children's passing. It might have been a better idea to go back and fetch a lantern. But that would mean relying on Hammersmith's patience, which had never proved to be of adequate supply.

They pushed on.

'Don't act like a baby,' Robert said.

They had made a construct of branches and small vines

covered with leaves, many of which were now dying and falling off, but it still looked enough like the surrounding trees that they felt safe behind it.

'But it's dark,' Simon said. 'And I want to go home.'

'We can't go home. The bad birdie man is there and he made them dead.'

'But our home's still there.' It sounded like Simon was going to cry and the wavering tone in his voice made Robert angry. He concentrated on the leaves, prodding them into place, filling in small gaps. The platform they had built, high up in the branches, was visible from below, but they had spent some time earlier in the spring, as early as the weather permitted, disguising it, painting it green, and Robert had returned without Simon to dapple it with grey and brown. The leaf curtain was meant to be temporary. Robert had ideas about fabric woven round sticks, if they only had enough money to buy the materials. Someday perhaps.

'We'll go home when it's safe,' Robert said.

'Tonight?'

'We're gonna stay here tonight.'

'In the wood?'

'It's all right. The wood is safe.'

'What if the policeman comes back?'

Robert glanced across their platform at the boulder they'd manoeuvered up with them, using a rope and a crude pulley. It had to weigh almost as much as Simon did. They'd originally been playing pirates, had set everything up as a game because they were bored and there were no other children to play with, but now it wasn't a game. Now they had a place to hide and they had a weapon, a rock that they could tumble down on top of anyone who threatened them.

'I don't know if that really was a policeman, Simon. We have to be careful.'

'But what if he comes back and it's dark and we don't see him?'

'He can't climb up without making noise.'

'And then the rock?'

'And then the rock.'

Simon stopped sniffling and moved closer and Robert put his arm around his brother, held him close. Robert was ten years old and it was his job to take care of Simon now that Father was dead, and Mother, too. He closed his eyes and made a silent promise to his parents. Nothing bad would ever happen to Simon.

'It's no use, Nevil.'

'Keep looking. We'll find them. Only I need a moment.'

'Your face is flushed.'

Hammersmith didn't answer. He sat, panting, on a fallen log, looking as if he might tumble off it at any moment. Day made him move over so he could sit, too.

'How's your chest?'

'My chest is fine,' Hammersmith said. 'How's your leg?'

'My leg's been worse,' Day said.

'I don't think they're out here.'

'They have to be.'

'Maybe we should be looking somewhere else.'

'It's late. They're out here, I'm sure of it, but we're not going to find them tonight.'

'If you're right,' Hammersmith said, 'if they're out here,

as you say, then we have to find them. We can't leave them to stay the night in the wood.' He started to rise, but Day put a hand on his arm and Hammersmith sank back down on the log.

'They know this area far better than we do,' Day said. 'They're more likely to do well out here than we are. And I'm worried about your health. You're supposed to be resting.'

'I am resting. Look at me resting.'

'That's not what I mean. You're overexerting yourself. You haven't caught your breath yet. And you're going to open your stitches if you keep at it like this.'

'If I do, Dr Kingsley can easily sew me back up.'

'Nevil, we're not going to find them like this. We might have passed them twenty times already. They don't want us to see them.'

'They're scared.'

'Of course they're scared. They saw their parents murdered. No, we have to out-think them if we're going to be of any use to them at all.'

Nevil slapped his hand against the dead tree's mildew-covered bark. 'Where are they, damnit? Why haven't we found them? I swear we've searched every square inch of bushes out here.'

'I'm tempted to start looking under rocks,' Day said.

'I actually did look under this log before I sat down.'

'We'll come back tomorrow, when it's light.'

'I hate to do that. I hate to leave them.'

'They'll be able to see us better. They'll see we're not a threat to them. They'll be tired and hungry. We'll have a better chance at coaxing them out of hiding.'

'Do you think so?'

'I don't see another choice, really. If we keep blundering through this wood all night, we'll collapse.'

Hammersmith didn't reply, but he nodded. He wiped his nose on his shirtsleeve and scratched his head.

'We'll come back,' Day said again. 'Don't worry. We'll find them when we have proper light.' He stood, putting more weight than usual on his cane, and held out a hand to help Hammersmith up. His former sergeant no longer seemed flushed. His face had gone pale, and Day worried that Hammersmith might pass out. There was no way he could carry Hammersmith out through the wood. 'Meet me here mid-morning. We'll take up the search again.'

'I'll meet you at first light.'

'No. Get some sleep.'

'I can't yet.'

'Well, why not, Nevil? Good God, man. Have you learned nothing after all your close shaves? You can't push yourself like you do.'

'I'm quite all right. Really. I've got someone to see, but I'll make it a short trip and then head straight home for a nap.'

'Someone to see? It can't wait till morning?'

'This is the most likely time to find him, really.'

'Who is it?'

'You'd rather not know, I'm sure.'

'Very well,' Day said. 'Send a message when you're up and about and ready to commence the search. Don't come out here without me. Promise.'

'I won't.'

'Nevil.'

'I won't. I promise I won't.'

Day took one last look around the clearing. He ran his palm over his stubbly chin and shook his head. 'Boys! We're leaving now! But we'll be back to help you!' He listened for a response, but when he heard nothing he turned and limped away after Hammersmith.

11

The Harvest Man found the new couple by accident. They were leaving a house on Garway Road, around the corner from Leinster Square. It was a small house, and old, but it had been kept up. The couple was smiling, happy to be with each other. She was pretty, with long brown hair done up at the back of her head, and he was tall and lanky with a giant Adam's apple that bobbed up and down as he murmured something in her ear. They held hands as they crossed the dark road and walked away. Neither of them even glanced in his direction.

He looked up at the house and clapped his hands together with joy. There was clearly an attic, with a single window that looked out over the front garden.

He waited until the couple was out of sight and then he went to the door and knocked. There was no answer. He looked up and down the road, but it was empty. Nobody was paying attention to him. He walked around the side of the house where a hedge obscured the view from the street and he stopped again. No one had followed him, no one was shouting. He wiped his fingers on a window pane, clearing the dirt and condensation, and peered inside, saw a small receiving room with nothing but a chair and a round table barely large enough for the lamp that sat on it. Nothing moved. The lamp was not lit and the sun was down, but nobody entered the room to light the flame.

He thought about the couple he had seen. They were doing well enough to afford a house to themselves, but they apparently didn't employ a housekeeper. Or if they had one, she'd been given the evening off. He didn't see evidence of children or a nanny. The couple was young, perhaps just starting out, which meant they might be living on an inheritance of some sort.

He used the point of his blade to pry the window open and slid it upwards on its runners. He put the blade away and tossed the plague mask into the room ahead of him, then hoisted himself up, balanced for a moment, teetering back and forth on his belly, his head inside the house, his legs brushing against the hedge outside. He heard nothing. The air inside was undisturbed. He smelled something sweet lurking beneath the usual stale quality of an empty house. He put the palms of his hands against the wall under the window and pushed himself the rest of the way in, dropped to the floor, turned and pulled the sash down. He picked up his mask by the strap, sniffed, and followed his nose to the kitchen, where a tray of fresh chocolate biscuits sat cooling on the sideboard. Moonlight streamed through the windows, lending the room a dim blue hue. The Harvest Man took two biscuits and rearranged the others so that they appeared to fill the tray. He crept about the ground floor, munching on one of the biscuits, getting his bearings. First, of course, he needed to know where the couple slept, and he was excited to find evidence that they occupied separate rooms at night.

He entered the woman's room first. Her bed was small and neatly made. A nearby table held toiletries and a hand mirror. A brush was tangled with long brown hairs, and a semicircle of the table's surface was lightly dusted with white powder. He ran a finger through it and smiled. The man's room was similarly apportioned, but the bedsheets were rumpled and unmade. A table that matched the one in the woman's room held a jar of shaving soap and a razor. The Harvest Man picked up the razor and tested its blade against his thumb. A dark bead of blood surfaced among the whorls and he tasted it. He folded the razor and slipped it into his pocket, then went looking for the door to the attic.

Hatty Pitt linked her arm in her husband's as they walked along the street. She had been Mrs John Charles Pitt for exactly two months and three days, and the taste of the name was still new in her mouth. She looked over her shoulder at their house – *her very own house!* – at the other end of the street, where she had left biscuits out on the kitchen table to cool. She thought she saw movement behind a window at the front, but she dismissed it as a trick of the setting sun, casting nomadic shadows where there was nothing.

The home of the Merrilows was only two streets over, and the night was bright and clear with no suggestion of rain. Hatty enjoyed the short walk and she tried not to think too much about their destination. John Charles was excited. She watched his Adam's apple bob up and down as he talked, waving his free hand about in the air to emphasize his points as he made them. She was aware that he and Eugenia Merrilow had indulged in a brief dalliance but, as he had assured her many times, that had ended months before his marriage to Hatty. There was, therefore, no reason for her to feel any jealousy. At least, this is what John Charles had told his seventeen-year-old wife. He had added that he thought jealousy was an old-fashioned emotion anyway.

Hatty supposed she was an old-fashioned sort of girl.

But she smiled and delighted in the cool evening air on her face. She was genuinely pleased that John Charles was so worldly about art and culture. She was learning a great deal from him – when she paid attention to what he said, which happened with less frequency during these past two months. She made a moue of irritation at her own fickleness. She would never learn a thing if she didn't concentrate on what her husband had to teach her.

John Charles misinterpreted her expression and fell silent until they came within sight of the Merrilow house. A sluggish stream of men and women dressed in their finery was flowing up the front walk. The door was open and light spilled out into the dark street, causing the guests' long shadows to stretch and caper like marionette puppets or *ombres chinoises*, the tops of their heads melting into the gloom. Hatty felt a sudden chill and hugged herself. She was surprised and pleased when John Charles noticed and put his arm around her.

'You needn't worry about Eugenia,' he said, still misunderstanding her. 'She's moved on every bit as much as I have. I hear she's involved with that fellow at the museum. What's his name? Frederick, I think. Met him once. Nice enough chap, though I can't for the life of me figure out what she sees in him.'

Hatty smiled up at him. 'I've hardly given Eugenia a single thought.'

'Well, no need to be rude. She is our hostess, you know.'

'I'm sorry, John Charles. I didn't intend any rudeness.'

'I'm sure you didn't. You simply don't understand what's expected of you. It's my own fault, really, for marrying someone so young. Don't worry. You'll catch on.'

He moved his arm from her shoulders and grabbed her above the elbow, steering her towards the big house. Above the door someone had hung two gold masks, one smiling and one crying. Comedy and tragedy, Thalia and Melpomene, the Muses of the theatre. And Eugenia had evidently hired extra staff for the evening. There was a new man on the door. He wore white gloves and his smile had a pasted-on quality that Hatty was afraid mirrored her own expression. He took her wrap and John Charles's boater and directed them to the drawing room, where most of the guests had already gathered. Hatty smiled at the people John Charles introduced her to and wondered how many she had already met and promptly forgotten. Did they remember her? She supposed she really was as rude as John told her she was. Poor John Charles, stuck with a silly little girl for a wife.

More men with white gloves circulated through the room carrying trays of hors d'oeuvres and tiny glasses of some clear sparkling aperitif. Hatty took a glass and wondered whether the biscuits waiting for her at home were cool enough yet to eat.

Fully a third of the drawing room had been rendered off-limits by the addition of a heavy burgundy curtain that ran from one wall to the other. Eugenia Merrilow was nowhere to be seen and Hatty assumed she was somewhere behind the curtain, readying herself for the tableau vivant, the night's scheduled entertainment.

John Charles leaned in and whispered, 'She's doing the Botticelli tonight.'

'What's that, dear?'

'Oh, I think you'll be quite impressed. I've seen her do

this tableau before, although it was for a private audience. It's her crowning achievement.'

Hatty nodded and sipped at her drink. It was sweet and burned her throat. At seven o'clock, the elder Mrs Merrilow, Eugenia's mother, stood and sang 'Woodman, Spare That Tree', the dark-red curtain framing her ample figure. She was in her fifties, Hatty was sure, and wore her hair in unfashionable ringlets that bobbed around her ears whenever she strained for a high note. When she had finished, the final notes (*Thy axe shall harm it not!*) lingering, there was an awkward moment of silence before the audience began to applaud. Nevertheless, Mrs Merrilow curtsied and came back for an encore of 'The Village Blacksmith' (*Under a spreading chestnut tree the village smithy stands . . .*).

When the clock struck eight, one of the white-gloved men stepped in front of the curtain and cleared his throat. Magically, the room went silent, all at once. Everyone turned towards the man and he nodded at them. '*The Birth of Venus*,' he said, and bowed, walking sideways with the curtain as he drew it open.

A gasp went up from the gathered crowd. A low platform, two feet off the floor, twenty feet long and ten feet deep, had been built under the windows, which were currently obscured by a flowery blue-and-green backdrop that filled the wall behind Eugenia Merrilow, who stood motionless, facing her audience astride an enormous pink scallop shell, its undulations framing her bare legs. Eugenia was entirely nude, except for a long red wig. She held one hand over her breasts and clutched the free end of the long wig in her other hand, pulling it around in front to cover her fanny. Lucy Hebron stood next to her holding up a salmon-coloured cloak as if about to drape it over Eugenia's shoulders. On Eugenia's other side, to her right but Hatty's left as she stood watching, George Merrilow was posed in mid-stride running towards his sister. He, too, was nude, but he had knotted a length of pale-blue fabric about his throat and wrapped the other end of it around his midriff. Another woman whom Hatty didn't recognize clung to George in an unseemly fashion. This woman wore a dark cape over her shoulders, but her left breast was exposed. Both she and George had somehow affixed wings to their backs. All four players in the silent drama stood stock-still, like mannequins, recreating *The Birth of Venus*, a painting which Hatty now recalled seeing in one of John Charles's books. The entire effect was neither shocking nor artistic as far as Hatty was concerned. It was merely ludicrous.

She heard herself snort with laughter and she clapped her hand over her mouth, but it was too late. Several of the guests closest to them glared at Hatty, and she felt herself flush. She dared not look up at John Charles; she feared his reaction to her outburst. An older gentleman ahead of her turned and winked, which made her feel a bit better. Still, her throat felt warm and she thought for a moment that she might faint. When she finally did look up, John Charles was stone-faced, staring straight forward at the stage. He had moved a pace away from her as if to distance himself from his wife, as if perhaps they had arrived separately and she was a stranger to him. For a split second, she wished the same.

At last, Eugenia Merrilow moved and the three other actors broke their stillness. Lucy Hebron stepped forward and finally covered Eugenia with the salmon cloak. The woman Hatty didn't recognize turned her back to them for a moment and tucked her breast away under her makeshift cape. When the four of them were presentable, they stepped to the edge of the platform together and took a bow. The assembly in the drawing room clapped and Hatty heard approving murmurs among them. One or two of the younger men hooted and the applause went on and on in waves until the palms of Hatty's hands began to sting. She imagined they would all have given Eugenia a standing ovation if they weren't already on their feet.

'She and Patience performed Thumann's *Three Fates* last month,' the kind gentleman said to Hatty when the applause had begun to die down. 'Along with the elder Mrs Merrilow. I wish you'd been here. I would've liked to see your reaction.' He smiled and Hatty looked away, embarrassed all over again.

At least now she knew the name of the third woman onstage, the one she hadn't seen before. Patience seemed a perfect name for someone whose idea of entertainment was to stand motionless for five minutes once a week.

John Charles moved quickly away without glancing back at Hatty and she spotted him a moment later embracing Eugenia. He whispered something in her ear that made Eugenia laugh, and Hatty put her head down. She wandered away from the kind gentleman and found a place near the door where she could lean unobtrusively. She wished someone would come around with more drinks.

After more than an hour, John Charles found Hatty again. She had not moved from her spot against the wall and no one had spoken to her since the end of the performance. At some point, all four actors had changed their clothing. Eugenia Merrilow was now wearing a shimmering yellow dress that barely covered her ankles. She giggled and flirted with the young men who had hooted at her earlier, putting her hand flat against their chests and throwing her head back as if they were the wittiest fellows she had ever encountered. Hatty noted with some satisfaction that Eugenia had no hips to speak of. She was as straight up and down as a boy. John Charles took Hatty by the elbow again, being a good deal rougher with her this time, and manoeuvered her to the door and out. He glanced back over his shoulder as they exited the drawing room and Hatty could well imagine what he must be looking at. Or, rather, *who* he was looking at.

John Charles did not speak to Hatty all the long way back to their home. It was much farther away than it had seemed on their walk to the Merrilow house and there were wispy clouds skulking about the moon now. When at last they reached their own house, John Charles held the door open for his wife and then disappeared into his study. Hatty hung her wrap on the coat rack in the entry and went straight to the kitchen, where she lit a lamp on the kitchen table and gobbled down two chocolate biscuits without taking a breath between them. At last she swallowed and poured herself a glass of water. She frowned at the tray of biscuits. She had eaten two and yet four seemed to be missing. She glanced, puzzled, in the direction of the closed study door and then shrugged. If John Charles had burnt his tongue on a hot biscuit before they'd even left the house, it served him right. She hoped it still hurt.

She left the kitchen and passed an open window in the hallway, which she pulled closed. She made her way up the stairs in the dark, brushing her fingertips against the wall all the way up. She changed into her nightdress and brushed her hair and settled into bed. She didn't know how long it would take John Charles to get over being angry, but she hoped she would have fallen asleep by the time he came upstairs. She didn't want him to come to her bedroom and she wasn't ready for a dressing-down. Perhaps by morning John Charles would forgive her and she would feel contrite and things would go back to the way they usually were between them. She closed her eyes and pulled her coverlet to her throat and listened with trepidation for John Charles's footsteps on the landing until, at last, she fell sound asleep.

13

There were four working women loitering outside the Whistle and Flute, and Hammersmith felt them sizing him up as he approached the front door. For a moment he was confused by their attention, until he realized he no longer wore a constable's uniform. As far as the women were concerned, he was no different from any other customer of the establishment. He felt a stab of anxiety that turned to deep sadness and he stopped short of the curb. In truth, he wasn't any different. He wasn't a policeman any more and quite probably never would be again. His dream, his life, everything he thought he knew about himself was all ended and he would have to start anew. He took a deep breath, set his shoulders and tried to put the thought out of his mind. He still had work to do, regardless of what he wore. At least for the moment. He would concentrate on the moment.

One of the women became impatient. She pushed herself off the building's façade and approached. 'Need some help up out of the street, love?'

'I'm fine,' Hammersmith said. 'Go about your business.'

'But you are my business. Come, let's have us a taste of gin and I'll give you a taste of summat else besides.'

'No.' He pushed his elbows in close to his body and walked past her, trying not to get caught up as she reached for him.

'Just a taste.'

'I said no.' He put his hand up and kept walking, ignored the woman, who was still wheedling. The others moved aside as he passed, seeing that he wasn't going to be persuaded. He opened the door and stepped through into the pub.

The ownership of the place seemed to change with the phases of the moon and there was always a different man behind the counter whenever Hammersmith visited. But the clientele remained the same: the same women working outside, whether they went by the same names or not, tottering in on the hour to spend their newly earned coins; the same four men in the darkest corner playing Happy Families for money, keeping a wary eye on newcomers; the same old gin-soaked sailor sitting by the door with his hand out. Hammersmith ignored the old man and the single tarted-up woman at the counter. He nodded at the barman and held up a finger. The man nodded back and reached for a glass while Hammersmith walked to the table in the corner and stood quietly watching the men play cards.

None of them looked up at him, but one clucked his tongue and said: 'Have ya got Mr Plod, the policeman?' Hammersmith could see the cards the man held and there was no Mr Plod in his hand.

'Yeah,' another man said. 'He's right here, but I don't want nothin' to do with him.' He threw down his cards and pushed his chair back and two of the other men stood up at the same time. They walked away in a group, passing the barman, who brought Hammersmith's beer and set it on the table at one of the now empty chairs. He took the penny Hammersmith offered, scowled at it and hurried away. Hammersmith sat down across from the remaining card player.

'You ruined my game,' the man said. 'And I was winning.'

'Looked to me like you weren't doing so well,' Hammersmith said.

'I had a strategy.'

'How have you been, Blackleg?'

'Been better'n you, from what I hear. And judging by the state of you, the rumours ain't far off.'

Hammersmith looked down at his torn and muddy clothes. 'I'm still alive.'

'Well, *I* won't be for much longer if you keep comin' in here askin' me questions.'

Hammersmith looked the man over. He seemed at home in the shadows, his back against the wall. He was imposing, with a heavy black beard and dark deep-set eyes. There was something slippery about the eyes, something amused and dangerous, like a big cat waiting for something smaller to move and give away its position. He had got his name, the only name Hammersmith had ever known him by, from his time spent crossing picket lines at the docks. Normally, it would have been an insult, but he wore it with pride and nobody dared to disagree with him.

Hammersmith took a drink of his beer and wiped his lips with the back of his hand. Then he unconsciously wiped his hand on the leg of his trousers. 'I can't meet you unless I go where you are. And you're always here. You used to be more careful about where we met. What do your friends think we talk about?'

86

'They think you're my brother,' Blackleg said. 'Only you was injured in the head when you was little and went wrong somehow, grew up a bluebottle.'

Hammersmith grinned. 'You know I'm not a bluebottle any more.'

'Still act like a bluebottle, askin' questions about things don't concern you.'

'That's got to worry them. Surely they don't like you talking to me, even if they do think I'm your brother. How, by the way, did they come to that conclusion?'

'Somebody told 'em you was. Might've been me told 'em. On account of the family resemblance.' He smiled at the weak joke. 'And they think I give you wrong information in order to put you off the scent of their business.'

'Why would they think you give me bad information?'

'Because I do.'

'You do?'

'Not all the time. If it was all the time, you'd never come back and then I couldn't give you wrong information any more, could I? Got to plant a little good in with the bad, a bloom here and there to distract you from the weeds.'

'I guess I need to be careful with you.'

'That makes us even,' Blackleg said. 'What're you here for today? I know you don't care much about the opium business. Or whores. You care about the kids bein' sold on the docks, but I don't got nothin' to do with anything like that, and you know it.'

'Murders.'

'Don't got nothin' to do with murders, either. And anyway you've got your friend, Inspector Dew, to help with all that.'

'His name's Day. And he's busy with something else. Somebody's cutting people's faces off.'

'The spider man. Yes, I know about that.'

'They're calling him Harvest Man.'

'For the spider, like I said.'

'You know where he is?'

'Now why would I know where he is?'

'Do you?'

'No.'

'There are two children missing. I've been looking for them all evening. If anybody can tell me where this madman is, I need to know it.' Hammersmith stared at Blackleg until the other man shifted in his seat.

'I'm not lying to you,' Blackleg said. 'No reason to. I've got no interest in that spider man 'less he tries to cut me own face off. If he does that, you won't be havin' no problem with 'im again 'cause he'll disappear off the face of the earth.'

'I believe you.' Hammersmith took another sip of beer. 'Anyway, that's not why I'm here.'

'Didn't figure so. You know I don't got nothin' to do with anything like that.'

'It's another murderer I'm after.'

'Like I say, I don't do murders that ain't called for. And none that's your business anyway.'

'It's the Ripper.'

Blackleg pushed his chair back. It hit the wall and he sat there, the sudden reaction followed by a silence that seemed just as sudden. Hammersmith nodded at him, but didn't speak. He worked on his beer and let Blackleg think. Finally the criminal pulled his chair back up to the table.

'The bloke you're talkin' of,' he said, 'it's the same one I'm thinkin' of? The same one . . . you know.'

'The very same,' Hammersmith said. 'Went by the name Jack.'

'He's gone. Dead and gone. Must be. Supposed to be more than a year now since the last time he cut anyone up.'

'No. He's alive.' Hammersmith looked around the room. The card players had found another deck of Happy Families and were busy at a table by the other end of the counter, well out of earshot. The girl had left, gone to join her coworkers at the curb outside. The old man was still at his post by the door, but he was snoring so loudly that the barman had gone to try to rouse him. Otherwise, Hammersmith and Blackleg were alone. 'He was being held prisoner. Jack the Ripper was. Somewhere underground. But now he's free and he's back at it.'

Blackleg held up a hand to stop him and motioned at the barman, who trotted over. 'Two whiskies,' Blackleg said. 'And one for my friend.' He turned back to Hammersmith. 'Tell me about him. What's happened?'

'There's a club,' Hammersmith said. 'A society of men. I don't know who they all are. Their membership is secret and closely guarded, as is their mission. They don't believe criminals can be rehabilitated.'

'Nor do I. A man is who he is and that don't change unless he gets religion, which is nothin' but its own kind of prison.'

'These men carry their conviction to its logical but frightening end. They call themselves the Karstphanomen and they specialize in beating the police to their quarry.

They capture murderers and rapists and the like, and they do unto them.'

'Kill 'em?'

'No. They torture them. An eye for an eye. They make the man feel whatever it is he's done to his victims, physically feel it. But they keep him alive, keep hurting him in the same ways, endlessly punishing him.'

'When you say they do everything the man done, you really mean all of it?'

'I mean everything and anything, short of death. My friend Day captured one of them and he told us more than I wanted to know.'

Hammersmith sat back in his chair as the barkeep set three whiskies in the middle of the table and backed away. Blackleg reached for two of them and pushed the third towards Hammersmith. Hammersmith picked it up and took a small sip. Blackleg downed one of his immediately, slammed the glass down and cupped his hands around the second whisky, regarded it as he spoke.

'I think I can guess,' he said. 'When these men got hold of Saucy Jack, they cut out his lady parts.'

'As close to it as they could,' Hammersmith said. 'They cut him over and over in the same places he cut those women, his victims. They let him heal and then they did it again. And again.'

'He didn't bleed to death?'

'Indeed,' Hammersmith said. 'They took measures to keep him alive. His death would have robbed them of their fun.'

'But then he got free of 'em. Otherwise you wouldn't be here talkin' to ol' Blackleg.'

'Yes. He got free. He ambushed Inspector Day and chained him up in the same place he'd been chained himself.'

'Didn't kill 'im?'

'Tortured him.'

'Like your secret club done to him in turn.'

'Yes.'

'You sayin' Day's one of these club members?'

'No. He stumbled upon what was happening and got swept up.'

'You got him free?'

'He freed himself. But he was badly hurt. Walks with a cane now.'

Blackleg sat back and pursed his lips, looked up at the ceiling and let out a long breath. 'That's bad news, bluebottle. That's bad business.'

'He's killed three men now. At least three.'

Blackleg brought his gaze down from the ceiling and levelled it at Hammersmith. 'Men, you say?'

'Two of them were Karstphanomen, we think.'

'Who was the other one?'

'A killer of children named Cinderhouse.'

'I remember him. No real loss there. I'd've killed that one myself.'

'No loss at all. But Jack still has to be stopped.'

'What about women? Saucy Jack was always a lady-killer. Sounds wrong to me, him killin' men.'

'I don't know. I don't know whether he's killing the Karstphanomen in addition to killing prostitutes again, like before, or if he's changed his intent.'

'Could be he's out for revenge now.'

'I'm sure he is. But if so he's got a completely different way of working, of thinking. He's got different reasons for doing what he does and that's led to different methods.'

'Which would make him as big a puzzle as ever, wouldn't it?'

'I think so.'

'But he's doing the same thing? Cutting 'em up? These men you're talkin' about he's after.'

'Not always. Not so far. He cut both Cinderhouse and a doctor into little pieces, took parts of them away with him. But this latest one . . . this one he choked to death.'

'How do you know it's him what done it?'

'I don't know,' Hammersmith said.

'But you think it's him. Why?'

'It's a bit complicated, but there's a clue. The Karstphanomen left signs for each other, right out in plain sight, signs that meant nothing to anybody but them. They used chalk, blue chalk, to draw numbers and arrows. They would hunt their victims using their network of men, pointing each other in the right direction.'

'Where was the chalk? I mean, they drew on buildings? On people?'

'How would you draw on a person?'

'If you killed him first.'

'No, nothing like that. They'd just make their mark on the street in front of a house or on the outside wall of a public bath, that sort of thing. And it wouldn't mean anything to anyone, except another one of them. Most people wouldn't even notice such a thing, but these men knew to keep their eyes trained to see them.'

'What does that have to do with himself? With Jack?'

'He's using it now. The blue chalk. I think maybe it amuses him. It's some sort of parody of their own game. Two of the murdered men had circles drawn in blue chalk near their bodies. I think the circles are zeroes. The number zero. I think he's saying that a dead member of the Karstphanomen is zeroed out, gone, nothing. He draws an arrow from the zero to the body. Just to make his point.'

Blackleg drank his second whisky. He licked his upper lip and motioned for another drink. He stared down at his hands on the table while they waited. 'A circle of blue chalk and an arrow,' he said. 'That don't say Jack the Ripper to me. That's nothin' like anything he ever done before. You thought at all you might be on the wrong track with this?'

'Of course. But he's out there. I know that for a fact. Jack the Ripper is out on the streets, wandering around this city. And those men, the men whose bodies we've found, were already suspected of being Karstphanomen. One of them, Adrian March, was certainly a member. He was a respected detective inspector of the Yard itself. The other was a prominent doctor.'

'He's killed a policeman?'

'Former policeman. March was retired and in prison. We found his body this morning.'

The barkeep put down another glass and took the empties away.

'Retired or not,' Blackleg said, 'a policeman's a policeman for all of his days. If this bloke's killin' bluebottles, the rest of you lot will be all over this, swarming about and lockin' up anybody looks at 'em cross-eyed. Remember what happened last time bluebottles was killed round here.'

'This is different.'

'I can't stick my nose in nothing that comes anywhere near the police. I make an exception for you 'cause we have history, you and me. Don't mistake my kindness and the trust I give you for weakness. I don't plan to go back to jail.'

'Nobody else is willing to believe it's Jack.'

'I don't know I believe it, either.'

'Meaning nobody else is looking for him.'

'So that's why you come to me.'

'I have no one else.'

'And you want me to do what?'

'Surely you hear about these things. You hear about crimes before the police do.'

'Some crimes. Maybe just enough before the police hear of 'em to get a hop and skip ahead. That's all. You lot are better equipped to track a man down.'

'I don't think that's true. And I have no resources any more. I'm on my own.'

Blackleg looked him over. 'You don't look the same without the uniform.'

'I don't feel the same, either. I always wanted to be a policeman and now I don't know what I am any more.'

'It's better. I think you were wasted on the police.'

'I wasn't good enough.'

'Depends what you mean by that. Anyway, what if I say I'll keep my ear to the ground?'

'You'll let me know anything you find out?'

'You're sure he's not still after women? Cuttin' up workin' women?'

'Honestly, I'm not sure of anything at the moment. I just want help stopping him.'

Blackleg picked up his glass and watched Hammer-smith over the edge of it. Hammersmith sat patiently. Finally, Blackleg swallowed his whisky and nodded.

'Finish your drink,' he said. 'I might have something to show you.'

Night

Day stood at the rail of a little wooden bridge and watched the moon float high over the trickling water of a tributary. Long branches hung across the water, casting it in shadow, and the moonlight scattered pearls on its surface. Day hung his cane over the rail and leaned forward, taking pressure off his bad leg. He listened to the chirp of insects as they woke up, one by one, and called out to one another; he breathed in the night air, thick with the scent of lilac and honeysuckle. Hammersmith had left long ago, but Day lingered. He hated to give up on the missing boys. He was convinced they were still hiding somewhere in the deep wood, or they were already dead, perhaps floating serenely along this very waterway. He pushed the morbid image out of his head and thought instead about his own children, wondered about the dangers he faced every day as a policeman, whether he would be alive when his girls took their first steps and said their first words, grew to adulthood, married and had their own children. And grandchildren.

Someone entered the bridge from the other end, a man moving slowly towards Day. Footsteps echoed up and down the wooden planks, deep and resonant, the sound absorbed by overhanging trees and magnified by the hollow space above the water. Day did not turn around. He recognized the gait of the traveller on the bridge, the confident, evenly spaced steps, and he felt the familiar aura of amused contempt emanating from the man.

Saucy Jack had found him again.

Walter held his breath. He gripped the railing tight and refused to look up from the water. He heard the man approach and then pass behind him without breaking stride.

That would have been the moment for Day to turn, plant his weight on his good leg, catch Jack off guard and put him in a headlock. But he didn't. Instead, Day kept his gaze locked on the beads of moonlight shimmering on the water below. The man continued across the bridge and on to the path beyond.

Then Day finally looked up, half expecting to see Jack standing there watching him. But there was no one. The path was wide and the view along it was shadowed but clear for several yards before it curved away into the trees. Jack was nowhere to be seen. The footsteps, the choking miasma of evil, it had all been a figment.

Day opened his mouth and took a breath at last, let it out and heard himself sobbing as if it were someone else in pain, in fear.

He patted his pockets until he found his flask and he drank until it was empty. He put it away in his waistcoat and took his cane from where it hung on the railing. He walked away from the deep wood, listening to the uneven bump of his own gait on the planks. He left the bridge and walked to the road where he knew he could still find a cab, get to his house where Claire would be waiting.

But he could not escape the sensation of being watched.

*

Whenever Henry Mayhew entered Trafalgar Square, his gaze travelled to Nelson's Column and the statue of the man at the top. Henry had always wondered who that man was and where he was going. He had one foot out as if he was about to step off the column into mid-air. It worried him that the man might topple from his perch and hurt himself. It made no sense for anyone to be so high up there against the sky. He could see the moon rising behind the statue, moving in tiny increments that were only visible because the column remained stationary.

Oliver swooped in from somewhere to the east and made a great show of landing on Henry's shoulder. His wings brushed against Henry's cheek. He reached up and rubbed the tickle out of his skin, then stroked the bird's feathered head, ran his fingertips over Oliver's black beak. The bird nuzzled his hand, looking for food, then flew away to the top of a lamppost at the southeast corner of the square. Henry smiled and followed him. He fished a key out of his pocket and inserted it into a keyhole in an almost invisible door. The door swung open to reveal a space barely large enough for two people to stand in, perfectly sized for Henry's giant frame.

He took a few kernels of dried corn from the ledge that ran along the inside wall of the post and held them up outside. Oliver flew down and perched on his arm, snatched at the corn. His beak was sharp, but it only whispered against the palm of Henry's hand as he ate. When the corn was gone, Oliver flew back to the top of the lamppost and began the long process of preening his feathers, preparing for sleep. Henry murmured goodnight and glanced around the square once more before closing the door and settling in.

Claire Day hesitated in the kitchen doorway, but didn't enter. She imagined a body lying on the floor, a blue uniform soaked in blood. She blinked and the body was gone, replaced by gleaming wooden planks. She shuddered. The kitchen maid saw her there and smiled at her, raised an enquiring eyebrow. Claire shook her head and turned and went down the hallway, passed the front room without looking in and crept quietly up the stairs to the nursery.

She held up a finger to quiet the nanny, then picked up the book she had left there and sat in the rocking chair next to the twins' cradle. She peered over the high railing at them. They slept curled together, touching each other's faces with their tiny chubby fingers, their round stomachs rising and falling. A silvery string of spit flowed down one of their chins, soaking the blanket their heads rested on. Claire used the back of her finger to stroke the drooling baby's cheek. She snagged the runner of drool and wiped it away. She felt calm now. She only needed to be near her girls, to blot out everything in the world but them.

With her free hand, she opened to a page in *A Child's Garden of Verses* and she tried to read, but the words blurred and disappeared. The nanny moved about at the far end of the nursery, folding the endless supply of little towels they used throughout the day, but Claire took no notice of her.

Her breathing evened out and she drifted off to sleep with her hand still draped over the side of the cradle.

*

Retired Inspector Augustus McKraken stood on the porch at 184 Regent's Park Road and watched the street. His eyes felt gritty in their sockets and his legs were like rubber. He wasn't a young man any more. Sometime soon he would need to sleep. But not yet, and hopefully not until he received some news about Jack the Ripper. He could hold out a bit longer. There were many men out looking for that fiend, and as much as McKraken wanted to join the hunt, he knew he was doing good work here protecting the Day family from harm. He leaned against the front wall and closed his eyes for just a moment, just giving them a rest. Within seconds, he was snoring.

14

Day passed the guard on his front door and went inside without waking the man. He crept as quietly up the stairs as his cane would allow and closed his bedroom door behind him. He felt tired all the way through his body, as if he might put down roots if he stood still. He changed into his nightshirt and sat at the edge of the bed. His cane rested against a chair on the other side of the room. He leaned forward and touched the fresh puckered scar that ran from his knee to his ankle. It was smooth, hairless and alien, spotted with blood. He poked at it with his thumbnail and dug into the damaged purple flesh.

'Walter?'

He jumped and turned to look at Claire. She stepped into the room and pushed the door shut behind her. Her long frilly dressing gown hung all the way to her bare feet, and her hair was down, cascading past her shoulders. He was struck anew by her beauty, as he was every time he saw her. He had never got used to the fact that she was his.

'What are you doing?'

'Nothing,' he said.

'Does it itch?'

'No. There's not much there, really. Sort of a trickle of sensation, like I'm dammed up somewhere inside.'

'You'll get it back.'

He smiled at her, but he didn't agree. She was too optimistic.

Claire approached the bed and sat next to him. She put her hand on his arm and he lifted it, drew her close and hugged her. His breath stirred her golden tresses and he blew the hair away from her ear. She drew back and clapped her hand to the side of her head.

'That tickles.'

He smiled.

'They're sleeping,' Claire said. 'The babies.'

'I haven't seen them today.'

'I barely see them myself any more. It's so odd having people here to help with the house. And with the girls. I think they're quite happy with their nanny.'

'What's her name? I can never remember.'

'Miss Powell.'

'Powell,' Day said. 'I'm sure I will have forgotten again by tomorrow. How long will she be here?'

'I think she's here for good. Unless you simply loathe her.'

'I couldn't possibly loathe her yet. I've barely even met her. I just worry we haven't the room here for a staff.'

'But we might. Mother's helped me to figure it all out. It's taken a bit of rearranging, is all.'

'Perhaps I don't want to rearrange my household according to your mother's whims.'

Claire frowned and stood up. She crossed the room and picked up his cane, turned and sat in the chair, laid the cane across her lap. 'She's only trying to help.'

'I appreciate that, but –'

'And it's temporary. When we have a bigger house –'

'Let's stop talking about things we can't do. I'm tired.'

'That's hardly a surprise. You're never here. You've barely said two words to my parents since they arrived.'

'I'm sure that's a great relief to them both.'

'I know you have work to do, but how will anything change between you if you don't at least make an attempt to get along with each other?'

'The only change they'll accept is if I disappear from the face of the earth and leave you to find a more appropriate husband.'

'There's no more appropriate husband for me than you.'

'Oh, I'm sure they've got someone picked out for you. After a proper period of mourning, they'll introduce you.'

'You're being beastly.'

'You know they can't stand the sight of me.'

'They simply don't know how to talk to you. You've nothing in common with them.'

'Exactly my point.'

'My father is trying very hard. He's suggested that we name the girls after –'

'Oh, so now he's naming my children.'

'He is not. He's made a suggestion. The babies are doing well after three weeks. They're happy and healthy and I don't think we're going to lose them. I think it's time we gave them names.'

'And what does your father suggest?'

'Margaret and Mary, after his sisters. They were twins, too, you know.'

'But they died when they were . . .'

'They were three.'

'That seems particularly morbid to me. And perhaps an ill omen.'

'Our neighbour's little boy was named after his own grandfather, a man he never got to meet. It's hardly an unusual custom.'

'Fine, then.'

'It doesn't matter anyway. I had other names in mind. What do you think of Winnie and Henrietta? Except she'd be Winifred, wouldn't she?'

'Who would be Winifred?'

'The small one. She looks like a Winnie.'

'And who suggested those names?'

'Nobody. I read them in a book. Fiona gave me –'

'So now Fiona Kingsley gets to name my children.'

'No, she has not. She gave me a book and there's a poem in it called "For Winnie and Henrietta". I think they're adorable names.'

'And what does your father think of them?'

'I haven't asked him.'

'Don't you think you'd better?'

'Walter . . .'

'After all, it hardly matters what I think. It's your father you'll turn to when you need something. His influence pervades every nook and cranny of my home.'

'You don't like –'

'It doesn't matter whether I like the names or not. They're my children and I'd like to name them myself, without his bloody meddling in it.'

Claire stared at him for a long moment. She swung the cane from her lap and took it by its end, extending the crook for him to take. 'I told you, my father had nothing

105

to do with the names I like. You're being hateful towards him. My parents are trying their best to be helpful. I know they can be difficult, but they're making an effort, however small that might be, and you are not. You've behaved worse than the babies ever since . . .' She indicated his leg with a glance. 'Well, anyway, you haven't been yourself in quite some time and, forgive me for saying so, I'm beginning to lose patience with you.'

'Well, that's just wonderful. They've turned you against me now. I knew they'd succeed at it eventually.' He snatched the cane from her and pushed himself up, hobbled to the door with greater difficulty than he really felt and opened it. 'If you want them here so much more than you want me, you may have your wish.'

'Oh, Walter.'

'Tell your parents they've won. The lot of you can name all the babies you want to name without any interference from me.'

'Walter!'

He stepped into the hallway and slammed the bedroom door behind him. He turned and saw a door at the end of the hall quietly close, with just a glimpse of one eye back in the darkness. One of the many newcomers to his household had witnessed their quarrel. His face flushed and he looked down, realized he was still wearing nothing but his nightshirt.

'Well, the hell with it,' he said. He was talking to the closed door at the end of the hallway. 'I will wear a nightshirt in my own home if I choose to wear a nightshirt. A man's home is his castle, and all that.'

Claire exited his room. She walked to her own room and shut the door without ever looking at him.

Day stomped to the stairs and started down, thumping his cane loudly against each step. Halfway down, he could see a light on in the study below. He hesitated, then turned and went back up and put on his trousers. A man's home was indeed his castle, but decency needn't be thrown out the window. There were, after all, several new women now under his roof. His second journey down the stairs was taken with a modicum of discretion.

Leland Carlyle was standing at the drink trolley when Day entered his study. The older man turned, but when he saw Day, he grunted and went back to pouring his drink.

'Port?' He spoke with his back to his son-in-law.

'I'll take a brandy,' Day said.

Carlyle stoppered the port and reached for another decanter at the back of the silver tray. 'I thought you'd gone up to bed,' he said.

'I did. I thought you'd retired as well.'

Carlyle ignored the implied question. 'Trouble on the home front?'

'None.'

Carlyle picked up the two glasses, crossed the room and set the brandy on a little table near the door, away from the chairs and the fire, as if he expected Day to take the glass up to his room. Day picked it up and took a large swallow. He wanted to turn around, go back upstairs and take Claire in his arms. He hadn't meant to be so disagreeable with her. He scowled at Carlyle's back as his father-in-law settled into Day's own favourite red armchair. Day had thought he'd be able to enjoy a few moments of peace and quiet, have an opportunity to settle his mind before gathering his courage to go and apologize to Claire. But life was simply one indignity piled upon another. He followed Carlyle, took one of the less comfortable yellow chairs and set his cane across his lap, realizing as he did it that he was mirroring the way Claire had held it only a few minutes earlier.

'Good port?'

'It'll do,' Carlyle said.

'It was recommended to me.'

'Yes, no doubt by another policeman.'

Day grimaced and swallowed another mouthful of brandy. He stared at his empty glass, at the flickering room barely glimpsed through its faceted surfaces. He considered hurling the glass across the room and ordering Leland Carlyle out of his study, out of his house.

The house Carlyle had paid for.

Day stood quietly and got his cane under him, thumped his quiet way to the drink trolley and poured another three fingers, watching the thick amber liquid swirl around itself and up, unable to escape its cut-crystal trap.

'I believe it was a barrister who recommended it.' He didn't turn around or look at Carlyle as he spoke, just stood there at the trolley and sipped.

'A barrister.' Carlyle's voice was deep and pleasant, his words clipped, even, measured. He was a man accustomed to being heard. His opinions were as good as facts. 'A barrister is only nearly as sophisticated as a policeman, wouldn't you say?'

'So you wouldn't have been any happier had your daughter married a barrister, then?'

There was a long silence behind Day. He didn't move. He was mildly shocked he'd said anything so bold.

'I meant no disrespect, Walter.'

'I understand your disrespect is implied.'

'You have daughters yourself now. One day you'll feel the same as I do. Nobody is good enough. Nobody.'

'But particularly not the son of a valet. Particularly not a policeman who can't afford to house your daughter properly.'

'Claire will always be taken care of. She will never want for anything, and neither will her children. And for as long as you remain married to her, you will not want for anything, either.'

Day turned and leaned on his cane. He opened his mouth to talk, but instead filled it with more brandy and waited. Carlyle continued in a hushed tone. Day could barely hear him.

'And should you choose to go your own way,' Carlyle said, 'you would never need worry about their welfare.'

'Should I go my own way?' Day barely moved his lips as he repeated the phrase.

'I think you understand me. In fact, there might be incentives for you to go, for you to pursue whatever kind of life you want, away from Claire and the babies. You're still young enough. Think of the freedom you'd have with a little money in your pocket and the world wide open to you.'

Day closed his eyes and imagined himself at the bottom of a deep well, surrounded by black water. He set his glass on the trolley, a lonely half ounce of brandy left swirling around at the bottom. The room spun and his stomach flipped over on itself. He felt his gorge rise.

'You'll excuse me,' he said.

He left his study, previously the only room in the house he truly felt he could call his own, and hurried down the hallway to the water closet. He jiggled the knob, but it was locked from the inside. Someone, one of the many new people in his home, was using it. Panicked, tasting the bile in his throat and fighting against the wave of nausea in his gut, he hobbled to the kitchen and through the meat pantry. He was bemused to see a rasher of bacon hanging there, expensive meat he was sure he hadn't paid for. He left the house by the back door and crossed the garden to the thin smattering of trees that bordered the property behind his own. He looked up at the stars, at a cloud that meandered across the sky, its misty fingers caressing the moon. Fresh air filled his lungs and quieted his stomach. He gained control over his gag reflex and resisted the urge to vomit.

It would have been a waste of good brandy.

Carlyle had made his offer so casually, in such a matter-of-fact way, as if it hadn't occurred to him that he could offend Walter Day. How could two men be of such entirely different species? Day leaned against a skinny tree trunk. The tree bowed beneath him, but didn't fall, and Walter allowed himself to trust its elastic strength. He took his weight off his bad leg and felt instant relief. The change in sensation alerted him to the fact that he needed to urinate and he glanced in the direction of his dark house, the occupied water closet somewhere in there.

He stood back up and unbuttoned his trousers and relieved himself in the tall grass. He looked up at the tree-tops, swaying above his head, and it occurred to him that there was something there, just out of sight. The treetops were trying to tell him something, the leaves rustling in a gentle breeze, chattering to one another.

The treetops.

Walter swallowed hard and grinned at the empty night sky. He buttoned himself back up and grabbed his cane and hurried as fast as he could back to the house. He went through the pantry, where he took the lantern that hung there, through the kitchen, down the hallway and past the parlour, past his study, past his father-in-law, who tried to grab his elbow. Day shrugged him off and kept going, to the front door and out. McKraken startled awake and gave him a sheepish smile. Day nodded at him and clomped down the steps. He was lucky. A two-wheeler rolled down Regent's Park Road just as Walter reached the street. He put out his hand and the driver stopped. Day pulled himself up into the carriage.

'Where to, sir?'

'Take me to Warwick Road, just off Sutherland Gardens,' Day said. 'I know where they are.'

'I know where they are, too, sir.'

'No, I know where the children are.'

'Which children's that?'

'Never mind. Just get me there as quickly as you can. They've already been through enough. They needn't spend the night in the wood after all.'

15

Blackleg led Hammersmith to a narrow street in a neighbourhood full of empty crumbling shops and people asleep under tents and awnings. Gas globes gave a faint radiance to the human shapes in the mist around them. Hammersmith saw a child eating something that resembled a squirrel, and a woman with scabs on her face reached out to him as he passed.

'A penny for a roll wiff me,' she said. 'A ha'penny, even?'

Hammersmith shuddered and looked the other way, but Blackleg stopped and gave the woman a coin. When he rejoined Hammersmith a moment later, he seemed embarrassed.

'Gotta help each other,' he said. 'Nobody else will.'

'But that woman . . .'

'She's got a baby to feed, don't she?'

'Does she?'

'Her name's Liz and her baby's name's Michael. The folks on this street are all the family she's got. Now shut up with that look on yer face and follow. Don't get lost or you're not gonna find yer way home from here.'

Hammersmith glanced back, but the woman was gone. He wiped the palm of his hand over his face and rolled his shoulders, then hurried to catch up to Blackleg, who was already halfway to the next corner. The criminal didn't look back, but marched purposefully to a building three doors down from the end of the street. It appeared to Hammersmith to be an abandoned textile warehouse, but smaller than any that he had seen before. The entire structure leaned to the west and the upper storey was half gone. He could see birds roosting in the exposed timbers of the roof. Blackleg beckoned for Hammersmith to follow him down an alley that ran between the warehouse and the next building over. A wedge of gaslight disappeared three feet beyond the alley's mouth and Hammersmith hesitated. Blackleg was a scoundrel and a murderer and he had never guaranteed Hammersmith safe passage. Still, to turn around and go back would be an admission of defeat. He might as well give up any lingering notions of being a policeman and instead settle in as a clerk or a shopkeeper. He took a deep breath and plunged into the shadows.

And almost bumped into Blackleg, who was standing against the wall in the dark.

'What is it? Why have you stopped?'

'It's behind me,' Blackleg said. 'You took a minute there. Thought you was lost.'

'Just wary,' Hammersmith said.

'Good. Wary's a good instinct. Now c'mon.'

He turned and, with a grunt, pulled himself through a half-open window. Hammersmith watched him disappear into the blackness of the warehouse. He shrugged and shook his head and jumped up on to the sill. He turned and sat, dangling his legs over the edge, then scooted forward and let himself drop into the room. He landed gently, but felt the impact in his chest, as if he'd broken open his wounds, doused them in kerosene and set them on fire. He took a moment to gather himself and heard the sound of his heavy breathing echo off the nearby walls. When he felt he could move again, he looked all about him in the inky dark, but couldn't see a thing anywhere, just a grey rectangle behind him where the window led back out into the alley.

'Blackleg?'

'Here.' A moment later, Hammersmith heard the *scritch* of a match against a striker and saw the orange flare of a lantern being lit. Blackleg closed the shutter and swung the light in Hammersmith's direction.

'Keep coming, bluebottle. It's over here at the other end.'

'We're liable to run into something. Or fall. This floor's probably rotten all the way through.'

'It'll hold you. It holds me just fine, and you figure to weigh about as much as one of my arms, boy. Look.' The lantern jiggled and swayed about, creating chiaroscuro patterns across the walls and in every corner of the room.

'Are you jumping up and down?'

'Aye,' Blackleg said. 'Showin' you the floor's solid.'

'Well, all right, then.'

Hammersmith shuffled carefully across the room. He pretended he was wearing skates, but the floor wasn't as smooth as an icy pond. Floorboards had warped and buckled. They stuck up at odd angles here and there, as if peeled away and discarded by some angry carpenter. If he tripped, Hammersmith was certain he'd get a face full of splinters.

Eventually he made it to the far wall, where Blackleg waited with the lantern. The criminal nodded at him and produced a key from his waistcoat, which he held up in the flickering light. He bent and inserted the key into a hole in a door and turned a knob and the door swung open, disappearing as it moved away from them. Darkness exploded at them, an eruption of wings and high-pitched screeches. Hammersmith ducked and covered his head. In a moment it was over and Blackleg grabbed his arm, pulled him forward.

'Bats,' Blackleg said. 'They won't hurt you. C'mon.'

They moved together into more darkness.

'There's stairs here,' Blackleg said. 'Might be slick with bat shit. Watch yer step and stay with me.'

'Oh, I'm following you. No plans to run off on my own.'

'See that you don't. I wouldn't wanna have to try to find you in here.'

Hammersmith kept one hand on the wall and put his other hand on Blackleg's shoulder and they started to move down.

'Wait,' Hammersmith said. 'Give me a moment, would you?'

'What's wrong?'

'I don't . . . well, it's tight spaces. They bother me.'

'Well, they should, too.'

'And I don't like to go below ground level if I can help it.'

'Who does?'

'And I don't care much for the dark.'

'You're not alone in that.'

'It's just . . . I need a moment.'

'We can turn back,' Blackleg said. 'Wouldn't be a bad idea anyway.'

'But what's down there? What are you so intent on showing me?'

'I seem intent to you?'

'Perhaps a bit.'

'I could tell you what's down there. But it's better to see it. Besides, if I tell you, you'll wanna see it anyway, I think, so I say we either go on ahead down and I show you, or we go back and forget the whole thing.'

'Is that what you want?'

'No,' Blackleg said. 'You're the only bluebottle I know of who might give a good goddamn and I wanna show you what we got down there. But you don't owe me nothin' and I don't owe you nothin' and you can come take a look if you want to, but I ain't gonna force you. That's that. It's your mind to make up as you please, isn't it?'

Hammersmith took in a deep breath, filled his lungs with stale musty air, then blew it all out until he felt hollow inside. 'All right,' he said. 'But take it slow. It's hard to breathe, isn't it?'

'Not particular hard, no. There's air down in there same as there is up here.'

Hammersmith gritted his teeth and took shallow breaths through his nose. He could see swirling dots of light from the corners of his eyes, but when he moved his head, they weren't there. His skull felt like it needed to be oiled, like it had rusted in place at the top of his spine. He moved slowly down the stairs, grateful that Blackleg was maintaining an unhurried pace ahead of him. The criminal blocked most of the lantern's light with his body, but Hammersmith could see the walls on either side of them as they slid into view below and then passed out of their bubble of light behind them. Blackleg's silhouette moved with confidence, as if he had travelled this way many times before. Hammersmith heard nothing but the sounds of their feet on the stairs and it occurred to him that he really did trust the barrel-shaped criminal. While it was entirely possible he was leading Hammersmith into some kind of ambush, it seemed unlikely. The dread that Hammersmith felt came only from the darkness and the closeness of their surroundings.

When they reached the last step, Blackleg asked Hammersmith to stand still while he hunted up another lantern. A moment later, there was the scrape of a shutter and a flare of light and the combined illumination of the two lamps shone all round the dry stone walls of a small chamber. The wall behind Blackleg was filled by a wide black mouth. It was the only possible exit, aside from the stairway they'd just come down, and Hammersmith felt the air pressing in on him from all sides. The lattice of scars on his chest ached. He looked up, but the solid stone ceiling did nothing to assuage his fears. If anything, it seemed much too heavy to remain where it was. He felt suddenly certain it was going to fall on him, crush him, fill his mouth with dirt and pulp his eyeballs, break his bones and bury him there for ever.

'You're all right,' Blackleg said.

'How do you know?'

'If I'm all right, you're all right. And I'm all right. Nothing's happened to me here, and I've been down in this cave dozens of times.'

Hammersmith swallowed hard. His face felt hot with shame.

'I understand,' Blackleg said. 'Lucky Eddy was in the

mines afore he came over and made hisself a shofulman. You know shofulman?'

'Counterfeit money,' Hammersmith said. His voice was shaky. 'A counterfeiter, right?'

'Aye. That. Wanted to put his operation down in here, but he couldn't stomach it. He'd pass out and wake up screaming.'

'Did it get better for him?'

'If it did, he can't tell us about it now. Got picked up by the rozzers and died in jail six months back. Don't matter, nohow. You can put up with bein' down here five more minutes, I think. Long enough to see what we got.' He jerked his head and swung the lamp in an arc, turned and beckoned Hammersmith towards the great black hole in the opposite wall. 'When it started, we didn't know it was gonna be more than one, but we knew it were possible. So we brought her here. The first one. She was alive then, but not for long.'

He stopped and Hammersmith almost bumped into him. They were just inside the hollow in the stone wall, twelve feet across and ten feet high and eight feet deep. A long bench, carved into the rock, filled the niche. Three women lay on the bench against the wall, their feet pointed out at Blackleg and Hammersmith. The women were wrapped in rough blankets, their hair plaited in braids, their eyes closed, and their hands crossed on their breasts. The fingernails on the nearest girl's left hand were broken and jagged, black beneath the tips. Hammersmith could see dark splotches on the blankets, deeper black at their centres, fuzzing out near the edges. Inky liquid that had soaked into the fabric, spreading out and drying in irregular patterns.

'Blood?'

'Aye, it's blood,' Blackleg said.

'What happened to them?'

'Kilt. Somebody came on 'em at night, up there on the street, and cut 'em up bad. Left 'em there.'

'And you brought their bodies down here?'

'I didn't. Some of 'em that found the girls brought 'em down here. Like I say, the first girl was still alive when they found her. They didn't know what else to do.'

'Tell the police. Get a doctor.'

'We got a doctor. Got our own man what won't go spreadin' rumours. Knows how to keep a thing or two to hisself. Nothin' he could do by the time he got to her.' Blackleg pointed to the woman in the middle. She looked to Hammersmith to be about nineteen years old, but the skin was slack on her cheeks and neck and he could see old bruises on her arms.

'But the –'

'We don't go to the rozzers,' Blackleg said. 'They come to us and it's never good when they does. Present company excepted, 'cept of course you ain't one of 'em no more, which is the only reason I care to show you this.'

'Surely you should have turned their bodies over to authorities after a time.'

'How long a time? We're still decidin'. Been a year since this happened the last time, ain't it? And the rozzers didn't catch the bloke then, did they?'

'When did these new murders happen?'

'Been happening for three weeks now. One a week. Every Sunday morning in the wee hours, like a sorta blasphemy. Lotta the girls are scared to go out any more. It's just like it was.'

Hammersmith understood what he meant. It was like the summer of 1888 when Jack the Ripper stalked the alleyways of the East End.

'Come closer,' Blackleg said. He stepped up to the bench and moved the blanket from the nearest woman's torso. Hammersmith averted his eyes, ashamed for the poor dead woman, but Blackleg caught him by the elbow and pulled him over. 'It's all right. I'm keepin' it decent. Just looka what he done.'

Hammersmith sighed and glanced at the corpse. Blackleg had kept the blanket bunched over her breasts and thighs, but had exposed her abdomen. In the lantern light it resembled an eclipse of the sun, ragged yellow flesh ringing a black maw.

'What, what am I seeing here?'

'He took it all,' Blackleg said. 'Took all her insides. Scooped 'em out whole. They're gone.'

'This wasn't the first one, the one who lived?' Hammersmith was horrified by the thought that anyone might survive for even a moment with such terrible wounds.

'No. That one he was gentler with, but he gets worse with every one he does.'

'I don't want to look at any more.'

'This is the worst of 'em. I just wanted you to see.'

Blackleg moved the blanket back over the hole in the woman.

'What were their names?'

'Their names?'

'Yes,' Hammersmith said. 'Who were they?'

'Well, this 'un's Betty. Little Betty, they called her. There's another girl named Betty who's a good bit heavier. That one's alive and well, thank the Lord. The one in the middle here's called Alice. Nobody knew her much. Only been around for a few weeks and kept to herself. And that one at the end's a complete stranger to us, but we took 'er down here with the others anyway. Still might be somebody who steps up and says they knows 'er.'

'You knew these other two, though?'

'Aye. I knew 'em. Knew Little Betty quite well, at that. I wanna say, it's good of you to ask their names. Decent of you. Like they was people.'

'Of course they were people.'

'Not how rozzers usually treated 'em, though, even when they was alive.'

'Yes,' Hammersmith said. 'I'm sorry.'

'Not your business to be sorry. Let's say no more about it.'

'All right. But this woman whose name you don't know. She's a stranger, you say. But she wasn't the first one killed?'

'No. She was the middle one in order of the killing.'

'Was there anything else unusual about her?'

'Nothin' I can see.'

'Where were they found?'

'Here and there. Round and about.'

'Would you show me exactly where?'

'If you think it'll help.'

'I have no idea. I'm no detective. It would be better if Inspector Day were here with us.'

'But you're all we got here. So you'll have to step up and be the detective now, won't you?'

Hammersmith pursed his lips and glared at Blackleg. 'Then show me the murder scenes. Where you found all three of them. I want to visit every spot.'

'I'll do it, but might be better to wait until there's daylight. Not gonna see much right now.'

Blackleg smoothed the blankets over the three women and recrossed Little Betty's arms over what was left of her chest. He looked down at her still form, then kissed his fingers and touched her forehead. It seemed to Hammersmith that the criminal's eyes were moist when he looked back up, but Blackleg shook his head, warning the former sergeant to be quiet. He marched past Hammersmith with the lantern held high and led the way back up the steps to the city, where there was fresh air and a wide-open sky above.

Hammersmith wondered how he kept finding himself underground. He hoped there would be no need to visit those three sad bodies again.

16

He was glad he'd thought to bring a lantern this time. The air was the deep green of underwater algae. It smelled of clean rot and fresh growth. He looked down at his feet sometimes to make sure he was clear of roots that might trip him, but mostly he kept his eyes up and peered as far as the lantern light reached into the branches above him. The trees gently swayed and occasionally revealed the moon, a bright sliver in the darkness. He wondered whether the children were still there or had moved on. If they had left the wood, he might never find them. He hoped they had no better idea than he did about where they might hide in the city.

An hour passed, two hours. He thought about stopping, thought about bringing Hammersmith to help in the search again. But finding the children was his responsibility, not Hammersmith's, and he needed to succeed, to get his nerve back. He hefted the lantern higher and moved slowly on through the trees.

It was after midnight when he reached a silent place in the forest. It took him a moment to realize that he couldn't hear squirrels chittering at one another, or birds calling. The breeze had not changed, but he heard leaves rustling somewhere nearby. He couldn't pinpoint where the sound was coming from, but he already knew where to look. He stopped moving and cast the lantern about in an arc, watching above him for movement. The rustling sound stopped and the wood became still.

'Simon?'

He listened for a reply or for the leaves to rustle again, for some indication that the boy had heard and reacted. But there was nothing.

'Robert?'

Again he listened. Again there was no sound.

'I know you're up there, boys. I'm not going to hurt you and I'm not going to chase you up a tree, but I'm not going to leave, either. I'm a policeman and I want to help you. I'm going to wait here until you acknowledge me.'

He looked around him and found a large stone. The ground near it had been disturbed; something else as large as the stone had recently been moved, leaving behind a muddy expanse of forest floor where there was no grass or brush. He went and sat on the stone and waited, his cane propped up next to him.

His mind wandered and he thought about Claire, thought about how he'd snapped at her. He had acted like a child. He winced at the memory. But he could still apologize to Claire and she would forgive him. Worse than his tantrum was the way he'd acted in front of Leland Carlyle. The man was an ass, but there was no reason to sink to his level. There was much he'd have to do to smooth things over when he got back home.

He looked around at the trees and smiled. Here it was peaceful. A man could disappear and never be found again. *Lost and gone for ever.* That certainly wouldn't be the worst thing he could do. Simply vanish and never have to deal with the emotional consequences of anything he'd said or done. He reached for his flask and remembered that he hadn't refilled it before leaving the house.

'Go away!'

Day jumped. His head snapped up and around. The voice had come from somewhere overhead, shrill and frightened. The voice of a child. He'd been right. The boys were hiding up above, in the treetops.

And they were alive. They were safe. He smiled at the trees.

'I'm not going to go away,' he said. 'And I'm not going to hurt you.' He waited again, but there was no response. 'Boys? Simon, Robert, my name is Inspector Day. I'm a policeman. I'm here to help you.'

More rustling from above. He stood and waved the lantern about over his head, trying to find them up there, but he only succeeded in casting crazy confusing shadows everywhere around him. He used his free hand to still the lantern and he closed his eyes, listening.

'Don't you want to come down from there and go home?'

'No!'

'Be quiet, Simon!'

Both of them had spoken. The first voice was higher pitched than the other. The youngest boy had less control and the older boy didn't want him to speak. Simon, therefore, was the one to talk to, the one who might answer back.

'Why don't you want to go home, Simon?'

'The birdie man is there!' The little boy's voice echoed down and around Day, lost and forlorn, coming from every direction at once.

'The birdie man?'

'He ate Mother and Father and he –'

'Simon!' Robert's voice.

'He wants to eat us, too!'

'The birdie man is gone now,' Day said. 'I won't let him come back or hurt you.'

'He'll eat you, too.'

'He won't eat me. I'm going to catch him. The other policemen and I are going to find him and put him in jail. He'll never be able to hurt you.'

'That means you haven't found him yet,' Robert said. The older boy was wiser than Simon.

'Not yet,' Day said. 'I admit we haven't got him yet. But we will.'

'No, you won't. You can't catch him. The birdie man can appear and disappear in the dark.'

'He's just a man.'

'No. He has a long beak that moves about wherever it wants and big round eyes on the back of his head and smaller eyes on the front and claws for hands.' Simon's voice now. 'He's not a regular sort of person and you can't ever catch him.'

'Did you see him, Simon?'

'We both saw him,' Robert said.

As they talked, Day moved slowly around the clearing. He was concentrating so hard on the sound of the boys' voices that he felt he could almost swivel his ears. As Robert spoke, Day stopped and laid his hand on a wide tree trunk at the edge of the glade. He looked up and saw a narrow board nailed into the wood just above eye level. Farther up was another board, and he thought he could make out some sort of platform, covered with leaves, high up where the trunk tapered towards the sky.

'I know where you are now, Robert,' Day said. 'Why don't you come down here? We should talk.'

There was a long pause before the older boy finally responded. 'No,' he said. 'I'm not going to. And even if you go away, you're only going to bring more people here and then the birdie man is going to know where we are. We can't let you do that.' Then, his voice softer and deeper: 'I'm sorry.'

Day frowned. There was a new sound above his head, something heavy rolling across wood. He peered up into the tree. There was the sound of branches breaking and in a split second he saw a flurry of leaves and broken tree limbs and a huge black shape falling directly towards him.

17

Alan Ridgway entered his room at the far end of the hall-way in the boarding house on Plumbers Row. He left the door standing open and fumbled with his free hand for the lamp on the table by the door, but hesitated when he heard someone breathing far back in the shadows at the other end of the room.

'It's quite all right, Alan Ridgway. Come in and close the door. But do let's leave the light off for now, shall we?'

Alan squinted in the direction of the voice, but couldn't see anything more than the vague shape of a man sitting in a chair under the window. 'Who's there?' He was certain he'd left the curtains open when he'd left that morning.

'I'd rather not say just yet,' the shape said. 'I'm still deciding whether we'll know each other long enough for it to matter.'

'You must have the wrong room,' Alan said. 'This one's mine.'

'Oh, Alan Ridgway, if you're going to steal from others, then you must learn to share in kind.'

'But –'

'Shut the door.' The shape's voice had lost its whimsical quality and dropped to a coarse whisper. Like the warning growl of a predator.

Alan moved his hand away from the lamp. He shifted his grocery basket to his right hand and backed up slowly, aiming for the door. But the shape was instantly out of its chair and had crossed the room faster than Alan could register the movement. Rough hands pulled him back into the room and the door slammed behind him. Alan felt a flash of heat across his belly and he let go of the basket. He lost his balance and sprawled on the floor. A single apple rolled away under the table. He heard the *snick* of a key in the lock. He probed his gut and wasn't surprised to find his fingers were wet. The man in his room had cut him, but Alan couldn't tell how deep the wound was. When he looked up, the shape was in its chair again, as if it had never moved.

'It would be unwise to test me again, Alan Ridgway.' The voice in the dark was relaxed and carried no indication that the shape had exerted itself. The merry tone of hail-fellow-well-met was back and Alan knew without a trace of doubt that he was being toyed with.

'I won't,' he said. 'I didn't mean to test you.'

'I won't be so gentle with you next time.'

'Who are you? What do you want?'

'The question is, Alan Ridgway, who are *you*? I know your name from the papers, the letters and journals you've carelessly left here for me to find, but I know very little else about you. For instance, how much pain can you endure?'

Alan shuddered. 'But I didn't purposely leave anything here for you. This is where I live.'

'Alan Ridgway?' A note of warning in the voice.

'What do you want to know about me?' Alan's belly had begun to hurt a great deal.

'Why are you pretending to be that which you are most patently not?'

'I don't know what you mean,' Alan said.

'Shall I cut you again? Somewhere different this time?'

'No.'

'No?'

'Please, no.'

'Then let us not pretend. You have made a clumsy attempt at mimicking my methods with three women recently. I was unfortunately detained and missed your first foray into the back alleys of Whitechapel, and I arrived a bit too late at the second spot to watch you work. But I was there when you did the third one.'

'You were there?'

'I believe her name was Alice. Am I mistaken? I never knew her full name, if she had one.'

'I didn't —'

'Don't lie to me again now, Alan Ridgway. If I decide to cut out your tongue, you'll be of no use to me whatever.'

'I mean to say, I never knew her name.'

'I see.'

It occurred to Alan that this shape might in fact be a policeman, in which case he had just confessed to a crime. But surely a policeman would have clapped him in irons by now. This person, this shape, claimed to have seen him murder a woman, had then broken into Alan's room and waited for him. It made no sense to Alan at all.

'How did you choose her?'

'She was alone,' Alan said.

'And?'

'Only that.'

'But was she ready?'

'Ready for what?'

'Was she ripe?'

'I don't know,' Alan said. 'I don't know what you mean by that.'

'You did the deed without knowing why you were doing it? That bothers me. Your imitations are appearing everywhere in my city now. You're stepping on my toes, you know, and I'm honestly getting weary just trying to keep tabs on you all. There's a fellow in Notting Hill and all about who's killing people at an alarming rate. Calls himself after some sort of spider. A Harvest Man, that's it. And here we have you, tallying up dead women one after another with no idea why you're doing it except you'd clearly like to be me, wouldn't you? Only you're not me, Alan Ridgway.'

And Alan suddenly understood who he was talking to. He actually gasped in recognition. He grinned and sat up, grunting with the pain. 'You're him.'

'Of course I am.'

'I mean you're Jack the Ripper.'

'I am sometimes called Jack. And you are always only Alan Ridgway. I would say it's so good to meet you, but I'm afraid it's not. Not for either of us.'

'But I've studied you.'

'Not well enough.'

'Why? What did I do wrong? I only did what you did. I did it all to honour you.'

The shape sniffed and sat silent for a long time. Alan checked his sore abdomen again and, although his shirt was soaked, the bleeding had stopped. Jack, that shape in the dark, knew exactly what he was doing. Alan smiled and tried to breathe in the scent of the room, tried to absorb Jack through the pores of his skin.

'Taste it,' Jack said.

'What?'

'The blood. Your blood. Taste it.'

'Why?'

Jack said nothing, didn't move. So Alan brought his fingers to his lips and licked the salty blood from them.

'What do you feel?'

'Feel?'

'What do you feel, Alan Ridgway?'

'I'm honoured.'

'How curious. Honoured by your own blood?'

'No, by your presence.'

'Feh. You still annoy me.' The shape leaned forward, hands across its knees. 'I'm this close to ending you, Alan Ridgway. Ending you! What does the blood make you feel, damnit?'

He floated a guess out into the room. 'Small?'

Jack sat back. 'Interesting. Yes, small, indeed. The blood humbles us all. Very good, Alan Ridgway.'

'But big, too.' Alan suddenly felt a need to talk, as if this person he couldn't even see might understand him, might even condone his choices. Who else would, if not Jack the Ripper? 'Powerful. It makes me feel like . . .'

'Like royalty?'

'Like a king, a king presiding over life and death.'

'Like a god, then.'

'Exactly, like a god.'

'Alan Ridgway, you are not a god. You are nothing, really. Not even a very good mimic.'

Alan blinked. The air in the room smelled like copper

and fish and ozone. As if lightning had struck a ship at sea. 'But I thought –'

'Don't think, Alan Ridgway. It doesn't suit you.'

'But I'm not just a mimic. I feel things. Dark awful nasty things.'

'Hardly. These dark feelings of yours are the blind impulses of an infant. You know of me. You worship me in your little way by doing the same sorts of things you think I do. Or rather the things I once did. But you have no understanding of my work and so you're only going through the motions, and how much pleasure can you derive from that?'

'I honour you. I do.'

'Perhaps you try. I am charitable enough to allow you that.' The shape nodded. 'But because you don't understand my process, you do us both a disservice. And you've done a disservice to those women as well.'

'You're here to kill me, then?'

'No, Alan Ridgway. I think you'd like that too much.' The shape sat silent for a long while and Alan waited. He sat quietly with his back against the door and his arm across his burning abdomen. Finally the shape shifted in his chair. 'I'm going to use you, Alan Ridgway. You're going to do something for me.'

'Me? Do something for you?'

'Yes. I find it useful to employ others from time to time. Some need money and have access to prison cells or private carriages, some long for notoriety and might be engaged to carry a message. Would you deliver a message for me, Alan Ridgway?'

'Gladly.'

'And then your symphony will have reached its climax. Better to take your bow and leave the stage, don't you think? No point in overstaying your welcome.'

'Symphony?'

'Oh, yes, Alan Ridgway. I have a plan for you. Isn't it good to be part of a plan for once, rather than blindly groping about in the muck, hoping for some clue about what you are and why you are?'

'I don't know. I suppose it is, now that you put it so baldly.'

'Good. I'm going to give you an address, Alan Ridgway, and you're going to do something clever for me. When you're done with that, I'll want you to deliver a message to an old friend of mine. His name's Walter Day, and I think the two of you will get along splendidly.'

Alan smiled, pleased that he had finally found a purpose.

18

Day didn't have time to react to the boulder coming at him. It weighed seventy pounds, more than enough to crack his skull, and more than enough to fall quickly through the leaves and small branches before a man could move.

The damp underbrush saved his life. He was just beginning to lean forward, trying to see the boys on the crude platform above him, when the tip of his cane slipped. He compensated by letting go of it and putting his weight on his bad leg just as the boys let go of their giant rock. Day's leg gave out and he fell against the tree's broad trunk. The rock plummeted neatly through the air behind him, grazing the tail of his overcoat and smashing into the ground, pushing mud and dirty water out on every side. The hems of Day's trousers were soaked. In the quiet seconds directly after, he worried he was turning into Hammersmith.

He got his balance and turned, sank back against the tree and stared at the rock embedded in the soil inches from his feet. It was as big around as his chest. His cane lay on either side of it and under it, divided into two big pieces and many more small pieces that were now a part of the forest floor. He was surprised by his own reaction, which was no reaction at all.

'Huh,' he said.

'Are you hurt?'

He looked up at the tree. There was a tunnel over his head where the rock had stripped away leaves and splintered branches on its journey to the ground. Water dripped down through the opening and on to his upraised face. It felt cool and pleasant.

'I'm all right,' he said.

'Good,' Robert said. Day still couldn't see him, but the boy's voice was clearer than it had been, and louder. 'We didn't mean to hurt you. Not really.'

'Yes, you did. You tried to drop this big rock on my head. You might've killed me.'

'We didn't really think about what would happen until we let go of the rock and by then it was too late. We didn't want to kill you. We just want you to go away.'

'How did you get this up there, anyway?' Day circled the rock, patted the top of it, and wiped it dry with the palm of his hand. He turned and sat and watched the leaves move overhead.

'We used a rope and pulley system.'

'That's quite clever.'

'I read about it in a book. We got the pulley from a farm west of us.'

'You didn't steal it, did you?'

'It was old and rusted. Somebody left it in a culvert.'

'We cleaned it up.' Simon's voice now, higher pitched and full of pride. 'It took a long time.'

'Then we clumb up to our secret place here and hung it in the branches,' Robert said.

'It took us three days to pull the rock up here,' Simon said. 'We had to keep tying the rope round the tree when we went home to bed.'

'Quite clever of you,' Day said again. '*Industrious* is the word.'

'Thank you,' Robert said.

'But it was wrong of you to drop it on me.'

'But we didn't drop it on you. We missed.'

'And it's a good thing, too.'

'We really are sorry,' Robert said. 'Will you go away now?'

'No,' Day said. 'But you're safe from me.'

'Safe?'

'I hurt my leg recently. I couldn't climb that tree if I wanted to.'

'You can't climb at all?'

'Not even a little bit.'

'Well, we're not coming down.'

'Why not?'

'Because he's still down there somewhere.'

'Is it all right, then, if I just sit here for a while and talk to you?'

There was a long silence. Day could hear faint murmuring from the platform as the boys discussed the situation.

'We don't want to talk to you,' Simon said at last.

'But we can't stop you from sitting there,' Robert said.

'This is what's known as a stalemate,' Day said. 'By the way, do you have any other rocks up there?'

'No. That was our only one.'

'Good.' Day reached for his flask by habit. He uncorked it and sniffed at its emptiness, but didn't put it away. He sat with the flask in his lap, and gazed away into the wood at a cluster of small green saplings that were deprived of

137

sunlight by the giant trees around them. They would never grow to full height until the previous generation of growth died away and gave them a chance. He wondered what would happen to the forest if all the tallest trees were felled, or simply disappeared overnight.

'Are you still there?'

'Yes, Robert. I'm sitting here on your rock.'

'Are you really a policeman?'

'I am. I'm an inspector with Scotland Yard. My name is Day.'

'But you didn't catch him yet,' Simon said. 'You didn't catch the birdie man.'

'You said he has a beak,' Day said. 'Is that right?'

'Yes.'

'I think he wears a special sort of mask. A plague mask. They have great long beaks attached on the fronts of them.'

'It's scary. If it's a mask, it's scary, even if it isn't his real face.'

'Yes. Plague masks are odd-looking,' Day said. 'But it really is only a mask. And he's only a man.'

'Why does he wear a plague mask? Is he sick?'

'Yes, he is, but not in the way that you mean,' Day said. 'At least I don't think he is. I believe he uses the mask to protect himself from a special kind of . . . well, a sort of gas that he uses to put people to sleep.'

'And then he hurts them.'

'Yes,' Day said. 'I'm afraid he does. But I won't let him hurt you.'

'Do you have any children?'

'I have two little girls. They're only babies, not big like

you. They could never have hauled this rock up there to where you are.'

'Of course not,' Simon said. 'Not if they're babies. Girls aren't strong enough anyway.'

'Probably not,' Day said. 'You must be very strong.'

'We are,' Simon said.

'Don't talk to us like that,' Robert said. 'You're saying nice things so we'll like you and come down from here.'

'You're right,' Day said. 'That's exactly what I'm doing. But I also think you must be strong lads. I honestly do. And I think you must be brave, as well, to run into the dark wood and keep each other safe for so long.'

'We don't mind the wood. It's quiet here and it's ours.'

'You did the right thing, coming here.'

'Do you think so?'

'Yes, I do.'

Day waited.

'Don't you have to go catch the birdie man?'

'Soon,' Day said. 'But right now there are hundreds of other policemen looking for the birdie man. Only we call him the Harvest Man and there are so many of us looking everywhere that he can't possibly escape. We'll get him.'

'You should go and help them look.'

'I will. But for the moment I'm here with you. I'm not going to go away from you until I know that you're safe.'

'We're safe.'

'No, Robert, you're not safe. The Harvest Man can climb trees.'

There was a sudden flurry of movement from above and more whispering between the boys.

'He won't know where to look,' Robert said. 'There are lots of trees.'

'But you've dropped a great rock here and there's evidence of activity under this tree. If I were the Harvest Man, I would climb this tree first and I would find you.'

Simon screamed.

'Stop it!' Robert's voice sounded shaky again. 'You're scaring him! Stop saying things like that!'

'I'm sorry, Robert. Simon, don't be frightened. The Harvest Man isn't going to climb this tree right now because I'm sitting here under it.'

'He'll kill you like he killed Mummy and Father.'

'No, he won't,' Day said.

'He'll catch you and cut you up. You can't run fast. You have a stick to help you walk like our grandfather did.'

'Well, I'm afraid I don't have a stick any more. But I have a revolver. I'll bet your grandfather didn't have one of those.'

'Do you really have a revolver?'

'I do. And if he tries to hurt anybody, I'll shoot him dead as you please.'

'You would shoot him?'

'If he comes near me, I will. Or if he comes near you, or anybody else I care about. I would just as soon shoot him as look at him, if truth be told.'

'Would you let me shoot him?'

'No, Robert.'

'Will you try to talk to him?'

'I don't know. It depends, I suppose, on what he's doing.'

'Promise you'll shoot him the moment you see him. Promise you won't let him get near you.'

'I can't promise that.'

'You must. Promise.'

Day smiled. He realized he was still holding his flask. He corked it and put it away. He pushed himself to his feet and looked with regret at the bits of his smashed and broken cane protruding from under the rock.

'I'll make you a bargain,' he said. 'If the Harvest Man stands very still when I tell him to and if he doesn't try to move until my friends and I tie his hands together, then I won't shoot him. But if he does try to move or tries to come close to me or you or anybody else, then I will shoot him.'

'Have you ever shot anybody before?'

'Oh, yes,' Day said. He crossed his fingers behind his back in case the boys could see him. 'I've shot many villains before. I'm very good with a pistol.'

'Stay there, please,' Robert said. 'We're coming down now.'

19

John Charles Pitt was lying in a hammock under a tree and the tree was spinning, sending the hammock around in great loops through the air. Around, and around, and around again. He smiled. Or he thought he might be smiling. Nothing seemed entirely real. His body was far away from him, but he felt secure. The force of movement didn't lift him from his hammock, didn't make him feel he might fall out and plummet to the ground. It was like an anchor weighing on him. An anchor in a tree? He could smell the vaguely antiseptic odour of the leaves as they fluttered down about him. He could feel the sun on his face, hot, burning him. He worried that he might be getting a sunburn on his cheeks. From far away, he could hear a troubadour singing some old popular song. Something he'd heard before, but couldn't place. He listened to the tune, strained to hear the lyrics. And as he listened he felt himself beginning to wake up.

He hadn't realized he was asleep.

The Harvest Man sang as he worked:

I heard the rippling brooklet sing among the poplar trees
I heard the willows whispering unto the evening breeze
Unto the evening breeze

It always surprised the Harvest Man to hear his own voice, deeper and richer than it ought to be. So he rarely spoke to his parents while he worked on them. But when he sang, it gave him a thrill. At first he had sung nursery rhymes to them or hymns half remembered from his brief time as a choirboy. But those soon gave way to parlour songs, which were far more appropriate-sounding when one considered how his voice had changed. He tried not to think about why it had changed or how it had changed. He concentrated on remembering the lyrics.

> Again I looked on the old old place
> Again I saw my darling's face

How apropos. He squinted at the man on the bed, wishing he might see his darling father's face, wishing his choice of song might be prophetic. Nothing so far. The man remained a stranger, his features unfamiliar. The Harvest Man made another cut, used his long curved blade to take off the tip of the man's nose.

He could hear the woman moving in the next room, struggling with the ropes that bound her to her bed, but he ignored her. It wasn't her turn yet.

> Again we wandered by the stream
> Again we wandered by the stream

He sliced off the man's left eyebrow and repositioned it. His father had often worn a quizzical expression and the eyebrow looked better slightly slanted across his forehead, pointed at the bridge of his nose. It was slick with blood and slid slowly down his face. Annoyed, the Harvest Man plucked it off the man's cheek and poked it back into place. This time it stayed put.

> It was a dream
> It was a dream
> Again I looked on the old old place
> Again I saw my darling's face

But he didn't see his darling father's face. He steeled his resolve. If it were going to be easy to find his parents, he would have found them by now. He was being tested to see if he was worthy of their love, if he deserved to have them back. He nodded to himself and resumed singing, taking comfort from the melody. He made tiny cuts in the man's lower lip, pulling the flesh apart as he went, tearing and repositioning, making the mouth wider, exposing the lower row of teeth. The man stirred and moved his head. Just a little bit, but enough to cause a cut to go too deep. Annoyed, the Harvest Man adjusted by making a corresponding slice on the other side of the man's face. He sat back and examined his handiwork, but it wasn't right. It wasn't only the new cuts he hadn't meant to make. The bone structure was wrong.

Perhaps it was just the ears. Maybe they needed to be adjusted.

> It was a dream
> It was a dream
> Again we wandered by the stream

It was a dream
It was a dream

The right ear complete, he moved around to the other side and cut the man's left earlobe off. He sliced the ear half away from the scalp, pushed it up, moulded it to the skull so that it looked smaller. He tossed the unused portion of ear over his shoulder, and heard it hit the floor. He sang louder.

I saw the wandering streamlet flow down to the cold grey sea
I saw the bending willows bow in welcome over me
In welcome over me
Again I listened to breeze and bird
Again my darling's voice I heard

The man made a noise. He grunted and one of his eyelids fluttered. The Harvest Man smiled at him before remembering the mask hid his features from view. He lowered his voice to a murmur and bent his head as if he might kiss the man with his beak.

We kissed beneath the moon's soft beam
We kissed beneath the moon's soft beam

This was not his father. He knew that now. And if this wasn't his father, then the woman in the next room could not be his mother. Once again, he had failed to find them.

It was a dream
It was a dream

He sucked a deep breath in through his teeth and tried not to be angry with the man and the woman who were not his parents. The strangers. He had gone with strangers again, something he had been told never to do. Still, perhaps the man hadn't meant to lie to him, hadn't intended the Harvest Man to mistake him for his father. He calmed himself with the ballad, closed his eyes, and concentrated on the lyrics.

> Again I listened to breeze and bird
> Again my darling's voice I heard

But it wasn't going to work. He felt the anger coming and he raised his voice, sang louder and louder, began to cut at the man's face without rhyme or reason now, using the blade to punctuate the syllables of the song, destroying the work he had done, no longer caring what became of his canvas. Another night wasted, another dead end, and it was his fault, *his fault, the man's fault, his father's fault. The man had misled him and why would he do that when all the Harvest Man wanted was to love him didn't he want to be loved and where was he hiding itwasadreamcomeoutcomeoutstophidingfromme itwasadreambutiremberitanditwasrealandwekissedbeneaththemoons softbeamandyoulovedme.*

John Charles Pitt came fully awake and his face was on fire. There was no sun, no tree, no hammock. There was a creature with a beak and two huge round eyes, but the man could barely see it through a haze of blood and pain. A candle flickered somewhere nearby, casting long dancing shadows of the bird creature as it bent over him. It was screaming at him, shouting the words of some drawing-room ballad. John Charles opened his mouth to scream, but he felt his lips tear open and he tasted blood. He gasped and blinked the blood out of his eyes and saw the creature's hand sweep down, felt fresh fire in his cheek, saw the hand raise up and slash down again and his throat erupted with pain and he couldn't breathe. He was choking, coughing up warm liquid that he knew could only be blood.

And still the creature screamed its song at him.

The tree shimmered back into view and the sky opened up and he was drifting away on his hammock again, being carried away from the grotesque thing with the beak and its horrible cry. He briefly wondered about Eugenia Merrilow, wondered where she was and whether she had a hammock of her own. Then John Charles Pitt relaxed and let himself drift and the song faded away on the breeze.

It was a dream
It was a dream

20

Robert stood beside him and steadied him with a hand on his back while Day reached up and plucked little Simon off the trunk of the tree. He gave the boy an awkward hug and set him on the ground. Robert brushed the leaves and bark from his brother's shirt, then took Simon's hand. The two of them looked up at Day with fear and hope in their eyes. He tried to smile, but was afraid he might be grimacing at them. His leg hurt more than it had that morning and he wondered if it would ever improve.

'Let's sit for a moment,' he said. 'If you don't mind.'

'We don't mind,' Robert said.

Day went back to the rock they'd tried to drop on his head and lowered himself on to it. Simon let go of Robert's hand and came and perched on the side of the rock, almost touching Day. Robert stood nearby, watching his brother, watching Day.

'Is that your walking stick?'

'Yes, Robert,' Day said. 'It used to be my walking stick.'

'We broke it with our rock?'

Day looked down at the shattered pieces of his cane. The bulk of it was probably beneath the rock he was sitting on, but the tip and handle were far away from each other, surrounded by splintered bits of wood.

'Yes,' he said. 'You did an excellent job of it. If that had been the bad man's head, you would have stopped him for good, I think.'

'We're sorry.'

'Think nothing of it. A cane is easily replaced. You two are not.'

'When will you take us home?'

Day sucked on his top teeth and looked away into the trees. 'I don't think I can take you home, Robert.'

'You're going to take us to the orphanage, aren't you?'

'I don't know. I want to be honest with you. I don't know what will happen now. Your parents . . . Well, your parents are gone.'

'We know. We saw.'

'You'll have new parents.'

'We don't want new parents, sir. All due respect.'

'Of course.' Day sighed. 'Of course you don't. This isn't a situation anyone would want. You shouldn't be here. You shouldn't have seen what you saw.'

'Will you take us home with you?'

Day rocked back and looked at Robert, his eyes wide. He turned his head and saw little Simon was staring down at his shoes. A single bright teardrop reflecting a spot of moonlight fell from his face to the top of his shoe, where it disappeared.

'I don't think that's the way this sort of thing works, Robert. I don't know that it's a possibility. Even if I had room at my house for you, I don't know that . . .'

'It's all right,' Robert said. He spoke quickly, embarrassed. 'I shouldn't have said –'

'No, no, it's not that I wouldn't, you know.'

'Just take us somewhere. Just let's get out of the wood.'

149

'You know, it's awfully late now. I believe I will take you home with me after all.' Day leaned forward, but didn't stand. 'I'm told there's more room there than I thought. Robert, you said you caught a glimpse of the Harvest . . . of the birdie man. You saw his real face beneath the mask.'

'Only for a moment, sir.'

'Could you describe him for me?'

'I don't think so. He looked sort of like a wee man, but different 'cause he wasn't, you know.'

'Oh, Robert, he is a man,' Day said. 'It was a man who did those awful things. And we'll catch him, I swear it. But I could use your help.'

'I don't know how to describe him.'

Day thought for a minute. The boys were still and silent, waiting to discover what their lives had in store for them. At last, Day smiled. He looked around and spotted a stout branch, knocked loose from the canopy above. He pointed at it and Robert ran, picked it up and brought it over to the rock. Day took it and poked it at the ground to test its strength. He stripped the remaining leaves and twigs from it and put his weight on it and stood. The top was rough and hurt the palm of his hand, but he thought he could probably saw it off and file it down and it would do just fine.

'I have an idea,' he said. 'Can you draw?'

'I'm not very good at drawing, sir. And Simon's not, either.'

'I am,' Simon said. 'I'm quite good at it.'

'You're not either, Simon. Not the way Mr Day means, at least.'

'I can draw anything.'

'You can draw dragons and you can draw wee people in tunnels. You can't draw what a person looks like just to show someone else. That's what Mr Day means, isn't it, sir?'

Day nodded.

'Oh, well, that,' Simon said. 'No, I can't do that so well.'

'Then what if you described the birdie man to someone else and they drew him for you?'

'Who?'

'I know someone who draws very well indeed. And if you tell her what the birdie man looked like, I think she might be able to create a picture of him for us. And then we'll be better able to catch him.'

'We could try.'

'Good man.' Day clapped his hand on Robert's shoulder and the boy flinched, but didn't pull away. Day nodded at him. He turned and smiled at the little boy still sitting on the rock and Simon rose and took his hand.

'You'll like this artist,' Day said. 'Her name is Fiona and she's very nice. We'll go see her first thing. You just tell her what you saw and she'll figure it out for you.'

'We'll try our best, Mr Day.'

'I know you will,' Day said. 'You're good boys.'

Robert walked a little ahead of them and Day could see the boy's shoulders shake as he silently cried. Day bowed his head and kept a tight hold of Simon's hand and let Robert lead them out of the forest.

McKraken gave Day a sheepish smile at the front door, clearly embarrassed that he had been caught napping on the job. The retired inspector leaned down and asked the boys their names, asked Day how long they'd be there in the house.

'I'm not really sure,' Day said. 'The night, at least.'

'Well, you'll be safe here,' McKraken said.

Simon shook his head. 'No. The birdie man can go anywhere he wants to.'

'Not as long as I'm guarding this door, he won't.'

'You stay here all the time?'

'Most of the time. I have to go to my own home sometimes to sleep and change my clothes.'

'That's when he'll come, then.'

'I only do that during the daylight hours when there are plenty of people about. Baddies tend to avoid places where there's lots of people. When it's quiet and lonely in a place, that's when the bugs come out.'

'Bugs?'

'That's what I call 'em. Bad people, they're nothing but little bugs trying to crawl out of the woodwork, but I squash 'em.'

Simon continued to look worried, but he nodded. Thinking of the Harvest Man as a bug seemed to put the murderer in a new perspective that he liked. McKraken straightened up, one hand on the small of his back to ease the strain. He patted the boys on their heads and held the blue door open. He closed it after them the instant they'd crossed the threshold.

Inside, the house was quiet and dim. Leland Carlyle had apparently gone to bed or had returned to his own place across the park. Both boys craned their necks and looked all round the entryway. Simon yawned, then scooted ahead of them to peer into the front room.

'I would like to look in the attic, please,' Robert said.

'Well, I'm sorry to disappoint you, but we have no attic here,' Day said.

Robert's eyes widened and he ran a hand through his unruly dark hair. 'No attic at all? Not even a little space?'

'There is nothing at the top of this house except a roof.'

'I'm hungry,' Simon said.

'Oh, well, of course you are,' Day said. 'I'm sorry. Come with me. Let's see what we can scrounge back in the kitchen.'

He was struck by how peaceful the house could still seem when there weren't so many people underfoot. It made him think of the early days of his marriage, when he and Claire had been alone together.

Someone had left a cold pork pie under a cloth on the butcher block. Day set the boys down and found two plates, two forks and two squat cut-crystal glasses in the cabinet. The rough stick he had acquired from the forest thumped against the kitchen floor and echoed back from the walls. He poured water for the boys from the pitcher on the kitchen table and sliced the pie into four segments, gave them each a quarter of it. The meat was encased in a thick layer of gelatinous fat under the pastry shell, salty and delicious. He ate his quarter of the pie directly from the tin and it was gone in seconds. He looked up, surprised to see that Robert had finished his piece as well. He lifted the last quarter of the pie out on to Robert's plate and watched the boys eat. Simon chewed every mouthful methodically, but Robert practically swallowed his food whole.

'Cook said that pie was meant for the morning.'

Day looked up at Claire, who stood in the kitchen doorway wearing a housedress, her hair up and her feet bare. He smiled at her.

'I'm sorry,' he said. 'It's been some time since our guests enjoyed a meal.'

'Then I think you'll have to settle for eggs at breakfast,' Claire said.

'I like eggs.'

'I like eggs, too,' Simon said. 'May I please have one now?'

'My, you must be hungry,' Claire said. She went to the pantry and emerged with a discoloured iron skillet and a bowl of brown eggs. 'How do you like them cooked? I warn you, I can only make scrambled.'

'I like scrambled,' Robert said.

'You're in luck. Except we've no milk for them, so they'll be sort of mixed rather than strictly scrambled. I hope you won't mind.' She cracked an egg and fished a piece of shell out of the skillet.

'I like poached,' Simon said.

'Then you, I'm afraid, are bound for disappointment, young man.' She frowned at the remaining eggs, then shrugged and began cracking them all, piling the pieces of brown shell beside the stove.

'This is Simon,' Day said. 'And this is his brother, Robert.'

'Hello, Simon,' Claire said. 'Hello, Robert.'

'They're going to stay the night with us.'

'How lovely.' Claire rummaged about in a drawer and found a wooden spoon.

'How are Winnie and . . .'

'Henrietta?'

'Yes,' Day said. 'Henrietta. How are they?'

'They're sound asleep without a worry in the world.'

'That's good.'

'Should I ask where your cane's got to?'

'A story for another time perhaps?'

'Just so. Walter, would you step outside and ask Mr McKraken if he would also like an egg, since we seem to be having an early breakfast?'

'Be but a moment.'

McKraken claimed to be no fan of eggs, and Day stopped in the study to refill his flask. When he returned to the kitchen, Claire was sitting at the table with the boys, a plate in front of her. Robert had finished his second piece of pork pie and he and Simon were both tucking into huge portions of eggs and cold sausages and bread. Robert in particular seemed to be a bottomless hole. Claire was talking and Day stood listening.

'. . . because it reminds me of something bad that happened.'

'I hope nothing too terribly bad,' Simon said.

'Our entire house will be like that,' Robert said. 'The whole entire place will remind us of what's happened.'

'I suppose that's why Mr Day didn't take us there.'

'I suppose it is,' Claire said. 'But now that I'm in here with you, this kitchen doesn't seem so bad after all. After tonight, maybe I'll think about how I made eggs for you instead of the bad things that happened here.'

'What were the bad things?'

'You know, you've managed to pop it all straight out of my head. I don't even remember any more.' Claire looked up and saw Day standing at the threshold and smiled at him. He smiled back. He went to the stove and checked the pan, but the eggs had all been eaten. He shrugged and joined the others at the table.

'If you like, I can find something else for you,' Claire said. 'If you're still hungry.'

'No, not really. Mostly tired, I think.'

'Cook's going to be terribly angry with us. We've eaten everything.'

Simon yawned again and this time it was contagious. Each of the others yawned in turn and Day stood back up, stretched and picked up his stick.

'I think that's enough eggs,' he said. 'Let's find a place for you two to sleep tonight.'

'I'll make up the daybed,' Claire said. She rose and took her plate to the counter. 'They should both fit if they don't mind sharing.'

'We need a bigger house, don't we?'

She looked at him and raised an eyebrow. Day cocked his head to the side and gave her his most disarming smile in lieu of an apology. She put her hand on his arm. 'Someday soon, but there's no hurry,' she said. 'We'll do just fine here for a little longer.'

'We share all the time,' Simon said.

'Then it's settled,' Claire said. 'Come with me and we'll get you settled in here.' The boys stood and followed her out of the kitchen. As she passed Day, Claire winked at him and he knew he was forgiven.

Day Two

The rain is falling all around,
It falls on field and tree,
It rains on the umbrellas here,
And on the ships at sea.

– Robert Louis Stevenson, 'Rain',
A Child's Garden of Verses (1885)

Day Two

Morning

Nevil Hammersmith trudged up the stairs next to the confectionery shop. The scent of chocolate already suffused the entire building as the early-rising bakers and sweet makers hurried to fill the front window with sweets, but Hammersmith barely noticed the smell any more. He unlocked his door on the landing and went inside, closed the door after himself and locked it. He found his way to the fireplace in the dark and lit the lamp on the mantel.

The flat seemed dimmer and smaller than usual and he suspected that was because he would be spending more time there in the future. He was suddenly paying attention to his surroundings. There would be no more Scotland Yard to retreat to, no work to bury himself in. He would eventually have to find new employment and he wasn't qualified to do anything else that might bring him a sense of fulfillment or usefulness. Grim days ahead. Still, he had enough money saved to allow him to pursue Jack the Ripper for another week or two. Surely that would be enough, especially with Blackleg's help. No madman, no matter how clever, could evade pursuit much longer than that.

There was no kitchen in the flat, but there was a low table under the window that overlooked the street. Half a loaf of stale bread gathered dust there, along with a hard wedge of cheese. Hammersmith filled the pot from a basin on the windowsill and put it on the hotplate to warm. He tore a piece of bread from the loaf and ignored the crumbs that showered the floor at his feet. He would have liked a spot of cream and perhaps a sausage, but the bread and cheese and strong tea would be enough.

After an hour or two of sleep, he would start again. He and Day would find the missing boys in the wood. And Hammersmith might even find Jack, too. Tomorrow, perhaps, he would begin the inevitable search for some new purpose in his life. He stared out of the window as he waited for the water to get hot, and he watched over his city as lights began to come on in the dark buildings across the street.

Alan Ridgway squatted in the shade of the tall tree across the street from 184 Regent's Park Road. His eyes hurt, but he was afraid to close them. He was afraid to fail the man Jack. Alan had been stationed beneath the tree watching the blue door when a cab had pulled up and a tall man who walked with a stick had helped two little boys down and escorted them inside the house. Alan felt certain the tall man was Walter Day, but he was confused. Who were the boys? And why had they been kept out so late at night? Alan had expected his first sighting of Walter Day to come in the morning, when the man left his home. Alan knew there were two babies inside the house, and the man Jack had told him all about Mr and Mrs Day, but now there were extra people and he wasn't sure what he was supposed to do about them.

Alan was not disturbed to find that there was a guard on the door, an older man with impressive whiskers. He'd been expecting that. The old man was much larger than

Alan was, and Alan could see that he wore a revolver in a holster under his arm. The guard looked as if he could handle himself in a fair fight, which was not the sort of adversary Alan preferred, but he had his orders and he knew better than to cross Jack.

He stretched and yawned and settled back against the tree. Alan would wait until Walter Day came out of his home again and he could deliver both his messages at once.

Dr Bernard Kingsley sat in his office at University College Hospital and frowned at his desk. He chewed his lower lip while he thought. He leaned forward and picked up an empty water glass, set it in the centre of the desktop and frowned at it some more. He rose and went to a cabinet against the wall, rummaged inside, and came out with a handful of small items: a letter opener, a bottle of ink, a pen nib, a ball of string. He set them on the desk next to the water glass and stepped back. Then he reached out and rearranged them, picked up the ball of string and tossed it half a foot in the air, caught it absently in his right hand. He looked at the string and smiled. He turned his head, looking for someone he could talk to, but he was alone. He nodded to himself and began to unwind the ball, quicker and quicker.

There was a single constable guarding the murder scene when Inspector Jimmy Tiffany arrived. Nothing had changed overnight. He paused in the doorway and crossed his arms over his chest, scowled at the broken fireplace on the wall across from him. Muddy footprints were tracked everywhere through the parlour and down the hallway next to it. He stepped inside and looked up at the ceiling, stalling before taking the trek up the stairs, where he knew the bits of gore would have hardened overnight and the pools of blood turned to tar. There was nothing left here. He would search the house one more time, but it seemed impossible that there could be a clue left undiscovered. He decided to vacate the place by afternoon and let the landlord clean it all out.

'Sir?'

Tiffany jumped and turned around. A young boy stood on the porch, just outside the open door.

'Is your name Tiffany, sir?'

'It is. You have a message?'

'From Inspector Day. He says to tell you that the boys is found safe and whole. He's got 'em now and they's asleep. He'll bring 'em round the Yard later today if you wanna ask 'em questions.'

The boy held out his hand, but Tiffany ignored him. He'd been paid already and didn't need to collect twice for delivering a simple message. He turned back to the fireplace, took a deep breath of the rank air inside the house and let it out.

And he smiled.

22

Hammersmith was mildly annoyed with himself. He'd managed a full three hours of sleep, but still felt exhausted. He hoped his lack of stamina was a result of the chest injury and that he'd eventually be back in fighting form, but he was afraid he might finally be falling apart, an old man at twenty-three. He trudged along the hallways of University College Hospital, trying to look like he belonged, like he knew where he was going, but he got turned around three or four times and ended up backtracking before he found Dr Kingsley's laboratory in the basement. It was empty, except for three bodies laid out on wooden tables at one side of the big room. Two of the bodies were missing their faces, skulls devoid of expression, staring up at the ceiling with empty sockets. Lamplight glanced across their cheekbones and scurried away into the empty sockets, where Hammersmith imagined he could still see their eyes, somewhere deep in the shadows, watching him. He shuddered and left that room, went upstairs and, after getting lost again, finally found the doctor's office. The door was open, but it was dark inside and Henry Mayhew sat on the floor in the hallway. The magpie, Oliver, hopped and strutted about in front of the giant, occasionally pecking at the clean floor, as if encountering invisible crumbs. At Hammersmith's approach, the bird fluttered up on to Henry's lap and cocked its head at him.

'I was hoping the doctor might be in early today,' Hammersmith said.

'Hullo, Mr Hammersmith.'

'Good morning, Henry.'

'I don't know where the doctor is,' Henry said. 'He's usually here by now.'

'So on any other day he'd be here.'

'Usually.'

'Just my luck. The one day I need him.'

'Did something bad happen?'

'What makes you ask that?'

'The police never want to ask the doctor questions unless something bad's happened. Did somebody get killed?'

'I'm afraid so. Three ladies are dead and I'm on my way to see where their bodies were found. I'd hoped Dr Kingsley might go along with me. He's more likely to find a clue than I am.'

'He likes clues,' Henry said. 'He finds them everywhere.'

'That he does. Well, I suppose I'll be off, then. Would you tell him . . . On second thought, never mind. No point telling him anything, is there? I'll have seen what there is to see by the time he gets the message.'

'You said you're going to where the ladies was killed?'

'I'm on my way there now.'

Henry hoisted himself to his feet, towering above Hammersmith. The displaced magpie squawked and flew up to perch on Henry's shoulder.

'I'll go with you, then,' Henry said.

'Oh, well, thank you, but there's no need.'

'No, I think I'd better go. The doctor would want you

to be safe. He went to a lot of trouble sewing you up when you was dead and he wouldn't want you to die again. If them ladies was killed, the bad person might still be there.'

'I assure you, whoever killed them is long gone,' Hammersmith said.

'Have you been there before? To the place they was killed?'

'No.'

'Then how do you know who's there?'

'I suppose I don't.'

'Then it's settled.'

'Ah.'

Henry stood perfectly still, like a statue of some Oscar Wilde fairy-tale character, staring down at him. Hammersmith blinked at him and decided there was no point in trying to argue. Besides, the giant might come in handy after all. He turned and walked away and heard Henry fall into step behind him. He led him down two wrong passages before finding the exit.

23

The sun had risen, but it didn't reach far into the narrow alley, and it never would. The alley floor shifted under Hammersmith's feet as he walked. Over time, the stones had been covered by a fine layer of silt, and stray seeds had taken root in the gloom. Tiny green shoots stretched upwards with misplaced optimism. Hammersmith stepped carefully as he followed the glow of Blackleg's lantern deeper into the dark. He trusted Blackleg well enough – after all, if the criminal wanted him dead, he could have killed him the night before and nobody would ever have found Hammersmith's body – but even Blackleg might be unaware of the dangers at the other end of the alley. Hammersmith wished he had kept the extra lantern from the warehouse basement. He reached for his truncheon and was momentarily surprised that it was missing. He was unarmed and without authority. But still, as always, in over his head. He was glad of Henry's comforting presence at his back. At last Blackleg stopped moving and stood in place over a spot in the haphazard shadow garden.

'Here it was,' he said. 'This is where we found her.'

Hammersmith glanced back at the shard of pale light at the mouth of the alley, then joined Blackleg and squatted on his heels to examine the ground.

'Hold that lower here, would you?'

Blackleg obliged, bringing the lantern down close to a patch where the silt and stifled greenery had been worn away.

'Your people trampled all over this,' Hammersmith said. He could hear Dr Kingsley's influence in his voice and almost smiled.

'Told you there wouldn't be much to see,' Blackleg said.

'Did you erase anything?'

'What do you mean?'

'Were there markings here that you or somebody else might've rubbed away?'

'What kind of markings?'

'Chalk.'

'Oh, that. No, nothin' like that. 'Course, I wasn't the first one in here. But I didn't see nothin' looked like chalk.'

'A circle? Blue chalk drawn in a circle. Maybe here on the wall beside the body.'

'No, not a bit of it.'

Hammersmith nodded and put his palm on the cool alley wall, leaned forward and squinted. It seemed logical to him that the brick and stone would show some sign of fresh wear if a chalk line had been rubbed away. He saw nothing but the normal effects of age. He swept his fingertips over the ground and dislodged a tiny methodical snail. It pulled its head inside its shell, protecting every part of itself except two wet probing eyestalks. Oliver changed his position on Henry's shoulder and cocked his head. Hammersmith closed his fist loosely over the snail.

'You didn't find anything else?'

'Just the body,' Blackleg said.

'You moved it right away to that place underground?'

Hammersmith suppressed a slight shudder at the thought of the subterranean tomb.

'Depends what you mean by "right away", but we didn't take our time about it.'

'Didn't stand around arguing over whether to call the police in?'

'That much never occurred to anybody, and I guarantee it.'

'And nobody lingered here when the body was gone?'

'Nobody I noticed. Of course, anybody could've come back later and done whatever it is you think was done.'

'I wish Dr Kingsley were here.'

'I wish he was here, too,' Henry said.

'I don't mind if you bring 'im,' Blackleg said. 'He's not a rozzer.'

'He might find something I'm missing.'

'What do you wanna do now, then?'

Hammersmith opened his hand and set the snail down safely out of Oliver's line of sight. He stood and kicked the wall, knocking dust off his boots. 'Let's take a look at the place where you found the second dead girl.'

Blackleg nodded and turned. Hammersmith had to trot along quickly to keep up with the bigger man.

24

After sending Walter off for the day, Claire spent some time in the nursery with the twins, who ignored her while they babbled at each other. She checked in on the boys, who were still sleeping at opposite ends of the daybed in the parlour. Simon stirred and whimpered. She sat and put her hand on his forehead, and he pulled himself farther under his blanket. When he was calm, Claire rose and went back through the house and wandered outside with her book of poems.

Her garden was exactly large enough to hold a young ash tree, as well as four white-painted chairs and a table roughly the size of a tea tray. It was not a suitable place for games or picnics, but she enjoyed reading there.

This morning, she found her mother sitting under the spreading branches of the ash with a newspaper. Eleanor Carlyle put the paper down, removed her spectacles and smiled at her daughter. She was all sharp angles, teeth and elbows and chin. Eleanor was wearing a mint-green dress with a subtle floral print and an enormous sun hat. The brim of it hid her eyes. From where she stood in the open doorway, Claire could smell her mother's lavender and talcum powder scent wafting through the garden.

'Come over here,' Eleanor said. 'I've barely seen you this entire week.' She folded her newspaper and set it aside on the miniature table, then patted the seat of the chair beside her. Claire reluctantly moved around the table and took the offered seat. She smoothed her skirts over her lap and looked down at the paper, tried to read it, though it was upside down.

'You know, I didn't sleep a wink last night,' her mother said. 'People in and out at all hours. And those babies of yours.'

'We've named them, Walter and I.'

'Mary and Margaret?'

'No. We've decided on Winnie and Henrietta. Winnie will be the small one.'

'Your father won't like that.'

'Won't he?'

'Do you want to tell him that you won't be using his dear sisters' names?'

'Why don't you tell him?'

'I'd be only too happy to. Well, whatever their names, can't you keep them quiet? The walls here are so thin.'

Claire had not heard the babies at all. If they'd been up during the night, the governess had swiftly responded to their needs. The twins seemed to thrive on each other's company and rarely demanded attention from anyone else.

'I'm sorry,' she said.

'Oh, well, it can't be helped,' Eleanor said. 'If one is going to have small creatures about, one must expect a bit of hardship. Have I told you your father's decided to get another dog? And just when the house has finally quieted down. I suppose I shall never sleep properly again.'

'Yes,' Claire said. 'A dog is much the same as a baby, isn't it?'

'What's that, dear?'

'Nothing, Mother. Only talking to myself.' She decided to wait a bit before telling her mother about the boys sleeping in the parlour. She could well imagine what Eleanor would have to say about that situation.

'Talking to yourself? Oh, the habits you've picked up here,' Eleanor said. 'I'm afraid this city's driving you mad.'

'I like the city.'

'You don't know what you like. Walter pulls you this way and that and you go along like a dutiful wife. It's to be commended, I suppose. He certainly chose well for himself.'

Claire stood. 'I believe I've had enough sunshine. I'm going to lie down.'

'Nonsense. You just now came out and you're deathly pale. Sunshine is exactly what you need. Come, let's talk some more.'

'About what, Mother?'

'Well, about anything you'd like, I suppose.'

'I don't think I have anything to talk about at the moment.'

'You have something better to do than talk to your poor mother?'

Claire sighed.

'I suppose you could be practising your needlework,' Eleanor said. 'You should, you know. You're dreadful at it.'

'Thank you.'

'Well, you are. Or perhaps you could take singing lessons. Tell me, do you sing to Walter after supper?'

'No. But we often talk to each other.'

'A man does not enjoy talking to his wife at the end of the day when he's trying to relax. A husband needs to be entertained. Sing to him if you want to be of any use.'

'Walter does enjoy talking to me. We discuss what's happened during the day.'

'But nothing's happened to you during the day. You take care of babies and mope about the house complaining of too much sunshine. You're morose, dear. What self-respecting husband would want to discuss the events of the day with you?'

'Oh, Mother.'

'I'm only trying to help, you know. You need to find something to do with your time, other than just filling a room with your presence and bothering your poor husband. No wonder he's . . .'

'He's what, Mother?'

'Never mind.'

'Walter is fine. And I do lots of things.'

'Like what, dear? What do you do?'

'I've been writing . . . Oh, never mind what I do.'

'No, I want to hear about it. You write something? Are you practising penmanship? Writing letters? That's lovely. A good way to pass the time.'

'Not letters. I write poems.'

'Poems?'

'Well, not poems. Rhymes for the babies.'

'How charming! And them with absolutely no understanding of poetry. The perfect audience for you, aren't they, dear?'

'I had thought . . .'

'What, dear?'

'Never mind.'

'No, tell me. What other ways have you found to occupy yourself?'

'I'm going inside now.'

'Suit yourself.' Eleanor clucked her tongue and picked the paper up from the table. She muttered something under her breath.

'What was that, Mother? I didn't hear you. Or were you talking to yourself?'

'I most certainly was not talking to myself. I said you're a very silly girl.'

Claire opened her mouth to reply, but closed it again. Anything she said to her mother would only prolong their conversation. She turned on her heel and left Eleanor in the garden. Inside the dim house, she bit her lip and closed her eyes, willed herself not to cry. She took a deep breath, wiped her fingertips across her cheeks to catch any escaping tears and walked to the staircase without glancing in at the parlour. She tried to dismiss her mother's nagging, but she was afraid there was a kernel of truth in what Eleanor had said. Claire was certain that Walter really did enjoy her company, but there might still be something she could do to be of use, perhaps even to bring in a little extra money for the household. An idea occurred to her as she looked up the stairs at the dark landing above. She pursed her lips and climbed the steps to the room where the twins slept. She took a chair beside their bassinet and gazed at their plump pink faces and let her thoughts wander far from the little house on Regent's Park Road.

25

Hammersmith stood and leaned against the wall. 'Three locations and no chalk anywhere,' he said.

'You still been looking for chalk this whole time?'

Hammersmith nodded at Blackleg. 'Blue chalk. But there's something wrong here. It's the same sort of thing he used to do, but it seems old-fashioned to me now, out of step with what he's been doing more recently. He's reverting to his old ways or . . .'

'You're thinkin' he woulda drawn them symbols if it's him.'

'Yes. Those three women you found were all mutilated in the same ways Jack the Ripper . . . Well, it's the way he worked.'

'Yeah, I don't got much doubt it's him,' Blackleg said. 'With or without chalk circles on the wall. He killed them three ladies, killed Little Betty.'

Henry grimaced and reached out, touched Blackleg on the elbow. 'Little Betty?'

'Did you know her?'

'She was nice to me when I didn't have a place to sleep,' Henry said. 'I haven't seen her in a long time.'

'She was nice to everyone,' Blackleg said. 'She didn't deserve to get carved up like a Christmas ham.'

Hammersmith's fingers went unconsciously to the scar across his chest. It itched. 'Nobody does,' he said.

'Especially not Little Betty,' Henry said.

'I'm convinced Jack's been different since he returned,' Hammersmith said. 'But these dead women . . . Maybe he's doing two things at once. Killing women for one reason and men for another.'

'Killers usually got cause to kill,' Blackleg said. 'And just one reason's enough.'

Hammersmith suspected the big criminal was speaking from experience. 'But I don't understand this at all. It doesn't make any sense.'

'No surprise to think he's a madman.'

'No. No surprise.' Hammersmith turned and surveyed the cobblestones again. 'Here, hold the lantern over here. Maybe I missed something.' He gestured and Blackleg swung the lantern around. Behind him, Oliver cried out and flew from Henry's shoulder, swooped to the ground and snatched something from the dirt. The bird circled around, soaring high up over the rooftops above them, and coasted back up the alley to land on his customary perch once more. Henry reached up and Oliver dropped the object into his hand. He held it out for the others to see.

'A silver cufflink,' Blackleg said.

'A clue,' Hammersmith said. 'You and your people must have stepped on it when you found the girl here, pushed it into the soil.'

'Bird's got good eyes.'

'Oliver likes shiny things,' Henry said.

'Could be from anybody,' Blackleg said. 'Could be unrelated to this thing.'

'Possibly,' Hammersmith said. 'Look. It's engraved.'

'*A-R*. A man's initials?'

'I hope so.'

'Be nice to know who A-R is.'

'It's a starting point, at least. More than we had before.'

'So, what now?'

'Now I think we have to ask for some help.'

26

Dr Kingsley's door was closed when Hammersmith returned. He knocked, but Henry reached out and turned the knob. Hammersmith was surprised to see Walter Day standing inside the office next to the desk. Fiona Kingsley was sitting in her father's chair, behind a pile of odds and ends, and she hurriedly grabbed a book from a stack on the desk. She slammed it down in front of her, covering something up, and shot him a guilty smile.

'I was looking for –' Hammersmith said.

'My father's not in.'

'I see that. But you're here instead, Inspector.' Hammersmith looked at Day and squinted as if to bring him into focus.

'I only just arrived myself,' Day said.

'Wasn't I supposed to meet you out at the wood to look for missing children?'

'No sense in that now,' Day said. 'I'm not there.'

'Clearly. And I'm not there, either. I had an early morning, after a late night, but I was going to head out as soon as I finished here.'

'No need.'

'You found them, then? Wonderful!'

'Last night. Only a few hours ago.' He held up the tree branch he was using as a cane.

'What's that?'

'My new walking stick. Fresh from the wood. It's a long story that I've just finished boring poor Fiona with.'

'So you went back there without me?'

'I had an idea of where they might be. Didn't really know how to get hold of you quickly and I thought, if I was wrong, it would be a waste of your time. Anyway, it worked out. They were up a tree. Literally, up a tree. They'd built a platform up there.'

'Ah, we were looking down,' Hammersmith said, 'when we should have been looking up.'

Day smiled. 'We were not very observant.'

'But who expected them to stay in a tree for hours on end?'

'At any rate . . .'

'You found them.' Hammersmith puffed up his cheeks and blew out a big sigh of relief. 'That's truly the best news I've heard in a long time. I take it they're all right?'

'Tired and hungry and scared, but otherwise two normal healthy boys.'

'That's good, Mr Day,' Henry said. 'I knew you would save those boys.'

'I told him about the children,' Hammersmith said. 'Henry and I have spent a good deal of time together this morning.'

'We found something important,' Henry said.

'Actually, I don't know if we did,' Hammersmith said. 'Where did you put them? The boys, I mean.'

'They're at the house with Claire,' Day said. 'Still sleeping when I left.'

'Glad I didn't go out to the wood first thing. I'd've

wasted the morning looking for them when they were happily napping miles away.'

'I promise I would've got a message to you before too much longer,' Day said.

He turned his attention to Fiona. She sat with her hands on the book in front of her, as if it might float away if she didn't hold it down. She had been moving her head back and forth between the three men as they talked, but hadn't interrupted.

'That reminds me, though,' Day said. 'It's why I'm here. I completely forgot when you showed me what you were –'

'Forgot what?' Fiona cut him off, her voice higher pitched than usual. 'Were you looking for my father?'

'No, in fact I was looking for you,' Day said. 'I wondered if you would stop at the house a bit later. You might be able to help the children remember something.'

'But how would I do that?'

'They saw the Harvest Man. You know . . . ?'

'I know who you're talking about. My father was at the latest murder scene all day yesterday. Those victims, the corpses, are downstairs now.'

'I saw them.' Hammersmith shuddered again. 'In his laboratory, early this morning. These villains are getting bloodier minded, aren't they?'

'It has begun to seem so,' Day said. 'Those victims were the boys' parents. The Harvest Man was at their home.'

'Oh, that's . . .'

'It's awful, is what it is. But they saw him, and that might be a good thing for us and for this monster's future victims. He lifted his mask and the boys saw his face. I need them to describe it, but they can't. I thought perhaps if you drew it for them, they might remember details that aren't coming to mind just now.'

'You mean, they would tell me what he looked like and I would draw whatever they say?'

'Yes. Maybe seeing a sketch of his features will help them remember even more about him.'

'You're going to make them scared again,' Henry said. 'Thinking about that man and looking at a picture of him. What they've been through . . .'

'But it might give us more information than we have right now,' Day said. 'We need to know what he looks like. He must be travelling somehow, going from house to house. That's when we can catch him, when he's out and about. Will you do it, Fiona? You're the best artist I know of.'

'That's kind of you,' Fiona said. 'I suppose I can try.'

'That's all I ask,' Day said.

'What time should I come?'

'Perhaps wait a couple of hours so they can catch up on their sleep and eat another meal. They'll no doubt feel safer once they're rested. But I don't want you to wait too long or they may start to forget.'

'We'll make sure to keep them safe,' Henry said. 'You tell them that.'

'I will,' Day said.

Fiona turned to Hammersmith. 'And you? Did you also come to talk to me?'

'Your father, actually,' Hammersmith said.

'I haven't seen him yet this morning,' Fiona said. 'He's left a dreadful mess here and run off somewhere.' She swept a hand through the air a foot above the desk, showing off the collection of bric-a-brac from Kingsley's cabinet drawers. The whole pile of junk was surrounded with a ring of twine that was still attached to a ball that had fallen off the desk and rolled halfway across the room.

'What was he doing with all this?'

'I haven't the slightest,' Fiona said. 'He scattered random things everywhere and then it looks as if he's made some halfhearted attempt to tie it all together.'

'Should we tidy up for him?'

'I don't think so. He prefers to have things just so.'

'I can see that,' Day said.

Fiona shrugged. 'I can write down a message for you and leave it here. But I can't guarantee that it won't be lost in this clutter.'

'Actually . . .' Hammersmith said. He passed a hand through his hair. 'I just realized I don't know what I'd say if we did leave him a message. I don't know if he can help me.'

'That sounds intriguing,' Fiona said.

'It's only this.' Hammersmith took the silver cufflink from his pocket and set it down on a reasonably clear area of Kingsley's desk.

'Oliver found that,' Henry said. 'He likes shiny things.'

'I thought the doctor might be able to detect something that I can't,' Hammersmith said.

'You mean the fingermarks he makes visible with black powder,' Day said.

Fiona leaned forward and peered at the cufflink. She looked up at Hammersmith. 'Is it a clue of some sort? From the Harvest Man case?'

'No,' Hammersmith said. 'Something else. I don't . . .'

'Of course, you aren't investigating the Harvest Man,' Fiona said. 'I'm so sorry. I didn't mean to . . .'

'Quite all right. I haven't got used to it myself, being a civilian.'

Day leaned forward to peer at the cufflink. 'Is it a clue about you-know-who?'

'That's just it,' Hammersmith said. 'I have no idea, but it might be. And if it is . . . Well, it's all I've got at the moment, so I thought it was worth bothering the good doctor on the off chance it really is something.'

Fiona narrowed her eyes at them. 'Who is "you-know-who"?'

'Another case. It's something I'm following up on now that I've got the spare time.'

'Well, at any rate,' Fiona said, 'I'm quite sure my father won't be able to find any fingerprints on this thing.'

'He can't?'

'Well, it's so small,' Fiona said. 'And even if he could find a little part of a fingermark, you've been touching this. They would be your marks he'd find all over it, wouldn't they?'

Hammersmith looked down at the cufflink and felt his face grow warm with embarrassment. 'I wasn't thinking. I should have been more careful.'

'It's all right.' Day laid a hand on his shoulder. 'Finger-marks aren't everything. If you've a reason to think this cufflink is connected to a crime, you'll track the man down, one way or another.'

Hammersmith sighed. Perhaps Sir Edward had made the right choice, after all, in dismissing him from the force.

He wasn't careful or thoughtful enough to be a good policeman.

'But there is an engraving on it,' Fiona said. She had picked the cufflink up and was examining it in the light from the window behind her.

'Initials,' Hammersmith said. He felt suddenly a bit more hopeful. 'At least, I think they're initials.'

'A man named *A* and *R*,' Henry said.

'There must be a thousand men in London with those initials,' Day said.

'At least we know it *is* a man,' Fiona said. 'Women don't have need of cufflinks.'

'Is there a way to track down the purchase of these? I mean, without a hundred constables at my beck and call, marching all over the city, questioning shopkeepers.'

'Perhaps if there were something unusual about them,' Day said. 'Or something different about the engraving process.'

'Does your father know much about . . . I don't know, clothing or engraving on silver?'

Fiona shook her head. 'But I think I know someone who does.'

'An expert?'

'You might say that. I could show this to him, if you'd like.'

'Could I meet him?'

'You could go with me.'

'If you wouldn't mind.'

Fiona stood up from behind the desk and picked up the cufflink. 'We'll go right away. And then I'll come round to your house as soon as we've finished, Inspector.'

'Bring your drawing supplies,' Day said.

'I always have those.' She slipped the cufflink into her pocket, grabbed her bag from the floor beside the chair and marched out of the office door. In an instant she was back. She ran to the desk and raised the book she'd been leaning on, scooped up something from beneath it and ran back out all in a flash. Startled, Oliver swooped out of the door after her and returned a moment later, looping through the office door as Hammersmith was trying to leave. Hammersmith ducked and fell back as the bird settled itself once again on Henry's broad shoulder.

Day helped Hammersmith to his feet, bracing himself with the stick, and brushed him off with his free hand. 'Well,' Day said, 'I suppose I'd better get moving, too. Lots to do.'

Hammersmith paused at the open door. 'You'll be at the house later?'

'I think I'll stop at home to check on the children and then I'll head in to the Yard. I'm behind on paperwork.'

'I'd rather not go by there, if I can avoid it.'

'What's on your mind?'

Hammersmith checked to be sure that Fiona was out of earshot. 'Three women killed in the East End. But recently. Matches his previous deeds.'

'But he's changed,' Day said. 'That makes no sense.'

'I know. I'd hoped you might have some thoughts.'

'Come to the house,' Day said. 'I want to know more.'

'I don't want to stay here,' Henry said. 'I don't know if I'm supposed to clean this up.' He gestured at the desk.

'I'm sure Dr Kingsley will —'

'I want to come to your house, too, Inspector Day,' Henry said.

'You do?'

'If that's all right with you. Mrs Day is nice to me and I'm hungry now. Maybe she'll give me food.'

'Um.' Day shrugged. 'Well, why not? The more the merrier, I suppose.' He looked at Hammersmith. 'You'll tell me if there's anything to this cufflink thing, right?'

'Of course,' Hammersmith said. 'I'll find you, wherever you are.'

He waved to Henry and rushed out of the office, hoping he wouldn't get lost in the hospital again before he could catch up with Fiona.

27

The street was empty, men off at work, children away at school or inside their homes carrying out chores, some women working, too, the rest watching their children or visiting friends. A four-wheeler rolled by and turned the corner and was gone, dragging silence in its wake. Dr Kingsley stood at the curb and looked up at the murder house again, at its wide-open shutters, its well-tended garden, its freshly painted trim. The windows of the attic above gave it the appearance of a face, watching over the bluebells and daffodils, and the creeping Jenny in early bloom. Kingsley unclasped his bag and approached the open front door, pulled out his tape measure and ran it across, then up and down. He put the tape away and stepped inside, sniffed to test the air. He still detected decay and the lingering body odour of many policemen, but the worst remnants of recent history were already wafting away out of the doors and windows. When the dust finally settled, there would be nothing left but a few stains and the memories held by neighbours.

'Who's there?'

Kingsley flinched in surprise at the sound of the rough voice and he strode quickly to the staircase. Inspector Tiffany stood at the top of the steps, looking down, poised as if to leap on trespassers. 'Ah, Tiffany,' Kingsley said. 'I thought perhaps I'd found some poor relative of the family, here to make off with the silverware.'

'I had the boys clean up in here a bit. Wanted to let the place air out before I closed it back up.'

Kingsley climbed the stairs and shook Tiffany's offered hand. They walked across the landing together and stopped in the bedroom doorway. The bed had been stripped of linens. A splash of dark brown marred the thin mattress. The sun streaming in through the open window behind the bed highlighted sticky smudges here and there across the floorboards. Fewer of them than Kingsley remembered.

'You could have left anyone here to guard this house,' Kingsley said.

'I wanted to take another look around,' Tiffany said. 'These murders don't sit right with me. Don't understand what he does or why he does it. I thought maybe . . .'

'Maybe there was a clue you'd overlooked.'

'It's possible. I had a little hope. Maybe with all the bodies out of here, living and dead both, well, maybe there was more to it all than a bloody madman slicing people up for no good reason at all. Used to be if a woman's dead, her husband did it. Go nab him at his club and the job's done. Now nobody's got a reason for what they're doing.'

'Jack the Ripper opened a gate.'

'Right,' Tiffany said. 'Exactly right. No reason we ever saw for what he did and he got clean away with it, too. Now every other madman out there's decided "if Jack can do it, I can do it", Makes it rough for the rest of us who just want a decent night's sleep.'

Kingsley nodded. 'And did you discover anything new here?'

'Aw, damnit, you know I didn't. If there was something here, you'd've found it yesterday, wouldn't you?'

'Who knows? The bodies, the living ones, do tend to get in the way sometimes,' Kingsley said.

'I apologize for Bentley. He was curious, is all. But I gave him what for, all the same. He shouldn't have walked all through here like he did.'

'What's done is done. No need to apologize. But I have an idea that might help us both with that very thing. I'd like your opinion and, if you agree with me, I'd appreciate your support when I present it to Sir Edward.'

'What is it?'

'Hold this for me, will you?' Kingsley handed his bag to Tiffany and reached inside. He drew out a cowhide pouch and held it up for Tiffany to see, then took the medical bag back and set it on the floor at his feet. He opened the pouch and walked to the bed and emptied it out on a clean section of the mattress. He pushed the items from the pouch into a small pile and plucked out a glove, tossed it to Tiffany, who caught it and frowned at it.

'A rubber glove,' Kingsley said.

'A what? I mean, I see it's a glove, but . . .'

'A *rubber* glove,' Kingsley said again. 'It's made completely of rubber.'

'Never heard of such a thing.'

'It's not common. But I frequently correspond with Dr Halsted in America, and he sent these over. The staff of Johns Hopkins has developed them in order to protect their hands from harsh chemicals, but these gloves have an additional unforeseen benefit. They're proof against the oils of the skin.'

'You don't say.'

'That means your constables won't leave the prints of their fingers on anything they touch if they wear these.'

'Oh, for . . .' Tiffany threw the glove back at Kingsley. 'Fingermarks again? Look, I've got nothing but the highest regard for you, Doctor, but this fairy-tale finger smudge of yours is too much.'

'I know you're not a particular champion of fingerprints in the –'

Tiffany held up his hands, palms out. 'No disrespect intended. Sorry if I misspoke. But it's my belief that criminals get caught because I chase after 'em. Where you come in is tellin' me which way to run. Fingermarks don't help either one of us do that.'

'They will,' Kingsley said. 'I believe they will. But we can disagree and still find common ground here. Before you finish passing judgement, I have more to show you.'

'Why me? I thought Day was your man. I wasn't even good enough for you to talk to yesterday, was I?'

Kingsley held a hand to his nose to mask the lingering scent of death and took a deep breath. He rolled his head until he heard his neck pop and a gratifying bit of tension left his shoulders. This was going to take longer than he'd expected. 'You have qualities, Jimmy,' he said.

'I do?'

'You do. You are closed-minded, you have trouble commanding respect from your peers, you frequently allow your job to overwhelm you, which in turn causes you to retreat from intellectual pursuits and give yourself over to the easiest answers that present themselves –'

'Oh, do go on.'

'But,' Kingsley said, 'you are dogged in your pursuit of the criminal element, you do not allow yourself to be swayed to any view but that of the law, you are not, in short, here to make friends. You are a perfect example of the modern policeman.'

Tiffany relaxed his stance and raised his eyebrows.

'You want to catch the man who did this thing,' Kingsley said. 'And so do I. And that's why I'm showing you this kit I've made up. I think it will help us both.'

Tiffany blinked and nodded and leaned back against the doorjamb. 'Let's see what you've got, then,' he said. 'Besides them flimsy gloves, I mean.'

'I should think some sort of rubber cover for your boots would be good, but I don't have such a thing at hand.'

'Aye, it doesn't do to have us tromping all through the stuff you're trying to look at, but I think that can be done just as well by trainin' the men better. Teach us to be careful where we step. Now I'm conscious of it, I watch where I put my feet.'

'Training will suffice, I suppose. Until I can come up with a solution.'

'Used to be, when I was just comin' up in the police, the public would turn out for a thing like this. We'd leave the bodies where they lay and everyone in the neighbourhood would file through for a good look. Like seein' their dead friends was high entertainment for 'em. Never understood it myself. But we didn't worry about findin' evidence.

Mostly, if there was any evidence, it'd be stolen anyways for a souvenir. We only worried about catchin' the one who did the deed. And I'll tell you, nine times out of ten, the murderer would be one of the ones walkin' through for a peep at the bodies. Imagine if things were still like that.'

'That was before my time,' Kingsley said.

'I'm not sayin' it was better then.'

'No.'

'Anyway, I'm not likely to stop and put covers on my boots. Much of the time there's a certain amount of hurry in what we do.'

'Point taken. But I've got this, as well.' Kingsley held up a small stack of envelopes with string fasteners.

'For puttin' clues in, right?'

'Exactly, Jimmy. When you find something important – say the Harvest Man had tracked something out of this room and you couldn't contain it or you needed to pick it up to keep it for me – you'd put it in one of these envelopes. And here's a grease pencil so you can write where you found it, the date, the case it's from, et cetera, on the outside of the envelope. A record of everything from start to finish.'

'And where would I put the envelope?'

'Back in the bag here,' Kingsley said.

'Oh, I didn't realize . . . You mean, you want me to carry that little bag with me everywhere?'

'Well, not necessarily everywhere. But you could keep a few like this at your desk. We'll make them up ahead of time. And when you're called out to a scene like this one . . .' Kingsley motioned with his hand to indicate the room and, beyond it, the entire murder house. 'When you come to a place like this, you'd just bring one of these along with you. It needn't be all that difficult.'

'Keep convincing me.'

'All right. Here, a pair of forceps.'

'Tweezers? What, in case I'm eating fish?'

'Fish?'

'Gettin' them little bones out of a fish so I don't choke.'

'No,' Kingsley said. 'To pick up small things and put them in the envelopes. Hair, threads, dirt, pipe ash, you know the sort of thing.'

'Go on.'

'Still not persuaded?'

'You got more there. Let's see it all.'

Kingsley picked up a measuring tape exactly like the one he carried, but new, without the myriad stains and overall threadbare quality of his own. He tossed it to Tiffany.

'Let me guess,' Tiffany said. 'When I pick up a clue, I can measure out where it was in relation to everything else.'

'Now you've got it. That's just what I'm driving at.'

'Or I can measure my fish before I take the bones out and eat it.'

'No, there's no fish. I don't know why you . . .'

'I'm havin' a little fun, Doctor. That's all. My apologies.'

'I see. Sorry. Yes, now for the last thing here. A spool of butcher's twine.'

'For . . .'

'For tying your fish,' Kingsley said. 'Before you roast it.' He smiled.

Tiffany grinned back. 'Right. That fish sounds tastier by

the second. What's it really for, though? This one's got me stumped.'

'One of the problems we still seem to have is people walking around these places and obliterating evidence. It's really not much better than what you described, when the neighbourhood used to parade through. Your men can't seem to keep everyone out –'

'They've got a lot of work to do and they –'

'No offence intended,' Kingsley said. 'I'm sure they do their level best, but sometimes outsiders will stray in and foul a scene before I can even get a look at it. Family, neighbours, witnesses, people are curious and they'll get around your men at the first opportunity to stroll around and ogle a dead body.'

'So we tie everybody up with butcher's twine,' Tiffany said.

'No. I think you're joking again. You work with Inspector Blacker quite a bit, don't you? His abominable sense of humour is wearing off on to you. No, what you'd do is tie off the entrance to this room or even the front door of the whole house. Both, if you want to be doubly certain nothing is disturbed. Just rope it across, like so . . .' Kingsley wrapped a loop of twine around the knob and stretched it across the open doorway, then twisted it around itself and wedged the loop into a crack in the wood, letting the rest of the ball drop to the floor. 'Now you've marked this room off and made it clear that no one is allowed to enter.'

Tiffany nodded and stroked his chin while Kingsley gathered the materials back up and put them in the little bag.

'And there,' Kingsley said. 'A compact package to carry

with you that will help us keep things orderly and undisturbed while we work.'

'Let me make sure I understand,' Tiffany said. 'Let's say it's yesterday and I arrive right here at this house. I got my bag here and I put on your rubber . . . Rubber, right?'

'Yes. The rubber gloves.'

'So I put on the rubber gloves and I walk around real careful-like and scour the ground for clues and then when I find one I produce my tweezers and pick 'em up and put the clues in an envelope.'

'Not all in the same envelope. You'd use a different one for each piece of evidence.'

'Right, so I juggle a handful of envelopes and then while I'm picking up the clues, I measure where they was at and then I get out my pencil and write all this on the outside of each envelope and put 'em all back inside this bag.'

'That's the long and short of it, yes.'

Tiffany nodded. 'I like it. It's a good idea.'

'You do?' Kingsley was astonished. 'You seemed so sceptical.'

'Oh, I am. I think we could do some different things, maybe have an extra thing or two to put in the bags in case there's different situations, maybe figure ways to do some of that faster or easier. But it's smart. One thing you are, Doctor, it's smart.'

'So you'll help me present it to Sir Edward?'

'Sure. But one thing, this twine isn't gonna work at all. It's like a spiderweb. Too thin and brown to get anybody's attention. People are gonna walk right into it, through it, not even notice it, just pull it out of the way.'

'Hmm. I see your point.'

'Maybe something thicker or with some colour. Some way to stick it here instead of poking it in a crack. Needs work.'

'An adhesive tape, perhaps?'

'I don't know. Just needs work. Other than that, you give me one of these bags and I'll use it.'

Kingsley almost hugged the surly policeman. If Tiffany could be convinced to use the new kit, they all could be.

28

Hatty Pitt was tied to her bed. Thick coils of rope wound over and around her, under the bed and back up, pinning her arms and legs. The rope was rough, wiry tendrils sticking off it in every direction, and it scratched her, made her itch. She was able to move her head, craning her neck to watch the narrow section of landing she could see through the partially open bedroom door.

Earlier she had woken when it was still dark and had heard someone singing, a voice she hadn't heard before, and she had heard John Charles cry out once. Then Hatty had passed out, and when she woke again the sun was up.

Now there was only silence.

Someone had entered her room in the night and bound her to her bed, then done something to John Charles. It occurred to her that the same someone might still be in the house.

Her mouth tasted terrible, like a rotten peach, and there was a lingering chemical scent in her nostrils. She snorted, trying to clear her nose, and turned her head to spit on the floor at the side of her bed. Propriety be damned. She was certain she would die soon and only wanted to feel a little more normal before it happened.

A great deal of time passed. Hatty watched a big black-and-green fly move across her bedroom ceiling. It grew braver when she didn't move, hopping and skimming above her, then spiralling down to land on her chest. She watched it groom itself, scraping its wings with its feet, rubbing its head, wiping its eyes, its abdomen iridescent in the pale sunlight. It stopped and sat very still for a long moment, then skipped towards her face. It took off again and drifted in a lazy circle and landed again, this time on her chin. She felt it; she could no longer see it, though she strained her eyeballs until they ached. It skittered up on to her lips and she blew on it and it retreated, up into the air for a few seconds, buzzing angrily at her, and then down on to her nose. She angled her lips and tried to blow it off her face again, but it didn't move. She crossed her eyes and could see its blurry black shape. It ran across her cheek and on to the bed beside her face and she lost track of it there. She worried that it was in her hair.

Her feet were free at the end of the bed. She could see her bare toes sticking up into her line of sight when she lifted her head all the way up and forward so that her chin touched her chest. She wiggled her toes and waggled her feet back and forth, then moved her legs, rocking them to and fro beneath the heavy rope. She swayed her hips, finding more room to do so the more she moved. She decided she was not as tightly bound as she'd thought and so continued to move parts of her body as much as she was able, straining against the ropes, feeling them give the slightest bit. Occasionally she would disturb the fly and it would drift upward into her line of sight and then settle down again somewhere beside her.

She found herself wishing that a spider would come along.

She lost track of time and was busy shrugging her

shoulders, tensing and relaxing, tensing and relaxing, creating slack in the rope, when she sensed a presence in the doorway. She stopped moving and swallowed hard before turning her head. A man stood there, stock-still, watching her. At least she thought it was a man. It was hard to tell because he was actually quite small and was wearing a plague mask, its heavy beak thrusting into the room. The creature cocked its head to one side and reached up, lifted the mask. Hatty stared at him for a moment and looked away. She guessed the man was in his early fifties, but he might well have been a puppet rather than a living, breathing person. His face was utterly expressionless, dark eyes hidden under a heavy brow, his thin lips nothing but a gash in his narrow face. He had a large nose and his whiskers were patchy and grey. He clearly hadn't shaved in weeks. His long salt-and-pepper hair stuck up every which way in sweaty spikes. Hatty closed her eyes and wished that he would go away, and when she opened them and turned her head, he was indeed gone.

She heard something bump against the floor in the other bedroom and Hatty watched the door, wondering when the man was going to come back and kill her. Quietly, she began pushing out against the rope with her elbows, continuing the work of getting herself free, though she was certain it was too late.

Sometime later, the man came by her bedroom door again. He was walking backwards, dragging something heavy along the floor. She blinked. The man had two corners of a blanket in his hands and, as she watched, John Charles's body passed through her line of sight, from his feet to his head and away across the landing to the staircase, which she could not see.

She heard the creak of floorboards and the steady thump thump thump as John Charles was pulled down the steps, one at a time.

Hatty redoubled her efforts, moving in mad patterns against the ropes, feeling them give way, but oh so slowly. She closed her eyes and thought about nothing but the ropes, willed them to loosen. Tears rolled down her cheeks and she hoped she might drown the fly with them, if that insect was still beside her on the bed. She felt her nose running, but couldn't wipe it. Her chest convulsed in sobs.

John Charles didn't have a face.

29

Hammersmith had never visited the Marylebone bazaar and he couldn't think of a thing they might have inside that he would ever want or need. He followed Fiona through the doors and waited for his eyes to adjust to the sudden shade. Electric lamps were hung everywhere, but the press of people absorbed the light. He wrinkled his nose at the smell of unwashed bodies and dust. Fiona pushed her way through the crowds – mostly women, Hammersmith noticed – to a stairway and up, without pausing to look at any of the distractions on display. Hammersmith was relieved, and had to hurry to keep up with her. He'd been afraid she was using him as an excuse to shop, but she appeared to be quite serious about their mission.

At the top of the steps, she led the way to the back of the broad landing, where an old man sat behind a meticulously arranged counter. He smiled at their approach.

'Lady Tinsley, isn't it? I never forget a name,' he said.

Hammersmith shot a puzzled glance at Fiona, but kept his mouth shut. The old man hopped off his stool and stepped forward far enough to rest his elbows on the counter. He stared up at Hammersmith and narrowed his eyes. Hammersmith felt self-conscious and used his fingers to brush his hair out of his face. He suddenly wished he'd taken the time to change his clothes that morning.

And another hour or two of sleep wouldn't have hurt him, he supposed.

'And this must be your young man,' the shopkeeper said.

Hammersmith's eyes widened and he looked to Fiona for help, but she was studiously avoiding his gaze.

'Mr Goodpenny,' she said, 'this is my friend Nevil Hammersmith.'

Hammersmith put out his hand and Goodpenny straightened himself and shook it.

'Don't shout at me,' Goodpenny said.

'But I haven't said a word,' Hammersmith said.

'Just so,' Goodpenny said. 'And when you do, you won't shout, will you? I like the look of him,' he said to Fiona. 'A bit rough, I suppose, but a few good meals and a proper laundering ought to take care of that.'

Hammersmith was confused. He felt like he'd stumbled into a conversation that was already under way.

'Actually, Mr Goodpenny, Nevil needs a favour, if you wouldn't mind terribly,' Fiona said. 'He'd like to get your opinion on something.' She glanced briefly at Hammersmith and nodded, and he felt a rush of relief when he realized that he finally knew what was being discussed. He groped about in his pocket until he found the cufflink Fiona had given him and set it on the countertop in front of Goodpenny, who leaned down over it.

'May I pick this up?'

'Please do,' Hammersmith said.

'Wouldn't want you to think I was stealing it,' Goodpenny said. 'Does this belong to you, Mr Angerschmid?'

'It's Hammersmith, sir. And no, it doesn't. I found it

and would like to return it to its owner.' He and Fiona had settled on this simple cover story during their journey to the bazaar. It didn't seem necessary to try to explain the circumstances in which he'd discovered the cufflink or the significance of it, particularly since it might have no significance at all. Hammersmith hadn't allowed himself much hope that the piece of jewellery would lead him to a suspect.

'I thought you might be able to help, Mr Goodpenny,' Fiona said. 'Since this is your area of expertise.'

'Oh, no no,' Goodpenny said. 'Not at all. I actually have a great deal of expertise in this sort of thing. Been at it for thirty years, though not always in this location, mind you. In fact, this cufflink is of the sort I carry. Made by a fine family in Cornwall. I visit them twice a year to buy silver.'

'There's an engraving on it,' Fiona said. It was clear to Hammersmith that she was fond of the old man, though she seemed to be acting cool towards Hammersmith now, virtually ignoring him, as if he'd offended her somehow.

'So there is,' Goodpenny said. '*A-R.* They're initials, I presume.' He looked up at Hammersmith and nodded. 'But not your own. Unless I put your initials on this in backwards order.'

'Do you mean to imply, sir, that you engraved this yourself?' Fiona sounded excited.

'It's possible,' Goodpenny said. 'As I say, this cufflink looks like one of mine. Here, let me show you.' He stepped back from his counter and scowled at it for a moment, then crouched down and reached inside. Hammersmith saw Goodpenny's hands and the top of his balding head through the glass as he peered about. He emerged after a few minutes with a handful of cufflinks, which he spread out over the counter. He grunted and picked one of them up.

'This is the very one,' he said. He held it out for Hammersmith and Fiona to examine. To Hammersmith's untrained eye it looked like the same design and style of work, a slightly squashed diamond shape with deep grooves around the edges and a smooth raised inner ridge. He picked up the one he had brought and set it in the palm of Goodpenny's hand, next to the new one. Aside from the engraved initials, the only difference he could see was the mud embedded in every indentation of the older cufflink. He looked up at Goodpenny's smiling face.

'Did you do this? Did you engrave this one?'

Goodpenny shook his head. 'I can't be sure. I do have quite a fine memory and I've got no recollection of these initials, so my first instinct is to say no to you. But if you'll wait but a moment, I keep a record of all my engravings. Stay here.' The old man patted the air between them as if settling them into their places, then turned and scuttled away behind a curtain at the rear of the little kiosk.

Hammersmith looked at Fiona and shrugged. She brushed a stray hair out of her eyes and opened her mouth to say something, but appeared to think better of it and looked away. Hammersmith turned slowly in a circle and took in the other little shops clustered around them, the ladies bustling from one spot to another, their baskets overflowing with sundry wares. He wondered how there were so many different things for sale. He glanced back at Fiona, but she appeared to be examining something behind the glass of Goodpenny's counter. She had swept her yellow hair back behind her ear and Hammersmith could see her pulse throbbing in her throat. Her long eyelashes fluttered and she licked her lips. He looked away, suddenly aware that he was staring at her.

'It would be quite a coincidence if the cufflink came from this very place,' he said. As the words left his mouth, he heard how inane they were and winced. Of course it would be a coincidence. He was making small talk, something he never did. He believed that if a person had something to say, he should bloody well say it. And if there was nothing to say, say nothing. He shook his head, confused by his own idiocy, but Fiona looked up at him and nodded. She seemed relieved.

'I do wonder how many places there are that engrave this sort of thing,' she said. 'Perhaps it's unusual.'

'In which case, it wouldn't be a coincidence at all, would it?'

'No. It would be fortunate, of course, but hardly coincidental.'

'Quite right.' Hammersmith felt an almost overwhelming and irrational urge to walk away and go back to his flat and start the day again without bazaars and cufflinks and foolish conversations. But before he could make any excuses, Goodpenny returned, clutching a leather-bound ledger book. The inexplicable awkwardness was immediately dispelled by his presence. He set the book down between them and opened it, then leafed through the pages, working his way backwards in the ledger.

'You see, I write down each transaction in this book, in case someone complains that I've engraved the wrong initials,' Goodpenny said. 'You might be surprised by how often that happens. People say one thing and expect something completely different to end up engraved on their jewellery.'

'Perhaps,' Fiona said, 'you ought to have them write their initials down for you themselves. That way there'd be no confusion.'

'That's exactly right, my dear, I write it all down to prevent confusion.'

'That's not what she said,' Hammersmith said. But Fiona motioned for his attention and shook her head at him. Hammersmith raised his eyebrows, but didn't pursue the matter.

They waited several minutes while Goodpenny pored over his journal of old transactions. Hammersmith shifted from foot to foot and drummed his fingers against the countertop. Fiona stood stock-still, her shoulders tense and her hands clasped together in front of her. At last Goodpenny looked up from the book and shook his head.

'Nothing here,' he said. 'A few initials, now and then over the years, but never an *A-R* at any time. I'm terribly sorry to disappoint you.'

Fiona blew out a lungful of air that Hammersmith realized she must have been holding for quite a while. She seemed to be as invested in his case as he was. She looked up at him, her brow furrowed and her jaw clenched. 'I'm so sorry,' she said. 'I really thought perhaps . . .'

'It was a good idea. Worth looking into, at any rate. For all we know this thing is entirely unrelated to the murders.'

'You said murder,' Goodpenny said. 'Murder? Has someone been killed?'

'Three women,' Hammersmith said. Their flimsy cover story didn't really matter any more, if it ever had.

'And you thought this was a clue?' He held up the dirty piece of jewellery and frowned at it.

'We hoped. Or rather it crossed our minds that it might be.'

'Oh, I do wish I could've helped you,' Goodpenny said. He handed the silver cufflink over to Hammersmith, who slipped it back into his pocket.

'Well,' Hammersmith said, 'we appreciate the attempt anyway. Good to have met you, sir.' He turned away, but Fiona didn't follow him.

'I wonder . . .' she said. 'You mentioned that you travel to Cornwall for your silver things, didn't you?'

Hammersmith perked up and grinned at her. If he hadn't been so tired, he might have thought to pursue the thread himself. But it was her idea, so he stayed silent, letting Fiona take the lead with the old man.

'Oh, no, my dear. I go to Cornwall. Twice a year.'

'Of course. Now I remember, you did say Cornwall. And you think this cufflink comes from there as well?'

'I showed you myself,' Goodpenny said. 'It's a perfect match, isn't it?'

'Yes, it is. But do you think there are other merchants who go there, too? I mean, might there be someone else selling the same sorts of things from the same place?'

'I see what you're getting at,' Goodpenny said. 'Yes, indeed. I, for one, always travel with my good friend Mr Parks, and I'm sure he finds splendid pieces of his own to bring back. Of course, sometimes our purchases overlap each other's, but a little healthy competition is good for the economy, wouldn't you say?'

'Quite,' Fiona said. 'Are there others, besides Mr Parks, I mean? Others who also deal with the family you deal with? The silversmiths in Cornwall?'

'Oh, I wouldn't know. Probably a few, but not too many. And they'd be spread about, you know. Not all clumped together here in the city. Good Lord, we'd be stepping all over each other to sell a cufflink. You'd be able to buy one for practically nothing and we'd all be in the poorhouse.'

'And your friend? He's a jeweller?'

'No, he's a hatter, my dear, but he carries a small assortment of accessories.'

'Could we . . . Would you mind terribly giving us his address?'

'Do you think he might be able to tell you something about this clue?'

'I doubt it very much, but it's worth a try.'

'Indeed. Give me a moment and I'll write down his particulars.' Goodpenny disappeared behind his curtain. He emerged in no time at all holding a small cream-coloured card with a familiar bit of filigree in one corner. In a small precise hand he had written the address of his friend on Jermyn Street. He hesitated, looking back and forth between them, unsure about who should be given the card, but Fiona reached across the counter and took it from him.

'Thank you very much, Mr Goodpenny.'

'I do hope this helps in some way. Mr Parks is a good man, though. I'm sure he'll do his utmost to be of assistance.'

Hammersmith tugged at his forelock and nodded at the shopkeeper.

'You'll let me know if you catch the murderer, won't you?'

'Of course we will, sir,' Hammersmith said.

'My prayers are with you, Mr Angerschmid. And good day to you, Miss Tinsley. Might I say, you're a most charming couple.'

'Oh, but we're not,' Hammersmith said. 'Not in the least bit.'

'My mistake,' Goodpenny said. 'Terribly sorry.'

Hammersmith turned to Fiona, but she was already gone. He spotted her several yards away in the crowd, already at the stairs, her blonde head bobbing down and out of sight. He hurried to catch up with her.

Halfway down the stairs, he had to stop. He was out of breath and he put his hand to his chest. He could feel the furrows and bumps of his still-healing wound through his shirt. He wondered if breathing too hard might strain his injured lung, cause it to burst open, filling his chest cavity with air and blood. Was that even possible? He saw himself collapsing and tumbling down the steps. He kept his head down and waited for the pain to let up. Somebody bumped into him hard, rocking him back against the railing. The man leaned in and whispered something low and unintelligible in Hammersmith's ear. Hammersmith snapped his head up and around, but the man was already walking away from him up the stairs, disappearing among the bustling throngs. Hammersmith shook his head and clutched the railing tight and descended to the ground floor.

By the time he managed to elbow his way through the shoppers downstairs and out into the sunlight, Fiona was halfway down the street. The pain in Hammersmith's chest had subsided and he half ran, half walked after her. When she heard him coming up behind her, she stopped and turned.

'Good thinking, you,' he said when he had caught his breath again. 'Getting that other name from him, I mean. You'd make a fine detective.'

'Well, that makes one of us,' Fiona said. 'You couldn't detect a soup stain if it was right under your nose.'

He looked down, surprised to see that he did, indeed, have a soup stain on his right sleeve. When he looked up, Fiona had gone again, stomping down the street with the little card in her hand and a slight breeze blowing her hair back over her shoulders. Hammersmith shook his head and let her get ahead of him. She acted like she was angry with him, but he couldn't for the life of him figure out why.

Puzzled, he drifted along in her wake.

30

The boys, Robert and Simon, had still been asleep on the daybed and Claire had cautioned him about waking them – *'After what they've been through, sleep is a blessing'* – so Day had returned to Scotland Yard, leaving Henry and his bird, Oliver, behind to help and amuse the new household staff. The corner of the main room that was reserved for use by the Murder Squad was empty, everyone else away from their desks and out in the city, presumably investigating things. Everything had been removed from the walls and set aside, waiting for the movers to take it all away to the new Norman Shaw building. There was a sense about the place of an ending, of people moving away and leaving it empty, devoid of all but dust and shadows, a party hall after everyone had gone home to bed.

Inspector Wiggins had taken full advantage of Day's new drudgery duties. He had left a stack of witness statements an inch thick on Day's desk, all to be sorted and abridged. And there were other odds and ends of reportage and paperwork left behind by some of the other police for Day to organize. He sat and stared at it all for a few minutes, then got up and limped to the back wall, beneath the coat hooks, where boxes of old case reports were kept on shelves, three high and twenty across. The bottom queue of cartons, which represented the oldest cases, had already been moved over to the new location.

Only the most recent files were left, as they might still be needed again soon. He hoisted the topmost box of archives from the end of the shelf and took it back to his desk, opened it and began to shuffle through the reports inside, not entirely sure what he was looking for, just aware that something was tickling the back of his brain.

He had barely begun sifting through the stacks of paperwork in the box when the door of the commissioner's office opened and Sir Edward Bradford stepped out. He was holding a box of his own, a large garment box, tucked under his arm. He was a thin man with a full white beard and friendly intelligent eyes under a high brow. He had lost his left arm, all the way to the shoulder, to a tiger in India and subsequently kept that sleeve neatly pinned up out of the way. He walked to Day's desk and Day took the box from him, cleared some papers out of the way and set it down. He lifted the lid and shook his head at Sir Edward.

'It's a constable's uniform.' His eyes went wide. 'Oh, no, you aren't –'

'Don't worry, Walter. I'm not making you walk a beat. Take it out and give it a look.'

Relieved, Day lifted the jacket out, leaving the corresponding dark-blue trousers in the bottom of the box, and unfolded it, held it up so the light from the window hit it. Two buttons were missing from the front and another from the left sleeve, a bit of thread left behind where the smaller button had been torn off. The cuff of the left sleeve was frayed and threadbare, a long irregular stain drizzled down the side from under the collar on the right-hand side, there was a rip in the lining in back, the seam had burst along the right shoulder, and there was a hole beneath the armpit.

Day smiled at Sir Edward. 'This was Hammersmith's?'

'Yes,' Sir Edward said. 'He returned it two days ago. I almost let him keep it. It's not good for anything but rags now. Except the hat. That we can use again. I can't very well pass the rest of this on to another policeman.'

'Yet you took it from him.'

'Well, perhaps we'll start a Sergeant Hammersmith museum one day. This will be the centrepiece.'

'I'm afraid to even look at the trousers,' Day said.

'Don't. They've fared even worse than the jacket, if you can believe it.'

'He'd come back, if you'd have him. You could just give the whole shabby thing back to him. He'd come today if you sent for him.'

'I know,' Sir Edward said. The glint of amusement faded from his eyes. 'He'd come back to work today, and tomorrow, given his reckless abandon, he might very well be dead. If not tomorrow, next week. I didn't sack him because I wanted to. I did it to protect him.'

'Sir, he'd rather die doing his duty than live by any other means. He's a born policeman.'

Sir Edward held his hand up and waved it, dismissing the subject. 'I thought you'd be charmed by the state of his uniform, that's all. I'm not ready to take up this discussion again. Let's at least allow the poor boy to heal from his wounds. It's a miracle he's alive at all.'

Day put his head down to conceal his excitement. The commissioner hadn't ruled out bringing Nevil Hammersmith back to the Murder Squad. He was still considering it as a possibility, at least, and Day knew better than to push him on it. He refolded the jacket, not taking any particular care with it. A few more wrinkles and creases weren't going to harm it. He laid the jacket back in its box and closed the lid, but Sir Edward didn't pick it up.

'You've heard about Inspector March.' It wasn't a question.

'Yes, sir,' Day said.

'Swallowed his own tongue.'

'Or had it fed to him.'

Sir Edward shook his head. 'Inspector . . .' He stopped and sighed and shook his head again. 'You know, it's not that I don't believe you.'

'About Jack, you mean? Jack the Ripper, still at large, still a danger to everyone in London? Hell, a danger to everyone in the country.'

'About that, yes. I believe that *you* believe that. And I'm not in a position to prove you wrong. But we've searched those tunnels, scoured them, for days, looking for any sign of the person you claim you saw there. We found nothing. We even had Dr Kingsley down there with his finger-ridge powder, whatever he calls it, and you know what he found.'

'He found the marks of Inspector March's fingers.'

'Everywhere. He found that Adrian March had been all over that dungeon where you were held, had handled the implements of torture we discovered there, had touched nearly every surface that was there to be touched.'

'Which doesn't rule out the presence of someone else there, sir, all due respect.'

'No. No it doesn't. But it doesn't help us find that

person, either. You yourself admit that you never saw this fiend who hurt you so badly.'

'He stayed in the shadows, but I heard his voice. So did Sergeant Hammer . . . Nevil heard it, too.'

'Yes. You heard a voice. And you were both in a great deal of pain. You'd lost a lot of blood. And Nevil had a scissors in his lung. He was practically unconscious.'

'That doesn't change the fact . . .'

'You must see that the logical conclusion is that Inspector March was your tormentor. Whether he was Jack the Ripper or not . . . That's not for us to know.'

'Did he ever tell you he was the Ripper?'

'He never told me much of anything, Walter. Nothing useful. And now he's gone, and he'll never have the chance. You know how much I respected him.'

'I know.'

'And I know that you respected him, too. It hurts me that he changed so much. It hurts me that he did these things to you, damaged you in your body and in your mind. And it's on me now to give you what you need to recover. You and Nevil, both. You think I'm punishing you with all this . . .' He pointed at the file box full of papers. 'But I'm not. And I'm not punishing Nevil by sending him away. I hope you'll see that someday.'

Day nodded, but didn't look up from the top of his desk.

'Anyway, we've discussed all this. I just wanted to make sure you knew about March. One day perhaps we'll both forgive that man for what he did. As it stands, it doesn't look like he was able to forgive himself.'

Sir Edward picked up the heavy garment box. Day was

impressed by the strength in the commissioner's fingers, to be able to hold the box closed and grip it so tightly. Sir Edward tucked it back under his arm and hesitated.

'And,' he said, 'I thought you might get a chuckle out of seeing the state of Nevil's kit. Lord knows we can all use a laugh round here.' He turned and walked back to his office, but paused with his hand on the knob. 'I'm going to miss this place,' he said. He didn't look at Day; his gaze wandered around the empty room, at the scuffed floor, the old gas fixtures, the grimy window panes and the faded green paint on the walls. 'It has character. I'm not likely to live long enough to see our new headquarters become so well used.' He shook his head and stepped into his office and closed the door.

Day stared at his box of archived files for a long minute, then went back to unpacking it, stacking the paperwork on his desk. The desk where he belonged.

31

Fiona sat across from him, but she stared resolutely out towards the front of the bus and refused to look at him. He had decided to give her time. Eventually she would either get over whatever was bothering her or she would tell him about it and he'd have a chance to smooth it over. Meanwhile, in the absence of any better clues, they jounced along in an omnibus headed for St James's and Jermyn Street. Hammersmith turned his gaze from Fiona to the woman next to her, who cooed at a baby in her lap, her free arm wrapped around a little girl who was busy pretending she didn't see Hammersmith. He grinned at her and looked away when he saw her trying not to smile back at him. On the other side of Fiona was an older gentleman, oblivious to everyone else, his nose in a newspaper.

Hammersmith closed his eyes and spread his legs wide, folded his arms over his chest, steadying himself as the bus swayed gently from side to side. He could hear the clop-clop of the horses' hooves and the clamour of other vehicles. He wished he'd thought to bring a book along. He had begun Jerome Jerome's *Three Men in a Boat (To Say Nothing of the Dog)* and had just come to the bit in Chapter Three where Uncle Podger made a mess of things while trying to hang a picture frame. Hammersmith imagined the character as his own uncle, whose name was Bamford, not Podger, and who wasn't anything like as clumsy as the uncle in the book, but who brought a form of benign chaos with him everywhere he went.

Hammersmith fell asleep while thinking fondly about Uncle Bamford's cluttered cottage, where he had spent many long summer afternoons. But he sank immediately into a murky nightmare scenario in which the cottage housed a street fair populated by enormous exotic creatures that bustled to and fro without looking where they were going. Hammersmith was lost in the midst of the steady flowing traffic of these blurry pink beings. He looked down and was not surprised to see he was wearing his old uniform, but it was much too big for him. His hat fell down over his eyes and he pushed it up, turning in small circles, trying to find a way out through the strange shoppers in front of him no matter which direction he faced. At last he spotted a rabbit hopping away from him, dodging the creatures' feet, its white tail bobbing up and down, swaying back and forth in a way that made him feel as if the floor he was standing on was moving. The tail was a beacon and he followed it, darting between giant legs, holding his hat up so he could see. The hems of his trousers tripped him and he used his free hand to hitch them up, bunching the extra fabric at his waist in his tiny fist. He seemed to be gaining on the rabbit, who grew larger as he drew closer to it. He now saw that it was much bigger than he was; its tail was the size of a two-wheeler and it was shiny, glowing. Then it disappeared and Hammersmith drew up short at the mouth of an enormous hole. He peered down into the dark, which he now realized was a mine shaft, and saw a glimpse of that giant rabbit's tail before it was swallowed by the inky blackness at his feet, like a flare snuffing out. He heard people moving out of the rabbit's way: people he somehow knew were miners working a vein of silver under the street.

Panicked, not sure whether he was meant to follow the rabbit down beneath the earth, Hammersmith looked all round him and saw that he was utterly alone. The strange creatures were gone and the sun was sinking on the horizon. All the booths and kiosks were shuttered. Bits of discarded newspaper blew along the empty avenue. One stuck to his chest and he grabbed it, held it up in the last rays of the setting sun, and read the headline: INCOMPETENT POLICEMAN GETS OWN FLATMATE KILLED! PRINGLE REVEALS MURDER PLOT! He threw it away and immediately felt another windblown page hit him, this one much heavier. He plucked it from his chest, but it was now too dark to read it and it was covered in blood anyway, and he dropped it. The blood was his own, seeping through the front of his chest, soaking his shirt, thick and clinging and sticky.

He wasn't alone any more. There was someone else nearby. A man-shaped hole in the darkness moved steadily towards him and then it was there, *he* was there, and he leaned in close to little Hammersmith, brushed his dead black lips against Hammersmith's ear and whispered a single word, then pressed something into Hammersmith's hands, something cold and metal. And then the man shape was gone. Alone once more, Hammersmith hefted the metal thing in his hands and knew that it was a pair of scissors.

He jolted awake and was surprised to discover that he was still on the bus and that his hands were empty. No scissors. Fiona was staring at him, a strange look on her face. The older gentleman next to her glanced up, annoyed, from his newspaper, made a great show of refolding it to a different page, then went back to reading. The little family on Fiona's other side had all fallen asleep, the baby held tight in the crook of its mother's elbow, the little girl slack-jawed, drooling on her mother's arm. Hammersmith motioned to Fiona and she got up, made her unsteady way across the aisle and sat beside him.

'Are you all right?'

'I'm fine,' Hammersmith said. 'A bad dream, that's all.'

'You shouted something just before you woke up,' Fiona said. She appeared to have forgotten that she was cross with him.

'What did I say?'

'I'm afraid I couldn't make it out.'

'Doesn't matter. It came to me while I was asleep.'

'What came to you?'

'Listen, when we were separated at the bazaar . . .' Hammersmith hesitated.

'Yes?'

'You got ahead of me on the steps there and someone bumped into me.'

'Did he hurt you? Is it your chest?'

'No,' Hammersmith said. 'No, nothing like that. It was a man, but I never saw him. I mean, I didn't see his features. He was already moving away from me, going up the stairs as I was going down. But he said something to me. Sort of whispered it in my ear.'

'What did he say?'

'He just said one word and was gone, and I didn't understand it when he said it to me, but I dreamed it just now. In the dream I heard what he said. And I think it's true. I think it's what he actually said to me there in the bazaar on the stairs.'

Fiona nodded impatiently. 'Right. And what did he say?'

'What he said wasn't as important as who he was. His voice was . . . I'd heard his voice before. You've heard it, too, back then, back when he stabbed me, but I didn't realize who he was until he was gone. Actually, I didn't realize it until just now when I dreamed him up.'

'Nevil, you're frightening me. If you don't explain yourself right now, I'm going to get off this bus and leave you here and never speak to you again.'

'Fiona, it was him. He must have followed us when we went to see Goodpenny.'

'Him.' She said it as a statement. He could see in her eyes that she understood exactly who he meant.

They said it together: 'Jack.'

He nodded.

'You saw Jack?'

'No,' Hammersmith said. 'I mean, yes, but I didn't see him properly, you know. Just the back of one side of him and then he was gone amidst all the other people. I never would have found him, even if I'd realized who he was right away and given chase. I don't know, maybe if I'd grabbed his arm before he could . . .'

'But he said something to you?'

'Just one word. He said, "Slowly."'

Fiona slumped against the back of the seat and silently mouthed the word in the direction of the old man's newspaper:

Slowly.

32

Day moved DI Wiggins's work to one side on his desktop and picked up a pile of papers from the archive box. He set the files in front of him and began sorting through them.

There were two killers in London, possibly three. The Harvest Man was a known quantity, even if little was known *about* him. The police, most of whom were out scouring the streets for him even now, were aware that the man was small and thin, that he crept into attics and killed sleeping victims. They knew that he was likely to be in someone's house at that very moment, either preparing to kill come nightfall or living with the aftermath of some recent prey. Day had no doubt that at some point, hopefully soon, they would find the right house and they would catch him. The kind of killer the Harvest Man represented, though clever and methodical, was also a danger to himself and his own freedom. He was unable or unwilling to deviate from his set pattern of crimes and would eventually be caught *because* of that pattern. He didn't just mutilate people's faces, he spent time with them, posed them in family settings. Day wondered if he had been frightened away from Robert and Simon's house when he had realized the boys were missing. Otherwise he might still be there.

The other killer was Jack the Ripper, and he presented

a far greater danger because there was no pattern, no rhyme or reason, to anything he did. He operated according to a design that only he could see, one that made sense only to him. And Day was not convinced that the three women killed in the East End had anything to do with Jack. At least, not directly. For Jack to return to a pattern he'd long since given up seemed wrong. It flew in the face of everything Day thought he knew about the man.

All of which might mean that there was a third killer at large. And, if so, Nevil Hammersmith's cufflink might be a clue to that third killer's identity. It was a huge leap of logic for Day to take and he knew it, but his hunches often turned out right. Dr Kingsley, that paragon of rational thought, believed in Day's hunches, and that gave him the confidence to shirk his duties for the afternoon and sift through old files on the off chance he could help stop a killer the rest of the police didn't even know existed.

Even sitting, the muscles in his injured leg throbbed, and he concentrated on the files in front of him, trying to ignore the pain. Whoever had killed the three prostitutes was either mimicking Jack's methods or celebrating them. Or perhaps the murderer thought he *was* Jack. Day had encountered enough delusional killers during his time with the Murder Squad to know he shouldn't rule anything out until they'd caught the culprit and heard his story.

The Yard had adopted the Bertillon system many years before, recording all of a suspect's pertinent physical data whenever an arrest was made: height, weight, hair colour, eye colour, moles, scars, and tattoos, et cetera. A man might change his hair colour and his weight, but he couldn't disguise the colour of his eyes or remove a tattoo. With enough information in the hands of the police, cross-referenced properly, criminals who had been arrested once were easier to catch again. Day had begun adding alienist information to these files as well, writing in elements of motive and mindset whenever those details were available to him. Just as a man couldn't rearrange the moles on his skin, he was unlikely to change his point of view. Most people were set in their ways and this made them prone to repeating themselves.

As Day worked his way through the files, working from most recent arrests backwards through the early part of the year, he paid close attention to the names of perpetrators and took notes regarding the crimes they'd committed in the past. He pulled out the records of anyone with the initials *A-R* and made a separate stack in his lap. He wasn't especially thorough, since Hammersmith's cufflink wasn't necessarily a clue at all; he just sped through the archive box, pulling arrest files for anyone that seemed reasonably likely. At the end of two hours, he had a stack of five reports in his lap. He put the discarded files back in the box and closed the lid on it, set it on the floor next to his desk and moved his small stack of paperwork to the blotter, where he could give them a more in-depth read-through.

The third report down in the stack gave him cause for excitement. But he set it aside and continued reading until he'd given all five the attention he thought they deserved. In the end, he set the other four files on top of the box, to be put away later, and picked up the file he'd set aside. A boxful of suspects, narrowed down to a single man.

He smiled and grabbed his stick, stood stiffly and got his balance. He put on his jacket and hat and took the file with him as he left the building, anxious to find Hammersmith and show him what he'd found. He was surprised to discover that flat grey clouds had rolled in while he was at his desk, obscuring the sun and threatening rain. It crossed his mind that he ought to replace his makeshift walking stick with a sturdy umbrella, something that could do double duty and help keep the weather off him.

He was so preoccupied that he failed to notice the figure waiting across the street from the Yard, a man who followed along after Day, easily matching the inspector's deliberate gait.

33

Henry was hot and out of breath and so he stepped out of the front door for a bit of fresh air. The policeman who always waited there smiled at him and held up his umbrella to cover them both.

'Would you like a cigarette?'

'No, thank you,' Henry said. 'Dr Kingsley says cigarettes aren't for gentlemen.'

'He does, does he? Well then, I suppose I must not be a gentleman, because I'm going to go ahead and have a smoke.'

Henry held the umbrella for him while the policeman lit his cigarette and took a deep drag on it.

'Ah, that hits the spot on a miserable day like this, doesn't it?'

'I'm Henry.'

'Yes. My name is Augustus. Augustus McKraken. It's good to meet you, Henry.'

They shook hands.

'I've seen you round here,' Augustus said. 'You're a big chappie.'

Henry nodded, unsure what he ought to say. He already knew he was big.

'Tell me, Henry, do you see anything under that tree across the way? Anybody behind it?'

Henry squinted into the rain. 'No,' he said. 'Is somebody hiding?'

'I think someone has been hiding there, but I don't see him now. My eyes are not what they once were and this rain makes it hard to see far.'

'Nobody's there.'

'Good. You know, I won't always be here.'

'Where will you go?'

'I don't know. Back to my home, I suppose.'

'Do you have a nice home? I like my home. It's very small, but I fit inside it.'

'That's good,' Augustus said. 'What I'm getting at . . . Your Inspector Day's a busy man. He won't always be here, either.'

'Where will he go?' The cigarette smoke was getting in Henry's eyes and making them water.

'Well, I don't know. But he might be gone and there are bad people out there. One in particular that worries me.' Augustus McKraken waved his hand to take in the entire street and perhaps the city beyond it. Perhaps the whole world. Henry wasn't sure how much of everything one sweep of the hand was meant to indicate.

'Mr Day catches the bad people.'

'Yes. I used to do his same job. But what I'm saying . . . I'm saying if he isn't here. If he's gone. Well, you seem to get on well with the family.'

'Mrs Day's nice.'

'She is indeed. You take care of her. And you take care of those children. You keep anything bad from happening to them, do you hear?'

Henry was confused. 'Mr Day will take care of them.'

228

Augustus seemed to be frustrated, but then he smiled and nodded. 'All right. You're quite correct and I'm just very tired. Yes, Mr Day will take care of his own family. But if you get the opportunity to help him . . . A man your size can be a great help. You can protect the women and children.'

'Yes, sir,' Henry said. 'I'm going to go back inside now.'

Augustus nodded at him. He threw his cigarette down and ground it beneath his heel. Henry left him there and escaped back into the dry, brightly lit house. *Augustus seems like a nice man, but he must be confused*, Henry thought. *Mr Day would never go away and leave his family.*

34

Hammersmith looked up at the low dark clouds that were moving fast over the tops of the buildings on Piccadilly. A raindrop hit him squarely in the eye and he reacted, then felt another hit the back of his neck.

'Starting to rain,' he said.

Fiona didn't respond. She was craning her neck, looking all round them at the mouth of every alley and the gloomy back of every vestibule in every doorway. Looking for Jack.

'He's not there,' Hammersmith said.

'Who?'

'We wouldn't see him if he was there. And if we did see him, we wouldn't recognize him. We've never glimpsed his face.'

'Just the same, I think I'd know him.'

Hammersmith understood what she meant. Saucy Jack radiated an aura of evil that seemed physical. But Hammersmith knew it was nonsense, a feeling generated by countless nightmares and waking fears. There was no such thing as an aura of evil.

Another drop of rain spattered against Hammersmith's shoulder and he reached out to take Fiona's hand, then thought better of it and shoved his hands into his pockets. He jerked his head in a southerly direction.

'It's up this way,' he said.

'I know,' Fiona said. She came with him, moving quickly but watching over her shoulder.

'Shouldn't be far.'

'Right around the corner,' she said.

They trotted along the footpath beside the road and turned east when they hit Jermyn Street. Hammersmith could see St James's Square between the tailors' businesses, the milliners' shops and the catch-all emporiums with their displays of women's clothing, men's bespoke suits and children's fashions. Beyond the square, he knew, was the larger park, and beyond that . . .

'We're right near the Yard now,' he said. He immediately regretted the words. They sounded pathetic, as if he yearned for little more than a glance at his former workplace. Still, he couldn't seem to stop talking. 'The old place, I mean. They'll be moving soon.' This sounded even worse. The Murder Squad would, of course, be moving without him. He would never have an opportunity to work in the new building on the Victoria Embankment. He winced and silently ordered himself to shut up.

He glanced at Fiona. She was looking up at him and he hoped it wasn't pity he saw in her eyes. She looked quickly away.

'That's it there,' she said. She pointed ahead, through the now steady shower of slow fat raindrops, and Hammersmith saw a sign for PARKS AND SONS, HATTERS. They ran for it as the sky opened up and they jumped through the big glass door, laughing and shaking their heads, their damp hair sending water flying three feet in every direction. Hammersmith noted that the hatter must be doing well for himself to have afforded so much plate glass at the front of the shop.

The inside of the place was dim and dignified: hats hung on pegs that covered every wall, there were shelves full of hat blocks of every size, bolts of felt scattered across a long cluttered counter, spools of ribbons and bins of some strange earth-coloured dust. Hammersmith guessed the powder must be used to season hats in some way. A door opened at the other side of the room and a man came through it, presumably the hatter himself. He was perhaps twenty years younger than his friend Mr Goodpenny and was wearing an American-style wide-awake hat. Hammersmith had only seen the likes of it in books and the wide brim would have seemed absurd on anyone else, but the whole thing looked like it had been crafted specifically for this man's head. And, of course, it must have been. Parks (if it was Parks) adjusted his spectacles on the bridge of his nose and peered at them, then broke into a huge friendly smile and held out his arms.

'Well, look at you,' he said. 'I'd say it's started to rain, hasn't it? You're a sight. Come, I've a fire going in the back and I've just put tea on. Warm up, dry off.'

They followed him back through the inner door into a room that was perhaps half the size of his showroom. He pointed at two low mismatched chairs in front of the hearth, where a crackling fire lent the room an inviting glow. Parks left them and went through yet another door. They heard him murmuring something to another person, but Hammersmith couldn't make out the words. A few moments later, a girl roughly Fiona's age brought out a tray heaped with teacups and scones and pots of clotted cream and raspberry jam. The hatter came behind her, carrying crockery.

'Sit,' he said, 'sit. You haven't sat yet? Here . . .' He put the plates and cups he was holding on a low table and hurried back through the door, emerging seconds later with two big soft towels, which he handed to them. Hammersmith dried his hair. The towel smelled clean and felt warm against his face, as if it had recently been hanging by the fire. When they were sufficiently dry, the girl took the towels from them and they sat. The hatter pulled up a third chair and sat between them, taking the closest spot to the hearth, and the girl left them.

'My daughter,' he said.

'You're Mr Parks, I take it,' Hammersmith said.

'The very same.'

'Your sign out front says "Parks and Sons",' Fiona said. 'Does your daughter work with you as well?'

'She does indeed,' Parks said. 'And she's turning into a better hatmaker than I am. My son's too young. Still in school.'

'You've only one son?'

Parks looked confused for a moment and then realization dawned and he smiled again. 'Ah, yes, that sign is misleading. I have one son and one daughter. But I've got to compete with the bigger shops around here. They're more established, been making hats for a century or more, passing the trade down through families. My business doubled overnight when I hung the new sign and claimed more children than I actually have.'

He turned to Hammersmith and frowned. 'Now, let's

talk about the proper hat for you. Do you always wear your hair so long around the ears?'

Hammersmith shook his head. 'Oh, I don't need a new hat, thank you,' he said.

'You don't?'

'He does,' Fiona said. 'But it's not why we're here.'

'I'm sorry,' Hammersmith said, 'but we were actually wondering about a cufflink. Mr Goodpenny sent us to you.'

'Goodpenny! You don't say. How is the old boy?'

'Seems to be doing well, I think.'

'Can't hear a word, you know.'

'He does appear to struggle.'

'But a more pleasant fellow you've never met. Excellent company, if you only keep your mouth shut and let him do the talking. Otherwise it can be a bit frustrating, the attempt to communicate and all that. We take the rail out together to Cornwall and it's the best trip I make all year. Look forward to it for weeks in advance.'

'You buy silver there?'

'Silver, yes . . . But specifically I buy silver items, not the raw stuff itself. Family there fashions the most exquisite little things.'

'A family? Do you mind telling us what their name is?'

Parks wagged a finger at them. 'If I tell everybody where I get my wares, nobody'll need me any more, will they? Go right to the source, won't they?'

'I suppose so,' Hammersmith said. 'Can you tell us, what kind of items do they supply you with?'

'All kinds.'

'Like cufflinks,' Fiona said. 'Isn't that right?'

'I deal primarily in hats, of course, but some of my better customers are also in need of accessories and prefer to come to me for everything: yes, as you say, cufflinks, as well as collar stays, the odd set of buttons or fasteners, even a small selection of walking sticks. All that sort of thing. And I'm glad to stock the stuff. Keeps 'em coming back to me.' He paused to pour more tea for them all. 'Goodpenny picks up a few items there as well, although we began these trips of ours because he was looking for letter openers and the like for his own concern. I was only too glad to go along with him. Not sure either of us makes a profit when all's said and done, but it's worth it anyway. We have grand adventures, Goodpenny and me. Have I told you the story of the goat on the tracks?'

'We've only just met you,' Fiona said. 'You haven't told us any stories.'

Parks sat back and blinked in surprise. 'Why, you're absolutely right. I forget I don't already know everyone in the world. And here I've forgotten my manners as well. As you've no doubt guessed by now, my name's Andrew Parks. And you've met my daughter, Hannah. Should've introduced you.'

'I'm Fiona Kingsley and this is my friend Nevil Hammersmith.'

'Hammersmith, you say? Unusual name. Never heard it on a person before now. I'd've guessed you were Welsh. There's a trace of it in your voice.'

'Well, you're certainly not hard of hearing, Mr Parks. I am from Wales, though my family wasn't originally. I was born there.'

'I thought so. I've spent a bit of time in Wales, now and

235

then, here and there. Do you know a gent name of Bamford?'

'Bamford? There's more than a few Bamfords round there, but that might be my uncle.'

'Wonderful fellow, if it's the same Bamford. Just wonderful. He ran his wagon over my foot once.'

'Why, that must be my uncle. It's just what he would do.'

'He didn't intend to do it, of course. Terribly apologetic about it.'

'How odd. I was only just thinking about him.'

Parks turned to Fiona. 'Coincidences abound if you open your mind to them. Did you say your name is Kingsley?'

'Yes. Fiona Kingsley.'

'Related to Bernard, by chance?'

'Dr Bernard Kingsley is my father.'

'Oh, he's a great customer of mine. Any daughter of the good doctor's is a friend to me.'

'Why,' Fiona said, 'you do indeed know everyone in the world, Mr Parks!'

He smiled at her. 'Feel as though I do, now I've met the two of you. What a delightful young couple you are. And here I'd despaired of meeting anyone new today. But you've actually come to ask me something, haven't you? If you'll tell me what it is, I'll do my best to help.'

Hammersmith fished the cufflink once more out of his pocket and handed it to the friendly hatter. Parks held it out to the fire, letting the light dance over its surfaces. It glowed yellow and orange, bits of blue flashed off its crenulations. The monogrammed initials stood out black against the reflective surface.

'I remember this piece quite well. It and its mate, both. Bought by a woman for her son's birthday. Strange thing, though, she was found dead only a week later. Fished out of the Thames, all cut up. It was such an odd occurrence that it stuck fast in my mind.'

Hammersmith tried not to seem too excited. He stared Fiona down and saw her swallow her happy smile. He didn't want the hatter to become guarded. The man had shown not the slightest sign of caginess, but Hammersmith had seen witnesses grow vague once they understood how valuable their information was.

'So you did engrave this,' Hammersmith said.

'No,' Parks said. 'Mr Goodpenny did.'

'But,' Fiona said, 'he has no record of having done it. He looked it up in his ledger for us.'

'Oh, he keeps terrible records, Goodpenny does. Just the worst at it. Lovely fellow, but terribly disorganized. He catches up his records on the train, so it's . . . what, once a year? Twice? And all from memory. Completely useless, that ledger of his. But no, I remember this one well. He did these cufflinks up for this woman, she was in an awful hurry for them, and then she dies immediately once she's got the things. Might've been on her son's birthday she died, for all I know. If not, it would've been right around that time. Must've been an 'orrible thing for the lad, mustn't it?'

Hammersmith heard a trace of a Mancunian dialect sneaking into the hatter's voice as he grew agitated. He wasn't the only person whose speech betrayed his origins.

'Why wouldn't Mr Goodpenny have remembered to tell us that himself?'

'I'm sure he would if you went back to him and nudged

237

his memory. And I'd bet he does have it in that ledger book somewhere, but these initials are *A-R*, so he'd probably have the customer written down as Helen Lidwedge or Calvin Whichway. I keep telling him to get a horn, hold it up to his ear when people speak.'

'Those names,' Hammersmith said. 'Helen Lidwedge, Calvin Whichway, they're similar. Why did you pick them?'

'Only because they sound funny to me, I suppose,' Parks said. 'I appreciate a good Dickensian name, same as anyone.'

'Ah,' Hammersmith said. He was a great admirer of Dickens himself.

'Also,' Parks said, 'because both those names sound a bit like Alan Ridgway, don't they?'

'Alan Ridgway?'

'*A-R,*' Fiona said. 'Alan Ridgway.'

'You remember the name?'

'Because the woman was found right after,' Parks said. 'If not for that . . . who knows?'

'So the woman's son was Alan Ridgway and this is his cufflink,' Hammersmith said.

'I'd say it is,' Parks said.

'And she was found dead . . . It sounds as if she was murdered after accepting this order from Mr Goodpenny.'

Parks set down his teacup and waved his hands in the air. 'Now, don't jump to any conclusions. Mr Goodpenny wouldn't murder a rabbit for his supper. I didn't tell you all that so you could go and –'

'No,' Fiona said. 'That's not what Nevil was suggesting at all.' She was sitting nearest the fire and her still-damp hair shimmered gold.

'She's right,' Hammersmith said. 'I didn't mean to imply anything of the sort. I was merely trying to figure out what happened and in what order. If this cufflink is related to those other murders, and I think it likely now that it is, then this Mrs Ridgway might have been the first victim.'

'Other murders?'

Quickly, Hammersmith and Fiona filled the hatter in on the three prostitutes who had been found in Whitechapel, and Hammersmith's discovery of the cufflink on the alley floor. Parks listened intently, then blew out a big gust of air and rubbed the back of his neck as if he'd been sitting in the hot sun.

'I'd say this calls for some real drink,' he said. He staggered out of the room and returned with a bottle of whisky. He unstoppered it and poured into their teacups, then raised his own cup and drained it before sitting back down. He had the look of someone who had just bumped his head against the lintel and hadn't yet got his bearings back.

'So,' he said at last. 'Do y'think this Ridgway fellow ever got his cufflinks before his mum was offed?'

'Could be,' Hammersmith said. 'Or it could be that someone took them from the mother before she was killed. Either way, it looks more and more like a clue after all.'

'Thanks to you, Mr Parks,' Fiona said.

The hatter smiled at her, but he didn't look happy.

'I'd hate to think she was killed just 'cause someone wanted a cufflink. What an 'orrible waste that'd be.'

Hammersmith sipped at his teacup full of whisky, his

nose full of the fumes. He watched as Fiona pretended to drink, but she set the cup quickly back down and made a face. He stifled a laugh and stood up.

'We've bothered you enough today,' he said. 'And Miss Kingsley's got an appointment that I've kept her away from all morning. Thank you very much for your help, Mr Parks.'

The hatter stood, too, and shook Hammersmith's hand. 'If there's anything else, please don't hesitate to drop in on me. I hope you catch this blackguard. Anyone who'd do that to a woman over a coupla pieces of silver . . .'

'Actually,' Fiona said, 'I did have one more question, if you don't mind, sir.'

'Not at all, young lady. What can I do for you?'

'Earlier you said you have a selection of walking sticks? Canes?'

'I do. Not many, but a few. It's a sideline, you know.'

'Of course. I was wondering if I could take a look at them.'

'You don't think any of 'em were used for . . . used for murder.'

'Oh, no,' Fiona said. 'Strictly personal reasons. Not related at all.'

Parks's face resumed its natural friendly expression and he motioned for her to follow, talking over his shoulder as he led the way out of the cosy little back room. 'As I said, not many of 'em, but what I've got's quality stuff. Did you have a price in mind?'

'I have two crowns.'

'Let's see what we can do for that. And I haven't told you the story of the goat on the train tracks yet. I promised you that, didn't I?' Their voices faded, but Hammersmith lingered for a moment by the fire.

He nodded to the hatter's daughter as she reappeared to pick up the crockery and the leftover scones. She blushed and hurried away and, embarrassed, Hammersmith hurried after Fiona.

35

Hatty Pitt finally kicked the last loop of rope from her hips down past her knees and ankles and off the tips of her toes. She was now able to buck her body up and down, loosening the ropes around her waist and chest. She hadn't seen or heard a thing from the world outside the bedroom since her faceless husband had been dragged past her door and away down the stairs. She worked her body up and down, from side to side, patiently inching her way up towards the wall behind her bed. At last her head touched the wall and she kept thrashing, *gently* thrashing, careful not to make too much noise. Whoever had taken John Charles's face away, whoever was wearing the plague mask, could come back at any moment to do the same to her. Her neck bent, and bent further as she pushed against the wall, and began to burn with pain. She tried moving diagonally now across the bed. At first she hardly moved at all, and she almost gave up. Her stomach hurt, the muscles clenched and sore, the back of her head hurt, her calves and ankles hurt. But she persevered. Gradually, her neck became more comfortable and she noticed there was slack in the ropes that she hadn't realized was there. She kept up her steady movements until she was able to roll from one side of the bed to the other. And then she stopped and began worming down the length of the bed, undulating from the waist, not caring that her skirts were riding up. If Eugenia Merrilow was willing to show the world everything, then Hatty Pitt could, by God, abandon modesty long enough to save her own life. She willed herself to flow from the top of the bed like a force of nature, like a stream that had been dammed and was now free, she was a body of water in the shape of a woman. The ropes dragged painfully up and over her breasts, but she kept moving. She tucked in her chin and closed her eyes and ignored the pain in her nose as it was tugged up and out of place. She heard it pop and felt a spurt of blood. She kept moving. Then she could taste the blood, spilling over her lips, down her chin and her throat. Blood soaked the ropes and trailed back into her eyes and her hair. Still she kept moving. And then the ropes were gone.

She sat up.

She swung her legs off the bed and tiptoed to the escritoire next to her bedroom door and opened it slowly, thankful that John Charles had kept the hinges oiled. There was still blood in her eyes and she blinked rapidly, trying to see through intermittent slits, her eyelashes painting her vision red. She groped about until she found a clean cloth and wiped her eyes with it, then pressed it to her nose while she found another cloth. The first cloth was soaked now and she threw it on the floor, squeezed the fresh cloth against her nostrils, and held it there.

Barefoot, she moved silently to the door and stuck her head out, looked both ways up and down the empty landing. She crept without breathing, willing herself invisible, pretending she was not, in fact, moving at all, only drifting on air, to the stairs and down them, letting the gentle pull of gravity dictate the speed of her progress. A feather on a light breeze.

At the bottom of the steps, she had only to make a ninety-degree turn to the left and she would practically be at the front door. She would be out on the street in an instant; she could find help. Instead, she turned right, stopped and stared down the length of the hallway. She moved her hand away from her face. The cloth stayed behind, stuck there, blood already drying along her upper lip and on her cheeks, and she wrenched it painfully away, ignoring the sparks she saw in her peripheral vision. There was a lot of blood on the cloth, but she could still see clean patches between the liquid red and she hoped that meant the bleeding had slowed. She turned the cloth over and applied pressure once more to her throbbing nose. She could hear someone talking at the end of the passage, low melodic whispers, and she listened. A man was in her kitchen; he was singing. She couldn't make out the words and so she crept down the passage and peered around the doorjamb.

For years to come, the scene she saw at her kitchen table would return to haunt her dreams. The small man, his sweaty hair plastered across his forehead, sat with his back partially to her. She was looking at his profile, his narrow nose and jutting chin. Part of his ear was missing and the skin had grown back in a shiny pink smooth ridge over the cartilage. There was a plate in front of him piled with the biscuits Hatty had baked the evening before, crumbs scattered all over the table and on the floor at his feet, where his boots had spread mucky streaks and clods of soil. This little man was singing, though his mouth was full, and he sprayed bits of mashed dough out on to himself and the table. She thought she recognized the song, but it was hard to make it out through his mouthful of stale biscuit.

> . . . But there was one of the children
> Who could not join in the play,
> And a little beggar maiden
> Watched for him day by day.

He paused to swallow and crammed another biscuit whole into his mouth, munched, and sang. An old-fashioned plague mask rested on the floor by his feet, propped up against a leg of his chair, and there was a wicked-looking knife on the table within easy reach. Hatty had avoided looking at the other end of the table, though she knew what she'd see there. She could almost make it out already, from the corner of her eye. Finally, she tore her gaze away from the singing man . . .

> She came again to the garden,
> She saw the children play.
> But the little white face had vanished,
> The little feet gone away.

John Charles was propped upright in his chair, his arms leaning casually on the table. There was a place setting in front of him, a single untouched biscuit on his plate. His skull grinned across at the singing man, a rapt audience of one. Pink streaks of blood were smeared across the pale bone, and ragged bits of flesh hung off his neck down around his exposed spine like some grotesque collar.

Still the little man sang:

> She crept away to her corner,
> Down by the murky stream,
> And the pale pale face in the garden
> Shown through her restless dream.

Hatty couldn't help herself. She gasped. The man stopped singing immediately, the words of his song: . . . *through her restless dream*, echoing in the empty kitchen, and he swung his head round to stare at her, his cheeks bulging with biscuits.

And then he was on his feet, the curved knife in his hand, his chair thrown back against the wall. Hatty dropped the cloth from her face and watched it for one frozen moment as it fluttered to the floor, then she turned and ran. She heard her feet slapping against the hardwood and – it sounded like he was right behind her, catching up with her – the *clomp-clomp-clomp* of the little man's heavy boots. Inanely, she thought about the dirt chunking off his boots, how hard she would have to work to clean the floor. She rounded the bottom of the staircase and there was an opportunity to look back, to see how close the man was, but she didn't. She focused instead on the front door and she didn't break her stride, though she could feel that her nose was gushing again, blood coursing in rivulets, splashing off her chest, spattering against the ground. She slipped on her blood, but reached out for the newel post and caught her balance and then she banged straight into the closed door and scrabbled for the knob. Behind her, somewhere back in the passage between this door and the kitchen, she heard a strange barking noise. She had seen a seal once at the circus, when she was a little girl. It had sounded like this. But she didn't turn to see why there was a seal in her house. She concentrated on turning the doorknob, which seemed to revolve in slow motion, slick with her blood, and then the door was swinging open and she was through it and it was raining on her. Rain was smashing into her forehead and into her eyes. It felt wonderful and cool.

She left her door wide open, ran and kept running, blind in the rain and the haze and the pounding of her heart, beating so fast, until she slammed pell-mell into the side of a horse and heard a man's voice yell, 'Whoa!' And Hatty fell unconscious beside a skidding carriage in the middle of the road.

36

The Harvest Man watched the Woman Who Was Not His Mother leave the house. Some part of him noted that she had forgotten to close the front door behind her. But he couldn't focus on her or the door because he was choking. He knew he ought not to have run from the kitchen with his mouth still full of biscuits. He should have sat and waited until he could swallow, perhaps taken a sip of water, before following the woman. She was small. He could have easily caught her before she went too far from the house. But he'd rushed things and now he would die here in the hallway. He supposed he deserved it because he'd been rude and left the table. Children mustn't forget their manners.

All of this flitted through his mind in the first seconds after the woman left him, and then blind panic took over as he tried to breathe. He dropped to his knees, his vision fuzzing out at the edges, darkness moving in. His chest convulsed and he crawled into the kitchen, moving on instinct, unable to think clearly. There was the Man Who Was Not His Father sitting at the little table. The man had not eaten his own biscuit yet, but he smiled at the Harvest Man. There was kindness in his face that was not a face. The Harvest Man raised his hands to the man, imploring him silently to help. The moment he moved his hands from the floor, he fell forward and slammed into the hardwood beneath him. The whole kitchen shook. The force of the impact expelled all the air in his lungs and a great gob of mushy biscuit dough flew from his mouth and skidded across the kitchen floor.

Exhausted, the Harvest Man rolled over and lay there on his back, panting, watching the Man Who Was Not His Father and who had not helped him. The man began slowly to move, leaning forward as if trying to get a better look at the Harvest Man, then, more quickly, the man toppled forward so that his head hit the plate. It looked like he was finally sampling his biscuit.

The Harvest Man sat up and rubbed his chest. He closed his eyes and got his breathing under control. After a few moments, he got his feet under him and stood. The front door was still open and he could see that it was raining quite hard now. Everything beyond the threshold was lost in a wet grey fog.

The woman had left him and now more people would come. She would bring them. They would take him away, back to the Bridewell place, where his parents never visited, and he would not be allowed to look for them any more.

He went to the window he had used to get into the house and opened it. Rain bounced off the windowsill and sprayed his face with a fine cool mist. He hoisted himself up and clambered through the opening, dropped to the ground outside and walked away.

37

Day had just started up the steps to his home, trying to move between raindrops, when he spotted two faraway grey figures approaching from around the curve out by the park. One was tall and painfully thin with a lot of wild dark hair. The other was petite with straight pale tresses. The shorter of the two had a parcel under her arm and neither of them was holding an umbrella. Fortunately, Inspector McKraken did have an umbrella and he shared it with Day, who waited impatiently on the steps for the other two to catch up, the file he'd taken from the Yard safe and dry under his jacket, keeping company with his revolver and flask.

McKraken cleared his throat. 'I don't want to alarm you,' he said, 'but there's someone been following you, lad.'

'Following me?'

'Seen him a time or two slinking round under that tree across from here.'

Day squinted into the rain. 'I don't see anyone there now.'

'Could be the rain's kept him away.'

'Well, we're right near the park,' Day said. 'Perhaps it was just someone relaxing in the shade.'

'Could be.'

'But do keep an eye out, will you?'

'It's what I'm here for,' McKraken said. And he winked at Day.

When Hammersmith and Fiona Kingsley mounted the steps, Day was already swinging the door open and they all hustled inside, leaving McKraken out on the porch under his umbrella. Day also left his makeshift walking stick outside, propped against the side of the house. Claire hadn't complained about it, but Day had noticed that the thing left big brown splotches wherever he walked. He must be making a mess for the new staff to deal with.

Before he could tell Hammersmith what he'd discovered in the Murder Squad archives, the housekeeper appeared with freshly laundered towels for everybody and Day was struck for the first time by her efficiency and usefulness.

When they were all reasonably dry and Hammersmith's hair was standing on end in a ruinous tangle that they all pretended to ignore, they left their wet boots by the door and adjourned to the sitting room, where Robert and Simon were playing with Henry, having only recently woken up and eaten a late breakfast. Oliver, the magpie, flew over and perched on Day's shoulder for a moment before returning to the mantel. The boys immediately stopped what they were doing and picked up all the cushions and pillows from the floor – where Day could see they had been building another fortress – putting them all back where they belonged on the furniture. The housekeeper bustled Henry and the children out of the room and returned with an armful of throws, which she draped over the sofa, daybed and chairs to protect them from wet clothing. When she had gone again, Day, Hammersmith and Fiona sat down.

'Nevil, I think I may have found something to help you,' Day said.

'Fiona and I have discovered something ourselves,' Hammersmith said.

'Your killer's name is –'

'It's Alan Ridgway.'

'It is,' Day said. 'That's just what I was going to tell you.'

'But how did you . . .'

'Here.' Day pulled out the slim file folder and passed it over.

Hammersmith opened the folder (Day noticed with regret that he'd accidentally bent a corner of the folder when he jammed it under his jacket) and began reading.

Fiona stood up and took a step towards the sitting-room door. 'We found his name by the letters on the cufflink,' she said.

'So it was a clue, after all,' Day said.

Hammersmith looked up, smiling. 'It would seem so.'

'While you two sort things, I'm going to check on Claire,' Fiona said. 'If that's all right.'

'Of course,' Day said. 'She'll be glad to see you. I wonder why she hasn't come down. Surely she heard us arrive.'

'I'll find out and be right back. Promise you won't say anything too awfully interesting while I'm gone?'

Hammersmith looked up again from the report on his lap. 'We won't,' he said. 'This Ridgway bugger is just as much your discovery as mine, you know. Maybe more so.'

She blushed and fled from the room.

Day pointed at the long parcel she'd been carrying, left

on the floor beside the daybed. 'What have you two brought?'

'Nothing to do with me,' Hammersmith said. 'Something Fiona decided on.' And with that, he went back to reading the file. Day had already looked it over. There wasn't a great deal of information about Alan Ridgway, but what was there was damning. After the standard physical description of Ridgway, there followed three items: Ridgway had been caught exposing himself to a prostitute in the East End in February. He'd been arrested and sentenced to two months hard labour on the docks. The week after he'd returned home, another prostitute had been stabbed near where Ridgway had originally been arrested. She had survived the ordeal and had described Ridgway in exacting detail. He had consequently been arrested once more, but his mother had given him an alibi for the evening in question and she could not be shaken on it. The arresting officer, Inspector Gerard, had decided that the word of a working girl could hardly be considered unassailable, particularly when weighed against that of the widowed Mrs Ridgway.

Day grew impatient watching Hammersmith read. He stood quietly and went out to his study, where he refilled his flask from the decanter there. He hadn't mentioned McKraken's warning to Hammersmith, but he was mildly concerned. He could think of only one person who might want to follow him. But that made little sense. Jack knew where Day lived already, knew where he worked. If he wanted to harm him, Jack could do it at any time; he didn't need to run around in the rain keeping tabs on him. Day hoped the person under the tree was nothing more than

McKraken's overactive imagination, but he was troubled just the same.

When he returned to the study, Hammersmith was still reading. After the second incident, the case had been left open and Ridgway had been set free. But days later, Mrs Ridgway had been found floating in the Thames. Again, Alan had been brought in for questioning – this time by Inspector Michael Blacker of the Murder Squad – but there had been no compelling reason to level charges. There was no physical evidence found on his mother's body and, after all, she was his alibi. Why would he have killed her?

Still, Inspector Blacker had made a note in the margin of his report, a note that made it quite clear he didn't like Ridgway and he didn't believe in his alibi. Blacker simply hadn't been able to find a reason to arrest him. He was certain Ridgway had, in fact, murdered his mother and he intended to keep an eye on the suspect.

Hammersmith closed the file and looked up. Day held out his flask.

'You're still wet, Nevil. Take the chill off.'

Hammersmith shook his head. 'No, thank you. There's no address in here for him.'

'I saw that. I checked and it seems Ridgway moved out of their home as soon as his mother was buried. It'll be a bit of work running him down now.'

'But we'll find him.'

'He's not Jack.'

'No.'

'But you like him for these new murders?'

'Oh, yes. He's the one.'

'I think so, too. Let's find him.'

'Find who, dear?'

Day turned to see Claire, Fiona and Mrs Carlyle entering the room with Robert, Simon and Henry. Claire came to Day and kissed his cheek. Hammersmith stood and nodded his head politely at Mrs Carlyle, but she didn't see him. She was busy watching the bird on Henry's shoulder. She appeared ready to cook it and serve it up. Day was certain that poor Claire had already received a lecture about letting animals in the house. With his wife in his arms and the sitting room full to bursting with people, Day felt a sense of comfort come over him that he hadn't felt in months. Perhaps a full staff of servants would mean more company in the house. And perhaps more company was exactly what he and his wife needed.

'Nevil and I were just discussing business,' he said. 'Mum, have you met Nevil?'

'No,' Mrs Carlyle said. She tore her eyes off Oliver and took a step back when she saw Hammersmith. 'What's happened to you, young man? Did you fall into a rubbish cart? You're a mess.'

Hammersmith smiled weakly. 'It's raining.'

'It is raining,' Henry said. 'We can't go outside any more today or we'll get messy, too.'

'Claire, run and fetch this boy a clean shirt,' Mrs Carlyle said. 'One of Walter's. I'm sure there's nothing we can do about his hair.'

'Oh, no, thank you,' Hammersmith said. 'I don't need a shirt. This one'll be fine. It'll dry.'

'There's a soup stain on your sleeve. That's already dried, unless I'm mistaken.'

'I've only recently had that stain pointed out to me.'

Day sighed and moved to change the subject. His mother-in-law was merciless. 'What have you been doing today?'

'Your wife has been staring out of the window and writing doggerel,' Mrs Carlyle said. 'Time well spent.' By the expression on Claire's face, Mrs Carlyle's sarcasm was not lost on her daughter.

'The boys have had a nice morning,' Claire said. 'Haven't you?'

Robert and Simon nodded in unison. They were standing side by side just inside the door, staring down at their shoes, suddenly shy in the presence of so many people. Simon perked up, though, and pointed at the parcel on the floor.

'What's that?'

'Oh, no,' Fiona said. 'I should have thought to bring the two of you something.'

'But you didn't even meet us until just now,' Robert said. 'How would you think to bring us gifts?'

'Just the same, I knew I was going to meet you today. I promise I'll make it up to you both.'

'But what is it?'

'Simon,' Robert said. 'It's not our business what it is.'

'It's all right,' Fiona said. 'That's a gift for Mr Day.'

'For me?'

'You can open it now, if you'd like.'

Day shot an enquiring look at Hammersmith, who shrugged. 'As I said, it's all her doing,' Hammersmith said.

He bent and picked up the parcel, handed it over to Day. It was cylindrical, four feet long, and Day already had a feeling he knew what it might be.

'You shouldn't have,' he said.

'You've been very kind to me,' Fiona said. 'I only wanted to do something nice to pay you back. After all, I spent months under your roof.'

'The whole time helping Claire.'

'Still, you were patient about the disruption.'

At the word *disruption*, Day's gaze went unconsciously to Claire's mother, who was standing back, still eyeing Hammersmith with poorly concealed distaste. Still, she had put her hand on little Simon's shoulder, giving the anxious boy a half-hug.

'Open it,' Robert said. He seemed excited, though the gift was not for him, and Day realized that this was a welcome good surprise, a balance, in some small way, against the horrific events of the past couple of days.

He smiled at the boys and tore the wrapping from the tube. He upended the parcel and a dark polished walking stick slid out into his hand. He tossed the empty tube on the sofa and held the cane up, admiring the way the light picked up deep red highlights in the wood. The end of it was capped with a simple silver knob.

'That's very . . .' he said. He had to stop and collect himself. 'You're too kind, Fiona. Really, I can't accept it. It's too much.'

'It was far less than you might think. The man who sold it to me got it for a song, he said, and he let me have it for almost nothing. Please, do take it. You need a new one.'

'You do need it,' Claire said.

'What, you don't like the tree branch I'm using now?'

'Open it,' Fiona said.

'But I did open it.'

'No, twist the handle and pull.'

Perplexed, Day did as he was told. There was the sound of ringing metal and the sharp scent of sparks and he pulled out a rapier from the inside of the cane.

'It's a sword stick!'

'I want one,' Robert said.

'I want one, too,' Simon said.

'You're always in danger, it seems,' Fiona said, 'and perhaps this might come in handy. It was the only one of its kind that the man had.'

'Walter's liable to stab himself in the foot with that,' Claire said. But she was smiling.

'Thank you very much, Fiona,' Day said. 'You're terribly thoughtful.'

'I have something for you, too,' Fiona said to Hammersmith. 'It's not quite complete yet.'

'Oh, I don't need anything.'

'You need a clean shirt,' Mrs Carlyle said.

Claire raised her eyebrows at Day and he took the hint. 'If you'll excuse me for a moment,' he said to the room. He limped over to his wife, testing the new cane. He grinned at Fiona as he passed her and she smiled back, clearly pleased that he was using the thing. Claire took him by the arm and led him from the room.

Out in the hallway, she leaned in close to him and whispered, 'She got something for Nevil, too, did you hear?'

'Yes. You know, I can't possibly keep this. It must have cost her everything she had.'

'You will keep it, Walter. She had to get you something, don't you see?'

'Had to?'

'Yes. Because she'd already got a gift for Nevil and she can't very well just give it to him. She's got to give something to someone else as well, and she chose you.'

'Why can't she give Nevil something?'

'Oh, you're hopeless. As bad as Nevil. Completely oblivious.'

'Oblivious to what?'

'Just keep the cane, will you? You'd be doing Fiona a favour.'

'If you say so. I do like it.'

'Then it's settled.'

'How have you been getting on with your mum? She seems ferocious today.'

'She hates everything. I think she hates me.'

'She loves you. She's just not comfortable with the sentiment and expresses herself poorly.'

'She's beastly about my rhymes.'

'I like your rhymes.'

'Do you really, Walter?'

'Yes, I really do. I think they're just the thing for children.'

'I do hope you're being honest with me, because –'

'I am.'

'Good. Because I want to publish.'

'Publish? Publish your poems?'

'I want to do a book of nursery rhymes. Fiona's convinced me to do it. I'm going to ask her to illustrate it for me, if she's willing. We can work on it together, she and I.'

'Why, that's a wonderful idea,' Walter said.

Claire's eyes widened and her cheeks pinked up. Walter was suddenly worried she might cry and he didn't understand why.

'Making a book is the very thing for you,' Walter said. 'And with your father's connections . . .'

'Oh, my father,' Claire said. 'He doesn't like the idea at all.'

'Ah. Well, who cares? Who cares whether two aged relatives like your nursery rhymes that are meant for children? Entirely the wrong readership you're testing these things out on. Read them to a child. We have two of them under our roof at this very moment. Well, actually, we have four, but the babies are probably too young to give you proper comments.'

'Oh, that's a wonderful idea. I'll see what Robert and Simon think of them. They're darling boys, Walter. I'm so glad you found them.'

'They don't seem to have reacted much to the death of their parents. That worries me.'

'They will. And we'll be here to comfort them when they do.'

'I'll have to turn them over to the proper authorities today.'

'Please, let's wait a bit longer. Surely they can spend another night here. It would be good for them.'

Walter sighed and rubbed the back of his neck. The house was crowded enough already. They didn't have room for two more. To keep the brothers any longer seemed irresponsible and possibly illegal. But perhaps Claire was right. One more night in a proper home, surrounded by people who cared about them, might not be so bad for the poor boys. He nodded. 'I need to make some enquiries about their placement anyway. I suppose we can wait a little longer.'

38

Alan Ridgway was tired of waiting. He had two very specific tasks set him by the man in the shadows and here was his opportunity to fulfill both of them at once. He'd abandoned the tree he was using for cover when the clever old guard on Day's porch had noticed him. Instead, he had spent the afternoon loitering in a doorway down the road and he couldn't tell who was coming and going through the rain. He knew, though, that Walter Day was at home, that his wife was home, too (she never seemed to leave the house), and that the old man was still standing at his post by the door. That was good enough for Alan. He thought he had seen other people arrive, but he couldn't wait any longer for them to leave. He was soaked through.

He had his blade in his hand by the time his foot hit the first step outside the house. The old man moved forward, blocking the door, holding up a hand.

'Here, you. What're you –'

Alan ran at him, yelling over the top of the guard's query. 'Die, Karstphanomen!'

Alan stabbed him in the throat. The old man fell to his knees, and Alan lost his grip on the knife. He grabbed for it and saw that the guard, even though he was dying and should have simply given up, was scrabbling for his revolver. The hilt of the knife was slippery with blood and rain and Alan had to try twice before he managed to wrench it from the old man's throat. A gusher of blood spurted up and over Alan's arm, sprayed over his face, got in his mouth – metallic and salty – and the guard stopped trying to find his gun, stopped moving entirely. He toppled face forward and slid partway down the steps, his feet angled up in the air. Alan almost laughed, it looked so comical.

Alan thought the whole operation had gone well. Aside from shouting his message at the old man and a few grunts and thumps, it had been a relatively silent affair. He spat out the old man's blood and fished in his pocket for the piece of blue chalk the man Jack had given him. He tried drawing a circle on the porch, as he had been told to do, but the conditions were not ideal, too wet. The chalk clumped and refused to make a smooth line. He was trying, down on his knees grinding the chalk back and forth in a semicircle on the brick, rain running down the back of his neck and into his ears and splashing down in the old man's blood, when the door opened and Alan looked up to see two little boys staring wide-eyed down at him. A pretty woman appeared behind them, grabbed the boys and pulled them back into the house. Almost immediately, as if he had been caught up behind the others, a tall thin man with feminine features rushed out through the door and, without pausing for even a second, launched himself from the top step and barrelled into Alan, sending him sprawling over the body of the guard. Someone shouted out the name *Nevil!* Alan bumped his head hard on the bottom step and rolled to his side, pulling on the dead man's arm, yanking the body up and over him for protection. He heard children crying from somewhere inside the house and a female voice again, this time screaming for someone named *Henry!* The thin fellow pushed the body away from Alan, but then made a deadly mistake. The thin man bent and checked the old guard for signs of life. Alan could have told him the chap was dead. It was obvious.

Alan lunged at the thin man, his blade at the ready, but a piercing scream startled him and he looked up to see yet another stranger in the doorway. This time, a blonde girl with a long graceful throat. Alan changed course immediately and bounded up the slippery steps at her. A small storm of black and white feathers, claws and a sharp little beak swarmed around Alan's head. He batted at it and someone called out the name *Oliver.* The bird disappeared. But the thin man was behind him now and had apparently satisfied himself that the old man was indeed quite dead. Alan's scalp felt as though it had caught fire. The thin man had a fistful of his hair and was yanking him back. Alan had no opportunity to brace himself and the thin man threw him back down the porch stairs and was on top of him in a flash. The thin man had acquired a stout tree branch from somewhere on or near the porch and now had it raised above Alan, about to bring it down on his face. Alan reacted, jerking his head up into the thin man's nose. A gusher of blood, and Alan rolled away, got his feet under him and brought his arm up, blade ready. The thin man was on his knees, disoriented and dizzy, bleeding heavily from his nose and blind with rainwater running into his eyes. Alan held the blade in both hands and thrust his knife arm down with all his might at the back of the thin man's neck.

He heard something crack, a loud retort that seemed to

be everywhere around him in the pouring rain. His head jerked back. He dropped the knife. He blinked hard and tried to remember what it was that had been so important only a moment earlier. There was a thin man hunched over on the ground in front of him. The man turned and Alan saw that he was quite good-looking, but his nose was bleeding. Alan smiled at the handsome man and then he saw bricks rushing up at him and everything was dark.

39

Day waited a second before he put his Colt revolver away, but Alan Ridgway didn't move. He lay still at the bottom of the steps. Day bent and looked at McKraken. The old man's eyes were open and sightless. Rain drummed off them, bouncing and spattering on his cheeks. Day put out his hand and closed McKraken's eyes for him.

'I thought you'd use your new sword,' Hammersmith said. He was out of breath and spoke each word as if it pained him.

'You'd've been dead by the time I got down these steps.'

'I'm hard to kill.'

'True,' Day said. 'Next time I'll wait and use the sword.'

'I should have come out of the door quicker than I did.' Hammersmith stared down at McKraken's body. 'Was he a good man?'

'I didn't know him well,' Day said. 'But Sir Edward thought highly of him. And he volunteered to guard my family. Nobody asked him to do that.'

'At least there was one man at the Yard who believed Jack posed a danger to you.'

'Now I wish he hadn't. He might be alive and enjoying his retirement.'

'It's how I want to go someday,' Hammersmith said. 'I never wanted to retire.'

Hammersmith's nose appeared to have stopped bleeding, but the front of his shirt was thick with blood. Day was pleased he hadn't given Hammersmith one of his own shirts to wear, per Mrs Carlyle's suggestion.

'Take off your shirt, Nevil, and let's have a look. I'm concerned you may have opened your wound.'

Hammersmith shook his head. He held up a finger and caught his breath before he spoke. 'No, my chest feels like it's on fire, but I think I'm all right. I didn't feel anything tear open. This fellow's in much worse shape than I am.'

There was a small round hole in the back of Alan Ridgway's head. Hammersmith rolled him over, pushing him with the toe of his boot. There was no corresponding hole in Ridgway's forehead. The bullet was still somewhere in his skull.

'He's still breathing,' Hammersmith said.

'You're joking,' Day said. He picked up his new cane from where it had fallen over McKraken's legs and limped down the steps. He and Hammersmith stood over Alan Ridgway and watched his chest move up and down. It was hypnotic. Neither of them moved.

'Walter?'

He looked up. Claire was at the front door.

'Everyone . . .' Day said. He felt very tired and had to start his sentence over again. 'Is everyone all right in there?'

'Physically, yes,' Claire said.

'Where's Henry? We could have used his help out here.'

'The boys were upset, Robert and Simon. They saw what happened to poor Mr McKraken and Henry refused to leave them.'

'Ah,' Day said. 'That's commendable, I suppose.'

'Those boys didn't need to see this,' Hammersmith said. 'They shouldn't have been out here at all.'

'No,' Day said. 'No, they shouldn't have. I was wrong. I should have taken them to the authorities first thing this morning. They wouldn't have been here.'

'No, you were right, Walter,' Claire said. 'They need to be around people who care about them. They've already seen worse than this.'

'We'll talk more about it,' Day said. 'Claire, please go inside and keep everyone there until we get this mess sorted.'

She opened her mouth as if to argue with him, but then thought better of it. She stepped back and closed the blue door, shutting Day and Hammersmith out in the rain with the two bodies.

'He's moving,' Hammersmith said.

Day tore his gaze away from his front door and looked down at Alan Ridgway.

'He can't be moving,' Day said. 'It's only the rain.'

But as he said it, Alan Ridgway's eyes opened and he smiled up at them. His lips moved. With some difficulty, Day lowered himself to his knees and leaned in closer.

'I didn't hear you,' Day said. 'What did you say?'

'It wasn't me.' Ridgway's voice was so soft that Day could barely hear him over the pattering rain on the footpath. There was a deep purple bruise spreading fast over Ridgway's forehead and his eyeballs seemed to be filling with blood. 'I was only the messenger. It was always you, Walter Day. Jack chose you, not me.'

'What? What does that mean?'

'Lost,' Ridgway said. 'Lost and gone for ever.'

Day stared at Ridgway. He no longer felt the damp of the rain or the discomfort of his leg. Instead, he felt a chill running along his spine, an electric thrill of fear and excitement. He stared and did not move until Hammersmith's hand on his shoulder broke the spell of Ridgway's words.

'Well, he's dead now,' Hammersmith said. 'He's finally stopped breathing.'

'Was he really breathing? Did he really speak?'

'I don't know how,' Hammersmith said. 'He had a bullet in his brain.'

Hammersmith was still holding the tree branch that, until recently, had served as a makeshift cane for Day. He used it to brace himself and helped Day back to his feet. Day felt dizzy and the pattern of raindrops pelting past him was disorienting. He wanted to lie down, but instead he turned to Hammersmith and tried to read his expression.

'Did you hear him? Did you hear what he said to me?'

'No. What did he say?'

Day hesitated and then shook his head. 'It was gibberish. The ravings of a dying man. I couldn't make sense of it.'

'Just as well,' Hammersmith said. 'I don't think I care what he thought at the end. I know right where he's headed to now and he can burn there.'

'I'm sure he will.'

'We need to send for the police. For more police, I mean.'

'If I hadn't already been inclined to move away from this place, I'm sure this would be the last straw. My neighbours will want me gone. Too much excitement lately for Regent's Park Road.'

'Let's have someone fetch Tiffany round here so we can get these bodies off the street.'

'Here's a boy now.' Day raised his hand and a young man, perhaps Robert's age, trotted up to him.

'I have a message for Walter Day,' the boy said.

'What?' Day was momentarily confused. He had a message for the boy to take, not the other way around.

'Inspector Tiffany sent me for you, if you're Walter Day. Said you'd have a cane. That you, then?' The boy glanced uneasily at the bloody bodies, but didn't look directly at them.

'Yes. Yes, I'm Walter Day. Tiffany sent you?'

'Said to tell you they almost have him, the Harvest Man. They've got a witness now. Young woman escaped him and Tiffany's right behind. You're to come there as quickly as you can.'

He recited an address from memory and held out his hand. Day rummaged in his pockets, but came up empty. Hammersmith stepped forward and pressed a coin in the boy's palm.

'Thank you, sir.'

'Would you be willing to carry a message back?'

'Of course, sir.'

'Please tell Inspector Tiffany that I'll be delayed here. And have a wagon sent round to this address.'

'For these dead fellows?'

'Exactly right.'

'Will do, sir.' The boy turned on his heel and sprinted off into the driving rain. He was lost to sight within seconds.

40

It took the police more than three hours to arrive, load the two bodies in a wagon and take them away. Hammersmith stood over Ridgway's corpse with McKraken's umbrella, trying to preserve the evidence, but the steady rain rinsed the blood away into the road. In the end it was decided that there was nothing left on the footpath or the porch for Kingsley to see. He would have to make do with the bodies themselves in his laboratory.

By sunset, the façade of number 184 Regent's Park Road had been washed clean, as if nothing untoward had ever happened there. But inside there had been a great deal of activity. Ants scurrying here and there, each with a singular purpose, reconstructing their hill after a careless footfall. Mrs Carlyle instructed the staff on the packing of overnight bags for her daughter and grandchildren. Claire packed a bag for her husband. Henry paced back and forth, checking every door and every window again and again, watching through the rain for danger. The bird, Oliver, flew from perch to perch after his master, but refused to sit on Henry's shoulder.

Fiona took the boys to the kitchen and fed them. When they were calm, she took out her tablet and gave them each a piece of paper and a crayon and let them draw. While they busied themselves, she asked them questions and she herself drew a picture. When she was finished, both Robert and Simon were able to recognize in the illustration the features of the Harvest Man. There followed another round of food and distraction.

At half ten, Leland Carlyle arrived with a pushcart. The luggage was loaded and taken away, followed by a procession down the road and across the park to the rented cottage of the Carlyles. Henry returned to his tiny room within the lamppost in Trafalgar Square and Fiona was sent home with a message for her father.

The new household staff was given a small stipend to find lodging at a nearby inn and number 184 was locked and abandoned.

'We'll find a new home for you tomorrow,' Mr Carlyle said. 'None of you will come back here again.'

This time Day did not argue with his father-in-law.

Night

Trafalgar Square was quiet. The man Jack emerged from the shadows and walked towards the southeast corner, his boot heels clocking against the wet stones. He paused at Nelson's Column and saluted, then continued across the square to a bulky lamppost. A bird was perched on the finial atop the rain shield, its head under its wing. It looked up and shook the rain off its feathers and squawked. Jack held a finger up to his lips and the bird went quiet. It cocked its head to the side and watched him with one beady black eye and then it lifted its wings and flew away into the night.

Jack smiled. When the bird had travelled out of sight, he raised his fist and knocked lightly on the small door that was set in the lower half of the post. He could hear someone inside moving about. He stood in the rain and waited.

Hatty Pitt had not spoken a word since she woke in a hospital bed surrounded by nurses and policemen. There had been a great deal of excitement centred on her for a time, but most of the people had gone now. The policeman named Tiffany had gone off and she could tell he had been frustrated by her lack of speech, but she didn't care. He had left a constable there by the door of the women's ward to guard her and she didn't care about that, either.

Anything could happen to her now and it wouldn't matter. She was a widow at seventeen. What was left for her in life? What did she care any more about other people or their wants and desires? She had no intention of ever speaking again.

She had begun to drift back to sleep when she heard a commotion and Eugenia Merrilow bustled into the room past the protesting guard, who followed her in.

'Hatty,' Eugenia said. 'Oh, Hatty.'

Eugenia came to the side of her bed and sat there. She leaned in over Hatty's stiff and unresponsive body and she hugged her. Eugenia's shiny aquamarine dress crinkled against Hatty's face. She smelled of orange blossoms and frankincense.

Eugenia did not let go of her. She sat there, bent awkwardly across the bed, and whispered in Hatty's ear. 'You poor dear. You shan't stay here another minute. You'll come home with me today and you'll stay there as long as you need to. As long as you want to. I'll take care of you. John Charles would have wanted me to.'

Hatty thought of John Charles at the kitchen table and she thought of the strange singing man who had eaten her biscuits. She suddenly remembered the name of the song. It was called 'The Children's Home'. Without understanding why, Hatty burst into tears. She lifted her arms and hugged Eugenia back and the two of them stayed like that for a very long time. Eventually, the guard returned to his post by the door.

Inspector Walter Day sat by his daughters' makeshift bassinet in his father-in-law's rented cottage and watched them sleep. One of them moved in her sleep, smacking her sister in the face with one chubby little paw. He smiled and put out his hand and she grabbed his thumb instead. She opened her eyes and he thought perhaps she smiled at him, but he wasn't sure if babies were able to smile. It might have been wind.

He sat and stared at his girls until his eyelids grew heavy. Claire entered the room and came up behind him. She rested her hands on his shoulders and he put his cheek against the back of her wrist.

Eventually he kissed each of the babies goodnight, blew out his lantern and allowed Claire to lead him out of the room.

Robert lay awake curled up next to Simon in an armchair before the guttering fire and listened to his brother whimper in his sleep. Mrs Carlyle and Mrs Day had piled extra blankets around the chair and Mrs Day had apologized that there was no room to put them somewhere more comfortable. The cottage was crowded and she promised that better accommodations would be found for them the next day. But Robert could see that Mrs Carlyle didn't particularly want the brothers there. He heard her arguing with Mrs Day about them. She didn't understand why her daughter had kept the boys for another night.

They didn't belong.

They didn't belong anywhere now. Their parents were dead and they didn't know any relatives well enough to want to go to them. There was nowhere for them in the world any more.

But Claire Day was kind to them and that was

something. She had fed them and given them shelter. Robert liked her very much.

Simon cried out and Robert reached for his hand. He lay there without sleeping and watched the fire die. He prayed that Mr Day would not take them some where he and his brother would be separated and they would have to start all over again. The orphanage did not sound nearly so nice as an armchair in any house with Mrs Day in it.

Final Day

The coach is at the door at last;
The eager children, mounting fast
And kissing hands, in chorus sing:
Good-bye, good-bye, to everything!

To house and garden, field and lawn,
The meadow-gates we swang upon,
To pump and stable, tree and swing,
Good-bye, good-bye, to everything!

And fare you well for evermore,
O ladder at the hayloft door,
O hayloft where the cobwebs cling,
Good-bye, good-bye, to everything!

Crack goes the whip, and off we go;
The trees and houses smaller grow;
Last, round the woody turn we sing:
Good-bye, good-bye, to everything!

– Robert Louis Stevenson,
'Farewell to the Farm',
A Child's Garden of Verses (1885)

Morning

The rain stopped just before dawn, but the sun rose behind rolling grey clouds and a fine mist clung to the ground. Primrose Hill was hushed and empty, as if all the blood spilled the previous evening had sent every living thing there into hiding. The only sound was that of the canal, filled by the storm and rushing through its channel.

Day stood when Inspector Tiffany entered the Chalk Farm Tavern. Tiffany looked about with distaste and made his slow way to Day's table at the back, passing those three solicitors who seemed to have made their offices at the counter. With Hammersmith the population of the tavern was now seven.

'I'm glad you made the time,' Day said. 'Thank you for coming.'

'Might've known you'd be found here,' Tiffany said.

'My neighbours have had quite enough excitement. This is less conspicuous than meeting at the house. Would you like a drink?'

'Early for me, but you go ahead,' Tiffany said. 'Mr Hammersmith, been a while since we saw you.'

Hammersmith nodded and shook Tiffany's hand. Day got the proprietor's attention and held up two fingers.

'So,' Tiffany said when they had sat down. 'You two have been up to old tricks. Killed some people last night, did you?'

'I had to shoot one man,' Day said. 'That's the extent of it. But he killed another before we could stop him. You knew Inspector McKraken?'

'He was a good man,' Tiffany said. 'Before my time, but I've heard he was an excellent policeman in his day. Up from the river police.'

'And he was possibly more than that,' Hammersmith said. 'McKraken's murderer was trying to draw a design in chalk when we stopped him.'

'We stopped him too late.'

'We did stop him too late,' Hammersmith said. 'I blame myself. I didn't act quickly enough.'

'You were first out of the door,' Day said. 'You were on Ridgway before I could even get my revolver out.'

'Whoever did whatever,' Tiffany said. 'What's this about chalk?'

'The Karstphanomen,' Day said. 'We think it's what Ridgway shouted at McKraken when he stabbed him. And the chalk is what's been drawn near some of the bodies we've been finding these last few weeks.'

The proprietor of the Chalk Farm Tavern appeared at Tiffany's back and reached across him to place two whisky shots on the table in front of Day and Hammersmith. Hammersmith slid his over to Day without looking at it. Day picked up the first of his two drinks and drained it in a swallow, smacked his lips and wiped them on the back of his hand. He let the second drink sit untouched for the moment.

'Your conspiracy theory,' Tiffany said.

'Well, however you'd like to explain it, there are indisputable similarities between some of the recent murders we've seen.'

Tiffany nodded. 'Aye, I'll concede that.'

'And McKraken's murder fits one of those patterns. Or it was staged to remind us of that pattern. Either way, we're meant to think that McKraken was Karstphanomen.'

'A secret society of torturers?'

'Who tortured the wrong man and are now being punished for it.'

'Whatever the reason,' Tiffany said, 'this Ridgway fellow killed McKraken and you killed him. Case closed and good riddance to bad rubbish. What irks me is I sent for you, Mr Day, and you never came.'

'By the time we sorted the bodies and got things cleaned up, it was late. By then I had no way of knowing where you were. I decided this morning was soon enough.'

'And now the Harvest Man has had another night to find another victim.'

'I had two very upset little boys, two bleeding bodies and a houseful of excited women. You had the entirety of the police force at your disposal and you're the one who insists I'm better off behind a desk than out making enquiries. I'm sure my presence wouldn't have mattered one way or another to your investigation.'

Tiffany sat silent, staring at the tabletop. Day took the opportunity to down his second shot. Finally, Tiffany looked up and sighed.

'All right, I admit it,' he said. 'There are some things you do pretty good. I've got a witness, someone who escaped the Harvest Man.'

'So I heard,' Day said. 'Congratulations.'

'Yes. It's a good break. But she's hysterical. Wouldn't talk to me at all. I thought of you. Thought maybe you could draw her out, get something from her that might help us. Kingsley puts a lot of store in your abilities and I thought we could maybe put 'em to the test.'

'I'd be glad to talk to her. But of course it's entirely possible she just needs time.'

'Time's not something we have a lot of. The house this girl came from is empty now. And he left behind another corpse. As bad as the others, maybe worse. Like he's getting angrier, impatient. It's not going to go well for his next victim.'

'It hasn't gone well for any of them,' Hammersmith said. 'Has it?'

'You stay out of it,' Tiffany said. 'Not even sure why you're here. You're not police and you can bugger off for all I care.' There was an awkward silence before Tiffany threw up his hands and slammed them back down on the table. 'Damnit,' he said. 'I apologize, Nevil.'

'No, you said what you meant. I respect that.'

'I bloody well did not. Just goddamnit tired of these killings. All these bloody goddamn killings. Pardon my language. I don't mean to lash out at everyone.'

'We have something for you that might help,' Day said. 'It's why I asked you round here.'

'What's that?'

Day reached into the pocket of his waistcoat and produced a folded piece of paper. He laid it on the table and carefully flattened it out before sliding it across to Tiffany.

'Who's this?'

'It's your killer,' Day said. 'It's the Harvest Man. What you wanted from your witness last night, a description of him, I was here getting from the previous witnesses. Or, rather, Fiona Kingsley was getting it from them.' He caught the proprietor's eye again and held up a finger.

'The previous witnesses,' Tiffany said. 'The children, you mean? They drew this?'

'Fiona Kingsley drew it.'

'That's Kingsley's little girl?'

'I wouldn't say she's a little girl,' Hammersmith said.

'But that's the one, right? You're saying the children told her what to draw?'

'Exactly right,' Day said. 'They described him to her.'

'They saw him?'

'He lifted his mask, his plague mask. He thought they were sleeping. He put a cloth with something on it on their pillow. They say it smelled bad. I think it was probably ether. That would fit with what we know about his methods. Anyway, he apparently thought it would keep them from waking while he did his business on their parents, but it was weak and didn't work. Maybe it was even the same cloth he'd already used on the parents.'

'And they saw him,' Tiffany said. His voice had changed from incredulity to triumph.

'And they described him,' Day said. A shot glass was set in front of him and was almost immediately emptied. Day's cheeks had begun to tighten, as if pulled back along the contours of his skull, and he felt focused.

'How good is the doctor's daughter? How accurate do we think this is?'

Day noted the use of the plural *we*. Tiffany had suddenly accepted them as his equals. Or he had joined them as one.

'She's very good,' Hammersmith said.

'Yes,' Day said. 'I've seen her draw from life and it's amazing work. Of course, in this case, she couldn't see the thing for herself, but we watched her at work and I think she got all the right answers from the boys. It's the next best thing to seeing the bastard ourselves. I'd suggest showing this to your witness.'

'I will,' Tiffany said. 'I may need to borrow your artist if Hatty Pitt sees anything here that ought to be changed.'

'Fiona's had a busy night. Nevil and I asked her to relay an important message for us to her father, and it would be good if she were able to sleep as much as she needs, but she'll no doubt return at some point to be with Claire across the park. Here . . .' Day took the illustration of the Harvest Man from Tiffany, turned it over and scribbled an address, then shoved it back across the table. 'My father-in-law's address. The children are there, too, but . . .'

'Hopefully, I won't need to bother with the children,' Tiffany said. 'Sounds like they've had a rough time of it lately.' He rose and pushed his chair back. 'Thank you for this.' He held up the drawing and nodded as if to himself, his eyes far away. He appeared ready to say something else, but then changed his mind, turned and stalked out of the tavern without a backward glance.

'I wish you'd kept that,' Hammersmith said. 'The picture, I mean.'

'Why?'

'I'd like to help look for the Harvest Man, of course.'

'Don't you have enough to do, Nevil?'

'I'm at an impasse. The cufflink was my only clue and it led to Alan Ridgway, not Jack. That wasn't Jack.'

'I know it wasn't.'

'It was a false clue.'

Day wasn't so sure. Alan Ridgway had been sent with a message for Day. The cufflink had been left in the alley for Hammersmith to find. Day was certain of it. They were being manipulated, toyed with, and Day felt cold panic in his gut. He had no idea what Jack was playing at, or why. Or when that monster would strike next.

'There's a hundred constables combing through every bit of shrubbery for the Harvest Man,' Day said.

'Only a hundred? Then they could use one more man, couldn't they?'

Day smiled and reached back into his pocket. 'Or perhaps two more men. What do you say to this?'

He produced another piece of paper and unfolded it. The shrewish features of the Harvest Man stared out at them.

'Fiona used carbon paper,' Day said.

41

Kingsley paused outside the Whistle and Flute and mustered his resolve. He had much to do today and there really wasn't time for this particular errand. But if what Hammersmith had told him was true – and he didn't doubt it; Nevil Hammersmith was among the most straightforward and guileless people Kingsley had ever known – this was important, too. He wondered where Henry was. The giant would be a comforting presence this morning, but Kingsley's assistant had not shown up at the office. The doctor assumed he was with Day and his family or perhaps somewhere with Hammersmith. It wasn't like him, though, to be absent without leaving some token, a message with a nurse or a student.

Kingsley focused his attention on the sign above him while he lit his pipe. The faded and peeling sign showed the two musical instruments crossed over the front of a suit of armour. An optimistic twist on the Cockney rhyming slang for the word *suit*. His first match sputtered out before the pipe was lit and Kingsley snuffed it between his fingers. It took two more matches to get the thing going. He deposited the spent matches in his pocket and found the letter Nevil had given him, then he stepped forward and pushed the front door open.

Although the pub was apparently open for business, it was not bustling with clientele. Kingsley was certain the door only remained unlocked so that the unsavoury people who used the place as an office could have free access. There was a barmaid hard at work cleaning chairs and tables, or at least circulating the dirt on them with the use of a filthy rag. She looked up at him with a scowl. He waved her off and she went back to her ineffectual occupation with a shrug. The only other person in the room was a sinister-looking man in the far corner, reading a newspaper in the shadows. It probably wasn't good for his eyes, but Kingsley decided he'd keep that advice to himself. The man didn't look like he much cared.

Kingsley made his way over to the man and stood at the table until he put his newspaper down and looked up.

'Yer in the wrong place, mate,' the man said. 'Move along.'

'Do you, by chance, go by the name Blackleg?'

'Aye. I do.'

'Here.' Kingsley held out Hammersmith's letter of introduction and Blackleg took it. He looked it over and tossed the letter on the table. It landed atop the abandoned newspaper. He pushed out a chair with his foot and Kingsley sat across from him.

'Your friend Hammersmith presumes an awful lot,' Blackleg said. But he was chuckling, a broad smile only partially hidden behind his bushy black beard.

'I'm offering my services,' Kingsley said. He puffed on his pipe. 'Take them or don't, I have other things I ought to be doing right now. I have the body of a murderer on my table. I have a victim, a separate victim, the subject of some other murder entirely, whose face has been peeled off. He's on another table. I have the corpses of two retired Scotland Yard inspectors to look at. One killed himself in prison. I'm told he swallowed his tongue. The other was stabbed to death on the front steps of my good friend's home. For his sake, I'd like to get to that one first. Besides all that, I have three bodies dredged up by the river police in the night, a child strangled in Coventry, and a woman who was crushed and then ripped in two when she fell off the dock in the path of an arriving skiff that scraped her along the pilings. I have a very busy morning ahead of me. So make no mistake, this is a favour I'm doing for Mr Hammersmith, not for you.'

Blackleg sat back and regarded Kingsley for a long moment while smoke wreathed the doctor's head, then he nodded and leaned forward, clasping his hands on the table.

'Would you have a drink with me?'

'No, thank you,' Kingsley said. 'As I said, I'm in rather a hurry this morning. I have –'

'Things to do, aye. Heard that. Our mutual friend says you're a doctor.' He glanced at the letter next to his folded hands. 'So answer me this: Why didn't he send the police? Why a doctor?'

'What would the police do in a case like this?'

'I 'spect they'd take the bodies of my friends away from me and stick 'em in some mass paupers' grave.'

'Yes, that's exactly what they'd do. If they didn't bring them first to me for my analysis.'

'I don't want that to happen. The paupers' grave or you pokin' round their innards. I don't like it.'

'And our friend Mr Hammersmith knows that. That's why he sent me here, instead of them.'

'You're better'n 'em?'

'No. But I don't bury people in mass graves. And I don't perform unnecessary autopsies. Our friend knows that.'

'He's a good chappie, that Hammersmith.'

'I'm fond of him myself.'

'So what do you plan to do, then?'

'I'll tell you what I'd ordinarily do,' Kingsley said. 'Under other circumstances, I would bring a large number of policemen with me and I would remove from you the bodies Mr Hammersmith claims you have in your possession, whether you liked it or not, and as far as I'm concerned you could go to hell. You are a criminal and I don't owe you a thing. But I owe the dead some justice.'

Blackleg stared at him, his eyes hot and angry under a jutting brow. His single eyebrow stretched across his forehead, highlighting a purple vein that throbbed at his temple. Finally, he threw his head back and laughed. Kingsley jumped in his seat and looked around, but the barmaid didn't react in any way. She was obviously used to Blackleg's theatrics. Kingsley sat back and concentrated on keeping his pipe lit.

'You're all right,' Blackleg said at last. 'Got a bit o' pluck. I like that.'

'I'm thrilled.'

'So that's what you would do. In other circumstances, like you say. But what do you actually plan to do?'

'The murderer is caught,' Kingsley said. 'And killed.'

Blackleg leaned back. The chair groaned under his weight. 'Killed?'

'Last night. Our Mr Hammersmith and Inspector Day –'

'I know 'bout him. He's friends with Hammersmith.'

'Yes. And my friend as well. And between them, they've dispatched the man who killed your friends. The three women you've got underground somewhere. That's the murderer I told you I have on my table right now. His name was Alan Ridgway.'

'Killed 'im.' It wasn't a question. 'Shot, stabbed, beat? What was it?'

'Shot. Day's bullet seems to have flattened against the villain's skull and travelled round his scalp under the skin. It lodged between his eyes. He bled to death fairly slowly, all things considered.'

'Serves the bloody bastard right, too. How'd our boy Hammersmith find him? He's a detective, he is. Or he would be if they recognized him right.'

'Actually, neither Mr Hammersmith nor Inspector Day needed to find him. He stalked them to a private residence and attempted to stab them. Nobody seems to know what his ultimate objective was.'

'Ultimate objective was being a nutter.'

'Be that as it may. The man who killed your friends is now dead. There is no investigation. There is no interest in the corpses you've kept preserved. And I might add that if you'd turned them over as you should have, maybe one or more of them would still be alive. I might have found some clue to his identity on their bodies. We could have caught him earlier.' Blackleg stared at him. The vein throbbed harder. Kingsley cleared his throat. 'But I promised Nevil I wouldn't delve into that particular line of accusation. I apologize, Mr Blackleg.'

'No. No, you're right. I should've given 'em over. But folks down here don't always get proper consideration.'

'I would have given them the same consideration I give everyone.'

'Maybe you would have at that.'

'It doesn't matter now. Justice has been served.'

'I'd like to know why he done it. What'd he have against them ladies? What'd they do to him?'

'I doubt very much they did anything to him. It probably had nothing to do with them. At least, not specifically. Tell me, have you heard of Gilles de Rais?'

'Frenchman. Murdered little children, didn't he?'

'Exactly right. He may have murdered scores of children, and for no greater reason than that killing them gave him satisfaction. That was centuries ago, Mr Blackleg. Creatures like that have no doubt prowled amongst us since the moment we dragged our primitive bodies from the surf. The likes of this Ridgway monster have always preyed on the innocent and the vulnerable. They pretend to be human beings, and they certainly look like us, but they take their pleasure from hurting others.'

'If that's the only way to get pleasure, a man like that'd be better jumping off the nearest bridge soon's he could walk there.'

'I think so, too. No one will grieve for Alan Ridgway.'

They sat for a moment. Kingsley puffed on his pipe. Blackleg reread the letter from Hammersmith. Both of them contemplated the human condition from opposite ends of the table. At last, Blackleg nodded and looked up at the doctor.

'Tell me what you plan to do with Little Betty and the others.'

'I have a private plot of land, Mr Blackleg. It is not a large property, by any means, but it was given to me, or rather to the hospital, to bury certain bodies we use in our studies. It is consecrated land and I would see your friends buried well.'

'You'd do that for me?'

'No. I would do that for Mr Hammersmith, and for my daughter, who brought this letter from him to me, and I would do that for the three women Alan Ridgway so cruelly used.'

'That's good enough for me, then. Come. I'll show you where they are.'

'Oh, I don't need to see where they are. I'll send people round to meet you and you can take them to the bodies. I'll make the arrangements.'

'No policemen. If it's rozzers you're sending round, they won't find me. I'll be gone.'

'I won't send the police. I'll send my assistant with some students from my hospital. They'll be discreet.'

'Send Hammersmith, too. I'd like to thank him myself.'

'I'll tell him so when I see him next.'

Both men stood and shook hands. Kingsley sidestepped the surly barmaid and hurried back to the street. He tapped his pipe out on the side of the building, took a deep breath of damp air and hailed a two-wheeler as it passed.

He fervently hoped Henry was already waiting for him at the office.

42

Henry woke and opened his eyes. Then he reached up and felt his face to make sure his eyes really were open. He was surrounded by pitch-black nothing. He could smell metal and dirt, thick in his nostrils, and somewhere behind the grit he could smell water. He got his hands under him and pushed and stood up, unsteady as the room rocked around him. His left arm was asleep and pinpricks ran up and down from his shoulder to his wrist. He flexed his arm and twisted his wrist, waiting for the tingling sensation to pass.

'Hullo,' he said. His voice came back to him in tinny echoes, deeper than he thought his voice really was, and he knew he was alone. And he knew that the room was very small.

He did not remember coming to this place. He didn't remember anything after closing the door to his little lamppost house and curling up to sleep. He had no idea how he might have come to be in yet another tiny room, but he knew he must be far away from Trafalgar Square.

When his head was clear and his arm felt normal again, he shuffled forward, his hands in front of him, patting the air to keep from running into a wall. He found a wall three steps away and turned to his right, felt along the wall until he came to a corner and turned right again. Nothing impeded his progress; there was nothing to trip over. He encountered the next corner and turned right again. Almost immediately, he came upon a metal doorway with bars that ran across it from side to side. He tested the bars, pushed back and forth, but they didn't budge. He felt for a knob or a key, and found a small flat plate joining the door to the wall beside it. He moved across and felt up and down, found the hinges holding the door. The whole thing seemed solid and locked and impassable. He moved on.

He went round and round the little cell without finding another way in or out.

'Hullo,' he said again.

When there was no answer, he sat down with his back against the wall opposite the barred door. He crossed his arms over his chest and put his head down and went back to sleep.

There was nothing else he could think to do until his captor revealed himself.

43

The police were combing the West End for the Harvest Man, but James Tiffany headed south instead, to 7 Great Scotland Yard and the stables of the Metropolitan Police. He chose a fine chestnut named Molly with a white blaze across her face and one blue eye, and the groom saddled her for him.

Tiffany mounted the horse and trotted her round the yard, getting a feel for the way she responded, then urged her forward past the ranks of police carriages and out on to Whitehall.

He had been an excellent rider in his youth, but it had been years since Tiffany had been on a horse. He and Molly took a few minutes to get used to each other. By the time they reached Trafalgar Square, Tiffany was riding easy, flexing his legs to counter the horse's rhythms. He urged Molly clockwise around Regent Circus and out on to wide Oxford Street, passing pedestrians and wagons at a steady clip. He had to keep one hand on his hat to keep it from flying off, and as he passed an omnibus the passengers inside goggled at him, unused to seeing a horse and rider in city traffic. He kept his head down, but tipped his hat at them, feeling a bit like a cowboy in an American novel.

They passed Hyde Park and the horse was working up a fine sweat, clearly enjoying the opportunity to run hard.

Tiffany turned his attention back to the investigation. Much as he hated to admit it, Inspector Day had hit on an important clue. Tiffany let go of the reins and patted the front of his waistcoat to make sure he still had the drawing of the Harvest Man in his pocket.

He stopped first at the latest murder scene, John Charles Pitt's home, and implemented some of Kingsley's new ideas about preserving the integrity of the place, but he didn't stay long. He showed Fiona's sketch of the murderer to Constable Bentley before jumping back on the horse and galloping away. He had a lot of ground to cover.

Sergeant Kett was coordinating the manhunt from the Yard and had posted policemen strategically throughout the neighbourhood. It took some time for Tiffany to make contact with them all. The route, which would have taken him the entire day on foot or even in a carriage, now sped by him, a blur of houses and trees, of children playing on footpaths and chasing each other across gardens. Tiffany stopped and talked to every man he saw along the way, but he stayed up on the horse while he did so. He leaned down again and again to show the illustration of the killer and he hoped they would recognize the man's features if they saw him on the street.

The Harvest Man had been flushed and Tiffany was determined to run him to ground before he could find a new place to hide, before night fell and some ill-fated couple went to bed for the last time.

Constable John Jones was patrolling Monmouth Road, going from door to door, checking window locks and exploring attics, when Tiffany caught up to him and gave him the sketch to look at.

Jones's mouth fell open and he stared up at the inspector. 'I saw him,' Jones said. 'I mean, I *just* saw him, not five minutes ago.'

'Where?'

'Here. Right here on Monmouth. He's odd-looking, has a funny ear, but he wasn't acting suspicious. Walked like he had something to do, in a hurry, not like he was looking at the houses, you know?'

'But which way did he go?'

Jones pointed south and Tiffany turned the horse around, used his heels to nudge her sides. He was excited. They had him. Molly whinnied and bolted down the street and Tiffany's hat finally left his head, sailing away behind them and fetching up against the curb.

Leinster Square loomed ahead, with its tall iron fences, dense growth sucking every bit of sunlight from the street. Tiffany rode along the outside of the fence until he reached a gate that led to a wide path through the square. He slowed Molly down and took her into the trees at a canter. He watched both sides of the path, turning left and right in the saddle, hoping to spot movement or a shadow that didn't belong.

He rode out at the opposite end and shook his head. Nothing. He dismounted and examined the soft earth at the edge of the path. There was a single boot print, but it was impossible to tell exactly how long it had been there. He stood, keeping hold of Molly's reins, and scanned the cobblestones. Ahead of him was Princes Square, smaller than Leinster, but a man could easily lose pursuit there, cutting across to any street beyond. To his right and farther away was Pembridge Square, and beyond it Ladbroke. To his left was Kensington Gardens Square. The Harvest Man could have gone in any direction, cut through vegetation anywhere and doubled back, leaving no trail to follow. Or he might even still be somewhere behind Tiffany, hiding in the thick greenery of Leinster.

Constable Jones came up behind him, breathing hard. He handed Tiffany his hat.

'You're sure it was him?'

Jones held up a finger and caught his breath before speaking. 'Sure of it. Matches that picture you showed me. Only difference is that ear of his.'

'You said it was odd?'

'Twisted like,' Jones said. 'Burned or torn, maybe, but a long time ago.'

'That ought to help us pick him out of a crowd.'

'No question of it.'

'Well, we've lost him for now. Or he's lost us. Still, he's nearby. He can't be far.'

Jones looked over the landscape, clearly reaching the same hopeless conclusions Tiffany had. 'He might be anywhere, sir.'

'He's close by. And we know what he looks like now. He can't travel easily, so he's got to take cover. Jones, I want everyone pulled in and stationed at every corner throughout this area.'

'That'll take some time.'

'Take the horse.' Tiffany handed the reins to Jones. 'Round everyone up and pull them into a tighter perimeter. And send a runner to Kett at the Yard. Get more men.'

'What are you going to do?'

'I'm going to protect our witness. Once we catch this bastard, we're gonna need her to identify him. For all we know, he might still be after her.'

'Aye, sir.'

Jones launched himself up and got a leg over the horse's back. Molly snorted and pawed the ground. Jones dug in his heels and they galloped away. Tiffany turned and entered the square. He walked slowly, watching the trees and underbrush, hoping for a glimpse of the killer. He balled his hands into fists. He'd almost caught him. He knew it. There wasn't much daylight left, but he'd be damned if another day dawned with the Harvest Man still at large.

He shouted at the tops of the trees as he walked. 'Can you hear me? I'm going to find you. This is the last time you'll ever see the sun!'

44

Leland Carlyle had to eat his plate of eggs standing up against a wall in the kitchen. Afterwards, he wandered into his rented parlour in a daze, the previous evening's newspaper tucked under his arm. He preferred privacy in the morning, but so far had been unable to find a room that wasn't already filled with people. He had opened his door for his daughter because he loved her, and for her babies because, well, they were babies and couldn't fend for themselves. His son-in-law had come along with Claire and the twins, which was to be expected, but the Day family had also brought with them an entire collection of hangers-on who had been in and out of the place all night long and all morning: an earnest young girl, a former policeman who didn't seem able to dress himself properly, those members of the new staff who hadn't been shunted off to the local inn, a couple of little boys who were always in whatever chair Leland chose for himself.

He had given up trying to remember everyone's names.

Fortunately, he had received good news from his solicitor. A house had just come open in Clapham. It was the right size and the price was acceptable. Leland was prepared to make an immediate offer. With any luck, he'd be able to pack Claire and her entire retinue off to a safe new home within the fortnight. Then he planned to sit wherever he liked and read the paper in relative peace.

Maybe Claire would even take Eleanor with her when she moved out. But that would be too much to hope for.

As expected, the two little boys were occupying the big armchair this morning. He hesitated in the doorway. He didn't want to wake them up, but he didn't know where else to go. There was no other room where someone wasn't asleep. The boys' dirty bare feet stuck out from beneath a throw: tiny pink toes, mud caked under their ankles. Leland was reminded of Claire as a child, always trekking in mud from the fields. He felt a swell of nostalgia for his daughter, for when she had belonged only to him, and he smiled. All she'd needed was the illusion of a simple life, the privilege of pleasant ignorance. She had been a happy child, strong and confident, and he was proud of the woman she had become. Even if he didn't understand all the choices she had made.

The boys woke up then and they both looked at him. Leland grimaced at them and took a step backwards.

'Hullo, Mr Day,' the smallest one said.

'Yes, hello,' Leland said. 'You're David, right? And Peter?'

'I'm Robert, sir,' the bigger one said. 'And this is Simon.'

'Ah. Well, I'm Mr Carlyle. Not Mr Day.'

'Sorry, sir.'

'Quite all right.' Though it was not, of course, all right. Leland did not want to be confused, even by children, with his son-in-law. He nodded at them and gave what he hoped was a reassuring smile. He didn't remember why they were in his house, why Claire had taken them under her wing, but it seemed to him something awful had happened to them.

'Did you sleep well?'

The boys both nodded at him, but their eyes were ringed with deep purple bruises. It was clear to him that their sleep had been interrupted by nightmares and that they had been crying.

'Glad to hear it,' he said. 'Well, I'll be off, then. I expect you'll want something to eat. No hurry, though. Cook's in the kitchen preparing breakfasts one at a time, as everybody wakes up. It's an unusual morning.'

'Are you eating breakfast now, Mr Carlyle?'

'Me? No. No, I'm off to look at a house. Thought I'd relax for a minute first, but it's clear that won't happen. I'd better get this taken care of.'

'Do you mend houses?' This from the small one, Simon.

'Oh my, no. I'm going to invest in a house for my daughter.' *And*, he thought, *try to sell off the house at 184 Regent's Park Road.* God willing, he might even turn a profit. Eventually.

'Mrs Day is going to move to the house you're going to now?'

'I certainly hope so.'

'Will we go with her?'

'Hush, Simon,' Robert said.

'Um,' Leland said. 'I really don't know.' He doubted it very much. As far as he could recollect, these boys were destined for the orphanage. But it wasn't his place to break the news. Why ruin their morning before they'd even had their eggs and sausages?

'It will have to be a big house,' Simon said. 'If we're to go with her.'

'I'm sure the house will be big enough.'

'Have you seen it? Does it have a garden?'

'I haven't seen it,' Leland said. 'I've just been told about it.'

'It doesn't matter anyway,' Robert said. 'It doesn't matter if it has a garden or not. Be quiet now, Simon.'

Leland could see anger and shame in Robert's eyes. The boy knew his fate, even if his brother did not. Leland looked away from the older boy's steady gaze and he recalled once more his daughter at their age. These boys had lost every chance to enjoy that pleasant ignorance all children needed.

'I'm sure it does have a garden, Simon,' Leland said. 'And it's near quite a lot of wide-open spaces. It's just the place for children to run and play, if my solicitor is to be believed.'

Robert threw the cover off them and scooted forward in the chair, stood up and turned his back on Leland. Clearly, he felt Leland was teasing them. And Leland knew that he was, but he couldn't help himself. He couldn't bring himself to shatter Simon's daydreams. The boy needed something to cling to.

Leland spoke again without thinking and he immediately regretted it. 'Would you like to come along and see the house?'

Robert turned around. A deep frown creased his face. 'Why?'

'To see if you like it. I could use your advice.'

'Yes,' Simon said. 'We'd very much like to see it, Mr Carlyle.'

Robert turned his frown on his brother, but didn't hush him this time.

'Good,' Leland said. 'Then it's settled. Get yourselves dressed and go eat something.'

'You'll wait for us?'

'I'll wait thirty minutes. No more, no less, so don't dawdle.'

'Yes, sir.' Simon jumped down off the chair and ran from the room. He smiled at Leland as he passed him in the doorway. Robert followed more slowly and did not even look at Leland. But the frown had begun to fade from his face, even if the deep furrows of worry were still etched across his forehead.

Leland went to the chair and sat. It was still warm. He opened his newspaper, but didn't read. He couldn't concentrate on the words. He had felt the need to be kind to those poor orphaned children and had given them a sense of hope, but he knew hope was a cruel gift. In the end, Robert and Simon no longer belonged anywhere with anyone and they were destined for many disappointments.

The eggs he had eaten no longer seemed to be agreeing with him.

45

Constable Bentley stood guard outside the house where the Harvest Man had killed John Charles Pitt. He nodded at Day as they approached, but ignored Hammersmith. A length of rope was strung from one side of the open garden gate to the other. A small hand-lettered sign hung from the centre of the rope.

'Bentley,' Day said. 'What's this?'

'Tiffany put it there, sir. Something new. Keeps the riff-raff out.'

'The riff-raff?' Day bent and peered at the little sign. It read: POLICE BISINES. KEP OUT. 'What kind of riff-raff?'

'Keeps boot prints and the like from ruining things before the doctor can come have a look at the place.'

'Hasn't Dr Kingsley been here yet?'

'Came and went. Had the body took out already, but said he had other business to take care of. He'll be back, though. And when he does come back . . .' Bentley pointed at the sign. 'Everything will be just like he left it.'

'Is anyone in there now? Did Tiffany beat us here?'

'He was here a few minutes ago. Showed me a drawing. Said it's the Harvest Man hisself. But then he went off again to show the thing to everybody else so they can keep their eyes peeled. If the picture really does look like him.'

'We'll find out if it does when we catch him.'

'Damn right,' Bentley said. 'Anyway, this place is empty right now.'

'Which way did Tiffany go? We'd like to help with the hunt.'

'Not sure. Guessing he's gonna want to check on the witness now she's out of hospital?'

'Where is she?'

Bentley waved his hand in a loose circle. 'Nearby somewhere. Can't miss the place. There's a scary sad face right on the front.'

'A face?'

'Sculpture, like,' Bentley said. 'Art or something, I suppose.'

Day looked at Hammersmith and shrugged. Hammersmith shook his head.

'I think I'd like to have a look inside anyway,' Day said. 'Only take a moment, but we'll have to remove your rope to get in there.' He pointed at his leg, which made jumping over the rope or ducking under it impossible.

''At's all right,' Bentley said. 'I'll put it back up. You can go on in, Inspector. But you . . .' He pointed at Hammersmith. 'You ain't a sergeant no more. You ain't nuthin'. You stay here with me while he goes in.'

'He's with me,' Day said.

'Tiffany's orders. You'd have to take it up with him. I just do as I'm told. And I'm told nobody gets in what doesn't belong.'

Hammersmith put a hand on Day's arm and shook his head. 'I don't need to see it,' he said. 'And Bentley's right, I've got no reason to be here any more. You go ahead and I'll wait.'

'I don't suppose I need to see it, either,' Day said. 'There's nobody in there to talk to. The only evidence right now is for Dr Kingsley to see, not me.'

'Might be something anyway.'

Day nodded, tired. It was easier to take a look at the place than discuss it any further. Bentley lifted the rope and Day limped up the garden path and into the house. It was dim inside and quiet. Day stepped carefully around a pattern of small red dots that led to the door from the hallway. Blood. There was some of it on the stairs as well, but Day didn't particularly feel like dealing with steps. Instead he followed the trail to where it ended in a small congealing pool halfway down the hall. A curved knife lay against the skirting. There was a boot print at the edge of the puddle of blood, but judging by what Bentley had said, Day guessed it was the Harvest Man's boot, not that of a policeman or witness. That rope at the garden gate was simplicity itself, and it might actually come in handy for weeding out the actual clues from the detritus of investigation.

A small brown ball rested in the corner between the floor and the wall. It was misshapen and surrounded by crumbs. Day squinted at it and got down on his knees to sniff it. It smelled sweet. If he had to guess, he'd say it was a gob of chewed-up chocolate biscuit. He pulled himself up to his feet again, leaning on his new cane, and made his way along the back half of the passage to the kitchen. Sure enough, there was a tray half full of biscuits in the centre of the table. There were two place settings and two of the chairs had been moved. One was on its back wedged against a cabinet behind it, the other had been pulled out into the room. Day could see traces of blood in the seat of the second chair. The plate that appeared to have corresponded to that chair held a single uneaten biscuit. The plate across from it was empty except for a ring of crumbs on and around it. Dried chunks of mud littered the floor under the table on that side. A plague mask rested against the leg of the table, propped up on its long beak, its leather straps hanging loose.

Day wondered what Tiffany had made of the scene. He guessed the Harvest Man had been sitting eating biscuits. This was apparently the creature's custom, killing a married couple, then living with their corpses for a day or two, eating with them before moving on. Day imagined the parody of family life being lived out in those sad empty houses and he shuddered. So the killer had sat across from his victim, but then had stood up in a hurry. It was possible the person across from him at the table had still been alive, had tried to escape, and the Harvest Man had reacted quickly. But that didn't quite fit what they knew about his methods. Inspector Tiffany had a witness somewhere, so it was most likely that person had stumbled across the scene in the kitchen and had run off. The Harvest Man had stood up in a hurry, knocking over his chair. Day looked at the upended chair, then turned and peered down the long hallway, at the wad of chewed-up biscuit and the blood trail. Whoever the witness was, she was lucky to be alive.

The victim had been carted off to Kingsley's laboratory, but Day doubted the doctor would discover anything they didn't already know. He contemplated the long climb to the attic, but dismissed the thought immediately. Any evidence up there would have been discovered by Tiffany and his men, and Day's leg had had enough already.

He bent and picked up the plague mask. Was there another reason the Harvest Man wore it, something beyond protecting himself from ether fumes? Day put the mask up to his face and snorted, pulled it back away. An assertive stench of old sweat and body odour had permeated the leather and become part of the thing. Day shook his head and blew air out through his nose, then took a deep breath through his mouth and held it. He put the mask on again and looked around the kitchen through the scratched and dirty lenses. Everything was overlaid with a brownish tint when viewed through the goggles: the sepia tones of a photograph. Day was reminded of the pictures of dead relatives that some families kept on their mantels. This was how the Harvest Man saw the world around him. Dead relatives, dead couples. Dead mothers and fathers across the kitchen table. Sad family meals and silent brown acceptance.

He pulled the mask off and breathed heavily, took out his flask and poured brandy into his open mouth, let it dribble off his chin and splash on the floor, let the scent of it waft up his nostrils.

He put the flask away and limped back down the passage – deep in thought but still careful to avoid the blood trail – and out of the house to where Hammersmith waited.

'He won't have gone far,' Day said when the rope at the garden gate had been lifted and replaced. 'He's left his mask.'

'Will he come back for it?'

'I don't think so, Nevil. But I do think this whole thing is about masks. It's about changing identity. Cutting these people up the way he does, he's putting masks on them. Or maybe taking them off. I don't know which. But I think he only feels he's himself when he's wearing a mask. So he can pass for a human being on the street, but I don't think he'll kill again unless he finds something else to put over his face, to hide himself from the people he's hurting and killing.'

'Right, he disguises himself so he can sneak up on people,' Hammersmith said.

'More to it than that, I think. He doesn't need to sneak up on anyone. He's already waiting until they're asleep. No, he wants to reveal himself, but he's afraid. Or he's waiting to do it. Whatever he needs from his victims, he's been frustrated every time so far. He doesn't want them to see his features until he's ready. He took off the mask in here, but he had it nearby. I think he was just eating at the table, not trying to play out the final act of whatever drama he thinks he's a part of.'

'Why do these people, these murderers, have to be so complicated? I long for the days when women killed their husbands for stepping out on them, and brothers killed each other for a little extra pocket money. Those are crimes I can at least understand.'

'There are still plenty of those, but they don't need us for them. Even Bentley could solve a murder like that.'

'Hey!'

'My apologies, Constable Bentley,' Day said. 'I thought you were out of earshot.'

'I heard my name. Don't suppose you had something nice to say.'

'I was only telling Mr Hammersmith that you're very good at the basics of your job.'

'Very well, then,' Bentley said. He went back to leaning against the gate and regarding his fingernails, which were apparently long enough for him to bite off.

Hammersmith chuckled. 'So where would our nutter get a new mask?'

'Any shops that might sell them would be located many streets over, too far for a fugitive to safely travel. So he would look for a mask inside a house. But who would own a mask and have it near to hand?' When the answer came to Day, he reacted physically, as if he'd been struck by an electric current. 'Tableau vivant!'

'Playacting?'

'Of course,' Day said. 'If this is a typical neighbourhood, there may be one house that acts as the centre for the evenings' entertainment. The people there would have costumes and some sort of crude stage, perhaps. And they would have masks.'

'Then to find him, we only have to find that house,' Hammersmith said. 'If we wait there, he'll come to us. Let's have another look at him.'

Day found the drawing Fiona had made for them. He held it out so that both of them could examine it.

'He's a queer one,' Hammersmith said. 'Ought to be easy to spot.'

'He's not gone far yet. He may be watching us right now.'

Alarmed, Hammersmith looked all around, at the shrubbery and the fences, the sun-dappled corners of the gardens that surrounded them. 'If so, he could be anywhere.'

Day looked up at the attic window. He imagined a sad little boy with a long beak gazing back at him through the faraway glass. Something nagged at him, soft lips brushing against his memory.

A black dot separated itself from the sky above the house and grew larger, came into focus. A bird swooped down and flew at Day. He started to duck, but the bird curved around behind him and landed on his shoulder, its claws digging into him through the fabric of his jacket.

'Oliver?'

'That is Oliver,' Hammersmith said. 'What's he doing here?'

The duotone bird swivelled its head, looking back and forth between Day and Hammersmith. It flapped its wings and dug its talons deeper into Day's flesh and squawked at Hammersmith, lowering its head and thrusting out its beak as if the former sergeant were prey.

'He's upset,' Day said. 'Something's got him agitated.'

'He's a mess,' Hammersmith said. 'Look how ruffled he is.'

'Perhaps he's lost.'

'Or Henry's nearby.'

'Where's Henry, Oliver?'

The bird screeched and flapped upwards, then settled back down. Day noticed that Oliver's talons had torn two small holes in his jacket. Claire was going to be unhappy with him when he got home.

'Is Henry in trouble?'

The bird shook itself. It sat for a moment, preening its feathers, then it beat its wings and took off. It flew back over the murder house, looped once around and was gone.

'Crazy bird,' Constable Bentley said.

'Something's wrong,' Day said. 'I'm worried about Henry.'

'What do you want to do?'

'We can't abandon the search for the Harvest Man right now.' Day was certain he'd been on the verge of an idea before Oliver had interrupted his train of thought. 'We'll have to trust that Henry can take care of himself for a bit longer.'

'We don't even know that he's in any trouble,' Hammersmith said. 'He's a big man. It's hard to imagine anyone hurting him.'

'Yes, but he's like a child, really.' Day steeled himself and nodded. 'Still, you're right. I'm sure he must be all right, probably out looking for his bird right now. But let's find the Harvest Man quickly.'

'You say that like it's an easy thing. Everyone's been looking for him for weeks now with no luck.'

'But we haven't looked yet,' Day said. 'Our attention's been divided, hasn't it?'

'A bit, yes.'

'Well, now that Day and Hammersmith are on the job, the Harvest Man hasn't a chance.'

He smiled at his former sergeant, but his thoughts were still on the agitated magpie. What had happened? The sky was clear now, no sign of Oliver. He shook his head and did his best to put it out of his mind. After all, it was only a bird and Day was not a superstitious man. He gave Bentley a cursory wave of his hand and hobbled down the street after Hammersmith.

46

'Henry Mayhew.'

Henry woke up and looked around. There was still nothing to see. Only darkness in every direction. 'Who's there?'

'It doesn't matter who I am, Henry Mayhew. I suppose you could say I'm a friend.'

'Let me out of here,' Henry said.

'Of course. Let me find the door. I'm in the dark, too.'

'Did he take you, too?'

'Who? Who took us, Henry Mayhew?'

'Jack did.'

'Jack? He sounds like a delightful fellow already. Taking people on marvellous adventures.'

'No, he's bad. He kills people.'

'Ah. Then we must escape his clutches.'

'Before he comes back and kills us.'

'Where do you think he went, Henry Mayhew? Why do you think he's left you and me here alone?'

'Maybe he's gone to kill somebody else.'

'Oh, maybe he has. You know, I think I heard him talking about that. I think I heard him say who he was going to kill next.'

'Who was it? Was it me?'

'No, I think he said he was going to go and harm Walter Day's baby girls.'

'The babies!'

'No, wait. I'm mistaken. Not both of them. Just one. The smallest one. He said that one is his goddaughter.'

'Oh, my goodness. Winnie is smaller than Henrietta. Not very much, but a little bit smaller. It's because she was born second.'

'Yes, that's the very one I mean. Winnie.'

'We've got to do something.'

'Well, Henry Mayhew, I think it's clear what you have to do.'

'It is?'

'You've got to take the baby before Jack does.'

'Take the baby?'

'Yes. Why, I'll wager if you were to go and carry Winnie away, take her somewhere safe, somewhere far away from Walter Day's house, it would be just as if you had rescued her from Jack.'

'I don't think that would be nice. I think Mrs Day would be worried and she wouldn't want me to take Winnie away from her.'

'Well, then you mustn't tell the baby's mother. What you'll do, you'll go to Walter Day's home . . .'

'But nobody's at Mr Day's home right now. Everybody's scared because of Jack and the man who came and killed Mr Augustus.'

'Well, that was speedy. It took him long enough to clear out of there, but then he goes and does it overnight.'

'What?'

'Nothing. Where are they now, do you know?'

'They're safe now.'

'Yes, but where? It's very important to know where.'

'Mr and Mrs Day and the babies are at Mr and Mrs Car-lyle's house. That's Mrs Day's family. Only it's not really their house. They're staying there because of the babies and now they get to see them all the time, so it's very nice that they're there.'

'Why, that's not far at all.' The man laughed. 'That's just across the park from Walter Day's house.'

'That's how they got there so fast.'

'Yes, of course. Well, you must go there now, to this new house, and you'll take the baby away, you'll take Win-nie Day for her own good, and when everything is safe and when there's no danger any more, you'll bring her back to her mother.'

'And Mrs Day won't be angry with me?'

'Henry Mayhew, how could Mrs Day be angry with you? After all, you'll be the hero who saved her baby from big bad fearsome Jack.'

'The hero?'

'Exactly that, Henry Mayhew. You're a hero, you are.'

Henry heard a bolt drag across the metal plate in the wall across from him. A door scraped open and Henry pulled himself to his feet and staggered towards the rect-angle of sunlight. A moment later, he found himself on the foot deck of a bright-red narrowboat drifting along on a canal, green water lapping at the side of the boat under his feet, fresh air wafting into his nostrils. He recog-nized the bend in the waterway ahead. He was in Primrose Hill, just under Regent's Park Road.

'Remember, Henry Mayhew, you must move quickly or it will be too late for little Winnie Day.'

Henry turned, but saw no one. The high superstructure

prevented him from seeing the other side of the canal boat.

'Go, Henry Mayhew, go!'

Startled, Henry jumped into the water and swam for the footpath just a few feet ahead. He scrabbled against the stone wall and found an iron ring set into it, pulled himself up and grabbed a low-hanging tree branch. He hoisted himself out of the water and stood for a moment, getting his bearings, then ran as fast as he could towards the steps that would lead him up into the park.

47

'You'll do the pictures for it, won't you?'

Fiona looked at Claire, unsure how to answer. Finally, she cleared her throat and shook her head. 'That's not the sort of thing I usually draw.'

'But I know you can draw my poems,' Claire said. 'You drew such a perfect little doll.'

'It was a doodle. It was nothing.'

'You would rather draw dead bodies?'

'It's not a question of what I would rather draw.'

'Of course,' Claire said. 'I'm sorry. But look, you can still render bodies for your father and do this, too. Do both. I mean, I can't pay you. At least not at first. But I'm going to get them published, one way or another, and help Walter with the household income. Your illustrations would help so much.'

Fiona smiled and looked away. 'Oh, why not,' she said. 'It might be fun.'

Claire clapped her hands and threw her arms around Fiona.

'But, Claire, don't blame me if my doodles ruin your rhymes. People will think you've written a penny dreadful.'

'Oh, they will not.'

Fiona shook her head again, but she was secretly very pleased. In her head, she was already composing pictures of little boys and girls at play, kites straining against the sky, stuffed animals resting on counterpanes, apple trees being climbed and puppies chasing butterflies.

It all sounded so much more pleasant than the endless crime scenes and victims, damaged flesh, and lost dreams.

She was about to ask Claire what poem she should illustrate first, but was interrupted by the front door of the rented Carlyle house swinging open. It hit the wall behind it with a bang and Henry Mayhew, Henry the Giant, appeared framed in the doorway, dripping wet, his clothing plastered to him, his eyes wide and his hair webbed across his forehead.

'Henry,' Claire said, 'what's happened to you?' She rushed to him and pressed the back of her hand against his forehead as if he might have a fever. 'Did you fall in a puddle?'

He shrugged her off and shook his head. He was panting, unable to speak.

'More like the canal,' Claire said. 'Well, go upstairs and dry off. I'm sure we don't have anything that would suit you – Walter's clothes would fit you like a sausage casing – but you can at least get a bit more comfortable.'

Henry nodded, out of breath, still unable to talk. He went quickly to the stairs and up. Claire turned to Fiona with a bemused expression.

'I wonder what happened to him,' she said.

'I'm sure we'll find out when he's calmed down,' Fiona said.

Claire went to the door to close it, but Henry was already clomping back down the stairs. He had something in his arms, but he kept his back turned to them and rushed out of the house before Claire could react. Fiona went to the door and looked out, but Henry was already across the road and hurrying into the park.

'What did he have with him?'

'I don't know,' Claire said. 'He was in an awful hurry.'

'Stop him!' The governess was hurtling down the stairs, jumping down them three at a time, her ample frame bouncing. 'He's got one of the babies!'

Claire stood frozen at the threshold, uncomprehending. Then she snapped to and grabbed Fiona's arm, shock written across her features.

'Go back and stay with the other baby,' Fiona said to the governess. Then she took Claire's hand and they ran together to Regent's Park.

But Henry Mayhew had disappeared.

48

Day struggled to keep up with Hammersmith, who trotted up and down every street in the neighbourhood, knocking on doors. At each house, Nevil showed the drawing of the Harvest Man to housemaids and ladies and to the occasional businessman, cook or governess they encountered. Children opened two of the doors and Hammersmith tipped his hat to them and went on his way. Even the illustration of a murderer might be too much for a child's sensibilities.

But there was no sign of the Harvest Man anywhere.

Constable Jones passed them twice on horseback. The third time they saw him he stopped and greeted them. 'He's close. Tiffany almost caught him.'

'The Harvest Man?'

'Indeed. The very one. Lost sight of him in the square up there, but we're tightening the circle now. He's not getting away again. Here, there's a drawing of him. Take a look.'

'We've seen it,' Hammersmith said.

'Good. Then I'd better get back to it.' With that, Jones turned the horse around and hurtled down the street.

The constable's excitement was contagious. Day felt a surge of energy and he picked up speed, easily matching Hammersmith's pace for a while. They spent another two hours in the search, occasionally criss-crossing the routes of other policemen, but with no luck.

Exhausted and hungry, they turned along a side street, hoping to find a fish-and-chips shop, and Hammersmith grabbed Day's jacket at the elbow. He pointed. 'Look!'

A big house at the end of the street was decorated with columns in the front, and above the door was a gold-painted mask of a frowning human face.

'Like the tragedy mask at a theatre,' Day said.

'Bentley's scary face.'

Day nodded. 'We've found Tiffany's witness. But there's usually a smiling face, too. The happy half. It goes with the sad one. I've never seen just one by itself.'

'Comedy, tragedy. They've only got tragedy at this house.'

'Wonder why.'

'What say we go ask them,' Hammersmith said. 'It might help to show our drawing to the witness.'

Hammersmith moved slowly down the street so that Day could keep up. Day knew he was holding Hammersmith back and he felt conflicted. On the one hand, he appreciated his friend's quiet support. On the other, he wished Nevil would just get to the damn house and ring the bell.

At last they reached the end of the street and Hammersmith pulled the cord. They waited. Day looked around at the houses. They were only five streets over from the most recent murder scene, but here everything seemed quieter, more refined. Blanketed in high shrubbery and flower beds and the hanging branches of pink-blooming willows, the homes were slightly larger, and better kept up. And no doubt exponentially more expensive. Day turned back when the door opened. A gentleman wearing white gloves bade them enter and closed the door behind them. The ceiling of the entryway was vaulted and a chandelier hovered over them, reflecting a thousand beams of sunlight from a high window.

'Tell me,' Day said, looking up past the chandelier, 'this house doesn't have an attic, does it?'

'No, sir.'

'I thought not.'

The gentleman took their hats and their names and led them to an antechamber, where he left them. Day immediately sank into the cushions of a sofa, but Hammersmith paced back and forth examining the canvas portraits that hung along the walls at eye level, all depicting the same woman in different costumes. The inspector and his former sergeant didn't have to wait long. Two women bustled into the room before Hammersmith had a chance to get impatient.

Day stood and clasped his hands over the silver knob at the end of his cane. One of the women was tall and buxom, recognizable from the many paintings of her around the room. She wore too much rouge and a wig that framed her face in mahogany ringlets. The other woman was smaller and seemed content to hover in her companion's shadow. Her nose was bandaged and her eyes were ringed with purple bruises. She might have been Fiona Kingsley's age, perhaps a year or two older.

The taller woman spoke first. She filled the room with her voice. 'Have you caught him, then?'

'We're only here to ask a question or two, if you don't mind,' Day said. 'I hope we haven't inconvenienced you.'

'Oh, then you haven't caught him. Damn it all!'

Day had the distinct impression she was trying to shock them with her language. 'Caught who, ma'am?'

'Whoever it is that murdered John Charles. And almost murdered poor Hatty.' At this, she thrust the smaller woman out in front of her, displaying her like a recently acquired pet.

'You must be Hatty Pitt,' Day said. 'I'm very sorry for your loss.'

Hatty opened her mouth to speak, but the other woman interrupted. 'Yes, of course this is Hatty Pitt. And I'm Eugenia Merrilow, as if you didn't know.'

'I'm sorry to disturb you.' Day could feel Hammersmith beginning to boil behind him and hoped Nevil would remain silent. Tact wasn't one of his strengths. 'We're looking around the neighbourhood and only stopped here to ask a question, as I said. Though of course we're terribly honoured to finally meet you, Miss Merrilow.' He had no idea who she was, but it was clear she thought he should know.

His flattery had the desired affect. She softened visibly and sat down in an armchair across from the sofa. Day took it as an invitation and reclaimed his seat on the sofa. He rested his cane across his lap.

'Is that silver? The top of your cane, I mean.'

'Yes, it is.'

'It's lovely.'

'Thank you. A recent gift.'

While they spoke, Hatty Pitt remained by the door.

There was about her the aspect of some wild creature, poised to run. Day noted that, while she had recently been bathed and had her hair brushed, her eyes were bloodshot and her hands trembled.

'Well,' Eugenia Merrilow said, 'what was your question?'

'We're looking for the man who . . . Well, I'm sorry, Mrs Pitt . . .'

'We're looking for the man who killed your husband,' Hammersmith said.

Day winced. He watched the girl, waiting for her to bolt from the room, but she didn't move. Her eyes cleared and she nodded. She was made of stronger stuff than Day had imagined.

'I saw him,' she said.

'Will you . . . Do you think you might be able to talk about him?'

'I don't . . . I'll try.'

Day looked up at Hammersmith, who nodded back at him.

'Miss Merrilow,' Hammersmith said. 'You have a lovely home. Would you mind showing me about?'

'Oh, I'll have Pritchard show you.' She aimed her carefully maintained face at the door and shouted: 'Pritchard!'

Hatty winced at the loud noise.

'Actually, if you wouldn't mind,' Hammersmith said. 'I'd much rather you showed me.'

Eugenia Merrilow looked Hammersmith over. She turned and glanced at Hatty, and Day saw something hungry in her eyes. He could see her weighing flattery against curiosity, struggling to decide between the pretty young man and the unhappy girl.

'Well, I suppose I've already heard all about what happened to poor Hatty. But let's be quick about it.' She rose and went to the door, patted Hatty on the shoulder, then reached out her hand for Hammersmith to take. Instead, Nevil put his hands in his pockets and followed her out of the room.

When they were gone, Hatty left her post by the door. She came and sat across from Day. 'I can describe him for you, if you like,' she said. 'The monster.'

'Did you describe him for the other policemen? The ones who talked to you this morning?'

'I tried, but ... Oh, I've forgotten his name, the policeman.'

'It would have been Inspector Tiffany.'

'Yes, that's the one. I didn't like him very much. I'm sorry. The other one, there was another one ...'

'Perhaps Inspector Blacker?'

'Yes. He was nicer. Tried to brighten my spirits a bit with terrible jokes.'

'That's Blacker, all right.'

'They visited me in hospital. But I didn't want to talk and I couldn't think just then. I couldn't remember very much about the one who chased me and who killed ...'

'It's all right. We understand.'

'He was going to kill me, too.'

'Yes. You must be very fast, and very brave. Only three people have escaped this man so far.'

'Two others?'

'Two boys. They got away from him, just like you did. Which means he's not a monster at all. He's only a man, and men make mistakes. And we can catch him.'

'Are the boys all right?'

'Perfectly fine. They're at my home right now.' This was not entirely true. They were at the home of Leland and Eleanor Carlyle, but that was more detail than Hatty Pitt needed to hear.

'I remember some things about him,' Hatty said. 'I've been trying to remember, but it's hard. He was very fast and he was running and I was running too and it was all so . . .' She broke off and put her hand up to her mouth. Her eyes wandered away to the rug at her feet.

'Those boys,' Day said. 'The boys I told you about? They remembered what he looked like. They described him to an artist who works with the police and she drew him.'

'She? You mean there's a policeman who's a woman?'

'Oh, no, of course not. But she helps us sometimes. With certain things.'

'There should be, you know. There should be a policeman who's . . . well, a policewoman.'

Day didn't know what to say to that. The thought had never crossed his mind and he doubted the commissioner would ever consider such a thing, but he only smiled at the poor girl.

'Could I see the picture? The picture she drew,' Hatty said.

Day took out the drawing of the Harvest Man and unfolded it. He hesitated before handing it to Hatty, but she reached for it and took it from him. She sat staring at the piece of paper for a long time before handing it back to Day. She didn't look up at him, but continued to gaze down at her hands.

'That's him,' she said. 'It looks like him. But he has a . . .' She reached up and touched her ear. 'It's bent or chewed or something. His ear is.'

'That's interesting. Thank you, Hatty. That's quite helpful.'

'You're going to catch him, aren't you?'

'I don't know if I will, but if I don't, Inspector Tiffany will, or Inspector Blacker, or my friend Mr Hammersmith. He's not going to get away, Hatty. He can't any more. He's done too much and left too wide a trail for us to follow.'

'But he can still kill more people until you get him.'

Day looked away. She was right and he didn't want to lie to her. But when he looked back at her, she was smiling. It was a small sad smile, but it made Day think there was hope for her.

'I'm sorry,' she said. 'I know you're doing your best.'

'We are. I promise we are.'

'Do you think he's still somewhere nearby?'

'I have to think he is. He can't have gone far out in the open. He's used to hiding. Or at least going unnoticed. There are too many people out looking for him. His instinct would be to go to ground somewhere.'

'In someone's house, you mean.'

'I'm afraid so.'

'But not in this house?' She was tense again, looking around at the corners of the room.

'No,' Day said. 'Not in this house, I don't think. He likes attics and there isn't one here.'

She visibly relaxed.

'Tell me, though, there's a face above the door outside, on the front of this house. A sad face . . .'

'Tragedy. It's from the theatre. Eugenia puts on performances for all the neighbours. Though I don't know why she hung those ghastly faces, since she so rarely actually does a story. There's no comedy or drama, only still-life portraits.' She waved a dismissive hand in a circle at shoulder level, indicating the many canvas likenesses of Eugenia Merrilow hung around the room.

'At least no comedy,' Day said.

'What do you mean?'

'There's only the tragedy mask out there.'

'No. She has both.'

'Are you sure?'

Hatty nodded her head and opened her mouth to respond, but looked at him and closed it again. Finally, she spoke. 'You're telling me one of the masks is missing. The smiling mask isn't there.'

'Yes.'

'It was there last night.'

'When did you come here?'

'Last night?'

'Today. When did you arrive today?'

'Eugenia brought me from the hospital this morning.'

'Did you notice the masks then?'

'I don't remember. I wasn't looking.'

'But it's possible the smiling mask was hung in its customary spot above the door when you came home with Eugenia this morning.'

'It's possible. I just don't remember looking up at them. I wasn't . . .'

'Of course, you had other things . . . Perhaps we could ask Miss Merrilow.'

'Do you think it's important?'

'Probably not. Nothing to get excited about. But I'd still like to know.'

'Then let's find her and ask.' Hatty rose and went to the door.

Day followed and she took his elbow. She seemed brighter at the prospect of having something to do and he hoped Eugenia Merrilow would plan activities for her in the next few days. She might never get over the murder of her husband, but she was a young girl and it was still possible for her to find happiness again if the Harvest Man was caught. Day allowed himself to be led away in search of Hammersmith and Eugenia, but his mind was elsewhere. He was certain the Harvest Man had come to this house, had taken the grinning mask from above the door. He needed something to replace the lost plague mask. But where had he gone after that? Day was confident they were close now. They were going to catch him.

49

The Harvest Man felt secure and comforted in the small space. It was even better than an attic, since it surrounded him on all sides. He was thankful he had never grown up big and strong like an adult. Only a boy could fit where he had gone. It was lucky, too, that he had lost the plague mask with its massive beak. He could never have brought it under here with him. The new mask snugged against his face, flat and close. It made him sweat, but sweat was good. He lay on his back and concentrated on breathing slowly, quietly, ignoring the heat.

A man and a woman entered the room and they stood talking perhaps two feet away from the Harvest Man. He could hear their voices almost on top of him and he wondered if he'd be able to touch their ankles if he only reached out and tried.

'Of course a larger room would suit me better,' the woman said. 'But we're still able to fit fifty people in here at a time.'

The man sounded bored. 'If you took out that platform, more people could fit.'

'Silly, that's my stage.'

'What do you do there?'

'I enact famous scenes from paintings and poems and sometimes from plays, although anyone can put on a play. I try not to be too awfully common,' the woman said.

'And people come here to watch you do that?'

'The whole street comes, the whole neighbourhood, and many important people from all over London. My performances are famously well attended.'

'Like a costume ball?'

'No, nothing like a costume ball. I swear, Mr Hammersmith, you act like you've never seen a tableau vivant.'

'Not sure I have.' The man's voice – the woman had called him Hammersmith – sounded disengaged. He was humouring the woman; even the Harvest Man could tell, but the woman kept talking about herself as if Hammersmith cared.

'We have fabulous sets designed by the great, and as yet undiscovered, George Bristol. Those go up behind the stage and we change them, depending on the performance. The next one we do, and I haven't decided what it shall be as of yet, but the next one we do we'll take down this curtain. And the new set, whatever it is that George designs, will cover those windows instead, you see?'

'Hmm.'

'And I design my own costumes. You should see me. The last one I did there was no costume. I was completely nude.' The Harvest Man could hear a change in her voice. She was flirting with Hammersmith, trying to get a reaction from him. The Harvest Man had heard his mother do that sometimes when she spoke to his father, but he was reasonably certain these two people were not his parents. His father had cared a great deal for his mother. It was clear that Hammersmith did not particularly like this woman. 'Well, I shouldn't say *completely* nude,' the woman said. 'I did wear a wig.' And she giggled.

'Is that so?' Hammersmith's voice was clearer now. He had moved closer to the Harvest Man's hiding place. 'What is this, three feet high?'

'Two and a half,' the woman said.

'What's under it?'

'We store George's old flats and cut-outs under the stage, in case we need them again. They stack quite well, but it's full now. We'll have to find a new place to keep them. Would you like to see? I can have Pritchard pull some out from under. In fact, if you'd like I can throw on one of my old costumes and give you a demonstration. A sort of private performance. You should hear me sing!'

'Oh, thank you, but no. I would like to take a look under there, though, if you –'

'Pritchard!'

The Harvest Man changed his grip on the razor in his right hand. He decided to wait until the little door at the side of the stage opened and then he would reach out and slash anything nearby. With luck, he'd be able to use the ensuing chaos to crawl out and escape.

'Ma'am?' This was a new voice. An older man.

'That was quick, Pritchard,' the woman said. 'You must have been right outside the room.'

'Indeed, ma'am. I was coming to inform you that we have another visitor. An Inspector Tiffany.'

'Tiffany's here?' Hammersmith was moving away from the stage now. 'What's he want?'

'He didn't say, sir. Shall I tell him . . .'

But now the voices trailed away as the three people left the room, their footsteps fading down the hall. The Harvest Man relaxed his grip on the razor and closed his eyes. The moment had passed. He had time now.

He would wait.

50

'Hammersmith,' Inspector Tiffany said. 'What are you doin', always underfoot? This is a police matter, not for you.'

'This isn't a crime scene,' Hammersmith said.

'Do you live here? No? Then what're you here for?'

'This is my home,' a Rubenesque woman said. 'Well, my mother's. I'm Eugenia Merrilow.'

'Pleased to meet you.'

'And this man is my guest.'

'He's been warned about interfering,' Tiffany said. 'He's not a proper –'

'He's with me,' Day said. He came limping into the entryway on the arm of Hatty Pitt. 'What brings you here, James?'

'Where've you been at, Day? Don't you know everybody's out lookin' for you?'

'For me? Why?'

'It's your babies,' Tiffany said. 'They've gone missing.'

Day came quicker across the room than Tiffany would have imagined he could. 'Babies? You're talking about the twins?'

'That's right,' Tiffany said. 'I think so, anyway. They told me it was a little girl.'

'One little girl?'

'I didn't hear. All I know, there's somethin' not right

with your babies. Somebody came and took 'em and they're gone.'

'Who? Who took them?'

'That giant friend of yours. Ran out the house with 'em.'

Day turned to Hammersmith. He was pale and shaking. 'Henry.'

Hammersmith shook his head. 'Henry wouldn't do that.'

'I'm sure it's all right,' Tiffany said. 'Some sorta misunderstanding.'

'The bird,' Day said. 'Oliver, remember? He was trying to tell us something.'

'He wanted you to follow him.'

'I should have.'

'No way of knowing,' Hammersmith said.

'I have to go,' Day said.

'I'm going with you.'

'No, someone has to stay here.'

'Tiffany can stay,' Hammersmith said. 'It's his job, after all.'

'It's why I'm here,' Tiffany said.

'Listen,' Day said. 'The Harvest Man is somewhere nearby. Very close by.'

'I know it. Jones and I almost caught him, too.'

'He's taken the smiling mask from the front of this house.'

'There isn't an attic, is there?' Tiffany looked up at the chandelier.

'No. But we're missing something, something about this one. I just can't figure out what. Regardless, I don't think Hatty's in any danger. He's never stalked anyone.'

'That we know of,' Tiffany said.

'I don't think that's how he works, how his mind works.'

'You go,' Tiffany said. 'Take care of your family. And if you see Jones out there, take his horse. It'll get you there faster than a carriage will. I'll coordinate the search from here.'

Eugenia stepped in front of Tiffany. 'My house is not a police station,' she said.

Hammersmith leaned in and whispered something to her and Eugenia's eyes widened. 'I suppose,' she said, 'it might make a good story. But I've never done an original production before.'

Before Tiffany could figure out what she was talking about, the front door banged shut and he realized he was alone with the two women. Day and Hammersmith had both gone.

'Good luck,' Tiffany muttered under his breath. 'And Godspeed.'

51

The sitting room of the rented cottage was crowded with people when Day and Hammersmith burst through the door. Claire stood in the middle of the room, surrounded by other people and holding one of the babies. Her mother was there, along with Dr Kingsley and his daughter, the boys Robert and Simon, and the twins' governess, who was sobbing uncontrollably while Eleanor Carlyle patted her on the back. When she saw her husband, Claire gave the baby to Fiona and rushed to him, throwing her arms around him.

'He took Winnie,' she said.

'Are you sure it was Winnie?' As the words left his mouth, Day realized how daft he sounded. Of course Claire was sure. And if she wasn't? What did it matter which of the twins was missing?

'He took her!'

Kingsley went to the decanter on the sideboard and poured Day a drink. 'Henry came here earlier in the day, a couple of hours ago, I think. He was wet and may have fallen in the canal. He went upstairs and took one of your daughters from her cradle, then left with her. My daughter was here and she and Claire chased Henry into the park. They lost sight of him there.' Day took the glass of brandy and swallowed its contents. He handed the glass back to Kingsley, who raised his eyebrows. 'Another?'

'Thank you, but not just now. Is anyone –'

'There's a search party being led by Mr Carlyle. I planned to join them myself, but wanted to wait until you got here. I'm going to give Mrs Day a sedative, but she insisted that she see you first.'

Day nodded. 'Yes, thank you.' He took Claire's arms and led her to the daybed, laid her down. He sat next to her and smoothed his hand along her forehead. Her eyes were red-rimmed and her hair was damp where it lay against her cheeks. 'Henry wouldn't hurt the baby, darling,' Day said. 'I can't tell you –'

'Why? Why did he take her?'

'I don't know why, but we'll find him.'

'I don't care about him. Only Winnie.'

'I understand. But don't worry now. She'll be just fine. I'm sure he's taken good care of her.'

'Oh, Walter, what if –'

'Don't let your mind travel down that path, darling. You rest. Nevil's here with me. And your father's out looking. Between us, and with Dr Kingsley's help, we'll find the baby.'

'Oh, Walter, don't let Nevil go. He'll be killed if he goes out there. Something awful always seems to –'

'He'll be fine.' Day looked up at Kingsley. 'Do you have that sedative?'

'Here.' Kingsley hovered next to them for a minute, blocking Day's view of his wife, then stood back, a syringe held neatly out of sight under his arm. 'That should start to work in a moment or two.'

'Walter?'

'Yes, dear. I'm here.'

'Walter, I can't go to sleep.'

'You must try.'

'If I go to sleep, I might never see you again. Just like Winnie.'

'That's not . . .' He stopped talking when her eyes closed and her breathing evened out. He sighed and stood up. 'Will she be all right?'

'She's had a shock,' Kingsley said. 'But the sedative will help.'

'Thank you, Doctor, but what will really help is if we find that baby while she's asleep.'

'I thought I might check Henry's home, that ridiculous room in the lamppost. It's possible he went back there.'

'You said he was wet when he arrived here?'

'Yes, that's what Fiona told me.'

'He might be hiding near the canal,' Hammersmith said.

'I have another idea where he might be,' Day said, 'but it's only the slimmest possibility.'

'One possibility is as good as another right now,' Kingsley said.

'If we split up, we've got a better chance of finding him quickly,' Hammersmith said. 'I'll head down to the water.'

'Take my revolver,' Day said. Claire's concern for Nevil echoed in his mind.

'I don't need it,' Hammersmith said.

'I'd feel better if you had it.' Day pressed his Colt on Hammersmith, who took it reluctantly, a sour look on his face.

'Now you'll be unarmed.'

340

'No, I have my new sword stick. Doctor, let's find something for you.'

'I don't like carrying weapons. It's against my oath to cause harm.'

'But surely for self-defence . . .'

'I'll be fine. Henry wouldn't hurt me. Honestly, he wouldn't hurt anyone. This isn't like him at all. He must believe he's playing some sort of game.'

'I think that's exactly what's going on,' Day said. He didn't give voice to his private fear. Henry really wasn't acting himself, which meant he might be acting on some-one else's behalf. He might not intend to harm Winnie, but if he was being used as a pawn in someone else's game, the baby could still be in grave danger.

Kingsley turned to Fiona. 'Watch Claire and take care of the remaining baby. Lock the door after us and do not let anyone in until at least one of us is back here.'

She nodded and Day saw her give Hammersmith a worried glance. The three men went to the door and out, and Day listened for the click of the bolt before he went down the steps to the road. Kingsley clapped Day on the shoulder and peeled off in the direction of Trafalgar Square without a word. Hammersmith shoved Day's revolver in his belt and shook his head.

'She's fine, Walter,' he said.

'I know.'

'We'll have her back within the hour. I promise.' And with that, Hammersmith turned and ran towards the canal. Day watched him disappear into the gathering darkness, then he limped across the road and into the park. He prayed that his child was still alive and that she'd be found in time. Alan Ridgway had delivered a message from Jack. Something about Day having been chosen, whatever that meant. But if Jack was toying with him, if he was behind Winnie's disappearance, Day thought he had an idea where he might find him.

52

There was a church on the corner. Hammersmith vaulted the low fence around its gardens and trotted to the back, where he knew he would find stairs down to the waterway. He could smell mildew and decay and freshwater, could hear the canal, full from the recent rain and lapping against its banks. He moved quickly and carefully down the dark steps and stood for a moment at the bottom, getting used to the gloom. The sun was going down and branches hung low over the water, filtering out all but a few diamond sparkles through the leaves and on the water. A red narrowboat bobbed up and down nearby, nudging against the stone embankment. Hammersmith moved towards it.

'You there!'

Hammersmith turned and saw Leland Carlyle running towards him. Hammersmith moved his hand off the gun in his belt and waited for the older man to catch up to him.

'What are you doing here? Do I know you?'

'We met once, sir,' Hammersmith said. 'I'm a friend of Walter's.'

'Is there news? Has the baby been found?'

'Nothing yet. I thought there was a chance he might have brought her here.'

'I thought the same thing,' Carlyle said. 'The fellow was apparently wet when he arrived at the house.'

'Exactly.'

'I've been all up and down this side, but I don't see anything out of the ordinary.'

Hammersmith glanced at the narrowboat and Carlyle followed his gaze.

'Yes,' Carlyle said, 'I thought of that, too, but it's empty. There's nothing here. I've encountered a few people walking along here, but nobody's seen a big man with a baby.'

'We'll find her, sir.'

'Will we? How can you be certain?'

'I have faith in Walter. He'll think of something. He always does.'

'I wish I shared your conviction, young man.'

Hammersmith shook his head and squinted at the water's surface. 'If they're not down here, perhaps we should go find Walter. He can't be far. Maybe he's on the right track.'

'Let's hope someone is.'

Trafalgar Square was sparsely populated, only a few clerks heading home from the office and a single straggling vendor, wheeling his oyster cart slowly across the square, hoping for one more sale before the day was done. Kingsley didn't even look at the man, but hurried straight across to the lamppost on the southeast corner. He hesitated at the low door before reaching up to rap on the dark window with his knuckles. He was afraid he'd find Henry here, and he was afraid he wouldn't.

After a long moment, Kingsley heard a soft noise from inside the hollow stone structure. He put his ear to the window and listened. The unmistakable fussing of a baby was clearly audible. He reached for the knob and rattled it, but the door was locked.

'Henry? Henry, if you're in there, open up.'

'No.'

'Henry, is the baby all right?'

'She smells bad.'

'Is she all right?'

'I think she messed herself. And we're hungry.'

Kingsley let out a sigh of relief and sagged against the post. 'Henry, you have to open the door. You've created a great deal of trouble for yourself.'

'I'm scared.'

'You'll be in more trouble if you don't open up.'

'No, I'm scared about the baby.'

'What about the baby?'

'She's in danger. The voice told me she was in danger. I'm saving her.'

'Saving her from what, Henry?'

'I don't know.'

'Who told you she was in danger?'

'I don't know.'

'Henry, somebody lied to you. The baby isn't in danger. I'm afraid you're the one who is in some trouble. And you're only making it worse.'

'I'm saving her,' Henry said again.

'Do you trust me?'

'Of course I do.'

'Then open the door now.'

Kingsley waited. At last he heard more noises from within the lamppost. A scraping sound, a click, and the door swung open. Henry crouched there in the dark, holding the little girl in his arms. Kingsley reached out and took her from the giant. Winnie Day kicked her legs and turned her face towards Kingsley's chest. He checked her eyes and they were clear and bright. He laid her on the low stone wall beside the lamppost, kept one hand on her to prevent her rolling off. He conducted a cursory examination of the infant and satisfied himself that she was healthy and hungry and unharmed. Kingsley didn't know what to think about his assistant. He'd always known the man was simple, but now he wondered if he might be deranged.

'Oh, Henry,' he said at last. 'What have you done?'

'I didn't hurt her.'

'No, I know you didn't.'

'Should we take her back to Mrs Day now?'

'I'm going to do just that, Henry. But you can't come with me.'

'Why can't I?'

'I don't imagine Mrs Day wants to see you anytime very soon. In fact, she may have you arrested. You'd better stay far away from her, and from Mr Day, too.'

'Until tomorrow?'

'For a long time. I don't think you'd better come back to work, either.'

'What will I do?'

'I don't know that. I'm very sorry, Henry. I don't know what to tell you just now. I'll do what I can for you.'

'Oh, that sounds very bad.'

'Mrs Day is a kind woman and I'm sure she'll forgive

you. But these things take time. Wait here until I send for you.'

With that, he walked away across the square with the baby in his arms, looking for a cab that could get him back to Primrose Hill. Behind him, he heard poor Henry sob.

53

The house was dim and quiet, but there was a strange electricity in the air, humming just beneath the senses, as if one only needed to turn in the right direction to see or hear or feel whatever it was that was waiting there at 184 Regent's Park Road.

Day closed the front door behind him and clomped down the hallway. He paused at the parlour door and stood watching the dark room until he was certain it was unoccupied. He could almost picture the dead man lying on the floor where Jack the Ripper had left him only weeks before. Where Jack had, in fact, disassembled the body and strewn its pieces about like an angry child upending his chessboard. Or like a messenger delivering a warning from somewhere humans could never set foot.

But there was nothing to see in the parlour except a memory. Day moved down the long passage to the kitchen. It was as empty as the parlour. Here, too, had been a body, this one simply discarded face down in a pool of blood. Constable Rupert Winthrop had been a good young man with promise and prospects. It was through no fault of his own that he'd been caught up in the web of madness and violence that seemed to surround Walter Day. Day retraced his steps, checking the study and the small crawl space under the stairs. Something about the crawl space nudged at him, tickling his brain. Something he should have thought of earlier. He stared through the tiny doorway at the odds and ends that were stored there, but could not think of what was bothering him about it. He closed the door and went to the bottom of the steps, made his slow way up to the first floor. He paused at the landing and listened. He heard his own breathing, laboured and nervous, but that was all. He moved on. His bedroom was empty, and so was the governess's room. At the last door, he paused. It entered his mind that he could simply retreat. He could limp back to the staircase and go down and out of the house and never come back.

But his daughter was missing. And so Day reached out and turned the knob and pushed the nursery door open.

'Hello, Walter Day.' Jack's voice, low and silky, somewhere deep in the pitch-black room. 'I knew you'd find me if I waited long enough.'

Day stood in the open doorway, aware that he was silhouetted at the threshold, a perfect target. But to enter the room would be no better. Jack's eyes were surely adjusted to the darkness, whereas Day would be stumbling about blind. He stayed where he was. 'Where's my baby, Jack?'

'Your baby? Oh, why is it always about *you*, Walter Day? There's always some bit of business you've got on your mind, never just stopping by for a chat, maybe a hand or two of Happy Families or a leisurely game of chess.'

'The baby. Tell me.'

'Well, what *about* the baby? Surely you can share her. I consider Winnie Day to be practically my own family.'

'She's nothing to do with you. You've gone too far this time.' Day could hear his own voice, flat and emotionless, a counterpoint to Jack's rich sing-song tones.

'But I always go too far,' Jack said. 'It's part of my not inconsiderable charm.'

'She's an infant.'

'What is it the Jesuits say, Walter Day? "Give me a child for seven years . . ." But what comes after that? I forget. "Give me a child for seven years and I'll most likely kill her anyway." Is that right?'

'Jack!'

'Why seven years? What a beastly long time to have to deal with a child.'

'Stop playing games,' Day said. 'Talk to me like a man. Do you have her here?'

'No. I don't have her here. Is this masculine enough, the way I'm talking to you now? I never dreamed you'd find me feminine.'

'That's not what I meant.'

'Enough, Walter Day. You're exciting yourself. Have a drink.'

'A drink?'

'From that flask you're so fond of.'

Day reached into his pocket and took out the flask. He didn't look at it, but let it drop to the floor at his feet. 'I don't feel like a drink right now.'

'Then let's get more comfortable. Why don't you come in here and shut the door behind you?'

'So you can murder me?'

'I would never murder you, Walter Day. You've always misunderstood our special relationship.'

'We have no relationship.'

'You wound me.'

'You've wounded me in far worse ways.'

'Touché! How is your leg?'

'Damn you to hell.'

'Holding a grudge, are we? Then perhaps a peace offering is in order: Your daughter is safe, Walter Day. She was always safe. Safe from me and safe from anyone else who might want to harm her. I promise that for the rest of her life, I will be there, always and for ever somewhere at the fringes of her sight, watching her and protecting her from wickedness.'

'The rest of her . . .'

'Always and for ever,' Jack said again.

'Leave her alone. Leave us all alone.'

'It's too late for that, Walter Day.'

'What is it you want from me?'

'I want . . . Let me think. I suppose it's possible I only want a friend. I've had vassals, toadies, mimics and suck-ups galore. How they weary me. Oh! Speaking of the like, you made quick work of Alan Ridgway, didn't you?'

'I'm not proud of that. I had to shoot him.'

'I knew you had it in you.'

'If you don't mean to harm me and my family, why did you send him to kill me?'

Jack chuckled. He had a pleasant laugh, melodious and clear, and it bothered Day that he could detect no evil or falsehood in the sound of it.

'Alan Ridgway? Kill the great Walter Day? No, that was never going to happen. I didn't send him to kill you, Walter Day. I sent him to *be* killed by you. He was an offering. And I sent him with an invitation.'

'An invitation?'

'And here you are. I wish you'd been a little quicker.

This rocking chair is not as comfortable as I'd imagined it would be.'

'You're in the rocking chair, then? Now I know where you are, I could shoot you from here.'

'But what if I'm holding little Winnie Day? You might shoot her by accident.' There was a false note of alarm in Jack's voice. Mocking Day, taunting him.

'You've already told me she's not here,' Day said. 'And you don't lie, do you?'

'Ha. No, never. You've got me there. Lying isn't kind, is it? But we both know you won't shoot me anyway. Even if you had your trusty Colt revolver with you, which you don't. You won't shoot me, because you're curious about me. You pride yourself on understanding people, on your grasp of your adversaries' minds, their methods, what they want and how they go about getting it. But me? You don't understand me at all. And you want to, don't you? You need to.'

'I only need my daughter. Tell me how to get her back.'

'If you're a good friend to me and do just what I tell you to do, Winnie Day will be returned this very evening to the house where your wife waits. My, but Claire Day is long-suffering, isn't she? You chose well with that one, Walter Day. I think a less patient woman would long ago have –'

'So you'll bring the baby back?'

'She has a name, you know. Why don't you call her by her name?'

'You'll bring her back.'

'I'll arrange it.'

'Someone else has her, then?'

'Yes.'

'Henry? Does Henry still have her?'

'That would be telling.'

'Where? Where does he have her?'

'I can't tell you that, either.'

'Contact him. Send for Henry. Tell him to bring her to me now.'

'That's not the arrangement I had in mind.'

'What then? What arrangement?'

'I want you to come with me.'

'With you? Where?'

'I have a little place picked out for us by the water. We'll talk and we'll become better friends and I'll teach you what's in here.'

'What's in where?'

'I'm pointing to my head. Sorry, you can't see me. It's terribly dark in here and your eyes still haven't adjusted, have they?'

'Not yet.'

'You could have tried to trick me just now, tried to make me think you could see. But you don't lie either, do you, Walter Day? Perhaps that's why I'm so fond of you. We're alike in some ways, you and I.'

'We're nothing alike.'

'You protest too much. You know, I think we could be even more alike if we take the time to learn from each other. We could be twins, Walter Day.' Day heard hands clapping. 'Just like your babies. How marvellous!'

Day's leg hurt and he was having trouble ignoring the pain. He wanted to lean against the doorjamb or sit down, but he was afraid Jack would see it as weakness and attack.

Assuming Jack hadn't already noticed how Day felt. The creature seemed preternaturally empathetic. Day concentrated on the cane, leaned harder on it, thought about what was hidden within its length. As long as Jack didn't know what was inside the cane, Day had an advantage. He only needed to wait until Jack got close enough to him. Jack had to leave the room at some point and he would have to pass Day in the narrow doorway . . .

It was as if Jack could read his mind. 'Walter Day, if you won't enter the room, then would you do me the great favour of taking two steps backwards?'

'Backwards?'

'If I have to ask again, I'll become displeased with you, Walter Day. I'm not as patient as your wife.'

Day did as he was told. He stood out in the open on the landing, squinting at the black rectangle of the nursery door, waiting for Jack to rush out of that darkness at him. He heard the rocking chair squeak.

'Now turn around,' Jack said. His voice sounded closer. 'Put your back to me.'

'I'd rather not do that, Jack.'

'I understand.' It was impossible to tell exactly where Jack was in the room. His voice seemed to bounce around from one wall to the other and back again. Day glanced to either side, but there was nothing nearby to step behind or to put between himself and the open doorway. 'You're going to have to make yourself quite vulnerable.'

'No, I'm not.'

'You are. Think of it as proof of your trust in me.'

'But I don't trust you, Jack. You know I don't.'

'Stop being so contrary. I'm trying to be nice. Now turn

around.' Jack's voice had lost its silky quality. It sounded now like the low growl of some forest predator. 'Turn around or our little game will end too soon and you'll never see your daughter again.'

Day swallowed hard. He tightened his grip on the heavy silver knob at the top of his cane and turned so that his back was to the nursery. The staircase was directly ahead of him. If Jack hit him from behind, Day thought he might be able to drop and roll to the stairs. Even if he fell down them, he'd put distance between himself and the Ripper.

But looking at the stairs, the thought he'd been trying to catch earlier came to him at last. Eugenia Merrilow's house didn't have an attic for the Harvest Man to hide in, but he wouldn't have risked moving on after stealing the mask. He wasn't brave or daring. He would have found the next best thing to an attic: a crawl space. The Harvest Man was there now in that house with Hatty Pitt, hiding almost within arm's reach, and Day knew it. But there was no way for him to do anything about it, no way to warn anyone, not while he was trapped here with Jack.

'Now walk to the stairs and down.' Jack's voice was immediately behind Day, in his ear. Day hadn't even heard the killer approach.

Could he spin around fast enough to catch Jack off guard? No, his leg wasn't trustworthy. The pain was too much. It would give out on him. If he fell, he'd be at a disadvantage, unable to use his hidden sword. So he did as he was told, limped to the top of the stairs and moved slowly down, one step at a time. He could not hear Jack behind him, but he was there somewhere close. How close? Was there time to unlock the top of the cane and unsheathe the blade?

At the bottom of the stairs he stopped. Jack's voice drifted down from somewhere above. 'Outside there is a carriage. Get in and close the door. Do not speak to the driver.'

Day hesitated.

Now Jack's voice was right behind him. 'Go now, Walter Day.'

'If I get in your carriage, you'll have the advantage on me, Jack.'

'I already have the advantage on you.' Somehow, Jack's voice was far away again, somewhere on the staircase behind them. 'Again, this isn't about you. This is about your family, and about doing what's needed to protect them. I know you'll do the right thing now. For their sake. Otherwise, I'll never give the word and little Winnie Day will never be returned to your dear wife. Of course, I'll keep my word to protect her from harm, but she'll never be seen again by anyone but me.'

Day took a deep breath and looked around at his house for what he was afraid was the last time. He wondered what Claire would do if he never returned, where she would go or where her parents would take her. He wondered whether Winnie would, in fact, be brought back, as Jack had promised. Day thought once again of his daughters growing up without him, calling another man Father and never knowing Walter Day.

He walked slowly out of the house and down the footpath, out by the garden gate. A black carriage was waiting at the curb, its windows covered by curtains, a midnight roan huffing up front. A driver sat above, immobile, his features obscured by a muffler and a tall hat. Far down the street, Day saw a fox run through the hazy circle cast by a gas globe. He wondered where it was going and what might be chasing it there. Day opened the carriage door and levered himself up and in, pushing off the street with his cane. He sat and the door closed behind him. He was plunged into utter darkness.

Jack's voice floated through the black from outside. 'I gave you my word, Walter Day. Your daughter is now safe. You have done what any good father should do and insured that nothing will ever disturb Winnie Day again in her lifetime. Bravo, my friend.'

Day heard the driver's lash crack and the horse's hooves clop against the cobblestones. The wagon lurched and Day was borne away for ever from 184 Regent's Park Road.

54

Hammersmith was standing outside the rented cottage with Leland Carlyle when Kingsley's cab pulled up in front. There were smiles all round when the doctor emerged from the carriage holding a healthy baby in his arms. Carlyle paid the driver and included a big tip, and the three of them – four with little Winnie – went inside.

The governess, whose name Hammersmith had never learned, wept openly at the sight of the baby. She ran to Kingsley and took Winnie from him. Fiona had Henrietta in a chair by the fireplace. She stood and handed Henrietta over to the governess, who sat with a baby curled in the crook of each elbow and began to rock them. The twins cooed at each other and fell asleep, while the housekeeper hurried away to fetch two bottles of cream and a fresh nappy.

'Henrietta's been fussing since you left,' Fiona said. She smiled up at Hammersmith. 'I suppose she must have missed her sister.'

'Walter isn't back yet?'

'No. We haven't heard from him.'

Dr Kingsley got his bag and knelt by the daybed. He opened a capsule of smelling salts under Claire's nose and she came awake instantly.

'Winnie's back home,' Kingsley said. 'And none the worse for wear.'

Once Claire had satisfied herself that both her daughters were safe, she settled back on the daybed and sighed. 'Was she with Henry?'

'Yes. He had her in his room on the square.'

Hammersmith stepped closer so he could hear them speak.

'Why did he do it? Why take her?'

'He apparently thought she was in some danger. I honestly think he meant well. He wasn't ever going to hurt her.'

'I don't care,' Claire said. 'I never want to see him again.'

'He said that someone told him to take her.'

'Who told him?'

'He didn't know.'

'And he didn't think to talk to me,' Claire said, 'or Walter? He just enters my home and steals my baby?'

'I think he'd like to talk to you now. He's quite upset about it all.'

'He should be. I won't see him. At least not now.'

'Well, give it time.'

'We should find Walter and tell him,' Hammersmith said.

'He'll come back when he's tired,' Leland Carlyle said. 'Or when he runs out of brandy.'

'Leland,' Eleanor Carlyle said. It sounded like a warning.

Carlyle put his hands up and shook his head. 'I apologize. These few days have been trying. Not at all the holiday in London we expected. Between the missing baby, the men murdered on my daughter's front step, three of my close friends murdered besides. It's too much.'

Hammersmith ignored him. 'Does anybody know where he went?'

Nobody spoke right away. Everyone looked around the room, waiting for a response. Leland Carlyle looked down at the floor. At last Kingsley cleared his throat. 'He went into the park. That was the last I saw of him.'

'Into the park or across it?'

'I don't know.'

'If he's in the park, he might be impossible to find,' Hammersmith said. 'But across the park . . . Might he have gone to check the house? To see if Henry took the baby back home?'

'It's possible,' Kingsley said. 'It's not a bad assumption, that Henry might return there, might forget the girl's parents are staying here now.'

'Even though he took her from here?'

'Exactly so. Henry's forgetful.'

'I'll go and look over there,' Hammersmith said. 'Be right back.'

Fiona caught up with him in the hallway as he was preparing to leave, his hat in his hand. 'Before you go,' she said, 'I have something . . . I keep meaning to give it to you, but the moment's never right.'

'I don't understand.'

'I gave Mr Day a gift, you know, the sword stick to replace his broken cane, and I had one for you, too.'

'But I don't need a cane.'

'It's not . . . Oh, here.' She thrust a small wrapped package at him and ran away down the hall and back into the sitting room.

He stared after her for a moment, then looked down at

the parcel. He put his hat on, freeing his hands, and unwrapped the package. It was a leather case, shiny and new, exactly like the wares carried by Mr Goodpenny at the Marylebone bazaar. He opened it and counted twenty ivory-coloured calling cards, each with a filigree design in the upper corner. He took one out and read it. Written in a clear and elegant hand, which he recognized as Fiona's, it said: MR NEVIL HAMMERSMITH, PRIVATE DETECTIVE.

He stood and stared at it and finally he smiled. He closed the case and put it away in his breast pocket, over the scar in his chest. He liked the weight of it there. It had the heft of a new chapter in his life.

He adjusted his hat and opened the door and went out into the night in search of Walter Day.

55

He lay under the stage and listened. For an hour or two —
he had no way of telling time — he drifted off. When he
woke up, the house was quiet. He stayed where he was, in
pitch black and surrounded by the smells of paint and
wood and dust. Spiders and silverfish crawled over his
face and he ignored them. At last the grumbling of his
stomach grew too loud. He worried that it would wake
the household. He pushed open the small door in the side
of the stage and held his breath, but heard nothing, no
reaction. He opened the door all the way and pulled himself out. He reached back in and retrieved the length of
slender rope he'd found. His skin was sticky with sweat
and he got the sense that, if he took off the strap holding
the mask to his face, it would stay where it was, a part of
him now. He thought about the mask and it made him
happy. He was smiling now, always smiling, and shiny. His
mask was gold. He was his parents' golden boy now, as he
was meant to be. And they wouldn't be afraid of him any
more when they woke up. They would see his happy
laughing sparkling gold face and they would smile back at
him. He used his fingers to brush the insects out of his
hair and went to the room's doorway. The hall beyond was
silent and dark. He crept forward, close to the wall, the
rope coiled in his hand. There were many openings all
along the passage, but he couldn't see or hear a single

person. Mother and Father must be upstairs, he reasoned, sleeping. He hoped he'd be able to tie them down before they woke up. He had left his ether behind at the last false home, along with everything else. Near the front of the house was a receiving room of some kind, a sitting room or parlour, and the Harvest Man stepped inside to regroup and plan his next course of action. Should he find something to eat first or get right down to business? He was surprised to see a man there, sitting upright in a chair, his back to the window. Lamplight from somewhere outside streamed in and backlit the man's body. The Harvest Man froze in place, one foot in the hallway, one foot in the room. He stood there for several minutes, waiting for the man to move. Finally, the man snorted and shifted position. He was asleep! The Harvest Man moved to the side of the chair without making a sound. He stood and looked down on the sleeping man. The man had a revolver, held loosely in his hand, and the Harvest Man took it carefully away, set it down on the floor behind the chair. The man did not have a kind face. He had a neatly trimmed moustache that made his features difficult to discern. Still, it was possible the bone structure was good, under the mask. Always under the mask.

The Harvest Man got to work right away, wrapping his rope around and around the sleeping man in the chair.

56

Hammersmith left 184 Regent's Park Road feeling vaguely unsettled. Day was not there, but Hammersmith had found his flask lying on the upper floor, still half full of brandy. It was enough to convince Hammersmith that the inspector had been there recently, but there was no other sign of him, nor was there a clue as to where he might have gone from there. Hammersmith took the flask with him.

Hammersmith had told Kingsley and the others that he would return to the Carlyles' cottage, but something was bothering him and he turned the opposite way from the cottage after leaving the house. Day might have accidentally dropped his flask, but he would have returned for it. He was fond of the flask and used it frequently. And it wasn't as if the two houses were far from each other. Even if he'd made it halfway across the park, surely he would have turned back.

But what if Day had been distracted or had found something else at the house? After all, why had Henry taken the baby? Had someone manipulated him? If so, who? And why? Henry wasn't a madman. There were too many questions and it occurred to Hammersmith that Day might have come up with an answer or two while searching his abandoned house. If he had a new idea, he might have tried to reason out where Henry would be now.

Day didn't know his baby had been found, but he knew that Hammersmith was searching the canal for Winnie. He knew that Kingsley was looking for the baby at Trafalgar Square. Other logical places to look might include Kingsley's office or laboratory, but University College Hospital was well staffed and Henry was known there. Someone would question why he was carrying a baby around. It was unlikely Henry would go there. The giant was a creature of habit and there were no other places he frequented. At least, no other places Hammersmith could think of. But what if Henry had been seeking help? Who would he have turned to? Dr Kingsley, of course, but Henry knew that Kingsley was working a murder scene. So maybe he would have sought out the baby's father, Walter Day. Walter Day, who would also be working a murder scene if he hadn't got the news about Winnie's kidnapping.

If, instead of returning to his home in the lamppost, Henry had tried to find the two men he trusted most in the world, he would have taken the baby to a crime scene. And, if that same thought had entered Walter Day's mind, he might have gone back there, too, hoping to find Henry and Winnie there.

It was all Hammersmith could think of. He saw a boy loitering near the edge of the park and tipped him a penny to run across to the cottage.

'Find a doctor there named Kingsley. Tell him that Day may have returned to the house where the spider was. Tell him Hammersmith has gone there to look for him.'

'I can't remember all that for a penny.'

Hammersmith snorted and gave the boy another penny,

watched him run off into the dusk and disappear into the trees. Then he turned and hailed a passing cab. Walter Day had certainly not walked away from 184 Regent's Park Road and Hammersmith didn't want to fall even further behind if he could help it.

57

Inspector James Tiffany woke up confused and groggy, thinking he had heard something, someone yelling nearby. He felt mildly embarrassed to have napped in a chair while on duty, but it had been days since he'd had a proper night's sleep. He shouldn't have sat down at all, should have known he might doze off. He tried to sit forward, but something held him back. He blinked and looked down. He was tied to the chair, lengths of rope wrapped round and round his torso and legs, his arms pinned to his sides.

Alarmed, he looked around the room, but he was alone. He couldn't feel his fingers or toes and he worried that the circulation had been cut off from his limbs for too long. He tried to arch his back and, when he couldn't do that, thrashed his upper body from side to side. But he only moved a fraction of an inch at a time. He was bound too tightly.

He forced himself to be still then and listen. From somewhere above him, he heard a woman scream. It was the same sound that had awakened him. It sounded like poor Hatty Pitt, who had already survived so much. It was obvious to Tiffany what had happened. The Harvest Man must have come back for Hatty, must have followed her to this house. A third scream was cut off and the house went silent.

Tiffany looked for something he could use to cut the ropes, but the closest thing was a fireplace poker and it was halfway across the room. There was no way to get it and no way to hold it. He was helpless.

He closed his eyes and thought of his loved ones. Then he opened his eyes and cursed Day and Hammersmith for leaving him here. He wondered where Constable Bentley was. Was he still guarding the other house? Was he close enough to have heard Hatty scream? Or were there other neighbours who had heard and would come to investigate? Probably not. That woman who lived here, Eugenia Something-or-Other, was a performer. No doubt there was enough high drama that the neighbours simply ignored unusual sounds.

Still. There was nothing else to do.

'Help! I'm a police officer! Help!'

He stopped and listened again. Footsteps on the stairs. Tiffany's breath caught in his throat and he bit his lip. A moment later, something very much like a man entered the room, but he was the size of a child and his grinning face was coloured gold. Lamplight from the window caught the planes of the face and shone brightly, cast the creature's cheeks and brow in shadow. The grinning thing moved quickly across the room towards him – it scampered, loose-limbed and nimble.

Up close, he could see the Harvest Man's sparkling eyes behind the gold mask. Pure madness. Tiffany opened his mouth to scream, but the Harvest Man stuffed a wad of fabric into his mouth. It tasted like paint and rancid oil. Tiffany gagged and closed his eyes, tried to work it out with his tongue, but the Harvest Man was pushing against it and Tiffany fought the urge to vomit. If he threw up, he knew, he would choke to death.

He felt something brush against his cheek and he opened his eyes again. The Harvest Man was petting him, stroking his fingertips up and down Tiffany's face. Tiffany concentrated on breathing evenly through his nose. The creature's body odour was nearly a solid substance. Like invisible jelly.

The Harvest Man cleared his throat and began to sing as it fondled him. Tiffany was surprised that his voice was so pleasant:

> He comes this way;
> Yes! 'Tis the night watch!
> Yes! 'Tis the night watch, his glim'ring lamp I see!
> Hush! 'Tis the night watch, softly he comes,
> Hush, 'Tis the night watch, softly he comes,
> Hush 'Tis the night watch, softly he comes!
> Hush! Hush!

And then Tiffany saw the straight razor in the Harvest Man's other hand.

> No, by heaven! No, by heav'n, I am not mad.
> Oh, release me! Oh, release me!
> No, by heaven! No, by heav'n, I am not mad.

The razor came down with a flash of lamplight as the Harvest Man began to cut.

58

Constable Bentley was still idling outside the murder scene, leaning against the garden gate and whistling something tuneless, so Hammersmith instructed the driver not to stop. They rolled past and turned the corner and went another five streets over. If Day had gone inside the Pitt house, Hammersmith felt certain Bentley would have followed him in, if only to relieve the boredom that came with guarding a crime scene. The only other likely possibility was that Day had gone to confer with Tiffany. Perhaps some new idea had occurred to him. Hammersmith hopped out and paid the driver and approached the door with its unhappy face hung above the lintel, a deserted golden twin. The house was dark, but as Hammersmith raised his hand to knock he heard a man singing somewhere within the house. The voice was fine, but had a stilted quality about it that sent shivers up and down Hammersmith's spine. He pulled Day's revolver from his belt and turned the knob. The door swung open and the lyrics of the song became clear.

> I loved her sincerely,
> I loved her too dearly,
> I loved her in sorrow,
> In joy, and in pain;

But my heart is forbidden,
Yes, it never will waken

Hammersmith stepped forward into the dark vestibule, its high chandelier tossing lamplight sparks against the walls. He recognized the song. It was called 'The Maniac' and he had heard it many times in various pubs. He didn't much care for it.

The mem'ry of bliss will ne'er come again.
Oh, this poor heart is broken!
Oh, this poor heart is broken!

He could hear something else now, a low whimpering, softer and almost drowned out by the singer. Hammersmith followed the voices to the front room and flattened himself against the wall outside. He crouched in the hallway and peered around the doorjamb. Inside the room, a small man was standing with his back to the door, bent over a person sitting in a chair. He was wearing something over his face – Hammersmith could see the strap at the back of his head – and seemed intent on whatever he was doing. Hammersmith took a closer look at the chair and recognized Inspector James Tiffany. At the same moment, Tiffany's eyes rolled to the side and he saw Hammersmith. Their eyes locked and Tiffany grunted. A rag had been stuffed into his mouth and the Harvest Man, for that was clearly who the small man must be, was carving Tiffany's cheek with a blade. Hammersmith gasped. The Harvest Man stopped singing and turned around. He was wearing the missing comedy mask and the grinning mouth didn't remind Hammersmith of anything happy or joyous. The killer's razor dragged across Tiffany's upper lip as he turned and the inspector let out a stifled scream around the wad of fabric in his mouth, his cheeks puffing out with the effort.

Hammersmith tumbled into the room, still in a crouching position, the revolver raised aimlessly. 'Jimmy!'

Tiffany tried to respond, but Hammersmith couldn't understand anything he was shouting. The Harvest Man changed his grip on the razor and rushed at Hammersmith, swinging it like a scythe. Hammersmith pulled the trigger and the recoil knocked him off his toes on to his back. Plaster dust sifted from the ceiling, but the flash and bang were enough to startle the Harvest Man, who hesitated. Hammersmith tumbled back towards the door, but the Harvest Man was moving again, coming at him fast. Hammersmith got his feet under him and stood, but a loud noise distracted him. He looked around to see that Tiffany had managed to knock himself over sideways and was now trapped half under the chair. When Hammersmith looked back at the killer, the Harvest Man was directly in front of him. The immobile smiling face thrust itself at Hammersmith, and the blade came down in an arc at Hammersmith's chest. Hammersmith raised the gun, but too late. He heard his jacket rip and felt the impact of the heavy razor directly over the scar in his chest. He fell backwards against the wall and the Harvest Man ran past him into the hallway. A moment later, Hammersmith heard footsteps on the stairs.

He felt the front of his shirt for blood, but he was dry.

He put the gun back in his belt and opened his shirt. Day's flask now had a deep furrow in it, metal shavings curled around a groove where the flask had deflected the Harvest Man's razor blade away from his heart. Hammersmith took a shaky breath, uncorked the flask and swallowed a mouthful of brandy. It burned all the way down his throat. He put the flask down and hurried to where the inspector lay, still trapped beneath the overturned chair. He removed the rag and Tiffany gulped air through his mouth. Hammersmith worked at the knot in the rope behind the chair.

'Never mind me,' Tiffany said.

'You're bleeding,' Hammersmith said. 'He cut you.'

'The women are upstairs. Get going, Sergeant.'

Hammersmith left the knot half untangled. He ran out of the room, down the hallway and leaped up the stairs, taking the revolver back out of his belt as he went. At the landing he was confronted with a series of doorways on both sides of a long passage, but only one door was closed and he made a beeline for it. He checked his grip on Day's gun and turned the knob, threw the door open and stepped into the room. Two women were tied to a bed against the far wall. As Hammersmith entered, the Harvest Man turned towards him, his stiff grinning mask slightly askew. Hammersmith took in the scene as he raised the gun. Both women appeared to be alive and reasonably well, though frightened. The Harvest Man stood perfectly still by the side of the bed, the razor held down at his side.

'Put it down,' Hammersmith said. 'Let it drop and show me your hands. I don't want to kill you if I don't have to.'

The Harvest Man said nothing, but he slowly raised his hands and put them out at his sides.

'Drop the razor,' Hammersmith said again.

The Harvest Man took a step back and crouched as if he might sit on the edge of the bed. Then he vaulted forward, bringing the blade up over his head, and Hammersmith pulled the trigger. The Harvest Man stopped in mid-stride. The smiling mask split in two and half of it fell away. The killer took another step towards Hammersmith, then sank to his knees. He set the razor down on the floor between them and collapsed sideways. He put his hands up under his cheek and lay still, like a sleeping child. Under the mask, contrasting the half smile left there, his mouth was open wide, white tendrils of spit connecting his lips, comedy and tragedy reunited. Tears streamed across his face in two directions, falling off the end of his nose and pooling in the hollows of his gnarled ear.

Hammersmith stepped forward and kicked the razor blade away. He went down on one knee and checked the Harvest Man's neck for a pulse, then lifted the remaining half of the mask over the killer's head and tossed it away. The Harvest Man's eyes rolled up and stared at Hammersmith. His lips moved and Hammersmith bent down closer so he could hear.

> Oh, release me!
> Oh, release me!
> She heeds me not.
> Yes, by heaven,

> Yes, by heaven,
> They've driven me mad.

A small hole in the Harvest Man's forehead suddenly released a trickle of blood and the little murderer relaxed, dead at last.

59

'Good riddance, I say.' Tiffany had freed himself and followed Hammersmith upstairs. Now he stood over the Harvest Man's body, looking down on him. Tiffany held a sodden rag against his jaw, but his upper lip bled freely. 'To think this little fellow killed so many people.'

Hammersmith didn't respond. He had the Harvest Man's folding razor and was sawing through the women's ropes. In a few minutes, they were able to sit up and Hatty threw her arms around Hammersmith. He hugged her and patted her on the back.

'You're safe now,' he said.

Hatty pulled back and surprised him by kissing him on the lips.

'Thank you,' she whispered. 'But I wish you had let me kill him myself.'

'I honestly didn't mean to kill him at all.' Hammersmith slipped out of Hatty's arms and moved around to Eugenia Merrilow's side of the bed. He began working on the ropes there. 'I would rather have taken him in. I wonder what was wrong with him to make him murder the way he did.'

'It doesn't matter,' Tiffany said. 'All that matters is he's dead and no more worries from that quarter.'

'Think of what people will say,' Eugenia said. She was able to swing her legs over the side of the bed now and she stood up. 'Imagine a tableau of this very scene!'

Hammersmith shuddered and didn't respond. Eugenia went on talking, but Hammersmith ignored her and left the room. Tiffany joined him a moment later on the landing.

'You did good work tonight,' Tiffany said. He wiped the back of his hand across his mouth, smearing his cuff with blood.

Hammersmith handed him the killer's razor. 'Evidence.'

Tiffany nodded and folded it up with his own blood still streaked across the blade. He put it away in his pocket.

'I only came here looking for Inspector Day,' Hammersmith said. 'Haven't you seen him?'

'Not since the two of you left together. Has his daughter been found, I hope?'

'She has. She's safe and sound. If you do see Walter, would you tell him that?'

'Of course,' Tiffany said. 'I'm going to recommend that Sir Edward reinstate you, Sergeant.'

Hammersmith shook his head. 'I'm not a sergeant any more.' He reached into his pocket and drew out the small leather case Fiona Kingsley had given him. He took out a card and stared at it before handing it over to Tiffany. Tiffany read it, then looked up at Hammersmith with a scowl.

'Private detective? Why would you wanna go and do that? Nobody likes a private detective.'

'Nobody likes an official detective, either,' Hammersmith said. He walked away from Tiffany and down the stairs.

60

Blackleg led a small group of five medical students through the alley to the broken-out window of the abandoned textile warehouse. One enterprising young man found a back door and together they cleared away the old looms, broken sewing machines and other debris and managed to get it open. Then they carried their lanterns to the underground burial chamber. They covered Alice, Little Betty and the unknown woman in clean white cloths and moved the bodies to stretchers. One at a time, they took them up and out of the building into the sunlight and set them in the back of a nondescript wagon. They did not re-barricade the back door, but left it open so that the building might be more accessible to the homeless of the neighbourhood.

The bodies were carried to an undeveloped plot of land behind St John of God Church. Three graves had been dug there and all arrangements had been made with a sympathetic priest. He had been made aware that the women were murder victims without families, but knew nothing of their lives before.

The graves were quietly filled and small stones were erected above them.

For years after, until the stones had broken and the

bodies had long since decayed, those three unremarkable graves were visited by men and women, in twos and threes, often very late at night. Chief among them was a burly man with a black beard and sad eyes.

Epilogue

I woke before the morning, I was happy all the day,
I never said an ugly word, but smiled and stuck to play.

And now at last the sun is going down behind the wood,
And I am very happy, for I know that I've been good.

My bed is waiting cool and fresh, with linen smooth and fair,
And I must be off to sleepsin-by, and not forget my prayer.

I know that, till to-morrow I shall see the sun arise,
No ugly dream shall fright my mind, no ugly sight my eyes.

But slumber hold me tightly till I waken in the dawn,
And hear the thrushes singing in the lilacs round the lawn.

> – Robert Louis Stevenson, 'A Good Boy',
> *A Child's Garden of Verses* (1885)

Hammersmith stopped and checked the address before knocking. He already missed the old blue door at the top of the porch steps. Too much was changing and he didn't like any of it. He waited, looking around him at the wide unfamiliar street, until the door opened and a housekeeper beckoned him in and took his hat. Claire met him at the bottom of the stairs and directed him to a front room that was arranged much as it had been at 184 Regent's Park.

The furniture was all the same, but the window at the front was bigger and sunlight gave the place a lemon-yellow hue. He started to sit, but straightened back up when he saw that Claire was too anxious to join him. She paced back and forth, picking at her cuticles. He could hardly blame her. It had been weeks since she had last seen her husband.

'Have you found anything?'

'Very little,' Hammersmith said. 'I'm sorry.'

'But he –' Claire was interrupted by Robert and Simon, who bounded into the room with Henry at their heels. Simon ran to Hammersmith and stood smiling up at him.

Hammersmith leaned down. 'Good morning, Simon. I wasn't sure if I'd get to see you this morning.'

'We live here now.'

'We have our own room,' Robert said. 'We never had our own room before.'

'I'm glad.' Hammersmith smiled. 'It's good to see you, too, Henry.'

'You, too, Mr Nevil.'

'Henry has been helping with the boys,' Claire said. 'Nanny has her hands full with the twins, and after all that's happened I feel more comfortable with a man around the house.'

Hammersmith nodded. He and Claire exchanged a look. He knew it hadn't been easy for her to forgive Henry and he was proud of her, happy to see his friends patching up their differences.

Something caught his eye and Hammersmith looked away out the window, where a magpie had landed on the sill. 'I wish I had good news to deliver,' he said. 'The police haven't given up and neither have I, but there's been no luck. Someone saw Walter get into a carriage at the old house, but it hasn't been spotted again. There's nothing to grab hold of.' The bird cocked its head to the side and looked in at him. Hammersmith thought it resembled Oliver and he wondered what had become of that loyal bird. It hopped to one side, pecked at the glass and flew away.

'You'll find him,' Claire said. Hammersmith wasn't sure if it was a question or a show of faith in his abilities. Either way, he felt he ought to answer her.

'I don't know that I will. I'm not the detective Walter was. I mean, he *is* the detective. I'm only his sergeant.'

'But you *are* a detective,' Simon said. 'Miss Fiona says so.'

'Is she about? Fiona, I mean? I wanted to say goodbye.'

'She was here earlier,' Claire said. 'I'm afraid you've only just missed her. A shame. She would have liked to see you.' Claire gave him a look he didn't understand. 'But what do you mean you wanted to say goodbye to her?'

'I've accepted a position,' he said. 'And I'm afraid I won't get much chance to come round in the future.'

'What? Where are you going?'

'It's not important.'

'Nevil, what position have you taken?'

'I'm to be a dustman. Beginning Saturday.'

'No!'

'It's honest work.'

'I can't let you do that.'

Hammersmith went to the door and looked into the hall, wondering where the housekeeper had taken his hat.

He turned back. 'It's done already. I've run out of funds and I need the work.'

'If you stop looking for Walter . . . If you stop, he'll be lost for ever. I know it.'

'Claire . . .' He looked down at his boots. He noticed that they were coming apart at the toes. He hoped Claire hadn't seen them. He didn't want her to know how bad things were for him, but he was going to lose his flat. He couldn't seem to find anyone to share it and Mrs Flanders had reluctantly given him notice. 'Mrs Day, my circumstances have changed somewhat. But you must know that I'm going to keep looking for Walter. I would never give up on him.'

'No, sir,' Henry said. 'You don't give up on anything, Mr Nevil. You never do.'

'Henry, please take the boys to the kitchen and ask Cook to get them something to eat,' Claire said. 'I have something I want to say to Mr Hammersmith.'

Henry took the boys by their hands and led them from the room. Robert looked back over his shoulder with a worried expression. Hammersmith couldn't blame him. He was worried, too, and he hadn't been through half what the brothers had.

'Now for you,' Claire said.

Hammersmith held up a hand. 'I know what you're going to say.'

'I have money,' Claire said. 'Or rather, my father has money and he has promised me whatever I need.'

'I won't take your money. Or your father's money.'

'You must. I know private detectives don't work for free.'

'This again? I never said I was any kind of detective.'

'Do you not have calling cards that say otherwise?'

'I do, yes, but I think I've been quite clear about –'

'So Fiona Kingsley has lied about you?'

'Well, no, that's not what I –'

'Do you really wish to be a dustman for the rest of your life?'

'Of course not.' He didn't want to be a dustman at all, going house to house, carting loads of refuse, but he had no choice if he didn't want to live on the street. Or worse, the poorhouse or prison. He'd had his shot at his dream job and he'd lost it. He bit his lip and took a deep breath.

'Well, then?'

'Claire, I appreciate what you're trying to do, but I can't let you. I don't want charity, no matter how it's disguised and no matter how well intentioned it is.'

'I'm not proposing charity, you bloody idiot. Will you look past your pride for even a minute? I want my husband back. Who will look for him if not you?'

'The police will. Walter isn't some clockmaker who disappeared on holiday. The Yard will never stop looking for him.'

'How many other crimes must they deal with every day? As time passes, Walter will be pushed further and further down the list of priorities. They think they'll keep searching. Jimmy Tiffany's been round here nearly every day telling me that very thing. But he's only looking for Walter in his spare time because his work hours are so full. People won't bloody well stop murdering each other long enough to let the police look for Walter.' She finally sat on the edge of the red chair that had once been the centrepiece of her husband's study. 'I'm not offering you charity,

Nevil. I'm asking you to work for me, because I know that you're as dogged and stubborn as a mule and you'll never give up until Walter's been found. He's your friend and I know he's counting on you. He needs the help of a single-minded policeman, not a bloody dustman. Please forgive my language. I didn't intend to let myself get so –' She broke off and her gaze went to the window. There was nothing to see there.

Hammersmith went and stood in front of her. He found the wallet in his breast pocket and took a card from it. He looked at it before handing it over to her. Fiona Kingsley's handwriting was as precise as printed text.

Claire took the card from him and closed her fist around it. She looked up at him and her eyes were rimmed with tears. 'Does this mean you'll do it?'

Hammersmith held out his hand. 'Nevil Hammersmith, private detective, at your service, ma'am.'

One Year Later

Over the borders, a sin without pardon,
Breaking the branches and crawling below,
Out through the breach in the wall of the garden,
Down by the banks of the river, we go.

Here is a mill with the humming of thunder,
Here is the weir with the wonder of foam,
Here is the sluice with the race running under –
Marvellous places, though handy to home!

Sounds of the village grow stiller and stiller,
Stiller the note of the birds on the hill;
Dusty and dim are the eyes of the miller,
Deaf are his ears with the moil of the mill.

Years may go by, and the wheel in the river
Wheel as it wheels for us, children, to-day,
Wheel and keep roaring and foaming for ever
Long after all of the boys are away.

Home from the Indies and home from the ocean,
Heroes and soldiers we all shall come home;
Still we shall find the old mill wheel in motion,
Turning and churning that river to foam.

You with the bean that I gave when we quarrelled,
I with your marble of Saturday last,
Honoured and old and all gaily apparelled,
Here we shall meet and remember the past.

– Robert Louis Stevenson, 'Keepsake Mill',
A Child's Garden of Verses (1885)

A telephone had been installed in Sir Edward Bradford's new office on the Victoria Embankment, but he had only used it twice in a year. It sat on the edge of his desk and he did his best to simply ignore it. He didn't trust the thing. When he talked to someone, he liked to look him in the eye. So much of a conversation was about body language. Sir Edward still used runners to deliver most of his messages. He liked the idea that some of the boys might grow up to join the Metropolitan Police, even become inspectors someday, but he could see that the old system would soon fade away. There would be no need to employ runners or nurture future generations of policemen. Time marches on and technology leads the parade.

So when the virtually unused telephone rang early one Tuesday afternoon, he jumped and upset his tea all over his lap. He stood and brushed the liquid off his trousers and sighed. He was reminded of poor Sergeant Hammersmith with his stained and soiled clothing. Sir Edward wondered what Hammersmith was up to lately. He hadn't seen the man in months.

The telephone rang again and Sir Edward grabbed the receiver.

'Stop it,' he said.

'I'm sorry?' The voice on the other end sounded timid. 'Is this Colonel Sir Edward Bradford?'

'Of course it's me. Who else would answer this thing? It's in my office.'

'Sir, this is Sarah at the exchange. You have an incoming call.'

'Oh. What do I need to do?'

'Please hold, sir, and I'll connect you.'

'Well, do it, then.'

'Yes, sir.'

There was a long pause during which Sir Edward could hear the shrill echo of machinery and multiple female voices, like ducks on a faraway pond. Then there was a click and he heard another voice.

'Hello,' the voice said. It was low and flat, almost a whisper, but Sir Edward recognized it immediately.

'Walter? Is this Walter Day on the line?'

'Please help me.'

Sir Edward's eyes widened. He could barely breathe. 'Where are you, Walter? Tell me where I can find you.'

There was no answer. After a moment, Sarah came back on. 'I'm sorry, sir. The other party has disconnected.'

Sir Edward set the receiver down on his desktop. He went to his office door and was surprised when it opened on a long dark corridor. For some reason he had expected to see the Murder Squad desks, all in their rows, as they had been in the summer of 1890. He rushed down the passage and grabbed the first runner he came across, a boy idling at the bottom of a staircase. He was probably the only runner in the whole building, there just in case the commissioner had a message.

'What's your name, boy?'

'Gregory Little, sir.'

'Get me Inspector Tiffany,' Sir Edward said to him. 'Of the Murder Squad.'

'Inspector Tiffany,' Gregory said. 'Right away, sir. What shall I tell him?'

'Tell him . . .' Sir Edward paused and ran a hand over his long white beard. 'Tell him I've just heard from Day. Tell him . . . tell him that our friend Walter Day is alive somewhere.'

'Yes, sir!' Gregory turned and ran.

Sir Edward watched him until he was out of sight. He put his hand on his chest and felt his heart pounding. He waited a moment to catch his breath and he nodded at the empty hallway.

'You carry on, Mr Day,' he said. 'We'll find you yet.'